Tempting Tara

Tempting Tara

Confession: Book Three

COZY DUBOIS

For those who keep going, out of hope or out of spite.

Author's Note

WELCOME BACK TO THE *Confession* series! Again, unless we're related, in which case: Thanks for the support. but please put down the book!

If you have not yet read *Loving Lee* and *Love on the Sunny Side*, I strongly recommend it before staring *Tempting Tara*. Many contemporary romance series feature interconnected standalones, where each couple has a book and past/future couples may make cameos, but they can be read in any particular order. The *Confession* series is **not** like that. This is an ensemble romance series that goes in chronological order, so while Lee and Antonio found their Happy Ending together in Book One, that's not the end of their story. Likewise, Sunny, Tara, and Blanche started their character arcs in Lee's book.

The *Confession* series is the story of Lee and Antonio's chosen families as they come-of-age a little later in life (as many queer people do), growing together and falling in love along the way. A central theme of this series is that queer love is more than just who we love romantically—our relationships don't necessarily follow heteronormative milestones; our family ties are not always bonded through blood or law, and friendships are powerful influences in our lives. Trauma isn't cured through the power of ~~dick~~ love, and people don't remain in stasis while their bestie gets their heart broken. Character arcs don't wait for someone else's happy ending before they begin, nor do they end with an "I love you." Their journeys continue together as their family changes and grows, even after they've found their happily ever after.

This series is an ode to the queer community I love and the people in it. LGBTQ people of color are the heart and soul of what it means to be queer in America and have always driven our community forward. My goal as a writer is to put more books with happy endings for queer people out into the world, but my lived experience as a white, queer, non-binary person is not reflected in this series. Through reading #ownvoices books, many conversations with trans and queer people of color from all backgrounds, and thoughtful reflection about my writing choices, I hope to have represented the spectrum of LGBTQ+ people from all walks of life in the series with dignity, admiration, and respect.

The series is *not* intended to depict a textbook perfect representation of anyone's experience—though the amazing sensitivity readers I worked with helped shape this into something that (hopefully) isn't horribly offensive and out of touch. Both Tara and Gabe have experienced neglect and abuse, along with joy and love. Tara's childhood, with housing insecurity and a parent suffering from addiction, and Gabe's life as a Native American, still impacted by the legacy of genocide and cultural disconnection, are outside of my own lived experience. I will never be the person who can write their authentic stories, so I encourage everyone to read works by authors who can. For recommendations, check out my B ookshop.org storefront: bookshop.org/shop/cozydubois (note: any and all affiliate earnings will be donated to the ACLU).

Content Advisory

This series centers queer joy. That said, the characters in these books haven't had the easiest lives and deal with the lingering impacts of past trauma. Proceed with caution if the below may be uncomfortable. If you see anything that may be a dealbreaker for you, I have a more detailed explanation (with some spoilers) on my website cozydubois.com/.

- Transphobia, biphobia, and homophobia, including sexual harassment, microaggressions, and deadnaming by unsupportive parents.

- Sexual harassment that results in physical violence.

- Off-page death of a side character.

- Sexual content between people of all genders to varying intensity, including a few aspects that may be more emotionally difficult or triggering to read than in previous books in the series: a coercive, exploitative professional BDSM arrangement with dubious consent during on-page sexual encounter; a flashback to sexual trauma during intimacy; less-than-safe sex that results in an unplanned but not unwanted pregnancy; a consensual BDSM scene involving alcohol.

- Difficulties managing mental health, including depictions of panic attacks, dissociation, flashbacks, and substance use to cope with emotions. This book explores recovery from sexual trauma more than previous books in the series.

- The main characters come in a wide range of body types and appearances. This book takes a body-neutral approach, however some characters have biases and insecurities. In particular, Gabe experiences more body dysmorphia than other characters.

- References to past traumatic events occur off-page but may be heavy for some readers, including trafficking, child abuse, abusive relationships, addiction, self-harm, and assault.

Saturday, March Sixth

Chapter One

TARA

THE BEST PART OF all this wedding planning shit was the snacks. Amidst the comfort and luxury of Gabe's kitchen—midafternoon sun streaming in the expansive windows, R&B playing softly on the speakers, the tile floor warm from the radiant heat running underneath—Tara was, as always, tempted. The freshly baked pastries on the table were too delicious to resist.

Her arm snaked around her laptop to grab a spinach puff, her fourth of the afternoon. Half-listening to Antonio wax poetic about Lee's vision board for the centerpieces, Tara bit into the flaky, buttery pastry with a contented sigh. Already three hours in, and they were only halfway through the agenda Gabe had put together to keep Lee and Antonio on topic.

As she ate, Tara stole a glance at the "master baker" (as Antonio always joked) sitting next to her. A carrot stick hung loosely between his full, pursed lips as he pointed to something on the screen. Unlike the spinach puff, some temptations had to be—

"Everything good?" Gabe waved the carrot stick in her direction with a quizzical look.

Shit. Her mind scrambled. No point in pretending she hadn't been looking; she just needed an excuse other than irrepressible lust. "Why are you eating a carrot stick?" Tara blurted out, gesturing with the pastry. "If I could make these, I'd be constantly eating them."

"You *are* constantly eating them," Gabe teased. With a snort, Tara smacked his arm. "Spinach puffs don't fit my macros. I made them for you." Gabe paused, pretty brown eyes flicking to Lee and Antonio across the small kitchen table from them, both wearing matching impatient smiles at the interruption. "So *all* of you would have something to eat while you're here."

Tara hid her wince with another bite. Pointing out that he didn't make them for her specifically was unnecessary; she *knew* that. Gabe was simply a good host.

"Not *all* of us," Antonio chimed in, tongue darting across his lips in longing. "Unless that spinach puff is dairy and gluten-free, you're forcing me to fit your macros, too."

"For the sake of all of us—especially me—stick to the carrots, babe," Lee teased his fiancée. He gestured to his laptop between them, the screen facing Tara and Gabe. "Can we focus on the centerpieces, though? Because option three is my front-runner."

Any relief that her moment of indulgence had passed unnoticed was undercut by her annoyance at Gabe's obsession with his macros. It wasn't like he was out of shape. His body looked even more built through his clothes than it had the last time she'd seen him naked—*No! Stop thinking about him naked. He's off-limits now.*

Nine months ago, Gabe had set a boundary: no more casual sex, no more charged flirting. Just their awkward tenuous friendship, while he focused on therapy. Tara had respected that boundary to the letter, keeping her feelings carefully masked behind their growing friendship. But even after he'd completed his treatment plan months ago, Gabe had never brought up the subject again. Nor shown any hint that he still liked her, no sign that he *wanted* her at all.

Stomach twisting in embarrassment for being so hung up on someone who only wanted her friendship, Tara stilled her face, an uncomfortable skill she'd acquired solely for Gabe's sake. The sweeter Gabe was (and he'd grown so incredibly sweet, considerate and patient since completing his therapy program), the harder contorting her heart into a friend-shape became. It ached, pressing against her ribcage, where it festered behind her mask.

"Why did we choose peach again?" Antonio asked, face souring as he compared the fabric swatches. "Why not pink?"

"Because 'pink and navy is giving baby shower'," Tara and Gabe replied in unison, shooting each other a knowing grin.

"Well, then why nav—"

"Oh my god," Tara grumbled, mentally preparing to convince Antonio of his own damn wedding colors for the umpteenth time.

"I got this," Gabe murmured with a friendly pat of her arm. He cleared his throat, "The stage decor you said you needed was more expensive in teal than navy." Turning his laptop around, Gabe presented an infographic of this constantly rehashed discussion, complete with quotes from Antonio. "You also thought that navy would be more consistent because you 'can't stand it when teals don't perfectly match.' And 'peach would be prettier than basic bitch blush'."

Tara and Lee laughed, but Antonio pressed his hand against his chest in mock offense. "You made a flowchart of my own words to use against me?"

Gabe grinned. "Maybe if you didn't keep bringing it up, I wouldn't need a visual aid. You're getting married in four months—little late to change the colors now!"

Tara snorted; that was an understatement. One of Gabe's spare bedrooms was already stuffed with navy and peach wedding decor.

"He's got a point, babe. We already bought a bunch of stuff, and I don't know if we can afford to switch colors," Lee rubbed Antonio's shoulder. "But if it's important to you—"

"Don't finish that sentence, Lee!" Tara checked the budget, mostly for show; she knew where every penny was going by heart. Gabe had taken over the annoying repetitive part of this constantly rehashed conversation. The least Tara could do was head up the part he struggled with: saying no. "You're already over budget on decorations, and your guest list is at two hundred and sixteen people of your invited one hundred. Unless you can find free shit, you won't be able to afford *flowers*, let alone all new decorations."

"And flowers are important to you," Gabe added, grinning as Tara chimed in unison, "At least, they were last week."

As the best men, Tara and Gabe were helping with whatever Lee and Antonio needed, mostly decision-making and reining in expectations. Antonio had too many ideas, and Lee wanted to say yes to them all. Gabe had the most experience with wedding planning of the four, and Tara was the most decisive, happy to naysay Antonio's more whimsical and extravagant dreams. Over the past months, the four of them had spent hours upon hours at Gabe's house, helping Antonio and Lee figure out which parts of their many vision boards they could afford.

It was a special torture, spending countless hours in discussions of love and commitment, while working alongside the one person Tara needed to stop thinking about. Yet here she was. In his picturesque house. With his cute dog. Gabe's pretty brown eyes, always on her, matched his friendly smile these days, though Tara could never forget how hungrily he used to look at her. How his gorgeous long dark brown hair felt between her fingers, those thick thighs between hers. How safe and precious that ridiculously hot body made her feel, holding her in his giant bed.

His dimples still made her heart skip a beat whenever Gabe smiled.

Instead of bashing her head against the table, Tara forced that painful mask of friendship back into place. Though her heart protested, she dragged her eyes away. The last nine months had been an excruciating test of her patience and willpower, neither of which had ever been Tara's strengths.

But for Gabe? For someone who'd become one of her closest friends? The person who had come to understand her better than anyone but Lee and Blanche? Tara had found the strength to endure. She'd wear that damn mask forever if he needed her to.

"Fine! Navy and peach, whatever. It's fine," Antonio huffed. Holding up two fabric swatches, he turned to Lee with a wink. "Which one looks best on me?"

Lee smiled softly. "You look great with both."

"Aren't you choosing napkins?" Tara asked, more waspish than she'd intended. But honestly, would the wrong shade of napkins really make their wedding less sickeningly romantic? "Why do they need to look good on you?"

"This one." Gabe pointed to the slightly more orange swatch.

"You didn't even look, Gabey." Antonio rolled his eyes as he held up the peach fabric to frame Lee's face. "But you're right. This one looks better."

"Final decision?" Tara asked, impatience making her feel like she was about to split out of her skin. Hippo huffed from his spot under the stable, stretching until his head rested on her feet.

Antonio let out a long contemplative sigh. "...yes?"

"Good. That color is on sale. I'm going for it." Tara added the napkins to the cart, burying her feet further under Hippo. "For a middle school teacher, you have champagne tastes."

"Don't forget—we're also famous musicians! We can afford to splurge a little!" Antonio winked.

One of the songs from the album they'd released last summer had gone mildly viral, courtesy of a trend where people shared their exes' red flags to the track. Between the money from their album and Lee's occasional bonus from Blanche's SubParty, their wedding budget had grown. To Tara's annoyance as the designated treasurer, their wedding dreams had kept pace.

"Famous musicians could afford a wedding planner," Tara teased, more at ease now that at least the napkins were under budget. "You were number ninety-nine on the house charts for one week."

"Don't dim my shine, Tara-Bear! That's a chart!" With a scoff of mock offense, Antonio turned to Gabe. "Speaking of champagne, Gabey, what are the odds that your parents would very generously gift us the wine for dinner? At least a discount? I hate to beg for free shit, but album streams have slowed down since our fifteen minutes of fame, so our royalty money is shrinking. I'm not above milking my network. Including your parents."

"It'll help ease the financial strain on Confession," Lee explained, looking anxious and sweaty, like he always did whenever he felt like a burden. "This hasn't been announced officially yet, but the other two owners got bought out by some investor recently, and Chas is under pressure to cut costs, including the discounted cash bar she said we could have."

Gabe nodded. "I'm sure I can convince them."

A chime sounded from Lee's phone. He glanced at the notification. "Oh, add two more to the guest list."

Tara pulled up the RSVP spreadsheet. "Who is it?"

Lee sheepishly scratched the beard he was growing for the wedding. "Uh... Mo and Hot Barber."

Tara smirked as she scanned the spreadsheet. "Is that his name, or is he a hot barber?"

Antonio huffed. "He is *a* barber. I met him over a year ago, and I still can't get his name out of him. Mo is no help. They think it's funny that Lee and I are both really bad with names."

"You're inviting someone you've known for only a year and don't know his name?" Gabe asked skeptically. "No wonder you're having budget troubles."

"Oh, uh... He's *my* barber," Lee muttered. "He and Mo are my friends."

"Oh." Gabe fiddled with his curls. "Sorry."

Lee pushed his glasses up his nose with a tight smile. "Don't worry about it."

Putting her hand over Lee's, Tara squeezed his fingers gently, hoping it wouldn't embarrass him. She was privately relieved that Lee would have more than their chosen family—Tara, Blanche, and Sunny—and his sister Jazz at the wedding; all of them were in the wedding party. Everyone else in attendance would be either from Antonio's side, or a mutual friend from Confession.

His brown eyes met hers with a smile. "Don't worry about me, Buttercup. I'll have my *real* family with me. That's what matters."

Tara smiled back. "I wish Auntie Alitrice could be there. She'd adore Tonio." Lee's aunt had taken them both in as teenagers. She'd been the first adult who had prioritized Tara, even though her nephew's friend was a strange, homeless white girl. Tara had never known what to do with so much attention, hadn't appreciated what she had until after Ali's death. Lee's asshole father had put them back on the streets with a mere hour's notice. "I miss her."

"I miss her too," Lee said softly, tangling their fingers together. His deep brown fingers were warm between her freckled ones. "But you know what she'd say, right?"

Tara smiled. "Suck it up, Buttercup." Her panic attacks had been far worse in her teenage years. Alitrice's advice may not have been the most trauma-informed approach, but "sucking it up" had worked for Lee's aunt all her life, so Tara had tried to make it work for her too. She was still trying, though hard feelings were much easier to "suck it up" than soft ones.

"Is *that* where your nickname came from?" Antonio asked.

Tara nodded. "It was her catchphrase. She hated to see us moping."

"She'd hate to see us moping over her now, too. She never understood why everyone let hard feelings linger. Speaking of, I've been thinking..." Lee hesitated, squeezing her hand almost painfully. "I might see if my parents want to come to the wedding."

Tara's heart dropped. She stared blankly at him, wondering if she'd heard him correctly. "What?"

Antonio met her eyes with a clenched jaw and an exasperated look.

"I just..." Lee sighed. "What if they want to be there?"

"Do *you* want them to be there?" Gabe asked as Hippo groaned. The affectionate pit bull got up to pace circles under the table, only to flop down on Tara's feet again. "Sorry, based on everyone else's reaction, I'm missing some context. But if you want them there, why not invite them?"

Antonio audibly sucked on his teeth.

"Yeah? I just... Maybe this is the right time to stop letting hard feelings linger." Lee winced, looking to Tara for reassurance. "Like Auntie Alitrice would want."

Tara stilled, masking her inner conflict (her newfound skill was useful for more than hiding her thirst for Gabe). Even on her deathbed, Aunt Alitrice had prayed every night for Leland Senior to see the error of his ways. Tara, meanwhile, had vowed to beat his ass if she ever met the man. Torn between protectiveness and supporting Lee in all of his choices, Tara smiled tightly. "I don't want you to get hurt."

"I won't be." Lee's thumb traced Tara's hand. "Even without Auntie Alitrice or my parents, I'll still feel loved, okay? I have my real family. You, Jazz, Blanche, Sunny, and now Tonio."

Tara remained unconvinced. "Maybe ask Jazz what she thinks? She knows them best."

With a sigh that Tara felt in her heart, Antonio kissed Lee's cheek. "If you decide not to reach out, or if they're not ready to reconnect, you still have my family."

"Don't forget Richard and me," Gabe chimed in. "You have us, too."

"Thanks, Gabey." Lee's soft smile across the table made Tara's heart melt, another reminder why this uncomfortable mask mattered. Gabe was entangled in her family; she couldn't ruin Lee's new friendships with her feelings.

Antonio threw his arms around Lee. "I hope you don't feel you need your parents at our wedding for my sake, but I love you and support your decisions, no matter what."

"What he said." Scooting her chair closer, Tara leaned into his familiar comfort. Her security blanket on their air mattress in Aunt Ali's living room. The best friend who had kept her warm at night when they took turns sleeping. The platonic soulmate who had pretended to be her boyfriend to keep them both safe.

"I feel left out." Gabe shuffled around the table to envelop all three of them. His familiar vanilla and oak scent washed over her. Surges of barely repressed yearning resurfaced just from his scent and his arm around her shoulder. Hugs from Gabe—which were frequent because Gabe was *so* affectionate—always brought up bittersweet memories and regretful desire.

Just keep showing up. This has to get easier at some point.

Lee's phone alarm disrupted the quiet; he silenced it with a wince. "I hate to interrupt the love fest, but can you two handle the rest of the list for today? We have a team meeting at Confession to introduce the new owner." Lee started packing up his laptop. "The main thing is ordering the supplies for making floral arrangements. I wish we could afford a florist, but grocery store flowers will have to do. I hope we can get enough peach carnations for the centerpieces."

Tara nodded. "The rest of this will take max five minutes without you two here."

"Oh! Gabe, ask my mom if she knows any florists!" Antonio stuffed the fabric swatches into his backpack. Tara fought a grin at the affectionate dismay on Lee's face as his precious linens wrinkled. "I think I have a cousin who owns a flower shop, but I can't remember who. And, like, I don't want to admit that I have no idea what my cousins do for work. But if *you* ask, maybe we can get a discount."

"Yeah, I'll text her. Don't worry about it." Gabe added a note to his to-do list.

Lee murmured a goodbye as he kissed Tara's hair, tentatively patting Hippo gently when the dog stuck his head out from the table to see where they were going.

"Have fun on your date tonight, Gabey!" Antonio said as he opened the sliding patio door. "I want to hear all about it later!"

Tara's heart constricted in her chest. *Date?*

Gabe groaned. "I'm not telling you anything again! Ever!" he called after Antonio, but the door had already shut behind him.

Antonio's voice still carried from outside as he and Lee walked around the house. "...that doesn't count as meddling! I'm just sharing information! Strategically!"

With a sigh, Gabe pushed the plate of pastries closer to her. "Here. Might as well finish them."

"Thanks." Tara grabbed one and stuffed it into her mouth. "You *haff* a *ay*?" Flakes from the puff pastry flew out of her mouth as she spoke. Hippo's snout nosed her hoodie and joggers, inhaling the bits of pastry in her lap.

"Maybe try talking when your mouth isn't full," Gabe teased.

Tara glared but swallowed the spinach puff, scratching the short gray fur between Hippo's ears. His giant blockhead rested comfortably in her lap. "You have a date?"

Gabe winced. "Yeah, my mom keeps setting me up on blind dates."

"You've had *multiple* dates?" Tara's eyebrows raised higher. She inhaled slowly, getting a handle on the whirlwind in her chest. She'd known this day was coming, had dreaded it. While Gabe had said he wanted to be with her one day, that day had never come. He'd said she was perfect and amazing, had looked at her with adoration and called her Kitten, which both annoyed her and turned her into a puddle of soft feelings—*No, this is your answer. That was when he didn't know the real you.* And now he did, and he wanted someone else.

Suck it up, you can't do all that relationship shit anyway. Ignoring the sting beneath her ribs, she forced a smile. "Meet anyone cool? Give me the details!"

Gabe ran a hand through his hair. "Not really. My parents think meeting more people would be good for me. And my therapist says I need to put myself out there more."

"Do *you* want to be dating?" Tara asked hesitantly.

He shrugged. "They're not wrong, I guess. I want... I want to be with someone." He chuckled. "I already know you're going to say this is corny, but I've always been a romantic. I want what my parents had—the epic love story and someone who understands me to grow old with. But I'm a terrible judge of character, and my mom knows more *good* people than I do."

"Oh, damn. Was I that bad?" Tara asked before she could stop herself. The casual delivery of his rejection was a slap in the face that left her reeling.

Gabe looked up with a sharp inhale. "What?"

"You said you were a terrible judge of character, and you and I..." She trailed off, shaking her head. Maybe there was a reason they'd never revisited the boundary; embarrassment burned hotter every second. Masking her hurt behind a smile, Tara hoped the tremble in her lower lip wasn't visible. "Never mind. I guess we didn't exactly *date*."

"I didn't mean it like that." Gabe tugged on his hair again, avoiding her eyes. "I meant that I don't have the best track record with relationships. That wasn't about you. At all. You're..." He sighed, scratching Hippo's ears, who'd abandoned Tara to support his human. "Can we change the subject? I'm not really sure what I want to say."

Ducking behind her laptop, Tara nodded. At least she wouldn't have to listen to him explain why he didn't want her. *Saved by Gabe's boundaries.* "Yeah. We should figure out this flower shit. Who knew weddings were so much work?"

"I mean, considering my parents operate a wedding venue, I did." Gabe's sardonic smile sent her heart fluttering. "Not that I'll ever get married, but I would absolutely elope. Or at least do something small. It isn't worth the time or effort to do all this."

"No big wedding for you? What happened to being corny and romantic?" Tara teased, swallowing her pain at the idea of Gabe eloping with some stranger. *Why am I doing this to myself? Oh yeah, we're friends.* Friends talked about their hopes and dreams and shit.

"No! I don't want the attention. My mom would kill me though. She never passes up the chance to embarrass, or as she calls it, 'celebrate' me." Gabe fussed with his laptop. "What about you?"

Tara shook her head with a too-bright laugh. "I never really thought about getting married. Too much dependency. I'd need a safeword or something to get out of anything legally binding."

"I think that's called a prenup," Gabe teased. "But if you *did* get married..."

"I dunno." Tara squirmed; she'd never considered the question before. "What about you?"

She expected the notoriously private Gabe to change the subject. But he kept his eyes on his laptop, speaking softly, "Probably something like my parents did. They kind of did a mash-up of Jewish and Cherokee traditions. Even though Dad isn't Cherokee, as far as we know, because we haven't tracked down his real name yet. But Chilocco, the boarding school he went to, was in the Cherokee Strip in Oklahoma, so most of the weddings he'd been to had a wedding vase and blanket ceremony, so my parents included that." He chuckled affectionately, the love in his calming timbre melting Tara's heart. Even though hearing about his hypothetical wedding sucked ass. "And Mom *really* wanted to build her own chuppah. She gets sentimental about big life milestones. I guess... I always imagined my wedding would have all of that, too." Gabe's cheeks pinkened as he glanced up, smiling uncomfortably. "Okay, your turn. I'm talking too much. Please say something."

"*If* I did..." Tara paused, uncomfortable with a game of what-ifs that would never happen. But Gabe had gone first, and actually shared something about himself for once, so she had to try. "I wouldn't want all this fuss that Lee and Antonio are putting themselves through. My wedding would be as cheap as possible. Like, one of those plastic rings from the toy machines at the grocery store, and a few friends hanging out outside. No big reception, just pizza and drinks right there in the park, or a backyard, or wherever. I certainly would not spend a thousand dollars on *flowers*!" She scoffed, exchanging an exasperated smile with Gabe.

"A thousand dollars is not nearly enough for the flowers Tonio and Lee want." Gabe shook his head. "About that... I have a proposal," he said cautiously. "For the decorations, I mean."

Tara raised an eyebrow at his tone. "Go on."

"Here," Gabe handed her a spinach puff. Narrowing her eyes, Tara took it, ignoring his obvious attempt to keep her temper at bay. She involuntarily moaned as she ate, listening with slightly less suspicion as he explained. "My mom works with a florist who may be willing to work at a steep discount. So we wouldn't have to figure out the flowers like Tonio and Lee had planned."

Tara looked at him expectantly. "But?"

Exhaling slowly, Gabe rubbed his forehead and looked at the floor. The rapport they'd built over the last nine months had become almost effortless as they'd learned which topics crossed a line, and which to avoid. But both of them had many lines that were easy to cross. Based on how long he was taking to mentally prepare, this conversation would be less than fun.

"Even at cost, it'd be at least four times what they budgeted—"

"No," Tara interrupted with a shake of her head. Money was the line most often crossed when they talked about the wedding, because Tara was the only one who protected Lee and Antonio's budget. "We can't afford it then. Lee and Antonio can't swing—what, four or five grand? On flowers! They don't *want* to swing it. Flowers are not a priority."

"If you let me finish, I could get my idea out!" Gabe ran his hand through his hair in frustration. "I'll pay the difference, and they won't ever know how much it actually is."

"Dude, do you hear yourself?" Tara was tempted to run her fingers through his hair, too. The curls had somehow grown more luscious in the past nine months, and touching his hair would distract her. Keep the panic and dissociation at bay, even ease the bile in her throat. Normally when they fought over the budget, Lee would see the early signs and hold her hand, give her something to eat or turn on music to distract her.

But Lee had left. Tara would have to do it on her own today.

Wiggling her feet under Hippo's belly, she focused on his warm body weighing her toes down, the pastry in her mouth—anything to forget what went wrong when the money ran out. Going over budget meant going hungry every weekend, because she only ate at school. Hiding under the blanket with her hands over her ears, while the landlord forced himself on her mom instead of evicting them. Her mom, puking and feverish, while Tara sold their food stamps to buy the stuff her mom needed to feel better. Lee turning tricks to afford Auntie Alitrice's morphine—

That's not going to happen anymore. Wishing Lee were here to calm her, Tara shook the memories from her head. She took a breath. *Focus. The decorations.* "Throwing money at it is not the answer. They set the budget. Not you."

Protecting the budget was protecting Lee's financial security, the roof over his head, his next meal. Even if it was Gabe's money, she cared about his financial security, too. *The mortgage on this giant house must be obscene!*

"I'm not throwing money at it. I'm *gifting* it to them for their wedding," Gabe replied testily.

"That doesn't make it better," her voice cracked. "Look, obviously you aren't missing any meals, but you should still care about where your next one is coming from."

"What the fuck is *that* supposed to mean?"

Tara couldn't answer. She breathed, focusing on her senses to keep the fear at bay.

Inhale, 2, 3, 4, 5. I feel Hippo lying on my feet.

Exhale, 4, 3, 2, 1. I smell the spinach puffs. And Gabe. His comforting vanilla and woodsy scent was omnipresent in his house.

Inhale, 2, 3, 4, 5. I see the wedding planning shit. And Gabe. His jaw worked back and forth as he glared at the table. *Shit. I pissed him off again. No wonder he doesn't want me anymore.*

Exhale, 4, 3, 2, 1. I hear... This wasn't working. She couldn't hear anything. The room was silent. When had the music stopped? Tara struggled to stay grounded. *Don't run, I'm safe. Fuck.*

A finger pressing on her nose startled her back to awareness. "Can we pause?"

Tara nodded, grabbing Gabe's hand. "Can I borrow this?"

Gabe laced his fingers through hers in response, his jaw still tight. Instead of simply holding her hand, he dragged his chair closer to hers.

Wood scraped the tile floor as he slid around the table and wrapped a warm arm around her.

Tara's breath and heartbeat slowed in the safety of his chest, the comfort of that oaky vanilla smell, the gentle affection of his chin atop her head. Even though he may not want her anymore, even though he may be pissed at her for...some reason he'd eventually share, he was still there for her. Still her friend who could tell when she needed a break, who would pause to let them both get control of their feelings.

They sat quietly, Tara gripping Gabe's hand like a lifeline as she breathed and tried to figure out where the conversation had went wrong. She ate another spinach puff to distract herself.

"Ready?" he asked when she finished, breaking the silence.

With their joined hands, she poked his nose. "Play."

A smile cracked across his face. "You or me?"

Her curiosity got the better of her. She still wasn't sure what she'd done to piss him off. "You."

"I think I got to the answer on my own, but for the sake of clearing the air..." He paused, his jaw working back and forth. "What did you mean by the 'missing any meals' thing?"

Tara wasn't sure what else it would mean. "That you're financially stable now, but that could change, so you should care about your budget?"

"So, it wasn't a jab at my weight?"

Tara jerked her head back to glare at him. "No!"

"I figured." Gabe shrugged. "It's a sore spot for me. After I took a minute, I knew you wouldn't mean it like that. But in the moment, it felt like a cheap shot about my body."

"What's wrong with your body?"

Gabe leveled a look at her.

"What?" Tara shrugged, gesturing to his body. "I mean, you don't have abs—at least you didn't the last time you let me see you naked—but you're proportionate to your height and build. You look good! You're always hot..." She trailed off, realizing she'd crossed the boundary between affirming his appearance and openly lusting after him.

Gabe's olive skin pinkened. "You can stop. Took it too personally, as usual. What about you?"

"The money thing again," Tara sighed, ignoring the smug glee that her shitty compliment had been enough to make him blush. "You're allowed to spend your money how you want. I just—it still blows my mind how much money they're spending on this wedding, let alone spending an-

other four grand on dead plants? Not that *they're* spending it, but..."
She trailed off again as their eyes met. "I care about your financial
stability, too. And a certain subscriber of Blanche's already leaves a
very generous donation once a month, amounts that happen to match
the bonuses Lee and I have been getting. You're already doing so much
for them." She raised an eyebrow, breath catching in her throat at how
close his face was to hers.

"Not sure what you're talking about." With an arch smirk, Gabe
squeezed her hand. His coffee-brown eyes were swimming with too
many emotions to identify. With a heavy swallow, Gabe tightened his
arm around her waist, drawing her nearer.

Tara's heart raced, unable to tear her eyes away from his. *Fuck. I'm
making a fool of myself.* Letting go of his hand was torture, but reading
too much into his affectionate nature was worse.

Fingers slipping from his, Tara looked down and shoved her hands
under her thighs.

Gabe fiddled with his hair, eyes downcast. But he kept his arm
around her, hand firm against her waist. "How about this? What if we
make a separate flower budget, without Antonio and Lee knowing?
That way you still get a say in where the money goes, and our friends
get a nice surprise on their wedding day. We don't even have to use the
florist my mom knows. We can figure out which of Tonio's cousins
has a flower shop, and see if we can hire them."

Tara considered it. "I wouldn't be mad about that, but you don't
have to. It's your money."

Gabe cracked a grin, meeting her eyes again. "I want to give our best
friends the wedding of their dreams. And you can help me do that."

"You and those damn guilt trips, dude," Tara huffed, hating that she
appreciated the care he took to include her. "You're right. This is about
Lee and Antonio. Not me. Sorry," she muttered. "What else is on the
to-do list, since we're not ordering stuff for floral arrangements?"

"Well, since Tonio and Lee are gone, I wanted to show you this
place for the bachelor weekend. Since we're going over Memorial Day,
I already booked it, but I can still cancel if you don't like it." Arm still
firmly around her, Gabe pulled his laptop over to show her a luxury
A-frame cabin on a lake, complete with a pontoon boat and swimming
dock.

"That's cute, but what about dancing?" Tara and Gabe exchanged a
put-upon wince, which turned into a laugh. For all their talk about a

joint bachelor party weekend, Antonio and Lee had opposite ideas for what they wanted.

Lee wanted to go out dancing at a club or bar, specifically one where it'd be safe for a group predominantly comprised of queer people of color to dance openly. Antonio wanted a quiet lake cabin retreat in the middle of nowhere. As their best men, it fell on Gabe and Tara to find something that would make them both happy.

Gabe flipped to another tab. "In town, a mere mile and a half away, there's a lesbian-owned bar with drag shows on Saturdays. It's not exclusively a gay bar, but it is a gay-friendly bar."

"Damn, that's good work." Tara laughed. "What's the catch? You saved this conversation for when we were alone together, there's gotta be a catch."

"Don't hate me." Gabe shot her a guilty smile, rubbing her shoulder in a blatant attempt to soothe her. "It's nowhere close to in-budget, but I am willing to pay for everything!"

"Gabe!" Tara swatted his chest. "We just talked about this. Stop throwing your money at shit!"

"I know!" He pouted at her, his deep-set eyes pleading. "But I can afford it, and how many lake cabins are we going to find with anything close to a gay bar in town?"

"We're not," Tara grumbled, flipping through the pictures of the adorable loft bedroom and private dock to avoid crumbling under his puppy-dog expression. Gabe's arm stayed draped around her shoulders, and she couldn't bear to pull away. "Ugh, fine. But just so you know, even if you're paying for this, this is costing me all my pride. You're making me look bad!"

"Tara, we have different strengths. Mine happens to be my trust fund." Gabe kissed her hairline. "Thank you for letting me do what I'm good at."

Pretending that her insides weren't melting to goo, Tara rolled her eyes. "You are doing more for this wedding than everyone else combined, and you know it. Between actually knowing how to plan a wedding and your secret donations to Blanche, this would be a disaster without you."

"I don't know what you're talking about," Gabe said archly. "Anyway, the other catch is that it's a bed short. There are four beds and seven of us—assuming the couples share—but I can take the couch."

"What, you don't want to bunk with me?" The words left her mouth before she could think better of it.

Gabe's arm around her stiffened. "I—"

"Sorry, forget I said that." Tara shook her head, kicking herself for being stupid. *Don't start flirting now.* Nine months, she'd managed to keep her hedonist impulses under wraps around him, mostly. Finding out that he was dating everyone *but* her must have put cracks in her willpower. "You don't need to sleep on the couch. I'll bunk with Blanche. Probably best if I don't wake up in a strange place alone, after all."

"If you're sure." Gabe scooted his chair away from her, leaving behind the ghost of his presence in the fading warmth and the scent of him on her clothes.

Fighting the urge to follow, Tara instead opened her own laptop to make the invite to the bachelor party weekend, while Gabe researched the area near the cabin. The sunlight around them slowly faded as they quietly finished what they could of Lee's extensive to-do list.

The snap of Gabe's laptop shutting made her and Hippo jump. "I should get ready for this date shit," he sighed, his expression wan.

Tara fought the impulse to tell him to stay home, preferably with her. She grinned too-eagerly instead. "Who is your date with?" *God, being a good friend sucks.*

"No idea, but Mom said I'd recognize them when I saw them." Gabe shrugged. "I'd be annoyed, but that's typical of my mom. She doesn't want to give me excuses to back out. The last guy she set me up with was a disaster though, so hopefully this one goes better."

"What happened?"

"He kept calling me Daddy." Gabe winced. "You know how I feel about that."

"'Under no circumstances'," Tara quoted with a sad smile, imagining some faceless man heaping praise and dirty talk on the star of her fantasies. Her stomach turned with jealousy that she promptly swallowed. *I should be happy for him. At least he's getting some.* "Was he hot at least?"

Gabe shrugged. "I guess. Silver fox, but a little vain, you know?"

"You had an *older* guy calling you Daddy?" Tara laughed despite herself. "Like if you were into that, it'd be cool, but..."

"Yeah. Try explaining to my very supportive and nosy mom exactly why I don't want a second date with the guy who officiates half the weddings at the vineyard." Gabe snorted.

"Can't imagine," Tara murmured awkwardly. She couldn't fathom having a nosy or supportive mom in the first place. "Should I go, so you can get ready?"

"No!" Gabe blurted out. "Uh, I mean, you can leave if you want to. But if you want to hang out while I shower and stuff, I can drop you off on my way." He opened his mouth, shut it, then finally gave her a half smile. "I wouldn't mind a second opinion on what to wear."

Tara couldn't swim, but she would rather cliff dive into the Mississippi than watch him get ready for a date that wasn't with her. But she couldn't let Gabe know that. It wouldn't be torture for a *friend*, and that's what Gabe needed her to be. Not trusting herself to speak, Tara forced a smile and a nod, hiding her face behind her laptop.

Chapter Two

Patting his cheeks, Gabe risked a quick glance in the mirror to make sure he hadn't missed any patchy stubble while shaving, zeroing in on the faded acne scars pitting his olive skin. The shadows under his eyes had bloomed darker from yet another sleepless night. If he cared more, he might pull out his concealer. But he barely wanted to go on this fucking date in the first place, let alone do more than the bare minimum to get ready for it.

Why am I doing this?

Because the person he'd fallen hopelessly in love with—*No, obsessed with. Can't love a stranger*—nearly two years ago was perfectly happy being friends. Because Gabe was finally in a place where he could concede that he deserved to be happy, instead of endlessly pining over someone who didn't want him. Because being friends with Tara was better than he'd ever expected.

Now, he had a close, supportive friend, instead of a casual hookup with the virtual stranger who would barely look him in the eye. Even if she brought his hopes up and dashed them to the rocks every time she joked about sharing a bed, or "letting her" see him naked again. *As if I'd ever deny her anything—*

No, that's not healthy. I could and would say no, even to Tara. That impulse to give her everything, every part of him—body and mind, heart and soul—when she didn't ask anything of him, was part of the reason he'd broken things off. Self-preservation had never been his strong suit, and his self-destructive impulses were still a constant lure. While he'd successfully fallen out of obsession with the stranger he'd called Kitten, he still loved the Tara he'd come to know.

As a friend.

Mostly.

Well, *predominantly*, he loved her as a friend. A friend who masochistically asked about her dream wedding. The delusional romantic in him had gleefully noted that there was no conflict with the one he'd imagined for himself as a kid whenever his parents talked about theirs, wishing for his own sweeping, romantic love story too.

Gabe caught his reflection again. The sad expression in his eyes belonged to that bitter, insecure kid, who had eventually accepted that an epic love story wasn't meant for him. Even if his reflection now belonged to a stranger.

Scrunching mousse into his damp curls, he left the bathroom and the threat of the mirror. From feel alone, he sectioned off his damp hair. The mane of waist-length brown curls was the one part of his body he was proud of, something he nurtured instead of maintained, his suit of armor protecting him from prying eyes. People looked at his hair instead of his flaws, seeing mere vanity instead of the scars underneath.

Safely in his walk-in closet with the hum of his diffuser drowning out his thoughts, Gabe laid out a half decent outfit. His mom had made reservations at a tasting room, which conveniently listed Cooper Winery on the menu (because why would his mother ever support a business that didn't support hers?). Thankfully, he could get by with a sweater and chinos there. It was bad enough he had to wear suits to work every day; dressing more like himself for a date was a relief.

Ready as he could be for inevitable humiliation, Gabe pocketed his wallet and phone from the kitchen table, but his keys were missing. Nor were they on the hook in the mudroom, the bowl in the entryway, or any of the other places he might have left them.

Leaning against the living room doorframe, he raised an eyebrow at Tara; blanketed by Hippo on the couch, she was watching yet another cooking show. He was tempted to change back into his joggers and join them, to have Tara curl up in his arms—*Don't go there.* "I don't suppose you know where my keys are?"

Without taking her eyes from the screen, Tara smirked and jingled them in her hand. "Can I drive myself home?"

"Promise to stay out of the bike lane this time?" Gabe couldn't resist talking shit. Tara wouldn't pass a driver's test by any means yet, but she wouldn't run anyone over. Probably.

"That was *one* time, and I didn't hit any—" Tara froze as she turned away from the television.

"What?" Gabe immediately looked down, checking for stains or wrinkles. He hadn't ironed, but the clothes had looked okay in the closet. Maybe he should have looked in the mirror again. "Too schlubby? Should I have gone for a suit? Or maybe a shirt and tie under the sweater?"

"No! Just strange to see you..." Her mouth hung open as her eyes raked over him. "I forgot how nice you dress when you go out. We normally hang out here."

"So I normally look schlubby?" Cheeks burning, Gabe screwed his face into a teasing smile to hide his discomfort, as she examined his appearance more closely than he wanted. "Thanks."

"Oh my god, you always look good." Tara huffed a laugh, her eyes tracing his body. "No, you look...great. Hot. Your date won't be able to keep their hands off you. Or their mouth."

Gabe's cheeks burned, wishing he believed her, that the naked desire in her eyes was real. Why hadn't she looked at him like this in all these months? His brain was lying to him. "You can stop. I wasn't fishing for compliments."

It was mortifying enough that she had found out he was going on these blind dates in the first place, set up by his *mom* of all people. He'd been hopeful for a hint of...some sign of discontent, jealousy or something. But Tara had been her normal, supportive, *friendly* self. It hurt more than he expected, even though that sting of inadequacy was why he'd agreed to these blind dates in the first place. Gabe wanted to be wanted, and Tara didn't want him.

Gabe cleared his throat. "You ready to go? Hippo, you need to go outside?"

Hippo groaned in protest, rolling onto his back between Tara's legs. *Lucky bastard.*

"I let him out when you were in the shower." Detangling herself from Hippo, Tara bent over, babbling in baby talk as she scrunched his face up and covered it in kisses. "And I fed him, in case he tries to convince you otherwise later on. Because you're a hungry, hungry Hippo! Yes, you are!"

"Thanks." Gabe forced himself to look anywhere but her ass in her leggings as Hippo's tail thumped the couch cushion. *New low unlocked—I'm jealous of my dog.*

Tara patted Gabe's chest as she passed. Those green eyes that always made his breath catch were upturned with a smile. "Seriously, Gabe, you look really good. I wasn't teasing. I just wish..." She paused, her smile twisting. "I hope your date is what you're looking for. The love story and all that from earlier."

He pulled her into a hug to keep her lovely eyes from seeing the truth, resting his cheek against her hair. "Thanks, Tara."

"You're getting dog hair all over your nice clothes." Her voice was muffled by his chest.

"Then they'll know Hippo is part of the package." Gabe injected a smile into his voice to hide the longing that somehow Tara would be the person waiting for him, just as he had every date before this.

But no. There was a reason Gabe was letting his parents set him up, instead of his friends. His parents had no idea that Tara existed, outside of the anonymous role of Antonio's fiancée's best friend. And that was how it would stay, because Tara didn't want more than friendship with him. If his parents caught wind that he'd been harboring feelings for someone, they'd encourage him; they were already hard enough to contain without external pressure.

But if Gabe went to his friends for dating help, they'd push him to pursue Tara. At the cost of their friendship and the equilibrium that had finally settled between their blended group over the last nine months. At the risk of falling for someone else who didn't love him again, returning to the altar he'd sacrificed himself on for every other love in his life. Everyone had been considerately pretending not to notice his feelings for her, presumably because they were one-sided.

An eternity flew by in a heartbeat, before Tara gave him one last oh so confusing smile and pulled out of his arms. She hurried down the hall, disappearing into the mudroom. "You coming? Don't want you to be late for your date."

Gabe fought to keep from reading too much into their long hug as he followed, just like he did with all their small moments that meant nothing to her, and everything to him. He used to be more decisive, more confident about what to say, more aware of his own mind, and more understanding of other people.

But that Gabe was long gone. Buried under years of doubt and insecurity, blocked by brain injury and mental illness, and made worse from one toxic relationship after another. Today's Gabe was stuck overanalyzing everyone's intentions, hidden between their words and actions. Trapped while he awaited signs from the universe that he was making the right decisions. Waiting for a sign from Tara that maybe he'd been reading her wrong all these months.

But those signs never came.

The silence was comfortable as Tara drove herself home. She cut in with a huffy "Yeah, I know!" any time Gabe was about to caution her about something, which never failed to make him laugh. From the moment they'd met, Tara had been an open book, expressive to a fault. He'd never had to question how she felt about anything. Anger, desire, hurt—her face, tone, and body said everything her words didn't. It made the past nine months painfully clear that even though he'd hurt her by breaking things off, she was happy being friends with him now.

If Gabe wanted any hope of finding someone who might grow to love him, he'd have to find someone who wanted him. Someone he was enough for. Someone who thought he wasn't too much.

Someone who wasn't Tara.

Lee

"Settle down everybody, settle down!" Chas ordered into the mic, as Jackie collapsed into the chair next to Antonio.

Lee greeted her with a tight smile, unsure if he'd ever seen Jackie sitting down before. All-staff meetings were rare; seeing the dozens and dozens of people who kept Confession thriving, seated together in the audience of the venue, was striking. It should be heartwarming, and yet...

"Shut yer pie holes!" Chas hollered. "The sooner we get this show on the road, the sooner y'all can get back to work!"

"Or go home!" Antonio quipped, flicking the LED candle on the table back and forth. The glow was barely visible in the afternoon sunlight streaming in through the leaded windows. But Lee could hear Antonio's anxiety in every *click click click*.

"Some of us can go home, darling," Blanche teased Antonio, sprawled back in their chair between Lee and Freddy. "You, however, have a show to star in tonight."

Lee wiped his hands on his jeans. That Blanche's presence was needed was not a good sign. They owned a small stake in Confession, but normally only got involved when Chas needed their backing in ownership decisions. Between Chas, Freddy, and Blanche, they collectively owned just over half of the gay bar.

Jackie sighed, putting her feet up on an empty chair and stretching her calves, shooting a baleful look between Freddy and Lee. "I'm so jealous that you two get to sit around all night."

Slouched in his chair on Blanche's other side with his arms crossed, Freddy shrugged, his mustache twitching. Lee shrugged with him. If Freddy wasn't going to correct her that they also did their share of physical labor, then he wouldn't either.

"Hey, my future husband has a very complex job," Antonio took up the fight on Lee's behalf anyway. "Have you seen all those buttons—"

"Hey!" Onstage, Chas pointed at their table, one thumb tucked into his belt. "Everyone except y'all managed to stop their yappin'. Hush up, now!"

With a huff, Lee covered Antonio's mouth before he could crack a joke in retort. Chas's tone was light but forced, and his shoulders were tense. As were Freddy's.

Antonio licked his palm. Lee gave his fiancée an exasperated, pleading look. He didn't take his hand away until Antonio's hazel eyes softened, and he kissed Lee's skin instead.

Antonio leaned close to whisper, "Sorry. Reading the room now."

"Thank you. I just got a bad feeling about this." He wiped his slimy palm on Antonio's leggings.

"All right, now that I have all y'alls attention," Chas boomed with forced cheer, "I've got a few things to say, so I'm gonna say 'em quick, and if you got questions or somethin' to say, come find me after, and we can discuss it private-like."

Lee's back prickled with sweat. He wished Chas would spit it out already, the anxiety of not knowing what the announcements were (even though he did know what the announcements were, courtesy of being close with the bosses) was making it hard to breathe. His anxiety had always been bad, but planning a wedding was making it so much worse. His jaw and neck pain had gotten so bad over the past few months, Antonio had been giving him massages every evening, just so Lee could sleep.

"First of all, thank y'all for coming. I know a lot of you are here on your day off, and the rest are here early or have better things you could be doing on the clock than listenin' to me. As always, I appreciate each and every one of you for the hard work you put in to keep Confession the best damn gay bar in Bellamy!"

Several folks, including Antonio and Jackie, whooped at that, but quickly quieted down again.

"Now, I got good news, and news news! It's not bad, *none* of it is bad news!" Chas quickly reassured everyone, which Lee did not find not very reassuring. "First of all, this may not shock anyone, but we're expectin' another new member of the Confession family to join us in September!" Giving everyone a chance to applaud and cheer, Chas patted his stomach. His bump had been visible for several weeks now, even though he was barely four months along. "Now, this ain't our first rodeo, so for those of you who are new and used to me stickin' my nose into everyone's business all damn day, here's how this is gonna go.

"For the four months I'm out, all the managers are gonna keep managin'. That means Jackie is in charge of front of house, Darla's got back of house, Carlita will still handle our promo and emcee the shows, Lee and Kat will coordinate show logistics, and anythin' they can't handle will go to Freddy. Easy as pie!" Chas held up his hands. "Now, I know what you're thinking! Don't Freddy get some parental leave, too? And yes, he damn well better!

"In the past, we've had Confession's silent partners, Todd and Mike, step in to help things run smoothly, and Freddy would take a month of leave. Which leads me to my second announcement." Chas's smile became even more forced. "As of the first of this month, Todd and Mike have decided to step away from Confession. So in their much-missed absence, I'd like to introduce you to Bryce Covey, Confession's newest *partial* owner."

To scattered applause and confused murmurs, out from the wings walked Blanche's patron.

Stomach plummeting, Lee stiffened. "What is *he* doing here?" His jaw clenched hard enough that pain shot through his skull. He'd known there was a new owner, but no one had mentioned that it was the piece of shit keeping Blanche trapped under his thumb. "What the fuck is he doing here, Blanche?"

With a resigned sigh, Blanche looped their arm through Lee's and rubbed his bicep soothingly. "Proving a point, darling. That's what he's doing here."

With a smirk, Covey glanced at Blanche, narrowing his eyes at their hand on Lee. The crowd of employees looked at him with trepidation. "Normally, I'm not one to get so *intimately* involved with my investments. But Confession, and everyone in it, Chas and Freddy especially, are so," Covey paused, looking right at Blanche with a cold smile, "*special*. I trust Blanche will work with me in lockstep around here, while Chas and Freddy are taking care of their family. Together, we can keep Confession successful. Right, Blanche?"

Fingers digging into Lee's arm, Blanche nodded with gracious serenity. "Trust me, sweetheart, I'll be watching your every step."

Covey smiled, and the dread that had been building in Lee's stomach curdled.

CHAPTER THREE

GABE

As the sun sank lower and the dusk deepened into darkness, Gabe tapped the wooden bartop as quietly as he could. Candles flickered in their votives, and the murmur of the room behind him grew louder as couples strolled in for a splash of wine after their dinner dates. The bartender wordlessly checked in on him yet again; Gabe shook his head politely. Anxiety slowly overtook his best efforts to breathe through his unease. Being in public—especially alone, with his back to the door—always made him feel exposed.

He'd given up turning around every time the door opened after the first fifteen minutes. By the time the ice in his water had melted, Gabe was on the verge of declaring himself officially stood up.

"Gabriel, I am so sorry!" A cloud of floral perfume, loose brown curls long enough to rival his own, and a skintight red dress collapsed into the empty seat next to him. "I got caught up in work for a wedding tomorrow, and then there was traffic, and I barely had a chance to shower or anything and—"

With a relieved smile, Gabe held up his hand to stop her. "Don't worry about it, Angie."

His mom's go-to florist for all of the vineyard's weddings, Angelica Garcia, smiled ruefully at him. Her red lipstick was bold against her russet brown skin. "Gabriel, let me apologize. I am forty minutes late. I'd be long gone if I were you."

"Apology accepted," Gabe smiled back, relieved that he finally wasn't alone, especially in the company of someone he considered a friend. He was far more comfortable with Angie than with the pushy officiant. "I should have guessed Mom would set me up with you."

Angie laughed. "She just wants a discount on flowers."

"She hasn't talked you into being a preferred vendor at the vineyard yet?" Gabe was surprised to find himself laughing along with her.

"For the weddings at the vineyard, of course! But she's been after me to do the spring flower displays at the museum, and frankly, the stipend isn't worth it." Angie wrinkled her nose. "It only covers the materials, so I'd be donating too much free labor for displays of that size. Don't get me wrong, I love creating more exciting arrangements than bouquets, but not for free!"

"It's for charity, Ang. I never expected you to be so cutthroat," Gabe teased. "You're still up for the youth class next weekend though, right?"

"Of course! *You* pay me a stipend *and* reimburse me for the cost of materials." Angie shot him a wry grin. "And it's a good cause, of course."

"Oh, sure," he mocked. "Don't try to pretend you're not in it for the money now."

Angie swatted his arm. "I run my own business in an industry with a very narrow profit margin, Gabriel. Not all of us have family money like you."

Gabe shrugged to hide his discomfort as the bartender brought them the first wine on the tasting menu. If he could give his trust away, he would. And did. Most of his monthly maximum went to Blanche's SubParty.

"Besides..." Angie continued with a soft hand on his arm once the bartender walked away. "If I teach your art class, I get to spend the morning with you."

Unsure how to respond, or if he even wanted to flirt back, Gabe smiled tightly as he sipped the full-bodied, fruity red. If he were designing the menu, he would have started off with a drier white, but it wasn't his business. After all, not even his overly-supportive parents wanted his input on the vineyard; who was Gabe to think he could design a wine menu?

Angie's hazel eyes stayed on his as she swallowed. *Maybe this will be fine.* Angie was easy to talk to and objectively gorgeous. They got along well. Perhaps their easy camaraderie could transform into more. Maybe his abstract yearning for love would finally overcome his aversion to being with anyone besides Tara. Maybe he could grow to want this for real. Maybe he could do this without it becoming toxic.

Dread pooled in his stomach at the reminder of his previous relationships— *Stop. Stay present.* Gabe cleared his throat and his mind. If he couldn't bring himself to flirt, he still needed to talk with Angie. "Hey, you know that quote I asked for? Would you be willing to uh...negotiate on a wedding coming up? I'm my friend's best man, and his budget is tight, so I'm hoping to help him out where I can."

"Negotiate, huh?" Angie winked and pulled up the calendar on her phone. "When is it?"

"June twenty-sixth."

Angie winced. "That won't work for me personally, but I could move some things around and have someone on my team deliver them. What's the time and location?"

"Six in the evening at Confession. It's a gay bar—"

"I am very familiar with Confession, Gabriel." Angie shot him a perplexed look. "You're Tonito's best man? Or Lee's?"

Gabe paused, confused. "You know Antonio?"

Angie raised an eyebrow. "Gabriel, what is my shop called?"

"Flores Flores..." Gabe trailed off. Garcia was Angie's first surname, but her second was Flores—he'd never made the connection before. "*You're* the florist cousin."

"I guess I should be glad Tonito didn't *completely* forget about his favorite cousin." Angie laughed and finished her glass. "Should I be offended that you're asking me professionally? Because *of course* I'll work at cost for family!"

"In my defense, I didn't know you were family. Tonio didn't mention *which* cousin was the florist. If it helps, you're next on the list...after yourself." Gabe chuckled. "Either way, he can't afford at cost. That's where I'm stepping in, but keep that between us." He shook his head, still in disbelief. "So that must be how you met my mom, then?"

"Yeah, Tia Paula introduced us, like, decades ago." Angie cocked her head at him. "So wait, if *you're* Tonio's best man, and his best man is his childhood best friend..." She gasped, slapping the bartop. "*You're* the Gabe that Tonio dated in high school?"

"Oh no." The dread he'd been fighting all day was nothing compared to the humiliation that burned through him now. Gabe pulled his hair in front of his face, hiding from the delight in her eyes. "Please say Tonio has two cousins named Angie."

A delighted laugh erupted next to him. "No such luck, Gabriel! I would not have recognized you in a million years, but I definitely remember you. Damn, you grew up!"

"Please stop." He threw back the rest of his wine, ignoring Angie's wicked grin. The floor could open up and swallow him whole any moment. His teenage self would be thrilled to be on a date with Angie; middle school Gabe had absolutely had a crush on her. Angie had been his friend's cool, intimidating high school cousin. But his teenage years had been humiliating enough, without the memories of stepping on her toes and ripping her hem while dancing at Paula and Oscar's wedding. Or the many times she'd walked in on him and Tonio fooling around. Or any of the other dozens of embarrassing adolescent memories she'd been involved in.

"Remember that time you, me, and Tonio split a bottle of tequila we stole from Oscar's special cabinet? I had no idea anyone could puke so much! You just kept going!" Angie laughed, pausing to thank the bartender who poured their next glass of wine. "Hey, why haven't I seen you around if you're still friends with Tonio? There's no way Tia Paula would let you escape her that easily."

Gabe shrugged, sipping his wine to bide his time as he considered his answer. "I go to his birthday and some holidays, but I'm not really a party guy anymore."

"That's a shame. You were always so much fun!" Angie rested her hand on his arm. "I'd love to dance with you again."

Tensing, Gabe fought against his indecision. He wished he liked the idea of dancing with Angie, flirting with her, or even being on this date with her. Wished he didn't hate the idea of dating, because he needed to move past that; everyone he dated would be the wrong person.

The problem was that anytime Gabe thought of dancing these days, only memories of dancing with Tara came to mind. The way all of her awkward limbs had flailed until he drew her close against him. How her blush had spread down her neck as her hands gripped his waist, and her thighs parted around his. How her green eyes had lost their hesitation as they moved together and turned dark with desire.

Even now, sitting with Angie—this gorgeous, funny, successful, *good* person actively flirting with him—he could never keep Tara far from his mind.

He swallowed heavily and took another sip of wine in lieu of an answer.

"This was fun, Gabriel." Angie pressed even closer to his side as he walked her home.

"I had a lovely time," he replied politely. The dread in his stomach pooled with every step closer to her apartment.

"Well, this is me." Gesturing to a brick fourplex, Angie took the first step up and turned around. Between her heels and the rise of the stoop, she was closer to eye level now. "Do you want to do this again?"

Gabe took a breath to stifle the "no" that threatened to spill out. It was just an instinct, rooted in the feeling that he was out with the wrong person. But the right person didn't want him. *I want love. I want happiness. This is how I find it.* "I think so. Do you?"

"Definitely." Angie smiled and pulled him closer.

A waft of lilac and rose overcame his senses a split second before her lips pressed to his. He stilled, fighting the urge to pull away. This wasn't Tara, with her myriad confusing rules that she'd break herself. He could kiss Angie to his heart's content without worry.

Fuck it. I have to try.

Gabe kissed Angie back, leaning into the scent of flowers that clung to her skin and hair. Hands encircling the curves of her waist, he pulled her against him. Her hands tangled in his hair as she parted her lips; the fruit notes on her tongue mingled with the lingering wine on his own.

Except his heart wasn't content. These weren't the lips that had woken him in a dream, when Tara had broken her own rule while he'd slept. The lush, soft lips sliding against his own weren't the thin, slightly chapped ones that had kissed him, body and soul. That had wrapped perfectly around his cock, sucked marks into his skin, and rendered comfort to his scars. The person in his arms wasn't the one he wanted more than life itself.

Heart clenching, Gabe took a step back, breathing heavily.

"Uh, wow. Damn." Angie panted, swaying with her hazel eyes blown wide. Her red lipstick was somehow still perfectly in place on her kiss-swollen lips. "Do you want to come inside?"

"I... Uh, I don't think so. Sorry." Burying a hand in his hair, Gabe couldn't hide the wince that crossed his face. "Nothing personal, just not ready for that. Or any of this really. I'm sorry. I shouldn't be doing this."

Relief washed over him as Gabe let the "no" in his heart escape. As much as he wished he was, he wasn't ready—not just for sex, or for Angie, but for romance in general.

But his relief stemmed from much more than that. He had just kissed someone, and felt only fond friendship, nostalgic attraction, and nothing more. Gabe felt exactly the same about Angie as he did before. Despite his long track record of "falling in love with anyone that got his dick hard" (Antonio's words, not his) he had just successfully kissed a gorgeous woman who, frankly, had gotten his dick hard. And Gabe hadn't fallen in love with her. His heart still belonged to himself.

If that wasn't a sign from the universe that he was healing, nothing would be. *I can't wait to tell my therapist that all the shit she puts up with is paying off.*

Angie tilted her head. "You're hung up on someone else, aren't you?"

"What makes you say that?"

"Partly to make myself feel better than you went from 'probably' to 'hell no' in one kiss." She shrugged with a soft smile. "And because reading people comes in handy as a florist. You didn't seem that into me, but I was hoping you'd at least be down for a hookup." Her eyes narrowed. "It's not Tonio, is it?"

Gabe shook his head with an emphatic, "No!"

"Just making sure." Angie shrugged, picking at her dress. "Why are you letting your mom set you up on blind dates if you're into some redhead?"

"How'd you know she's a redhead?"

"This was on your sweater." Angie held up a single curly red hair with a triumphant smile. "Don't worry. I'm not taking any of this personally. More curious why you'd agree to a date with me if you have feelings for someone else."

Gabe probably shouldn't be eager to tell the woman he'd just made out with on the sidewalk about the person he'd been in obsession with for years. But talking about it with someone other than his therapist, or strangers online, would be a relief. That Tara's hair had made it onto his sweater from one hug... Well, maybe that was a sign from the universe, too.

"I guess… She and I are really good friends. And she never indicated that she wanted more than that." Gabe paused, then amended, "Emotionally anyway. I'd hate to ruin a friendship I value when she doesn't feel the same."

Or ruin himself by giving in to the attraction he'd imagined in Tara's eyes earlier, when she didn't want more than sex.

"And yet, her hair ended up on your sweater right before you had a date with someone else. I get why you might feel hopeful." Angie rubbed his shoulder affectionately. "You know, your mom set us up because she wants you to be happy. And I can see what she means. Don't take this the wrong way, but frankly, the Gabriel in front of me is a shadow of that boy I used to dance with." Her smile softened. "People change, but not that much. You are in dire need of more happiness in your life. Would being with your redhead make you happier?"

That was something Gabe had questioned himself countless times. Yes, because the idea of being with Tara was like basking in the sun, or a warm blanket. She was a swell of music that made his heart ache, the lightness of dancing that freed him from the weight of the world, a nap on the couch after a good meal. The problem was that Gabe didn't remember what happiness felt like, and perhaps all that passion and comfort existed only in his imagination. A romantic ideal, projected onto a person simply because he wanted her.

Love and happiness had always been mutually exclusive. Love was miserable and desperate, resentful and demanding. Love hurt inside and out.

But unlike his exes, Tara had never needed him to be anything other than himself. Tara had taken exactly what he was willing to give without question or protest or demand for more. She accepted him for who he was and wanted to be.

His jaw tightened. Maybe Tara had done that nine months ago, when he'd said he could only give her platonic friendship. Maybe she had been respecting the boundary he'd set, just like how he had respected all of hers. Maybe Tara was waiting for Gabe to break it.

That irrepressible hope blossomed again, stronger than ever. The music in his heart sang, and his feet itched to dance. The uplifting balm at the dream of loving Tara was nowhere close to the restrictive pain of his nightmare ex. Of course, being with Tara would make him happier. But until now, Gabe had never let himself consider that she might want him back. If he'd been reading her wrong, and Tara had been waiting for him to see her heart... "I think so."

"Then pursue your happiness, Gabriel." Angie hugged him. "Now, get out of here. If you don't want to fool around with me tonight, I'll find someone who does. Maybe a cute redhead of my own."

Feeling lighter than he had in months, years maybe, Gabe laughed and hugged her back. "Thanks, Ang. And uh... Good luck getting laid."

"I don't need luck." Angie winked. "Do you see how good I look in this dress?"

TARA

"NOT WATCHING THE SHOW tonight, Tara?"

With a jump, Tara tore her gaze away from her whiskey to find Jackie raising an eyebrow at her. The muscles in her broad shoulders rippled as she wiped the stainless steel bartop.

Tara shook her head. "No, not really feeling it. I would have stayed home, but Blanche is recording tonight."

Being in public when she wanted to hide from the world under her blanket was painful. But less painful than replaying and overthinking every second of her *friendship* with Gabe, with the sound of Blanche flogging a sub in the background. Confession was her home away from home, so she was processing her racing thoughts in her second-favorite place in Bellamy. And because it was Saturday, her processing was aided by liquor.

"Well, glad you're here!" Jackie refilled her whiskey without prompting. "It's been a while."

Tara grinned. "Did you miss me?" She would often come here before when Blanche sexiled her, but now she had Lee's apartment to go to. Wedding planning and driving lessons with Gabe also kept her busy. On the rare occasions she did come here alone, Tara usually worked in the offices upstairs. She'd missed late nights out bothering Jackie; she'd never considered that Jackie might miss her, too.

"Don't read into it," Jackie grinned. "I hate change, and you're a regular I haven't seen in a while. It's nice to have some symbol of reliability."

Stomach twisting, Tara nodded in sympathy. Lee had blown up her phone earlier with the news of Confession's new owner. Every employee was probably feeling nervous about it too. Even if they didn't fully understand why a pharmaceutical executive was personally investing in Confession. Yet another reason to hate Covey. "Yeah, I haven't really gone out as much. Usually, Lee has to drag me out of the house."

Jackie laughed, tossing her long braid behind her. "I'm surprised you're not upstairs, hanging out with him and Freddy."

Tara shrugged. She was in her feelings, mostly because she couldn't stop thinking about whatever Gabe might be doing on his *date*. Since he was anxious, Lee would make her talk about those feelings, so he could avoid thinking about his own problems. And while she was somewhat getting better at identifying her constantly shifting moods—thanks to the many pauses Gabe needed to figure out his own—she wasn't ready to talk about *that* subject with anyone, especially Lee. He'd be too damn...supportive.

Tara shot Jackie a smile. "Maybe I wanted to hang out with you tonight."

Jackie leveled a look at her. "Do I need to remind you that I'm ace?"

Tara surprised herself with a laugh. "I wasn't hitting on you, I promise. No, I'm not here to get laid. Just here for a few drinks."

Jackie raised a skeptical eyebrow. "Girl, when have you ever come here alone for platonic company?"

Tara's cheeks burned. "Give me some credit, Jackie. When's the last time I hooked up with someone here?"

"Hell if I know. I don't keep track of your sex life!" Jackie laughed as she headed to take someone's order. "I'm sure tonight, like every night, will be your lucky night."

Tara doubted it. She may have a reputation, but it'd been a long time since she'd last made any effort in sex or dating. Once Lee had moved in with Antonio, Gabe had fallen back into existence, turning her one-night stand from long ago into Antonio's best friend. And later, her occasional lover.

Not that she held any fidelity to Gabe, even if she had some lingering unexamined feelings for him. But the abstract star of her fantasies suddenly becoming a very real and constant part of her life... It had been jarring, to have her fantasy walk into her best friend's new home.

Her motivation for dating had lost all momentum at the stark reminder that the happiness she wanted had ripple effects. Real people could resurface in unexpected ways. The nameless man with pretty brown eyes, who had melted her brain with his tongue, could suddenly become inescapable in her daily life.

And while Gabe wasn't off-limits per se—hell, their friends had tried their hardest to force them together—Tara couldn't give him what he needed. And he would have given her more than she could handle. Reality was messy. Complicated. Especially when Reality had turned out to be even easier to fall for than her Fantasy had been. Until Reality had broken her heart to protect his own.

"You're looking at that drink like it killed your dad."

Tara jumped at the rich voice next to her. A curvy Black woman, in a devastating red dress that hugged her curves with an equally bold red lip, smiled from the barstool next to her. Tara must have been really in her head if she hadn't noticed someone sitting next to her, let alone someone who looked like *that*.

"Did I scare you?" The woman laughed. "Sorry."

Tara shook her head. "Just startled me."

"What's your poison?" The woman nodded to her half-empty glass. "Let me buy your next one to make it up to you."

Tara hesitated. She was already on her second drink. That was her first and most important rule: Only drink on Saturdays and special occasions, and never get drunk in public. But she could drink the next one slowly, so it wouldn't bring her from tipsy to drunk. "You don't have to, but I won't say no."

The woman grinned as she got Jackie's attention. "What's your name?"

Trying to hide her wince behind a smile, Tara replied, "That's need-to-know."

Her second rule: Don't give personal information to strangers. She'd learned that one the hard way, and at far too young of an age.

Thankfully, the woman laughed. "Mysterious, huh? I'll call you Red, I guess." She reached up to wrap a lock of Tara's short hair around her finger. "You have nice hair."

"I washed it this morning."

A laugh quickly muffled by a cough told Tara that Jackie had overheard. "What can I get you?"

"I'll take a paloma, please." The woman, whom Tara decided to call Red right back on account of her dress, gestured to her. "And another of whatever she's having."

Jackie raised an annoyingly smug eyebrow at Tara as she worked.

Tara shook her head, hoping her exasperation showed through her impassive expression.

"So," Red sipped her paloma once Jackie walked away. "Tell me about yourself."

"Not much to tell." Tara had her evasive replies down to a science. "What brings you here tonight?"

The woman tossed her long hair over her shoulder. "To be honest, I'm hoping to get laid."

Tara choked on her whiskey. "Oh?"

"Yes! I look fabulous, but the date I had earlier didn't pan out." Red huffed. "I'm a busy woman! I cleared my schedule for tonight to have a good time. It'd be a waste of this dress, or the amazing job I did on my hair and makeup, to go home early by myself!"

"Your date was a fool. You're hot as fuck." Tara mentally kicked herself for her honesty. She'd been trying so hard to learn to control her mouth for Gabe's sake, and here she was, unintentionally flirting.

"Thank you!" Red turned to her. "He's a sweet guy, just not interested. Can't fault him for that. So how about you?"

"Oh," Tara shrugged. "I'm just here to kill time."

"No, I mean, are you interested?" Red gave her an appraising look, her hazel eyes roaming over Tara's appearance.

"Oh. Um..." Tara froze. The Tara from two years ago would have already been tongue-deep between her thighs in the Confessionals.

But the Tara from two years ago had also pretended that Rule Six (When you need to feel something, have sex) wasn't a crutch to avoid acknowledging her feelings. And as annoying as her emotions could be, Tara had to admit she was stronger for facing them. That desperation to feel alive, wanted, in control, to feel *anything,* was less sharp now than ever before.

Still, sex would be fun. And Gabe was probably getting some from his date tonight. If he was dating everyone but her, why shouldn't she move on, too? Red seemed more than willing.

"I'm going to be honest, an 'um' is not as validating as calling me 'hot as fuck' was," Red teased, leaning closer. "What can I do to convince you?"

Tara ducked to avoid her kiss, ending up with red lips on her temple instead. Red's hair tickled her face, filling her nose with the smell of lilacs and a note of vanilla that reminded her of Gabe. "Oh, I don't kiss."

"I'm sorry, what?" Red sat back, confused. "You don't kiss?"

Tara's rule against it was an addendum she'd quickly added to Rule Six. Fucking strangers made her feel alive. Kissing them reminded her just how vulnerable she was. And she hated feeling vulnerable. "Not on the mouth."

Red rested her chin in her hand, lips parted in curiosity. "But making out is the best part."

"Hard disagree," Tara laughed, as her phone buzzed in her pocket. Relieved at the excuse to avoid defending herself, she pulled it out to check the text.

> You busy next Saturday morning? The florist I told you about is teaching the art class I volunteer at. Want to come?

> Dude, why are u texting me when ur on a date? Don't be rude.

> Date's over. I'm home.

> Tell Hippo I said hey. why are u home already? That was quick. How was it? Were they hot? Did they call u Daddy?

> Lmao I'm never telling you anything again. Please don't tell Tonio about that. I'd never hear the end of it.

> No promises! soooo… hot or not?

> Why do you care about my date?

Because Tara was a fucking martyr. She sighed, unsure what to say.

Im a supportive friend. And living vicariously through u.

I guess the date went well, but I doubt there'll be a second. Yes, she was hot. No, she did not call me Daddy.

No second date? But she was hot AND she didn't call you Daddy! Why not?

Tara! I did not text you to debrief. Art class? Yes or no?

Yes. Can I drive?

No. I'll pick you up at nine on Saturday.

That's so early dude I need my beauty sleep.

You really don't.

Tara's cheeks burned, and she fought a smile.

"You know, I was going to keep flirting, but I see I have no shot."

Tara jerked back to the stunning woman sitting next to her. "Sorry, a friend texted me."

Red raised an eyebrow. "Sure, because I smile like *that* anytime a friend texts me." Red laughed in exasperation. "Tonight is not my night. First, my date is hung up on his friend, and now the hot stranger at the bar is, too."

Her cheeks had to be noticeably pink, but Tara didn't know how to reply. Red wasn't wrong. Gabe had become the exception to every part of Rule Seven: Don't get attached to hookups—no repeats, no one from real life, stay in public places. Not only was he a repeated hookup who she knew in real life, but she'd gone to his house, met his dog, and made herself comfortable in his bed.

She'd gotten attached.

"So, are you a regular here? Is the bartender single?" Red nodded toward Jackie.

"Yeah, but she's ace." Tara snorted at Red's groan. "Maybe she'd make out with you?"

Red considered it with pursed lips, then shook her head. "I love a good make out sesh, but maybe I'll cut my losses and spend some quality time with a smutty romance novel and my vibrator."

"Cheers to that." Tara held up her still-full whiskey neat with a snort. She'd probably go home and do the same, to thoughts of someone who was supposed to be a platonic friend. She'd reconciled her guilt over *that* vice months ago. Gabe's boundaries didn't say anything about her imagination.

Red laughed and clinked her bubbly, peach lowball against Tara's glass.

Sunday, March Seventh

Chapter Four

Sunny

Grinning in anticipation, Sunny flashed the laser pen along the wall.

The blur of orange fur burst from under the couch, flying around the room after the red dot. Dumpster was, as always, chaos incarnate amongst the monochrome greige walls and boring black leather furniture that Richard thought was classy. The sweet cuddly kitten, who had wormed her way into Sunny's heart and Richard's condo, had grown into a hyper demon cat. With a yowl, she leapt six feet in the air, backflipping off the wall and onto Richard's coffee table. Her gymnastics knocked his book to the cold tile floor.

Sunny beamed; Dumpster really was her baby.

Towel slung low around his waist, hair and body still damp from his shower, Richard stalked into the living room. Crossing his arms, he glared at her expectantly.

"Hey there, handsome!" Sunny batted her eyelashes, admiring his blond, slicked back hair, and the tattoos decorating his muscular arms and wiry shoulders. "Wanna drop the towel and come join me on the couch?"

"No." Richard's fingers tapped his elbow. "I want to take a shower without the drain clogging."

Sunny grimaced. "Sorry, I forgot to clean up my hair ball. I'll get it next time."

"You shouldn't need me to remind you to pick up after yourself, Sunny."

With an arch look, Sunny set the laser pointer down. Her annoyance was already spiking at his condescending tone. Sure, Richard had asked her nicely many times. But the way he talked down to her now rubbed her the wrong way. "And what are you going to do if I don't, Dicky?"

"What will it take to get you to remember?" The edge to his voice went beyond condescension now, sparking a hum of anticipation. "What will it take for you to be good?"

Skin prickling, a shiver ran down her spine. Sunny fought her smile, raising an eyebrow. "That depends. What's in it for me?"

Richard's blue eyes narrowed as he stalked toward her. Her heart raced. "Maybe ask what's in store for you if you're *not* good."

Sunny's skin burned with the thrill humming through her veins.

Before she could find a bratty retort, a crash interrupted them. Dumpster zoomed away to hide from her own destruction under the bed. The seahorse sculpture that lived on the top shelf of the bookshelf was on the floor, split in two.

"Shit!" Richard rushed over to pick it up. Muscles in his back tight, he stared at the decapitated ceramic seahorse in his hands. Shuddering, he let out a single, wrecked sob.

"Are you okay?" Sunny rushed over. Her stomach squirmed with guilt for getting Dumpster so worked up. "Did you get hurt?" Richard was always so stoic; he must have been on edge already if a broken sculpture was making him cry. A year together, and she was still putting her own wants before his needs. She bit her lip. Why had she left the hair in the drain?

"Stop chewing your lip," Richard muttered as he perched on the edge of the sofa. Drying his eyes on the corner of the towel, he took a deep breath and straightened his shoulders. "I'm fine. Just tired."

Eyebrows raising, Sunny failed to mask her skepticism. He'd been tired many times, but the one and only time she'd ever seen him cry was after after her disastrous introduction to his family. He might be too proud to admit he was upset, but Richard wasn't fine. Swallowing the urge to call him out on the lie, Sunny sat next to him instead. "What's going through your head right now?"

His robin's-egg blue eyes were almost green against the red rimming them as he held out the pieces of seahorse in his hands. "I can't replace it."

Richard could be a little materialistic, but he was—in most regards—a minimalist. Sure, there were his designer clothes and extensive shoe collection that he cared for meticulously. But they were still mere possessions. In the past year, the only things that truly upset him were when they argued, or when Gabe was sad, or when their friends had problems he couldn't fix. For Richard to be this upset about a sculpture... It must be important.

She took the pieces and held them together, inspecting the damage. A few spots were bright white where the colorful ceramic had chipped off. "With some super glue, we can probably get this back together without much noticeable damage. I have some nail polish this exact gold color in my bag."

Before he could protest, Sunny left the room to get super glue from Richard's meticulously organized office supplies, and nail polish from her overnight bag. After a year together, her purple backpack merely held her makeup kit and clean underwear. She spent enough time at Richard's condo that most of her femme clothes lived there, along with her cat and gaming computer (and her hair in the drain).

Comparing the chipped parts of the statue to her nail polish, Sunny lost herself to the task. Lining up the chips just so, analyzing if she should paint or glue first, matching the colors as closely as she could—it all became a puzzle to solve. Glittering Gold for the line around the seahorse's head where it had fallen off, Jungle Green for the chip in the kelp, and Aquamarine Blue for a few dings on the base.

"So what's the deal with the statue?" Sunny asked as she added another layer of the gold polish. It was a pretty close match, so long as no one noticed the extra glitter.

Curling around himself, Richard gripped the towel covering his lap. "Seahorses are one of the only animals where the father carries the babies. Metaphorically, that helped me with my dysphoria when I was deciding on what I wanted from my transition. I can be the birth parent and still be a dad. Seahorses are the scientific precedent."

"Typical Dicky, justifying your choices with scientific precedent," Sunny teased, hoping their usual banter would bring him back to his normal, relaxed self. Well, as relaxed as Richard got, anyway.

Richard gifted her with his rare, crooked smile. "Gabe made this for me in his sculpture class junior year. Even as a fake boyfriend, he always gave thoughtful gifts."

Sunny's brow rose as she glued the pieces back together. "I had no idea Gabe was an artist. No wonder it's irreplaceable."

"For someone as brilliantly smart as you are, you really don't listen to your friends when they talk, do you?" Richard snorted. "Gabe went to the same arts high school as Tonio, and minored in art in college. Volunteers at the art museum. The past few months, he's basically had a side gig doing wedding photography at his parents' vineyard."

Pleased Richard was feeling like himself enough to tease her in return, Sunny tossed her hair over her shoulder. "Thank you. I am brilliantly smart."

He huffed. "Seriously, what *do* you know about Gabe?"

Sunny screwed her face up, confused why Richard cared so much. "He took your v-card in college, and he was your fake boyfriend to keep your parents off your back while you transitioned. You guys work together, but I don't really know what he actually does there. Or what you do, for that matter." Sunny paused, scouring her mind for what she knew about Richard's best friend. She didn't need to know every fun fact about Gabe to be his friend. "He's...tall. Plays League. Has a dog..." she trailed off.

Richard waited expectantly. "That's it?"

"Yup!" Sunny shrugged, pressing the pieces together and wiping away the extra superglue with her fingertips. "Should I know more?"

"I guess not." Richard merely shrugged—to her annoyance, because why did he ask if he wouldn't explain *why* he asked—as Dumpster tentatively crept back in.

Sunny was very proud of herself for letting it go, when really, she wanted to bicker more. Instead, she put on a bright smile. "Here, good as new." She set the seahorse on the coffee table once the glue was dry. "But maybe this should go in a different spot, until our bratty daughter stops destroying everything."

Picking up Dumpster, who purred and headbutted his chin, Richard chuckled. "She takes after her mother in that regard."

She swatted his arm. "You like me bratty and destructive."

"I do." Richard kissed her cheek. "Thank you for fixing this. Sorry I lost my head for a second."

"You're allowed to feel emotions, Dicky. I am honored I got to witness you actually expressing them for once." Sunny ruffled his still-damp hair as she got up. "I should go. I promised Mae I'd be home for dinner tonight. But I'll clean my hair from your drain first."

Richard opened his mouth, hesitating as if he wanted to say something else. Instead, he simply nodded and went to get dressed, while Sunny packed up her nail polish.

Something was itching the tip of her tongue too. Several tabs had popped open, and questions were coalescing, but Sunny was reluctant to voice anything before they were fully formed. Richard was in an odd mood, as if part of him had cracked along with the seahorse. Forcing a conversation before he understood his feelings would likely lead to an argument; that was the last thing Richard or Sunny needed tonight.

Sunny sighed as she packed her bag. She'd never left before on this weird, unsatisfied note; usually she floated home in lovedrunk contentment. Any thrill from their flirty argument had completely dissipated under the reality of the weekend ending.

THE MOMENT SHE'D WALKED through the door, her mae had immediately asked when she planned to clean the bathroom. Or put the dishes away. Or if she'd remembered to pay the bill that Sunny had told her multiple times was set up for auto-pay. Instead, Sunny had quietly retreated to her room and her tablet. Birdie's terse interrogation was decidedly less fun than getting nagged by Richard.

To her delight, her online bestie was waiting for her. Messaging him would distract her from being a contributing member of her mother's household, at least until it was time to eat.

Sunnywith0meatballs: Sup. Howsit hanging?
Black_Hawk_Up88: Surprisingly good?
Sunnywith0meatballs: Why surprisingly?
Black_Hawk_Up88: When am I ever good? I feel good. It's weird.
Sunnywith0meatballs: Did you get laid or something?
Black_Hawk_Up88: You really have no filter, do you? No, I didn't get laid. I just feel like I have a direction for the first time in a while. Like I know what I want. Is this...hope?
Sunnywith0meatballs: Oh, you're existentially good. Weird.
Black_Hawk_Up88: ...Yeah? It's so uncomfortable. lol.

Sunny hesitated, debating bringing up the various, confusing brain tabs that kept popping open since her latest flirty argument with Richard. Black_Hawk was the person she usually went to when she couldn't ask the real people in her life for advice.

After leaving everything so unresolved with Richard, and the little digs from her mae about avoiding her responsibilities, Sunny was frustrated. She was tired of living torn between two places. The urge to pack up the rest of her shit and move in permanently, to let him spoil her every day, was tempting.

But Sunny wouldn't like the version of herself who took the easy way out. While a serious relationship was in their future, things between them were still fun and light. The version of Richard's home she wanted to escape to was just that, an escape. Maybe that was why today felt so...unsatisfying. It wasn't the unresolved sexual tension, it was the break in their usual pattern: She'd been the caring, doting partner, instead of Richard. Guilt made Sunny squirm, because that shouldn't feel so uncomfortable. She was the responsible one all the time, just not with Richard.

Their lives were still so different, though over the past year, the gap had narrowed. Richard had no younger sister to pay tuition for, no elderly relatives counting on his income, no expensive surgeries to save for oh so *painfully* slowly. With two masters degrees and a decade of work experience, Richard had a steady career trajectory, was satisfied with where he was on his gender journey. He was ready for The Rest of Their Lives. He'd been patient, giving her time and space, while he waited for Sunny to catch up.

If Sunny moved in, that would be a milestone—a sign that things were serious. That she was ready for Wifey status.

But she wasn't. Not yet. Sunny was nowhere *close* to ready for that.

Black_Hawk_Up88: Sunny? You there? Or am I freaking you out with my halfway decent mental health?

Black_Hawk_Up88: Are you only friends with me because I'm depressed?

SunnywithOmeatballs: Can I ask a personal question?

Black_Hawk_Up88: Can I stop you?

SunnywithOmeatballs: Haha /s You've been in at least 2, maybe 3, serious relationships since I've known you, right?

Black_Hawk_Up88: Have I? Damn, it's been that long?

Sunnywith0meatballs: You and J split up like a month after we started gaming together, and then E. And this other person you've been seeing.

Black_Hawk_Up88: There's no other person.

Sunnywith0meatballs: I thought you were having a thing with the mind-blowing, life-changing hookup you caught feelings for mid-nut?

Black_Hawk_Up88: I told you that ended a while ago.

Sunnywith0meatballs: But it happened.

Black_Hawk_Up88: But it wasn't serious. (At least for them... T.T) All of these are very sore subjects btw, so can you get to the point? This trip down memory lane is not exactly fun.

Sunnywith0meatballs: Yeah, sorry. How does a relationship become serious?

Black_Hawk_Up88: Ooh, I am a bad person to ask. Every relationship I've had has gone from first kiss to moving in together way too soon.

Sunnywith0meatballs: Are you... are you a lesbian?

Black_Hawk_Up88: Lmao no, just a chronically romantic doormat.

Sunnywith0meatballs: Tragic

Black_Hawk_Up88: Tell me about it. I'd rather be a lesbian. Anyway, why do you ask? Maybe I can still help.

Sunnywith0meatballs: Well, so my lover and I have been together for like a year, and they're ready for The Rest of Our Lives, and I want to be, but I'm not.

Black_Hawk_Up88: What makes you think so?

Sunny sighed. When she imagined The Rest of Her Life with Richard, she imagined she'd be more mature than she was. Someone more like her mae, who could be responsible, and take care of her husband and their cat and their future kids—instead of being spoiled rotten by her hot, sweet, rich boyfriend. Like how she had fixed the sculpture for him earlier. She'd helped. That had been Serious Relationship Sunny.

But Sunny still wanted to have fun. To tease him and annoy him, to have him follow through on the spanking he'd threatened her with earlier. Richard was so sweet and caring, the perfect gentleman. Except for the moments when he wasn't. And those moments when he wasn't made her feel giddy with anticipation. She wanted to push him, see how long his careful control would last. Find out what happened when he let go of his inhibitions. The consequences if she pushed him far enough.

The truth was Sunny *had* noticed the hair in the drain. Thought about it, imagined how annoyed he would be, and then left it there. She had wanted him to tie her to the bed and swat her ass so hard it hurt to sit for a week. To call her a good girl when she knelt down and promised to do better in the future, before she made it up to him with her mouth.

Which was so immature of her! Except she sensed Richard wanted that too.

She liked how they were now, but she also wanted *more*. More serious *and* more fun, though it seemed impossible to bridge the two. Richard liked her bratty and destructive, but when she finally upgraded to Wifey status, things would shift. Serious Relationship Sunny would simply take the damn hair out of the drain.

But where was the fun in that?

I really hope Black_Hawk doesn't read too much into this. Her online friend had shared very little about his sex life; this felt like crossing a boundary. *But I'm gonna ask anyway, because since when do I care about shit like crossing boundaries?*

SunnywithOmeatballs: TBH, I solve most of our arguments by bratting.

Black_Hawk_Up88: Oh. Okay. Love that for you.

SunnywithOmeatballs: And that doesn't seem very mature. Like, a serious relationship would probably mean talking things out and being responsible for my own actions, but sometimes, I just don't want to. And I don't know how to go from bratty girlfriend to future wife.

Black_Hawk_Up88: Why do those have to be mutually exclusive? Like, you could plan a scene where you can be bratty, and still have mature conversations outside of that.

SunnywithOmeatballs: We haven't really planned scenes like that though. I don't think they'd be into roleplaying.

Black_Hawk_Up88: You're just bratting in the wild without discussing anything?

SunnywithOmeatballs: Lol yeah?

Black_Hawk_Up88: O.o I'm honestly impressed you haven't run into issues with this before.

> **Sunnywith0meatballs**: Wait, so are you into BDSM yourself? Like dom/sub shit like that specifically?
>
> **Black_Hawk_Up88**: Wow, personal questions again. I had a few bad experiences that turned me off. A little impact play is fine, but nothing too intense, especially not the D/s parts anymore. I don't think I could go to that headspace again.

After being friends with a professional domme for so long, Sunny should probably know more about kink. But Blanche never liked talking about work. Even during their fling, Real Blanche had solidly kept Sunny away from Work Blanche. Until their breakup anyway. Which was part of the reason *why* they broke up. Sunny wanted more, but Blanche couldn't give it to her—

A tab popped open in her head. Surprisingly, not the most embarrassing one, where Blanche had shut her down hard. But one with a memory of the next day, where Blanche said they'd help her negotiate a contract when she found someone who would give her all of that. *Maybe I should ask them.* With a satisfied nod, Sunny closed the tab. Reminiscing about their breakup was still humiliating.

> **Sunnywith0meatballs**: TBH, we've been dancing around talking about it, and maybe that's the reason it's frustrating. How do I bring it up?
>
> **Sunnywith0meatballs**: (Side note, I like how this went from "how do relationships get serious?" to "how do I ask my partner to dominate me?")
>
> **Black_Hawk_Up88**: Literally just ask. Be honest about what you want and listen to what they have to say.
>
> **Black_Hawk_Up88**: And whatever you do, negotiate everything out first. Don't go into it hoping the scene will go the way you want, you gotta talk about it first and get on the same page. Trust me on that!
>
> **Black_Hawk_Up88**: And research shit. Idk if you're familiar with SubParty, but I recommend Blanche Van Horne's page. They're an experienced Domme and have some checklists and shit you can download.

Sunny blinked. Did she seriously just find a fan of Blanche's out in the wild? She'd never actually watched Blanche's content; watching her ex's BDSM porn was a weird boundary to cross.

> **Black_Hawk_Up88**: Sorry if this is getting TMI, but you asked lmao Don't judge me for subscribing to a kinky site when I just said I'm not into BDSM. lol
>
> **Sunnywith0meatballs**: Lol I'd never kink shame. I'll check them out.
>
> **Black_Hawk_Up88**: Take a lesson from me and communicate your boundaries in advance. And keep communicating.
>
> **Black_Hawk_Up88**: I might have had shitty experiences, but there was a reason I was drawn to it in the first place. You can become a whole new person and completely change a relationship dynamic, so honestly, you might get two birds with one stone by doing this. Watching Blanche's more educational stuff has been therapeutic for me because I get to understand better what fucked me up both in kink and vanilla relationships.
>
> **Sunnywith0meatballs**: Every time I learn something new about you, the image I have of the neckbeard gaming in his mom's basement falls apart.
>
> **Black_Hawk_Up88**: Lmao. Please, I'm an adult. I game in my own basement.

Sunny laughed. Black Hawk always seemed to have the advice she needed to hear. Hopefully, Richard would be open to the suggestion. Because Sunny was tired of feeling torn between their current happiness and future lives. Split being the responsible Sunny whose family depended on her, and the fun version of herself who had Richard at her back to lean on.

Maybe bridging the gap wouldn't mean sacrificing their fun. Maybe by making the easy, escapist parts of their relationship a priority, they could take everything to the next level. After all, Sunny was curious what Richard would be like if he finally stopped being such a gentleman. How the hard edge of his voice might sound, if he allowed himself to truly use it.

Maybe Richard was feeling torn, too.

Chapter Five

Antonio

Balancing the stack of take-out containers against his chest, Antonio tucked the leftovers from the Flores family dinner into the fridge. Sometimes, he considered learning to cook some of his stepdad's recipes. But honestly, he never ran out of food long enough to need to.

He poked his head out of the kitchen. "You want anything, Angel?"

Lee lay stretched out on the couch, his glasses and phone on the coffee table. Opening one eye, he gave Antonio a halfhearted smile. "Yeah, no, I'm okay. Thanks though."

Waving a hand, Antonio preemptively shushed his demons before they had a chance to say some stupid shit. Lee had been quiet since the meeting at Confession yesterday. He was always quiet, but rarely so withdrawn. "What's wrong?"

With a soft chuckle, Lee shook his head. "Nothing."

"Liar." Antonio crawled on top of him, resting his head in his favorite spot on Lee's chest. Lee's arms automatically encircled him.

"I'm not lying…" Lee sighed. "I'm just anxious about things I can't control. And the things I can control. And the things I'm not sure if I want to find out."

"About the Covey bullshit with Confession?" Antonio asked. "We could run him off. Venus offered to plant drugs in his car, and I've got a ton of pranks I used to pull at school that might work. I got my biology teacher to quit in tenth grade."

"Yeah, no, we're not doing that," Lee laughed. "He's a billionaire, not an overworked and underpaid science teacher. You'd probably end up getting everyone fired."

Antonio grinned, proud of himself for getting a genuine laugh out of his future husband. "Still, I want to do something!"

"I know, babe." Lee cupped his jaw, brown eyes dark in the dim light. The scar under his cheek was barely visible. "But please, don't make this harder for Blanche than it has to be. They're already beating themself up for the situation, even though it's not their fault their patron forced his way into Confession as a power move. We can't make it worse."

With a reluctant nod, Antonio kissed his wrist. "Fine. But I'm not happy about it. Is there no getting out of this? Wasn't Phin looking into it?"

Lee shook his head. "No, yeah, Blanche emailed him a few months ago, and he said that unless they can come up with half a mill, or Covey breaks it, there's no getting out of their contract. And considering that he now owns almost half of Confession, I don't see him breaking it."

Antonio's jaw dropped. "Half a million?"

Lee nodded. "Don't tell Blanche you know that, I don't think Phin was supposed to tell me either. But you know how Phin talks when he's..." Lee trailed off, a guilty wince crossing his face.

Antonio tapped his nose with a silent question.

Lee nodded. "He always says he's just gonna stick to drinks, but then..." He trailed off again. "Sorry, you probably don't want to hear it. You know better than I do how he is."

Antonio pressed a kiss to his chest, murmuring his thanks. He really didn't want to hear it. He knew Phin's habits too well; they were the same ones Antonio used to share.

"Anyway, the point was, I'm worried this guy is going to be looking for any excuse to take more control of Confession. So, if you can, try and keep everyone backstage in line?" Lee winced. "At least until Freddy and Chas are back from leave, and things go back to normal."

"I hate doing nothing, but if that's what Blanche wants..." Antonio nodded. "I'll do what I can. I am pretty persuasive."

Lee laughed, scratching his jaw. "You are. That's how I ended up growing a damn beard for you. This is so itchy!"

"You look so good though!" Antonio winked, and murmured, "I'm sorry you feel so anxious about it."

With a sigh, Lee's jaw tightened, his body tensing underneath Antonio's. "That wasn't the main thing making me anxious. I'm just over-thinking, so I'm stuck in my head."

Fingers tapping Lee's chest, Antonio raised an eyebrow, waiting for an explanation.

Lee shook his head. "It's gonna make you upset."

"Tell me, Angel," Antonio insisted. "I can manage my own feelings."

He let out a slow sigh. "I hate to ask Jazz to get involved, but I want to give her the heads-up that I'm going to reach out to my parents."

"Going to, huh?" Antonio held his breath, trying to mask his frown.

"I told you you weren't gonna like it," Lee groaned.

"Well, damn, Lee! I wonder why?" Antonio cried, exhaling his frustration into Lee's chest, so he could speak more gently, "This is supposed to be the happiest day of your life, and you want the people who hurt you, who abandoned you there? Am I supposed to be excited about it?"

"Yeah, no, of course not!" Lee's thumb swept across Antonio's cheek. "I appreciate that you're worried about me, but please, I don't want to argue about this."

"So I don't get a say?" Antonio asked, heart aching.

"Of course you do! But..." Lee threw his head back with a groan. "Look, we have over two hundred guests coming, right?"

"Yeah, and you had a say in every person on that list!"

"I know, I know," Lee murmured. "My point is, we have all of these wonderful people who are showing up for you, most of whom don't even know me. And I'm happy that you're bringing all these people to my life, and I can't wait to meet them all, because even if we have nothing else in common, we all love you. And I'm..." His sigh trembled. "Aside from the people standing up with me, there will be two guests who I can call mine, three if you count Phin, and I don't even know one of their names!"

"You don't have to bring more than yourself!" Antonio pleaded. "You don't have to do this for me! I just want *you*, it's not a competition."

Lee winced. "I don't want Jazz to have to keep—"

"Jazz wouldn't want you to—"

"Antonio, please," Lee interrupted. "Please, don't argue, just listen!"

Antonio slammed his mouth shut, heart in his throat, humming his Intentions Song instead of snapping back like he wanted to. Normally, he had to dig and pull Lee's feelings from him, like stubborn roots. And here Antonio was, talking over Lee the one time he wanted to open up.

"All of the things you're going to say, I've been saying them to myself for months." Lee sighed, with a quiet grumble that resonated in Antonio's chest. "And you're right. It's not for you, or Jazz, or because I feel like I'm not pulling my weight. I know I don't need them. I know I'm setting myself up to be hurt, to be angry, and they might be a huge shadow over our wedding day, but... I have to try." His baritone turned raspy. "It's been over a decade. Jazz says they're not the same people anymore. If I can't extend an olive branch now, when can I?"

Never, if Antonio had any say in it. But this wasn't his choice, so he stayed quiet, pressing a kiss into Lee's sternum. Lee trusted Jazz's judgment, and Antonio would have to, too.

"And if they reject me, if they never acknowledge my existence, if they hurt me again, then I know. But at least then I'll have closure." With a heavy swallow, Lee shook his head. "This has been on my mind every day since we got engaged, Tonio. I'm tired of thinking about it! I want to start our marriage without regrets and what-ifs."

"Okay," Antonio murmured with a nod, even though he wanted to reassure Lee that he didn't need the parents who had hurt him. That *he'd* protect him and love him the way they hadn't. He had to trust Lee knew that, and still wanted this. "How can I support you?"

"Just be by my side, and listen to me, and have my back. Support me like you always do." Lee kissed his cheek, holding him close. "I'm not going to invite them without your blessing, because you do have a say. But I want us to meet them, if they're open to it. If it goes well, we can discuss if inviting them is something we both want to do. I need you to tell me if I'm overlooking my dad's bullshit. And if he comes to the wedding, help me make sure Tara doesn't commit assault."

A laugh burst from Antonio. "I can't control Tara, but you have my support on everything else." He bumped his forehead against Lee's, even as the inaction Lee was asking of him grated. As much as he was tempted to collaborate with Tara instead, he wouldn't.

For Lee—and for Blanche—he would listen. Be his rock, the way Lee was for him. After all, Antonio had reluctantly embraced inaction for the past nine months, not meddling (mostly) in the obvious pining between Gabe and Tara. If Lee needed him to be there to lean on, Antonio would be at his side.

Tuesday, March Ninth

Chapter Six

Richard

Midway through the stir-fry Richard had brought for lunch, three of Gabe's friends rounded the corner into the break room, buzzing with gossip as they made a beeline for their table. The trio power walked through the sterile white room, salads and oversized water cups in hand.

With a sigh, Richard put his headphones on. They weren't there to talk to him, and honestly, it was better for everyone if he listened to music. He and Gabe usually ate in a comfortable silence, but Gabe was friendlier than he was. Through college, grad school, the New York office, Gabe had always attracted a flock of straight women as lunch companions.

The first bars of Ponyboy played just as the three women—Jaida in HR, Beth?, and someone he'd never been introduced to—sat down around Gabe, ignoring Richard completely. As usual.

"How was your date last weekend, Gabe?" Probably-Beth asked without a hello.

Richard turned the music off, but kept the headphones on, pretending to be engrossed in his well-worn copy of *The Count of Monte Cristo*. He'd been waiting for Gabe to talk about his date for days, but Gabe hadn't so much as mentioned it, much like the rest of his blind dates. There was no way Richard was passing up the chance to eavesdrop.

"Oh, you know, first dates." Gabe shrugged. "How was your weekend?"

"You gotta give us more than that!" Jaida insisted. "Where did you go? Was he nice? Are you gonna see him again?"

Was he even a he? Richard kept his face passive. Gabe was openly queer, yet for some reason, everyone at work had assumed that meant exclusively gay. But Gabe never corrected them, so Richard wouldn't either.

"We went to some wine bar. It was nice, but I don't think it's gonna go anywhere." Out of the corner of Richard's eye, Gabe's hand drifted to the end of his hair. So the date hadn't gone well. Or maybe it had? Gabe could be anxious about either outcome.

"Why not?" Probably-Beth asked. "Bad lay?"

Gabe tensed as Jaida hissed that she shouldn't ask that at work, even on break. "No, I've honestly..." he paused, turning slightly toward Richard. "Dogs are better than cats."

Still as a statue, Richard held his breath, staring hard at the page. Damn, Gabe had almost gotten him. Sure, he was always annoyed at Dumpster for the constant mess, and knocking his glasses behind the bed every night, and the statue thing. But that was Sunny's cat, and therefore, Dumpster was perfect. Far better than Hippo, who stank and drooled and shed like crazy.

"Okay, cool," Gabe turned back, talking in a quieter voice. "I've honestly had feelings for someone for a while, and I just... I never knew if they had feelings for me—still don't! They're so hard to read, you know? But I want them to, because I don't know if I'm ever gonna get over them."

Richard felt everyone else at the table look at him, and calmly turned the page. Goddamn Gabe. This would not help the rumors about their alleged secret relationship; it was the gossip fodder for half the office. Richard could speak up, say it wasn't about him. But the first dozen times he'd done so had made no difference.

"I've known them for a while, and I figured they weren't interested, but what if I'm wrong? Not that their behavior has changed, but I'm kind of a hopeless romantic, so I'm probably seeing signs that aren't there." Gabe sighed, pushing his fruit around its glass container. "I just don't know what to do."

Tell her you love her, dumbass! Richard couldn't remember how long he'd been on this page; he turned it without reading a single word. After over a year of mutual pining, Gabe might finally be on the verge of doing *something* about his feelings for Tara. He'd been in a really healthy place lately, more energetic, laughing more. Even going on these dates was a good sign that Gabe's mental health had taken a turn for the better. If not now, then when?

Richard had been worried how Gabe's new dating life would shift the group dynamics, especially if Gabe caught feelings. Granted, the group dynamics were at risk either way, and Richard thought Tara and Gabe would suit very well. Frustratingly, doing anything to encourage them would only end up discouraging their equally stubborn asses; Richard and Sunny could only monitor from a distance.

"Do you guys ever hang out?" the third woman asked around a mouthful of spinach. "Maybe ask him to come over, just the two of you."

"Yeah, all the time!" Gabe nodded.

"Have you ever, you know?" Probably-Beth asked, making a rude gesture that Richard couldn't see because he was staring at his book.

"You seriously can't ask that around me!" Jaida scolded her, then added with a smile in her voice. "But if you wanted to share..."

"Uh..." Gabe shifted in his chair, turning away from Richard. "We, um... Attraction is not the issue. Definitely compatible in that regard."

The women squealed.

"So, then, what *is* the issue?"

Gabe's sigh was so heavy, Richard felt it in his bones. "What if they don't want anything serious? The idea of putting myself through heartbreak again... It might be too much."

"Hey, you're a catch, babe!" Jaida reached across the table and took Gabe's hand. "Any man would be lucky to have you."

"Thanks Jaida. Maybe I will..." Gabe sputtered. "I dunno, say something?"

"You're so gorgeous, all you'd have to do is bat your eyes, and anyone would fall for you," the third woman chimed in. Her glare at Richard was apparent in the tone of her voice. "Assuming he's a man with a heart, of course. Instead of a black hole in his chest."

"Yeah, anyone who doesn't treat you like a king is a fool!" Probably-Beth said, a little too pointedly.

The conversation fell. Richard looked up; everyone but Gabe was looking at him with a scowl. He pulled his headphones off. "What? He's not talking about *me*!"

"Seriously? I *knew* you were listening the whole time!" Gabe smacked his arm.

"I was pretending not to!" Richard smacked him back. "If you wanted it to be my business, you'd talk to me. You're welcome for not getting involved!"

Jaida, Probably-Beth, and the other woman all sneered at him. With a shake of his head, Richard returned to his book and pulled his headphones back on.

BLANCHE

"ARE YOU FUCKING SERIOUS?" Blanche huffed as their phone chimed with an incoming text. They grabbed it off the coffee table, mostly to confirm that it was, indeed, their patron. "Now?"

Instead of his usual hour warning, which had been growing shorter and shorter the past few months, the text simply read:

> omw

"What's wrong?" The tone in Tara's voice told Blanche that she already knew. With a nod, Blanche crawled out of their chair to grab their pills.

"What's up?" Jazz asked from where she sat next to Tara on the couch, looking up from the biology textbook in her lap. This semester, Lee's sister had started coming over after classes to avoid being home for dinner. She didn't have work today, and her friends all had classes until late in the evening, so Blanche and Tara were happy to keep her company. They usually sat together in easy silence. Jazz did her homework, Tara worked on editing Blanche's footage, and Blanche responded to subscriber messages.

Until today, when they instead had to get ready for a scene, with the piece of shit who was clinging to Blanche like gum on their shoe.

"Sorry, Jazzy," Blanche winced, downing a blue pill dry. "I'm going to have to kick you out. My patron is on his way, and I'm not sure how long we have. He's en route, but I'm not sure where he's coming from."

"Oh, no worries! Sorry, I'll get out of your hair!" Jazz closed her textbook, stuffing it into her bag, while Tara scurried out of the room to put her laptop away and put real clothes on. She looked quizzically at the bottle in Blanche's hand. "You okay? Headache or something?"

Blanche laughed, cheeks burning. "No, this is my uh... Well, trade secret, so to speak."

Tucking her short locs into a beanie, Jazz looked at them blankly. "It's Viagra."

"Oh!" Jazz's eyebrows raised as she zipped up a pink and orange fleece. "You take that every time?"

"I take it any time I need to...perform, especially with someone I'm not that attracted to." Blanche's cheeks burned; Jazz's naivety was endearing, but being the one to disillusion her was awkward. Lee would probably not be thrilled with this conversation. They probably shouldn't share that they took more than most sex workers on account of being intersex; Jazz didn't need to know all that.

"Doesn't it have a lot of side effects?" Jazz hefted her bag over her shoulder. "That doesn't seem healthy."

"Probably, but needs must." Blanche shrugged. "Honestly, a little dizzy spell every now and then is the least of my worries."

"If there was an alternative, would you be open to it?" Jazz asked hesitantly.

"Are you dealing drugs, Jazzy?" Blanche teased, pulling their hair up into a high pony.

"No!" she laughed, tugging on the straps of her backpack. "I've gotten into alternative medicine lately, experimenting with herbal supplements, that kinda thing. There's a tea blend that might help."

Blanche smiled at her sweetness. Maybe a tea would be enough for someone who wasn't intersex, but it would take one hell of a tea to get Blanche hard on demand. Still, Jazz looked so eager to help, and Blanche had been trying to be better about being helped, instead of always helping. "You know, I've been struggling a lot with headaches lately. You got a tea for that?"

Between trying to find a therapist they clicked with over the past nine months, the bullshit their patron was putting them through, and growing their SubParty, the headaches had grown infinitely worse. Blanche's head was so full of bullshit, there was no escape from the tension. Not even weed was helping these days.

Jazz nodded eagerly. "Yes! Do you have any prescriptions besides the Viagra?"

"It's sweet you think this shit is prescription," Blanche teased. "I buy this from my weed guy at the Kum and Go down the street."

To Jazz's credit, she simply waited for their answer with a patient smile.

"No, no prescriptions." That'd require going to a doctor, and that was the last place they wanted to go. Going to a therapist was already bad enough. "But you really don't have to make me a tea, you know."

"I know!" Jazz grinned. "But my friends are sick of tea. It'll be nice to have a new customer."

Tara appeared in a hoodie and joggers. "Ready?"

"Oh!" Jazz looked surprised. "Am I going with you?"

"Where else you gonna go? Home?" Tara snorted derisively.

Jazz shrugged. "I figured I'd go to a coffee shop or something?"

"Nah, we're going thrifting now," Tara said, slipping on her shoes. She passed a pair of thigh-high boots to Blanche from the hall closet. "Sunny and I were gonna look for wedding outfits tonight anyway. We can get a head start, which will save us like, six hours. Blanche, you want me to look for anything for you?"

Swallowing the urge to refuse help from Tara—something several of the many therapists Blanche had seen over the past nine months had said they should work on—Blanche slid the leather heels up their leg, zipping it up under their robe. "Oh, now that you mention it, if you find any navy satin in the fabric section, grab it. I figured I'd make my own outfit."

"You got it!" Tara looped her arm through Jazz's and pulled her out the door. "Come on, the sooner we find something to wear to this wedding, the sooner I can take this underwear off. I fucking hate elastic, but your brother says I can't go commando in a fitting room..."

As Tara's voice disappeared down the hallway, Blanche ditched their robe in the bedroom, pulling the outfit their patron preferred from their closet. In the beginning, the priest roleplay had been an escape for Blanche. A way to reclaim power and cling to one last, lingering connection to Daisy, who had arranged the first meeting with Covey before her death. Now the satin and velvet vestments had become iron chains.

Blanche sighed, swallowing the sour twist in their gut. It was one thing to ask Jazz for help, but asking Tara, Lee, or Sunny had been a hard barrier to overcome. It was a role reversal Blanche couldn't quite wrap their head around. Before, they'd always made sure to do more for their ducklings than their ducklings did for them. But their latest therapist had suggested Blanche stop keeping score about who was more helpful. And while Blanche fully planned on breaking up with her as soon as they could replace her (because she was quite judgmental about Blanche's career, and weed habit, and gender expression, and *everything* really), her insight was valid.

Still, it nagged at them as they laced up their corset, perfectly molded to their body over all these years. Because while Blanche had been trying to accept help, everyone else had started refusing theirs.

Tara wasn't confiding in them anymore, at least not about the things Blanche knew were bothering her. Namely, her feelings for Gabe. Lee and Antonio kept insisting that the only help they wanted from Blanche for the wedding was to officiate the ceremony, even though Gabe and Tara got to help constantly. Richard was perfectly capable of taking care of all of Sunny's whims. And Gabe honestly was more help to them than they could ever be to him; giving them reference for therapist after therapist, connecting them with his lawyer friend who Blanche had emailed a few times, and letting them hang out with his dog was more than they could have ever hoped for.

Perhaps that was something they could discuss with their therapist, even if Blanche wasn't fond of her. They had been putting off saying much more until they got off the waitlist for another one, but who knew when that would be? Blanche pulled the bloodred vestments over their head, the satin cool against their skin as they put those thoughts aside.

On cue, a key entered the lock to their apartment door, and Blanche tucked their real thoughts, real feelings, real life problems away. As a final step in their transformation, they adorned themself with a plain linen stole. Entrenched fully in their Work headspace—the righteous priest, releasing the anger and resentment that constantly festered in their soul—Blanche went out to greet their patron.

Chapter Seven

Sunny

After four thrift stores, Sunny was beginning to think that finding navy satin *anything* might be a tall order. Jazz had patiently tagged along while Sunny and Tara scoured the formal wear; Antonio's sisters had invited Jazz months ago to join in their idea to all wear infinity dresses together.

While Jazz was happy to be included, Richard was waiting in his Range Rover in the dark, because the smell of the second store had given him a headache. Sunny scowled as the hangers squeaked under her fingers, willing any of them to turn into navy satin.

"You okay?" Jazz asked.

"Huh?" Sunny looked up. Tara looked surprised too; both of them normally ignored each other's bad moods, unless they were crying or on the verge of violence. "I'm a little annoyed that we're not finding anything, but nothing serious. Why?"

"You just growled at the clothing rack," Jazz bit her lip to hide a smile.

"Did I?" Sunny asked Tara.

Tara nodded. "I'm used to it."

"I guess," Sunny huffed. "I feel bad for making Richard wait in the car for us. He's being nice and driving us to the suburbs, and I gave him a headache."

"You didn't give him a headache. That obnoxious perfume gave him a headache," Tara corrected. "And he says he's fine, so he's fine."

"Yeah, but he's not actually fine," Sunny insisted. "He's toughing it out for my sake."

"And?" Tara ducked behind another tall, circular rack of dresses.

"He does that shit all the time, and I appreciate it, but he's..." Sunny paused, searching for the words. "I feel bad."

"Because he's doing something nice for you?" Tara snickered from around the rack. "Tragic."

"It's not just shit like favors, Tara-Bear," Sunny snapped. "He's always fine with everything. He supports whatever I want or need, and I... I don't do that back. And I don't like it, because now he has a headache, and he wouldn't if I hadn't bugged him about driving us out here."

"If I can try," Jazz said hesitantly. "It sounds like he's been meeting you where you're at in a lot of ways, and you haven't been meeting him halfway."

"Yeah!" Sunny snapped. "Exactly! Like, I tell him what I need in our relationship, and he does it, and I feel like I'm not doing that for him. But I can't get him to open up about what he wants or needs."

"What's wrong with that?" Tara asked, strangely defensive. "If he couldn't handle it, he'd say something, or tell you no."

"Because more often than not, we end up arguing, because he keeps it all bottled up inside for my sake." Sunny flipped her hair over her shoulder. "And I'm better at arguing than him, so I always win."

"It doesn't seem sustainable," Jazz added. "My mom always did whatever my dad said until he kicked Lee out, and that broke her. And because my dad is an asshole, he doubled down until after Auntie Alitrice's passing finally sank in, and then that broke *him*, and they're still not back to normal."

Sunny stared dumbfounded at Jazz; even Tara poked her head around the clothing rack with a confused expression. "Are you comparing Richard and I to your *parents*?!"

Tara flipped her off. "Bitch, Jazz just opened up about something personal! Be nice!"

Jazz's eyes widened. "I wasn't trying to compare your relationship to my parents! Sorry! I was just trying to say, you might need to show more consideration for him if he won't advocate for himself."

"Wouldn't that cause the opposite problem?" Tara asked, ducking around yet another clothing rack. Sunny never understood how Tara could tell there was nothing worth finding without looking at anything closely. "Instead of Richard taking on everything, Sunny would."

"Yeah, no," Jazz laughed, reminding Sunny so much of her brother. "There's this thing called communication. Not every relationship is going to be fifty-fifty all the time, and Sunny doesn't need to take on the burden of everything. Sunny can tell Richard where she's at, meet him where she can, and encourage Richard to open up about his wants. As long as you're honest about what you both need and want, then you can figure out where you meet, or help with each other's slack."

Personally, Sunny liked Black Hawk's idea of roleplay more than Jazz's advice. But maybe, they could do both. Planning a roleplaying scene and aftercare would probably be easier with honest conversations, and she should probably practice those, too. That way, Sunny could still get under his skin and on her knees for him, and hopefully...

Clearing her throat, Sunny wiped the dreamy smile off her face before Jazz and Tara made fun of her. She and Richard would hopefully figure out how well they worked when things were serious, too. This wasn't just about kinky sex, though that was a pretty high priority. This was about their future together. She had to remember to be Serious Sunny, too. And to ask Richard if he would be interested. Because she still hadn't done that.

"Here." Tara handed her a cocktail dress, with a knee-length navy satin skirt. "It's your size."

"Hell yeah!" Sunny held the lace bodice with a sweetheart neckline up to her body with a squeal. "Did you find anything for you?"

"Yup!" Tara held up a navy satin sleeveless jumpsuit with a corset top. "Looks like it'll fit."

Sunny and Jazz exchanged a skeptical look. "Tara-Bear, with all due respect because they're very cute, your mosquito bites are not gonna fill that top."

Tara shrugged. "The rest should fit though, and it has pockets, so I'll figure it out. The only person with a view will be Gabe, and he'll have no problem keeping his eyes to himself." Before Sunny could tease her that no, he wouldn't, Tara turned to Jazz. "How do you know all this relationship shit anyway? Got something to share with the class?"

Jazz let out a flustered laugh. "Nope! Not at all!"

"I think you do!" Tara smirked.

"We don't tell Lee," Sunny teased. "Come on, who are they?"

"No one!" Jazz made a beeline for the fitting rooms. "Come on, don't you want to try those snazzy outfits on?"

Relieved Richard wouldn't have to suffer for her sake much longer, Sunny exchanged a knowing grin with Tara as they followed through the sea of clothes. Probably for the best that Jazz kept her love life low-key. It didn't matter who Jazz dated; Lee would be pissed out of principle.

BLANCHE

SINKING TO HIS KNEES in the living room without even removing his suit jacket, Covey looked up at Blanche with his thin lips parted and expression wrecked. "I'm here to confess."

"Get up," Blanche snapped, anger burning along their skin. While it was a relief to have an outlet, Covey's blatant manipulation by starting the scene without so much as a hello enraged them. They'd let him get away with so much shit over the years; his entitlement was a habit they could no longer break. "We need to talk."

"Please," he whispered. The lines deepened around his blue eyes as they narrowed, his desperation dimming with annoyance. "Goddess Divine, hear me."

Blanche shook their head. "We talked about this, Bryce. You can't just show up without warning. You agreed you'd give me at least an hour's notice."

Covey's mouth closed in a wry sneer. "But I need to confess." He crawled toward them slowly, reaching out for the hem of Blanche's vestments. "I'm on my knees for you, Goddess. You will hear me, won't you?"

"Don't touch me, scum," Blanche hissed. Kicking his hand away from them, they pinned his fingers to the floor beneath their boot. The satisfied expression on Covey's face as he hissed in pain made their stomach churn.

Pushy as always, their patron knew Blanche would never force a sub into a conversation about their arrangement during a scene. They couldn't even call him out for the late notice, let alone his bullshit with Confession. Blanche's moral compass may be shaky, but they had limits, and Covey used that against them. As he had done many times before, Covey forced their hand.

Blanche growled as they dug their stiletto heel into his palm until he cried out. "You disgust me. A simpering little bitch, always crawling back, begging for forgiveness you don't deserve."

"I know. I'm revolting and disgusting. I don't deserve to gaze upon your holiness." Covey closed his eyes with a smile, breathing deep. The zipper of his pants was already straining. "Will you hear my confession?"

"Confess to your wife!" Blanche let his hand up before they caused real injury. Any permanent marks had to be left out of public view.

Covey's eyes snapped open, a sneer crossing his face. "Don't go there."

"Why not?" Blanche stepped toward him. "I've trained her myself, just for you. You married her, made vows of fidelity and devotion. She is eager and willing to fill my boots. Make *her* forgive you, you lying sack of shit!"

Covey's laugh was low and sweet, tinged with a groan. "But she loves me too much. Her forgiveness means nothing. No one hates me like you do, Goddess Divine."

"Then stop doing shit that needs forgiving." Blanche led the way to their bedroom, snapping for him to crawl behind them. They wished they could bring him to the playroom, where all of their other clients had their scenes since they'd turned Lee's old room into their recording set. But Covey insisted on being in their bedroom; Blanche's inner sanctum was defiled by him and him alone. "Get therapy so you hate yourself less."

"Perhaps I could get therapy," Covey murmured, waiting for instructions on his knees at the foot of the bed, hands behind his back. His smirk turned cold. "Or perhaps I could go to Confession. Aptly named, I think. I wonder what secrets could be revealed there."

"Fuck you!" Blanche growled, protectiveness for Freddy and Chas roaring through them. "You're taking this too far."

"Stop fighting this, my divinity," Covey shook his head. "I wouldn't have to threaten you, if you hadn't gone behind my back with my wife to try and leave me. I need you, and you need me. What we have is stronger than any marriage would ever be. My wife loves me for who she wants me to be. I am infallible in her eyes. You see my soul, your Grace, you see me for the worthless scum I am, and you still love me." He took a shuddering breath. "Please, let me confess."

Blanche sighed, too tired to keep fighting someone who refused to bend. "Grovel then. Accept your punishment, and repent."

Covey eagerly stripped naked, crawling up onto the wooden bench at the foot of Blanche's bed to kneel, while Blanche lit incense and candles. They grabbed a wooden paddle, and waited.

Clasping his hands together, as if praying to some power higher than Blanche, Covey confessed all the evil weighing on his soul since the last time he'd coerced his way into Blanche's bedroom, mere days ago. Unleashing the rage they'd so carefully kept buried, Blanche put their anger into the flogger, striking his ass and thighs as he spoke. Degrading him the way his soul needed to keep persisting in his greed and lust for power. His groans of pain and pleasure echoed louder than his confessions.

All the while, Blanche internalized his guilt. Perhaps this was how gods felt, when people prayed to ease their consciousness. But Blanche was only human, and Covey's guilt ate at their soul as he used them to free himself from it. The dozens of lawsuits from parents grieving children, who'd overdosed on the opiates his company produced, burrowed under their skin like worms. The sales exec who'd leapt from his office window that morning brought a lump to their throat. His own son, back in rehab again, made their chest tight.

That was the final admission that made Covey break, and as always, the wall protecting Blanche's heart broke with him. Sobs wracked his body as he begged Blanche for forgiveness. Their anger evaporating, Blanche dropped the paddle and backed away, sinking down into the chair in the corner of their bedroom. Pity weighed them down. The disgust and resentment that had been fueling Blanche drained away. The trust he placed in them was so precious; how could Blanche not cherish it? At their beckon, Covey fell to the floor. Crawling to them, he buried his face in their lap as he cried.

Blanche stroked his hair. "You're forgiven, sweetheart," they murmured, letting him cry his pain out until it soaked through the vestments to their thigh. "I forgive you, it's okay."

The words, as always, rang hollow. Who were they to forgive Covey's sins, other than the transgressions against themself? But Covey whispered his gratitude as if his soul hung in the balance, already touching himself. Groaning into Blanche's lap, he mouthed their cock through the fabric. Blanche winced, resisting the urge to push him away.

"What's wrong?" he asked, when Blanche barely reacted to his ministrations. Anger darkened his voice, "You said I was forgiven."

"This is why you need to give me enough time, sweetheart," Blanche sighed, willing their body to cooperate. But their erection never came. If they'd had more notice before his arrival, they could have taken another dose, endured the migraine that would follow after. "Or perhaps a sign to seek forgiveness from your wife."

"Why would I, when I have you to save me?" Covey groaned as he stroked himself, nosing at their chest until Blanche adjusted their vestments, easing a breast from their corset for him to suck on instead. "You're my peace, my salvation, my love. Why would I ever let you go?"

Faking pleasure as they always did for him, Blanche stroked his hair. The confusing whirl of emotion got the better of them as he came with a groan around their nipple. His cum splattered their boot. They whispered praise and affirmations as Covey lapped it up, looking up at Blanche with his tongue dragging up their boot like they were holy. As much as Blanche despised and resented him, after seven years of being tied to this sad, weak, broken man, a part of them loved him, too.

Just as they'd loved and hated Daisy.

Blanche put him back together, treating him like the fragile, precious wretch he hid from everyone, except Blanche. After they had absorbed all of his guilt and anguish, locking it all away in their heart like he needed them to, Covey stood tall at the door. Exhaustion and gratitude shone behind the blue eyes looking down at them. He kissed them slow and sweet, as if Blanche really was his mistress, instead of his domme.

And as always, Blanche kissed him back, hating themself for loving him.

"Thank you, Blanche. For everything." He pressed one last soft kiss to their forehead. "I do truly love you, I hope you know that."

"Then let me go," Blanche pleaded in a whisper. Their soul was on the verge of cracking, just as his had been, when he'd knelt at this very spot mere hours ago.

"You know I can't do that," Covey murmured. "But we will talk about our arrangement, see if there's ways to make this easier for both of us, okay? We'll talk first next time."

Blanche nodded, knowing that was a lie, but too tired to call him out. He always said that; there'd never be a next time.

Saturday, March Thirteenth

Chapter Eight

TARA

Following Gabe into the Education wing of the Modern Art Institute, Tara sipped the coffee he'd handed her when she'd climbed into his Outback. Notes of chocolate and hazelnut rose up in the steam. The bagel that had come with it was long gone. "When you said you volunteered at a youth art class, I didn't realize you ran the whole program."

With a shrug, Gabe unlocked the classroom door, holding it open for her. "I don't run the whole thing, I just find guest teachers and coordinate permission slips. Admin stuff."

"I'm pretty sure that's running the whole thing," Tara teased as she stepped past him. Her heart swelled with nostalgia at the familiar space.

The MAI was her favorite safe place in Bellamy—after Confession of course. Rule Eight (always have an escape route) could be difficult in public places, but Tara had long ago memorized all of the emergency exits in this beautiful maze. She had spent countless hours here as a teenager, taking classes with Lee in this very room. Sitting in the light-filled atrium overlooking the Mississippi, or wandering through exhibits, Tara had found peace here, getting lost in brush strokes and color composition, or eating tacos in the sculpture garden on a sunny day.

Thinking about Gabe being so involved here was strange, like he shouldn't belong in this place where she'd made so many memories. Yet, he looked just as at ease as she felt. Flicking on the light switch like he'd done it hundreds of times before, he tossed his messenger bag on the back table like it was routine.

The classroom hadn't changed much since Tara had last taken a class a decade ago. The podium with a computer and the smartboard were new; when she'd been a student there, the projector had overheated after an hour. Otherwise, the neat gray carpeting and clean white walls were unchanged. As were the beige tables that could flip vertically when the lever underneath it was pressed just right. The splotch of blue acrylic paint that Lee had accidentally flung at the ceiling was still there.

Standing close enough behind her that his chest brushed her shoulder, Gabe followed her gaze up. "Yeah, my mom has been after maintenance to replace that ceiling tile for years."

"No! Leave it!" Tara protested, leaning back to look up at him, the soft wool of his dark green sweater brushing her ear. "Lee will be so embarrassed that it's still here!"

Gabe shot her a quizzical look. "That's from *Lee*?"

Tara smirked over her shoulder. "We had a battle of wills over a fan brush."

He gave her a soft smile. "Well, in that case, I'll cancel the maintenance—"

The door burst open with a bang. A cart, stacked high with an explosion of flowers, pushed through the door frame. "Gabriel, a little help, please? I've got a box full of sharp objects about to fall."

Gabe hurried to prop the door open, taking a box that appeared from behind the flowers. The room filled with the scent of greenery as the cart trundled into the room. "You're on time this morning, Ang. You feeling okay?"

"Shush, I'm only late after lunch." Hidden behind the tower of blossoms, the florist pulled Gabe down into a one-armed hug as the door swung closed.

Tara hung back, unsure what—if anything—she was supposed to do as the florist parked the cart next to the table at the front of the classroom. The woman finally stepped out from behind the towering flowers. Her orange wrap dress swirled around her rounded hips as she unloaded two buckets full of carnations onto the table.

They both froze as their eyes met over the blooms.

The florist smiled before Tara could regain control over her face. Her red lipstick was as bold as it had been last Saturday night, at Confession. "Oh, hello. *You* have red hair!"

Tara's hand drifted to her curls in confusion.

After a muttered, "Are you fucking kidding me," Gabe loudly cleared his throat. "Tara, this is Angie Garcia, the florist I was telling you about and, in the most convenient coincidence, Tonio's cousin. Angie, this is Tara Sanderson, Lee's best man and acting CFO of the wedding planning committee."

"A coincidence indeed." Angie's smile grew wider. "So, you do have a name."

With a heavy sigh, Gabe looked between them in dawning realization. "I take it you've met."

Angie nodded, not taking her eyes off Tara. "I bought her a drink at Confession after our date on Saturday."

Tara whipped around to look at Gabe, jaw dropping in disbelief. "*She* was your date?!"

Gabe shrugged, his jaw tight, and gave a reluctant nod.

"Dude, what is wrong with you? She is beyond hot!" Tara crossed her arms, unsure if the frisson in her veins was relief or insecurity. If he didn't want someone like *her*, why would he want Tara?

Angie's laugh was rich and throaty. "Yeah, Gabriel. What *is* wrong with you?"

Gabe gripped the ends of his hair. "Can we focus on the flowers? Angie, I'm willing to pay you however much you need, but because Antonio and Lee don't know we're hiring a florist, Tara gets the final say in who we book." He smiled nervously at Tara. "Assuming this is still all right with you?"

Tara snorted, embarrassed that Gabe was being so considerate; really, she had no say in how he spent his own money. "I've had a week to come around to the idea. My mind is as open as can be."

"Good." Gabe's dimples deepened before he turned back to Angie. "Can I set up for you while you talk?"

"Well, since you asked!" Angie handed him a stack of small plastic buckets and a pitcher of water. "These vases go on the tables, fill them up to the line. Each gets one of the bouquets on the bottom of the cart. Once you're done with that, I've got elastic, wire, scissors, pins, and greenery tape that needs to be distributed." Angie hopped up on the table with a brochure and patted the spot next to her with a wink. "Tara, come sit with me so I can *convince* you."

Hesitantly, Tara leaned against the table. Gabe set down each of the small vases with an audible *thunk*, stuffing them full of flowers. Angie handed Tara the brochure, leaning in close as she explained her vision for the wedding. Trying to focus on the brochure, and not the view down Angie's dress (while Tara's heart yearned for Gabe, she still had eyes, and it was quite the view), Tara pulled out her phone to ask all of the questions she'd prepared.

While she was less forward than she had been Saturday, Angie flirted outrageously—paying loud compliments to the color of her hair, for some reason—as they chatted about the arrangement options and process for the wedding. Gabe resolutely refused to look at them, distributing the supplies louder than necessary. Confused, Tara bantered back, trusting Angie wouldn't read too much into it, considering they'd parted with a friendly hug after their drink.

After Angie had finally won her over with (mostly professional) answers to her many questions, and photos of lush centerpieces in every shade of peach, the only other thing Tara wanted to ask about was money. But that was Gabe's business. His financial contribution was his decision, not hers. But he'd been right; Angie would be perfect for the wedding.

Tara waved Gabe over from distributing scissors. Fiddling with the end of his braid, he approached hesitantly, his coffee-brown eyes searching her face for approval.

"You're going to give yourself split ends." Tara pulled his hand away to stop him, burning hot when Gabe held tight to her fingers instead. Tearing her eyes away from their joined hands, she stilled her face into the mask of friendship she'd been practicing for months. It did not stop her heart from thumping wildly behind her walls. "I'm willing to concede that hiring Angie will be way less stressful than buying everything and making all of the arrangements ourselves."

"Why, Kitten, I never thought you'd admit I was right," Gabe teased, squeezing her fingers as his thumb traced her knuckles.

Warmth exploded in her chest and a quiet laugh bubbled out of her as her mask slipped. He hadn't called her Kitten since they ended their...thing. And he'd always been careful not to say it around other people. But he said it so casually, so *intentionally*, with Angie right next to her. Her confusion spiraled, laced with hope she shouldn't allow herself to feel. Tara tried to hide her relieved smile behind a scoff, but the heat in her cheeks had to be giving her away. "Don't get used to it. Besides, it's your money. If you want to spend it on flowers for Tonio and

Lee, I won't stop you. Roses and ranuncus, or whatever they're called, will look way better than grocery store carnations."

"Ranunculus," Angie supplied. "But most people call them buttercups."

"Buttercups?" Gabe smiled softly at Tara. "I bet Lee would love those."

Not trusting the lump forming in her throat, Tara could only nod in agreement.

The door burst open, and a group of teenagers strolled in with greetings of "Hey Coop!" as they headed for the tables. Dropping her hand, Gabe turned to greet them.

Tara drew it to her chest, confused by how it stung when he'd let her go. They held hands all the time. This was no big deal. But normally, her heart was safe. Now, it was soaring, and Tara couldn't control it even if she wanted to.

"Are you making corsages with the class today?" Angie asked quietly, eying Tara up and down.

"That's the plan." Tara edged away from her. Gabe had just smashed through her mask with a single pet name; this close examination was too much. "I know nothing about flower arranging, though."

"Good." Angie's smile widened as she hopped off the table. Her Cheshire cat expression was distinctly *not* flirty; it reminded her more of Blanche when they were scheming. "This will be so fun!"

"All right everyone, find your seats!" Gabe called as the last teenagers filed in.

Tara hovered to the side with Angie while Gabe got everyone's attention, unsure where she was supposed to go.

Standing at the front of the class, Gabe hushed the kids with a wave of his hands. "Everyone, this is Angelica Garcia, who owns Flores Flores, a flower shop on Broadway over Eastside. She's here to teach you about the history of flower arranging and show you how to make your own arrangements. She'll also show you how to make corsages and boutonnieres to wear to prom—"

"What if we're not going to prom?" a kid interrupted, spurring a wave of titters and fidgeting from the class.

"...or just for fun, if I'm allowed to finish my sentence without interruption." Arching one eyebrow, Gabe gave the class a mock-stern look.

Tara smiled as they all dropped the flowers and tape they were fussing with, their hands slapping on the tables to show they were paying attention. Gabe seemed surprisingly comfortable—confident even—leading a group of teenagers. Kids who, just ten years ago, *were* her. Tara shifted to her back foot. As close as they'd become over the past year, there was still so much about this sensitive, considerate soul to discover.

"Syl," Gabe hid the name in a fake cough at a young boy, too busy trimming his bangs with the scissors Angie had brought to listen. The kid jumped and dropped the scissors with a guilty smile, brushing the hair off the table. Half of his forelock stuck in the air, cut comically short. Gabe sighed. "Ms. Garcia, this is the very *respectful* and *polite* youth art program from the Eastside Community Center."

Tara's inhale was sharp. Gabe wasn't just running a program similar to the one she had taken as a kid, he was running the *exact* same program. She and Lee had signed up for dozens of classes at the Eastside Community Center to make Auntie Alitrice feel better about them not going to school. They'd joined this exact program—where she had learned graphic design, and Lee had found his calling with music. This class had been their last vestige of childhood innocence, one that had offered dreams of their future. And *Gabe* was running it?

Gesturing to give Angie the floor, Gabe put his hand on the small of Tara's back, guiding her to the back of the classroom.

Still struggling to process everything, Tara muttered under her breath, "Dude, you work with kids from *Eastside*? I'm surprised you've lasted this long. I would have torn your sensitive heart to shreds if you were my teacher when I was young."

Gabe snorted as he pulled out a chair for her at the back corner table. "Not much different as an adult, then."

Head spinning, Tara merely sat next to him, instead of asking what he meant.

Angie was just beginning to explain the origins of flower symbolism, when the kid who had been cutting his hair pointed at Tara. "Hold up, sorry. Who are *you*?"

"Syl, can you think of a more polite way to get that information?" Gabe asked, his teasing sarcasm barely detectable. "Maybe without interrupting the instructor or pointing at anyone?"

Syl ignored him. "I thought you were another flower lady, but Coop didn't introduce you. So what's your deal?"

"Who wants to know?" Tara asked, raising an eyebrow and fighting a smile. Talking with these kids was more comfortable territory. She had been Syl. Still was. He was smart to be suspicious of new strangers. There was a reason Rule Nine (keep the circle small) existed.

Gabe rubbed his forehead. "Please don't tell me you're about to argue with a kid."

Tara kept her eyes on Syl. "Depends on the answer."

Looking away, Syl finally muttered, "Just curious. Coop's only ever brought his mom here before."

Angie muffled a laugh.

"Thanks, Syl," Gabe sighed.

Tara stifled her own laugh. "I'm Tara. I'm here to learn about flowers, same as you. Now can Ms. Garcia get on with her class?"

Syl nodded, mollified. "Coop, you should keep her around. You give away everything so easy."

Tara shot a grin at Gabe. He tried to scowl back, but a smile played on his lips.

With a beaming grin, Angie restarted her lesson, explaining how different cultures used plants and flowers to send messages. "Let's put this into practice. So, using the symbolism guide in front of you, what flowers would I put in a bouquet to tell a lovely lady that she's beautiful, and I want to get to know her better?"

Syl raised his hand. "Roses!"

Angie nodded, her lips pursed. "Roses could work, depending on the context of the other flowers. *Red* roses might be a little too forward for the talking stage. If I'm just shooting my shot at a pretty woman, I'd probably go with orange roses, which mean fascination or desire." Angie pulled half a dozen deep peach roses from the buckets of flowers on the cart, placing them on the table next to the vase.

"Heather," a girl near the front said, raising her hand.

"Good, purple heather represents admiration." Angie fished a few more flowers out of another bucket.

"Orchid?" another girl asked.

"Orchid, very nice! It can symbolize adoration and beauty." Angie's smile turned apologetic. "But I didn't bring orchids with me today."

"Blue Saliva?" a boy offered with a confused laugh.

Angie pulled a few flowers from the buckets, gently correcting his pronunciation. "Excellent. Blue *Salvia* means 'thinking about you.' That will look pretty with the heather."

"Camellia."

"Yes, good. Pink Camellia means 'longing for you'."

Angie explained her aesthetic decisions as she snipped the stems, tucking them carefully into a small vase. "See how the heather and salvia add dimension, while the camellia and roses help make up the bulk of the bouquet? I'm going to tuck some ferns in here, too. Ferns represent fascination, and they'll add some greenery to create a more elegant shape."

Angie rotated it, showing off her final display as she walked it to the back of the classroom. She set it in front of Tara with a wink. "Here you go, lovely lady. Shooting my shot."

Tara's cheeks burned, politely thanking Angie amongst the wolf whistles and "oohs" coming from the kids. Maybe Angie had read more into her flirting than Tara had intended.

"Now, based on Mr. Cooper's expression, what flowers do you think *he'll* send to her?"

The kids laughed. Tara shot him a confused look. Gabe's olive skin was tinged red. He covered his eyes with one hand as he shook his head.

"Yellow hyacinth or maybe marigold?" someone called.

"You got it!" Angie pulled some flowers out. "I have yellow hyacinth with me. Marigold doesn't have the nicest smell, so I would leave those out unless you know the other person likes them."

Tara looked at the chart in front of her. Both meant jealousy. *But Gabe said he didn't plan to go on another date with Angie?*

Gabe's jaw worked back and forth as he glared at Angie, tugging on his braid.

"But yellow hyacinth alone isn't attractive enough." Angie's smirk never left Gabe. "He's gotta win her over now that he has competition. What flowers could he include to convince Tara to stick with him, instead of me?"

Tara's heart dropped, crashing with the panicked butterflies in her stomach. *Wait, I'm "her"?*

"Red carnations?" Syl guessed.

"Great, red carnations would tell her his heart aches for her." Angie dramatically held her hands over her chest. The kids laughed.

Wondering what the ever-loving fuck was happening, Tara burned hot. Gabe buried his face in his hands, not denying any of it.

"Can we do red roses too?" someone else asked.

"Yes! Red roses were too forward for me, but in Mr. Cooper's case, we'll use darker red or burgundy roses, because they show devotion. He's gotta let her know he's serious, right?" Angie hummed to herself as she found the right ones. "The last two I'll add are red salvia, which means 'forever mine,' and tarragon for greenery, which means 'lasting interest'," Angie explained her process again as she assembled the bouquet. "See how I arranged the lighter colors around the outside? That way the deep, passionate feelings are in the heart of the bouquet."

With a teasing grin, Angie practically danced to the back of the classroom to set it in front of Gabe. "Here, Mr. Cooper, you know who to give this to."

The kids laughed again. Still refusing to look at her, Gabe slid it in front of Tara.

Heart pounding, Tara lost the fight against her smile, her neck and face burning. "Thanks, Coop."

Using the kids' nickname earned her a playful glare. The hint of dimples was a win, as far as she was concerned. Even if Gabe was frustrated and embarrassed, those coffee-brown eyes were still looking at her with affection.

Sashaying her way back to the front, Angie flashed them a smug grin, before she turned to the class. "All right, now that you all understand the symbolism, I'll show you how to make corsages and boutonnieres, then you'll make your own arrangements. You have some flowers at your tables to choose from, but you can have anything I have up here." Angie demonstrated how to wrap the stems with ribbon and wire to attach them to the elastic wristbands.

Eager for a distraction, Tara scanned the chart, wondering what she should make. She'd been planning to make something for Blanche, but now... Well, she had a bouquet to take home instead. She wasn't sure if she was *supposed* to take a bouquet, but she definitely was now.

Selecting a yellow carnation from the bucket of flowers in front of her, she attached it with some greenery to the elastic. As she worked, Gabe sat quietly, not making anything. "You okay there, Coop?" Tara asked softly.

"After my dignity was flayed alive with an audience of teenagers? Yeah, I'm okay." Gabe fiddled with a spare scrap of elastic. "Would you, um..." He huffed. "Would you want to teach a class on graphic design?"

"I don't know if I'm qualified to teach, but I'm down." Tara nodded, trying to ignore the heavy weight of imposter syndrome. She wrapped a ribbon into a neat bow to help secure the elastic to the flower, and added softly, "That class changed my life."

Tara kept her eyes on the corsage, feeling exposed under Gabe's quiet, examining gaze.

"Good," he finally said. "We have a spot open next month. I'll send you the details." As the kids worked not-so-quietly on their arrangements, Gabe stood. "Excuse me, I need to tear Angie a new one. I'll never hear the end of it if my mom catches wind of this."

Tara snorted. "Can you bring her this from me?" She held up the corsage she made.

Gabe frowned, but he delivered it to Angie at the front of the room. Angie laughed as she slid it on her wrist, holding it up for the class. "Everyone, I got a reply to my bouquet. A yellow carnation. What did she tell me?"

"Damn, you got rejected!" Syl jeered. "What are you making for Coop?" he asked Tara.

"I haven't decided yet," Tara said, honestly. "But I'm out of yellow carnations."

Gabe shook his head, but he wore a small smile as he pulled Angie aside. Their hands gripped each other's elbows as they stood close. The easy camaraderie of teasing smiles and bickering was so similar to how Gabe was with her. Maybe Tara had been reading too much into the bouquet...

And yet, her chest was so full of hope, Tara was about to burst. Because Gabe had said he wasn't interested in a second date with Angie. And Angie's date had been hung up on his friend, and the bouquet in front of her was lush, full of devotion and jealousy and longing.

And Gabe had given it to Tara.

Tara picked through the bucket, hoping one of the blooms would feel right. She wasn't sure how she felt about Gabe in words, let alone flowers. The cool fragrance of a white rose settled her nerves. The difference between the charged tension she felt for Gabe, and the lighthearted flirting with Angie, was too overwhelming to contemplate. He was so much more of *everything* to her.

Her throat tightened as Tara wrapped the white rose together with three burgundy rosebuds and a sprig of the tarragon from the bouquet, pinning the ribbon around the stems to form the boutonniere.

The last pin slipped as she stabbed too hard, pushing through the stems and pricking her finger. With a hiss, Tara sucked the dot of blood into her mouth before it could stain the ribbon. *I should go.* She'd spent too much time thinking about her feelings while picking the damn flowers for Gabe; her chest ached from trying to breathe, her head still light and spinning. Breaking down in front of kids, who had their own shit to deal with, wouldn't be a good move. Managing her familiar dissociation was old hat, but Tara needed to get out of here if she was making mistakes like stabbing herself with pins.

She set the boutonniere in Gabe's empty spot and stood up to go.

Hesitating, Tara picked up the bouquet Gabe had "given" her; the one from Angie was nudged to his side of the table. Both were vibrant and lovely, but she wanted the devotion and aching longing and jealousy. Even if she was reading too much into Angie's teasing, at least in bouquet form, Tara could pretend her feelings weren't one-sided. And if Gabe took her gesture to mean she was interested in him? Well, he wouldn't be wrong.

Slipping quietly out the back door, Tara found the nearest exit without an alarm, hoping Gabe would understand why she'd left without a word. That he'd somehow understand her feelings, even if she didn't understand them herself. Everything about today confused her. Gabe seemingly wanted her—something she'd been longing for for months. And yet, if someone like Angie didn't interest him... Tara buried her nose in the bouquet, inhaling the floral scent to keep her head.

The exit led her through a concrete tunnel out to the riverwalk. Blinking as it emptied into daylight, Tara found herself in the amphitheater outside the MAI. Dodging a kid on a skateboard, she oriented herself, wondering how to get from the riverwalk up to street level. Her plan, to walk the mile and a half home and hide in her bed the rest of the day, was forgotten when she spotted a man in a top hat and peacoat sitting in the sunshine.

"Walter, long time." Tara set the vase next to her as she sat down beside her oldest friend. The cold concrete seeped through her jeans, but the sunshine warmed her face.

"Who's that?" Walter squinted at her, blinking. "Sorry, cataracts got shittier over winter."

"Tara," she hesitated, because Walter always remembered people in relation to others. And for Tara, that was her mother. "Anne's girl."

"Oh! Anne's girl!" His deep-lined face broke into a smile. There were a few more teeth missing than the last time she'd seen him. "How you been, sweetie?"

"I'm good, Walter. Yourself?" Tara smiled back, even as her heart ached at how haggard he looked. Since the last time she'd run into him, Walter's normally ruddy skin had grown ashen, his eyes milky. Still, that smile gave Walter an aura of peace she'd always envied and admired.

"Been better. Can't see shit, can't breathe worth a damn, and I get dizzy whenever I stand up," Walter sighed, leaning back against the concrete. "But not much I can do about it without taking those damn pills the doctors give out, and you know how I feel about that."

Tara nodded. "Side effects are worse than the illness."

"Exactly. That or they'll try to keep me there, and I can't sleep cooped up with the machines and the lights and all that. Luckily, the folks here let me sleep in the employee entrance, out of the wind a bit." He shrugged, nodding to the tunnel Tara had just exited. "Not as comfortable as the old bus, and it floods when it rains, but it's safer than anywhere else I've found."

"Good. I'm glad you found a spot."

"Me, too." Walter coughed. "This city's changed. No one's decent to strangers anymore."

Tara scoffed. "You're no stranger. Everyone knows you in Bellamy. You and Wanda won that City Icon award, remember?"

"Oh yeah! We pawned that. Only got twenty bucks." His laugh turned into a coughing fit. "Maybe they used to know me, but there's too many new people now. There's no bum on the sidewalk if they pretend I'm not there."

Tara knew what he meant. Everyone had done the same to her and her mom, their eyes passing over them as if they didn't exist. Walter was right; it was probably worse now. Bellamy had grown. Even Eastside wasn't Eastside anymore. Losing the encampment had been the writing on the wall. "You can always stay with Blanche and me."

"That's nice of you, sweetie, but being inside gets too loud in my head. I get panicky. Outside is quiet, even if it is cold and wet." Walter patted her hand. "How's your fella?"

"Lee's good! He's... Well, he's getting married. Not to me!" Tara added in a hurry. "You know he's not really my fella, right?"

Walter chuckled. "Yeah, figured that out a while ago, on account of how often I run into him outside of that gay bar up the street. He's got himself a husband, then?"

"Yeah, his name is Antonio. He and Lee are sweet together."

"Good." Walter nodded in approval. "How about you? You and Daisy's gal living together as friends or..."

"Oh, yeah, Blanche and I are just friends." Tara laughed. "We're both very single."

"That's a shame. You two never had enough people in your lives. That Daisy passed long ago, and your mom left even longer than that." Walter waved a hand to silence the protests before they left her mouth. "I know you have each other and your fella and all, but who do you have that's yours? That's what I miss most about my Wanda—we were always each other's above all else. There's nothing like that feeling in the world."

Tara sat silently, fiddling with a red carnation in the vase.

A shadow fell over her. "Tara? You're still here?"

The stem of the carnation snapped off in her hand as Tara jumped. She squinted up at Gabe. "Oh! Hey! Sorry, I just...left."

"No, it's okay." Gabe smiled. "I'm glad you didn't go far."

"Who's that?" Walter asked. "He's too tall, I can't see him."

Tara wasn't sure how to answer, but Gabe crouched down. Curling his giant frame around his knees, he set down the bouquet she'd left for him next to hers. The boutonniere she'd made was pinned to his sweater, the creamy white and rich burgundy framed by soft, forest green wool. "Oh, sorry. Gabe Cooper, John and Miriam's son. Not sure if you remember me."

Remember him? Tara blinked. Why did Gabe know Walter at all?

"Oh!" Walter's face broke into a smile again. "I haven't seen you since you were shorter than Wanda! Your mom said you'd grown as tall as your dad, but it's another thing to see you in person! How is he? Your mom stops by to chat sometimes, but your dad hasn't been around lately."

"He's good, busy as ever. I'm sure you remember how he is." To Tara's bewilderment, Gabe and Walter exchanged a knowing grin and a nod. "They built a house at the vineyard, so he doesn't come to the city as much. I'll tell him you said hi."

Fiddling with the broken carnation, Tara could only watch as she struggled to process their exchange. The closest thing she'd ever had to a grandfather had known Gabe as a kid, was friends with his parents. Yet again, Gabe had leaked out of the many compartments she'd tried to keep him in—as the stranger she'd hooked up with, as the friend of a friend, as her friend with benefits, and so on. With no effort on his part, he'd become entwined in every aspect of her life.

"Do... Do you want to get lunch?"

Tara stiffened as she realized Gabe had directed that question to her. Scolding herself for reading too much into it, she forced a friendly smile. "Are you sure you don't want to get lunch with Angie? You really undersold how hot she is."

Gabe shook his head with a laugh. "And yet, I'm asking you."

"She'd love to," Walter answered for her, digging an elbow into her side. "Watch out—if he's anything like his dad, he's going to trick you into living with him. Wanda and I once ended up staying in their garage for six weeks, while John took his sweet-ass time towing our bus to the winter camp by the mounds."

Gabe laughed. "I remember that. I was like, seven or eight, I think? You were so mad once you realized. You're still welcome to stay anytime, Walter. Even at the vineyard—we can set you up wherever you're most comfortable."

"See what I mean? Just like your dad. No, I like my freedom." Walter nudged her again. "Now go on, you're always hungry. Go get a free lunch with this nice young man."

"Unless *you'd* rather go to lunch with Angie." Despite his teasing smile, Gabe tugged his braid. "You could still catch up to her."

"I don't want to get lunch with Angie, Coop." Tara handed the snapped-off carnation to Walter. "Take care of yourself, all right?"

With a toothless grin, Walter tucked it into the buttonhole of his peacoat. "Thank you, sweetie. You tell your fella congratulations for me, and say hi to your mom if you see her."

"I will." No point in reminding him that her mom had taken off years ago; Walter knew. Standing up, she wiped the grit of the concrete off her jeans. "So where are we going?"

Gabe picked up both vases, handing her the bouquet made of his jealousy and longing. "I hadn't thought that far ahead yet."

She fell into step beside him, cradling the vase to her chest to bury her nose in the burgundy roses. Lunch with Gabe should feel like no big deal; they'd eaten together many times, spent hours in each other's company. Their friendship was so comfortable, even if her heart secretly ached. But never before had Tara been so hopeful that Gabe was asking her to lunch as more than friends. She wrenched the shattered pieces of the mask back on. "Can I drive?"

Gabe laughed. "No."

"But I need practice in parking lots."

"Even more reason to say no." Gabe's smile was teasing, easy as ever. But his deep brown eyes lingered a little too long, his expression a little too soft for mere friendship.

Biting her lip to hide her foolish grin, Tara swallowed. "Please?"

Gabe snorted, putting an arm around her shoulders. "Fine."

Chapter Nine

Antonio

Arranging their wedding planning binder and laptops, Antonio and Lee settled into the sofa in Blanche's apartment, ready to tackle the next item on their to-do list: the ceremony itself. Everything else—the vendors, the color schemes, the catering—had needed to be booked and decided on so early, the details of their actual wedding had fallen off their radar. Until Blanche had sent them a list of questions they'd never considered before.

Laptop balanced on their knees, Blanche sprawled over their armchair as they squinted at the screen. "Are you planning to write your own vows?"

"I think so?" Antonio looked to Lee for confirmation, who nodded. Anxiety tightened Antonio's throat. Strange, because he'd been performing his whole life. Why did wedding vows seem so monumental? "Can I sing my vows?"

"As long as you don't steal my vows like you did my proposal, you can do whatever you want," Lee teased. "But you can also write them down, you know. I'm not going to memorize anything."

Antonio shrugged, entirely unashamed that he'd unintentionally plagiarized Lee's private speech when he'd proposed at their album's launch party. "You said it so perfectly, everyone else needed to hear it."

Blanche rubbed their neck. "And will anyone be doing any readings? Or perform any songs? Anything like that? Prayers?"

Antonio exchanged a shrug with Lee. "Not that I planned. Should we have that?"

"Definitely no prayers," Lee said. "But we haven't talked about the rest. Should we have all of that?"

"Depends on how long you want the ceremony to be." Blanche snorted. "I can talk shit about you two all day if you want, but you might want to have other friends or family members do a reading to break up the parts of the ceremony and make them feel more involved."

"Do we have any friends who don't mind public speaking?" Antonio asked Lee.

He shrugged, pushing up his glasses. "What about your family?"

Antonio winced. As hard as it was to go against his nature as a mama's boy, he'd endeavored to minimize his family's involvement. It felt unfair to Lee. Even *if* Lee invited his parents (and *if* his parents showed up), Antonio wouldn't want them to do a reading. Or speak at all. Antonio supported Lee's every decision, but if it were up to him, the people who had abandoned his future husband would never get the opportunity to hurt him again, let alone on the happiest day of their lives.

Besides, from what Lee had told him, given the opportunity, they'd find a way to work a prayer into it; Lee and Antonio had both agreed to keep religion out of the ceremony. Antonio's family knew not to expect the usual Catholic pageantry of the Flores family milestones. And asking any of his siblings or cousins to do a reading would also mean wading back into the politics of favoritism.

His sisters had understood why he'd asked Cassie to be an attendant, but his mom was pushing him to find other ways for his siblings to participate. Antonio had already given in and asked his youngest brother and Cassie's daughter to be the ring bearer and flower girl, and the rest of his siblings were now ushers. But the disappointment in his mom's eyes had filled him with guilt; she'd probably imagined walking him down the aisle. Poor Gabe had been a saint, reassuring Antonio that he was making the right choice anytime indecision struck again (whereas Lee would just say it was fine, because he didn't like to cause conflict).

The Flores family presence would already dominate the event. Walking down the aisle with any combination of parental figures—flaunting his healthy, loving relationship with his parents and stepparents, while Lee had been wracked by indecision about extending the merest olive branch to his own—felt cruel. Out of all the ideas Antonio had suggested, Lee liked the idea of walking down the aisle with Antonio the best, so that's what they would do. Thankfully, none of Antonio's parents had pushed back.

"If I ask one, I'd have to ask, like, twelve people." Antonio smiled brightly. "Let's stick to friends, if anything. Otherwise this ceremony will never end."

Lee leveled a look at him. "You don't have to do that. It's fine if you want your family involved. Don't worry about me."

Pressing a kiss to his cheek, Antonio teased, "Try and stop me. It's my job to consider your feelings." He rubbed Lee's arm. "I'd say maybe someone from Confession like Venus or Jackie, but Lord only knows what they'd say. Maybe Phin? He's a lawyer. He can probably give a decent speech."

Lee grimaced. "Maybe we just don't do readings?"

Antonio nodded. "We can get to the fun part faster that way. Besides, there'll be speeches during the reception."

A knock on the door sounded.

"Who the fuck is here? I'm not available today," Blanche groaned as they got up to answer it, shoulder cracking as they stretched. "Oh, Jazz! Come on in! Your brother's here."

Lee's eyes tightened briefly behind his glasses. His sister, bundled up against the lingering winter winds in a cream coat and hat, followed Blanche into the living room. A small storage bin was tucked under her arm. "What are *you* doing here?"

"Good to see you, too." Jazz rolled her eyes and gestured to the tub. "Sorry, I should have checked to make sure you were free, but I wanted to make a delivery to my best customer."

"Aren't I your only customer?" Blanche teased.

"You're the only one who paid me. Ergo, the best one."

Antonio cocked his head, looking at the dried flowers in the storage bin. "Is that weed?"

Blanche laughed. "Please—no offense Jazz—but I exclusively buy weed from the guy at Kum and Go. He's the only grower I trust now that the government's selling it. No, I've been exhausted lately, so she offered to make me a tea blend."

"An herbalist came to one of my botany courses as a guest speaker last semester," Jazz explained, shedding her layers to reveal a tight, low-cut lilac sweater. "I've gotten a little obsessed, but I can only drink so much tea. And Blanche asked for something to help with their headaches and stuff, so I made a new blend for them."

Lee leaned back against the couch cushions, crossing his arms. "You hang out here without me?"

Jazz set the tub down with a *thunk*, putting a hand on her hip. "I'm not exactly eager to go straight home after class, and Blanche and Tara are cool with me hanging out here. Is that a problem, Lee?"

"I guess not." Lee shrugged as Antonio rubbed his arm. As easygoing as Lee was, his patronizing, overprotective attitude toward his younger sister drove Antonio up a wall. He could only imagine how Jazz felt.

"I'm so glad you approve," Jazz scoffed.

Blanche settled back into their armchair, returning their laptop to their knees. "We're planning the ceremony if you want to hang out for a bit."

"Oh fun!" Jazz squinted at them. "You want me to make you a cup? You don't look like you got much sleep. Tension headache?"

"Honestly, the same headache I've had for days," Blanche nodded. "Tea sounds lovely."

"Anyone else want one?"

Lee declined, but Antonio accepted, his curiosity piqued.

Jazz busied herself finding the old kettle in the kitchen. "Where's Tara today?"

Blanche smirked. "At the art museum. With *Gabe*."

"Wait, really?" Antonio asked eagerly, excitement bursting in his chest.

Gabe hadn't told him about any plans with Tara. Then again, he'd only dug for details on how Gabe's latest blind date had gone; he'd gotten none other than "it was fine," and "no, one date was enough to know it wouldn't go anywhere." Not unexpected. Gabe rarely offered up any juicy details about his love life.

"He picked her up at nine." Blanche grinned. "Yes, Tara was not only awake that early, but she ventured out in public! And wore real clothes for once—or at least jeans instead of joggers. It's after one, and she's *still* not back."

"Is this, like, a date?" Antonio asked.

They shrugged. "She didn't say it was, but she didn't say it wasn't."

"What an interesting turn of events!" Antonio's grin matched the one Blanche wore.

"Or maybe she's helping at his volunteer gig?" Lee suggested with a weary sigh. "Maybe it's totally platonic, and you two are reading way too much into it?"

Antonio patted his thigh. "Angel, I love you, but let me have hope that my best friend finally made a move on the woman he's been pining over for a year. Why do you think I wished him luck on his date right when we left last week?"

Lee opened his mouth to scold him, but Antonio cut him off with a finger to his lips. "And before you start in on me again, that was not *meddling*, just sharing information. Maybe I happened to strategically share it on our way out the door, in hopes that it would spark a private conversation about how available he is. But that's not meddling!" Ignoring Lee's skeptical look, Antonio took the mug from Jazz as she sat next to them on the couch. "Either way, we are allowed to read into it, because *that's* not meddling, either."

"You're not allowed to meddle? That's boring." Jazz slurped her tea. "Mmm, tell me what you think of this. At first I wasn't sure about the flavor balance, but it's grown on me."

"I better like it—you brought me a year's worth." Blanche laughed.

Antonio took a sip and forced himself to swallow, instead of spitting back into the mug. He and Blanche exchanged a meaningful look over the rims of their cups.

"I don't like that expression." Jazz looked between them with a wince. "What is it? Tell me, I won't take it personally."

"Um..." Antonio sniffed the steam and took another tentative sip. It was somehow worse than the first. "It tastes both like soap and dirt."

Blanche took another sip, grimacing as they swallowed. "Maybe if I add some honey?"

"I put a lot of honey in it already." Jazz sighed, "I'll take it back and keep playing with it."

"No! I'm sure I'll get used to it!" Blanche insisted. "Maybe it's an acquired taste. See? Better with every sip."

That is a bald-faced lie. Antonio took another sip to make sure, and yes, it was still disgusting. "What's in it anyway?"

"Lavender, chamomile, ashwagandha, St. John's wort, lemon balm and catnip. And a little honey and lemon juice."

"Catnip? Oh, Jazzy, I wonder about you sometimes," Blanche laughed. "I guess the lavender explains the soap taste. What's causing the um...earthy notes?"

"It's dirt, Blanche. Don't dress it up by calling it earthy." Antonio put his cup down. "Sorry Jazz, I'm out on this one. Someone else can acquire the taste."

Lee picked up Antonio's cup and took a tentative sip. "Yeah, that's dirt all right."

"Well, they're not all winners," Jazz laughed. "Probably the ashwagandha. It's really helpful for stress, but you might want to add milk next time you make a cup. Your half-and-half is expired, by the way. And I couldn't find anything dairy-free for Antonio."

"Well, thank you! I'm sure this will help with the fatigue." Blanche bravely kept drinking the awful brew. "I'll try and remember to get more creamer."

"Jazz, can I ask a favor of you?" Lee asked.

Jazz nodded. "Of course. Unless it's coming to your bachelor party. Tara texted me the formal invite a couple days ago, but I have the...you know."

He shook his head. "No, I know. Mom's annual family reunion is Memorial Day weekend. And, frankly, I'd sooner you don't come to the bachelor party. No offense."

Jazz held up her hands. "None taken. I'd rather not witness all that."

"So..." Lee paused, pushing his glasses up.

Antonio rubbed his thigh in encouragement.

"Lee, spit it out. I'm getting anxious."

"Do you think Mom and Dad would come? To the wedding? If I invited them?" Lee scratched his growing beard. Already handsome, Lee was irresistible with it, but his fiancée was still getting used to having facial hair. "I'm still not sure if I want to reach out to them, but if there's a time to rebuild bridges, it's probably a wedding, right?"

With a tight smile, Jazz sighed. "Honestly, I'm not sure. They still don't talk about you, but that doesn't necessarily mean they're still in the same place as they were ten years ago. They've changed a lot, Lee. If I had to *guess*, Dad is stuck in his ways, and Mom allows it. They don't want to have to reconcile their guilt, let alone consider if you'd forgive them. Not knowing how to contact you lets them continue to avoid it." She fiddled with the amethyst pendant around her neck. "How about this? I'll just ask!"

"No, don't put yourself at risk!" Lee shook his head. "If they're not even talking *about* me, I can't imagine what they'd do if they found out you were in contact with me this whole time."

"But if I don't tell them, and they *do* want to see you, then we'd have to act like we haven't been in contact the whole time for the rest of our lives." Jazz grimaced. "It's your decision, but we're going out for my birthday this week. Let me bring it up to them in public, and if they react too poorly, I'll come stay at your place instead of going home with them. Okay?"

After a long pause, Lee nodded. "Okay. Thank you."

Antonio leaned into Lee in silent support. Even if their reunion was sunshine and rainbows, with all of their problems resolved over the course of a meal, Antonio doubted he could ever forgive his future in-laws. Lee would never tell them about the lasting mental scars: the nightmares, the panic attacks, and the obsessive need to be constantly perfect and accommodating. The easygoing Lee would want to smooth everything over, without holding them accountable.

But that was Lee's decision. If Lee wanted the parents who'd hurt him over and over back in his life, then Antonio would support him, protect him, and take care of him when they were back in the safety of their home. At least, that was what he and Tara had decided when she'd cornered him at Confession last Sunday to vent (having someone to bitch all of his less-than-supportive feelings to had been a relief).

"I'm glad you're doing this." Jazz took Lee's hand. "It's really sucked pretending you don't exist for this long. One less secret to keep."

Lee's smile was wary. "I just don't want you to get put out for me."

"I'll be fine. And if not, I have you to take me in, right?" Jazz elbowed him. "By the way, y'all free on Friday? My friends are dragging me out to some bar for my birthday, if you guys want to come."

Blanche grimaced. "I have—"

"A recording session with a client?" Jazz interrupted with a teasing grin. "Wait, no, it's Friday, so a livestream?"

"You guessed it! A livestream *with* a client." Blanche snorted. "I'll try to reschedule if I can, but no promises."

"I figured." Jazz shrugged with an easy smile. "Can you two make it? Everyone is invited—Sunny and Tara and their SOs, too."

"I can rope Richard and Gabe into coming!" Antonio offered, eager to do anything not as tedious as the endless decisions about their wedding, as heavy as his inner conflict about Lee's parents, or as grating as doing absolutely *nothing* whenever Covey made an unwelcome appearance backstage. At least his friends would always be there for him to annoy.

"To clarify, Tara and Gabe are not together," Lee interjected, then snorted. "But he'll go anywhere Tara does, so yeah, he'll be there."

Chapter Ten

GABE

Tara was stretched out on his couch like a satisfied cat, head resting on Hippo's shoulder. The infuriating bouquets Angie had made decorated the coffee table. The artfully arranged stems stood innocently in the bright afternoon sun, as if his heart wasn't bursting in those blooms. But Tara was still here. She'd gone to lunch with him, had even suggested coming home with him, so maybe he should thank Angie. Despite the familiarity between them, being here by themselves, with no other pretense, felt like uncharted territory. Frisson ran through his muscles, like he was on the edge of a cliff.

With her hoodie riding up her midriff, Tara nudged Gabe's thigh with her foot. "I can't believe you made me eat salad."

Gabe patted her calves as he sprawled out on the chaise of the sectional, letting his hand rest on her ankle. "You made me eat french fries. I'd call it even."

Tara groaned. "It's not the same thing at all. Fries are *good*."

Gabe snorted. They'd eaten at a cafe near his house he'd always wanted to try, but had never had anyone to go with. The fries had been delicious, but that was a slippery slope. However, the sacrifice to his macros had been worth it; Tara had reluctantly agreed to have a few bites of his grilled chicken salad, on the condition that he had a few of the fries that came with her bacon cheeseburger. "Salad is good for you. Especially since your ass never eats vegetables. Your insides are probably crying in relief."

"Potatoes are a vegetable." She grabbed the remote on the coffee table and tossed it to him. "What are we watching?"

Gabe turned on the TV, trying to shake the anticipation thrumming under his skin. *There's nothing to anticipate.* "Let me guess, a cooking show."

Tara shot him a grin. "I like to pretend I know how to cook."

"I could teach you. You won't learn how to cook if you never try." Gabe found the one she'd been watching the weekend before. Whenever their friends came over to hang out together, Tara always turned on some show related to food, once everyone but he and Sunny had tired of gaming. Gabe always teased her for it, but he secretly thrived on it. For everyone else, it was background noise. But for Gabe, the semi-private conversations next to her on the couch, about if he could cook that recipe or if she'd ever had that dish, were stolen moments of connection with the real Tara.

"Or maybe if I watch enough of these shows, I'll magically know how."

"I don't think it works like that, Kitten." He mentally kicked himself for letting that nickname slip again, but Tara kept her eyes on the screen. Her only reaction was a light pink tinging her cheeks and the barest hint of a smile. Unlike at the museum, when the "kitten" while Angie had been flirting with Tara hadn't been entirely accidental. But Tara had outright giggled and blushed so hard that her freckles disappeared. Her obviously pleased reaction had made him feel a bit better about being a jealous asshole; he'd had to fight to keep still, instead of dancing or rubbing it in Angie's face that Tara liked *him*.

Still, he'd half expected Tara to turn down his invitation for lunch. Especially after she'd disappeared from class while he was confronting Angie, who'd pretended she had no idea what he was talking about when he'd accused her of meddling. *Hypothetical situation, my ass.*

After the kids had filed out for the bus back to Eastside, Angie had pinned the boutonniere to his chest and tried to explain it. Allegedly, Angie had *tried* to pick Tara up after their date. But Tara had been blushing and smiling at her phone when a friend had texted her, coincidentally around the same time that Gabe had been doing exactly that. The reassurance that nothing had happened— *No, it doesn't matter if they did hook up. They're adults.*

All of the messages in the flowers Tara had left—that Angie had sworn up and down were signs that Tara was into him, a green light to make a move—still confused him. Here he was, practically cuddling with the woman he'd been heartsick over for years, and he was stuck overanalyzing some damn flowers.

By leaving the bouquet Angie had made, Tara might have been "shooting her shot." Or it could have been a complete coincidence that it had moved over a few inches to his side of the table. And the boutonniere? According to Angie, white roses could mean new love (or as Gabe pointed out, sympathy). Burgundy could mean devotion or beauty. With the tarragon, the combination could mean Tara liked him and wanted to give them a chance (Or, as Gabe's pessimism rationalized, "I still think you're hot, but sorry bro, no dice."). Or it had simply meant that Tara thought white and burgundy roses looked good with tarragon. In the past few hours, he'd dissected and overanalyzed every combination, worked out every possible meaning. But he was no closer to clarity.

At least Angie's corsage had been clear-cut; Tara's rejection of her was reassuring. *He* didn't get any yellow carnations. So he had hope. Maybe he *wasn't* overthinking it. Maybe she *was* trying to tell him something. She'd taken his bouquet with her after all, the one that Angie infuriatingly made to expose all of his feelings. Angie had seen right into his heart and bared it all to Tara in a bouquet. Maybe she *wanted* the bouquet that said Gabe was hers, devotedly and passionately and eternally hers.

Ignoring the cooking show completely, Gabe squeezed Tara's ankle. His thumb idly traced the skin at the cuff of her sock. He was reluctant to hope, unsure if Tara had realized that he'd been asking her on a date, or if she thought this was a normal hangout between friends. They didn't often hang out without their other friends, or some pretext like driving lessons or planning the bachelor party. By design, on his part. Until his EMDR program had ended, Gabe hadn't trusted himself to not throw himself at her feet and confess his eternal, obsessive feelings—

Stop. That's too much. Dial it back. At least now, he could better manage his reactions. His previous therapy programs had helped him recognize his unhealthy thought patterns. But when it came to Tara, recognizing the pattern hadn't stopped the resulting reckless behavior.

"Coop." Tara nudged his thigh.

"Yeah?" Gabe asked, wondering if he should read into the new nickname. "Coop" wasn't exactly romantic, but Tara was not the most sentimental person. Gabe couldn't think of any other nicknames she'd given anyone, so he would hold on to "Coop" like the precious gift it was.

"You got a blanket?"

"You cold?" Gabe rubbed her feet, which she'd pressed against his thigh. They did feel cold through her socks, though his house was fairly temperate. Tara's hands were always cold; why wouldn't the rest of her be?

Tara nodded. "I always get cold after I eat. And blankets are cozy."

"I have just the thing." Gabe headed to his bedroom, taking the opportunity to change into his joggers and hoodie while he was in there. Boutonniere carefully pinned up to dry next to his bed, he grabbed the spare blanket from the linen closet.

"Ugh, you look so comfortable. I'm jealous." Tara pouted as soon as he sat back down on the sofa and started unfolding the blanket. "Jeans were a mistake. I didn't want to embarrass you in front of your class, but these have so many seams."

"Yeah, today's class would have been *so* humiliating if you were more comfortable," Gabe drawled, burning with embarrassment all over again at Angie's meddling. "Wanna borrow some sweatpants?"

"No, that's okay. I want that blanket, though." She reached out for it without getting up.

"Get closer then. We're sharing." Gabe's heart thumped, cursing himself for being a martyr. "Do you have a weighted blanket?"

"No? What's that?" Tara scooted up the couch, pressing against him as Gabe. Swallowing heavily, he waited until she was curled up under his arm—right where she belonged—before spreading it over them.

"Oh, my god!" Tara moaned, leaning harder into his side.

"Yup. That's a weighted blanket." He hoped the shuddering of his breath wasn't audible. The casual moans she constantly threw around always made visions of every time he'd made her come—on his fingers, mouth, thigh, and cock—flash through his head.

"You kept this a secret? You've been depriving me of heaven. Oh, this is like a hug."

Gabe laughed, pulling her closer with an arm around her waist, grateful for the blanket obscuring his lap. "My mom got this for me when...when I first moved home." He'd never appreciated his well-intentioned mom so much as in those first months of inpatient therapy. When he'd first moved back to Bellamy, the weighted blanket had gotten him through endless nightmares and countless nights without sleep. Normally, he tried not to think about that time, but it was doing wonders for getting rid of his semi.

"Where do I get these? How much are they?" Tara wiggled closer until her thigh was practically in his lap.

Gabe closed his eyes, trying and failing to think of anything depressing. *Was my dick always this hard to control, or is this from lowering my SSRIs?* "You can have this one."

Tara shook her head. "I'm not taking your magical blanket, dude."

Gabe smiled. "I insist. I upgraded to a king-size for my new bed, so this one doesn't get used much anymore."

"Are you sure?" Her green eyes met his as she turned in his arms to face him. Gabe nodded, heart pounding in his throat at how close her face was to his. How her body was pressed against him. "Well, um... Thanks."

"Don't worry about it," Gabe muttered. She kept her hand on his chest as she turned back to whatever was on the TV. Tentatively, he laid his hand on top. He'd stopped paying attention to the show before he'd even turned it on, and having her so close... Tara's thumb began to trace his.

"So, how do you know Walter?" he asked, desperate to think of anything other than how much he wanted her like this. The domesticity of it made his heart ache.

"Oh, uh..." Tara shrugged. "He's always been around."

He chuckled. "That's not an evasive answer at all."

"Fine, Nosy," Tara huffed. "Walter looks out for people, and he's always looked out for me. Or, us, I guess. Lee and Blanche, too." Tara shifted next to him. "He and Wanda were always there when I needed them. Wanda was the one who taught me about art and shit. She let me paint with her sometimes. I got to do the three blind mice on that mural she did along the riverwalk."

Gabe vaguely remembered his mom recommending Wanda for that commission when he was in middle school, so Tara must have been...six or seven. Far too young to be spending so much time in the encampment with Walter and Wanda. His hand tightened over hers.

"Walter had me and the other kids read the books for her, while she was planning the installation. He said his eyes were too old." Tara chuckled, her ice-cold thumb still rubbing gently against his fingertips. "In hindsight, they were probably making sure we learned how to read."

He waited for her to share more, unsure of what he was allowed to ask.

"So how do you know him?" The definitiveness in her voice told Gabe that Tara was done.

Gabe blinked, trying to process her question. "Uh, my dad met them in the early eighties. He was hitchhiking from San Fran to Bellamy. Hitched a ride in a school bus full of hippies who were looking for a destination from the universe, after the land their commune had been on was sold."

"Why the fuck would he leave California for *Bellamy*?" Tara asked.

Gabe laughed at her skepticism. "He was involved in a bunch of AIM stuff back then—still is, I suppose, but it's different now—and caught wind of some real estate developer from New York looking to build right along the burial mounds. So he headed there to help the effort to protect them, convinced the real estate developer to focus her efforts downtown and turn the mounds into a public park instead, then eloped with her."

"You weren't kidding when you said your parents had an epic love story," Tara said with a smirk. "Let me guess, nine months later, you came along?'

"Oh no, I came along *years* later. Accident baby." Gabe preemptively shrugged off the questions and sympathy that everyone always gave, because for some reason people thought he should feel unwanted. "They didn't think they'd be good parents, so they never planned on kids. My mom was raised by nannies, and my dad was uh, 'scooped' as a toddler and grew up in boarding school. They weren't perfect, but they did their best. Even if they were kind of busy, they were always supportive and encouraging. Better than most parents I've met."

Tara looked at him thoughtfully, her green eyes pensive. "I mean, you turned out okay. They must have done something right."

Gabe snorted. "That's questionable, but any flaws are on me, not their parenting."

"You're always so down on yourself," Tara grumbled, turning back to the TV. "If you're looking for validation from me, you're not getting it. I just said you turned out okay, Coop. That's as good as it gets."

"I wasn't fishing for validation, but noted." A smile tugged at his face. "And thank you."

They fell into an easy silence as the next episode started. Hippo's snores from the other end of the couch grew louder than the TV. Gabe's thumb traced the soft curve of Tara's waist where her shirt had ridden up, so close to her— *Stop thinking about her naked. You don't even have the courage to make a move.*

Easier said than done. Especially when she let out a soft sigh as she nestled into his side. Her head lay on his chest, and her back arched to press further into his touch. He swallowed hard as her shirt slipped over his hand. His thumb grazed the soft swell of skin on the underside of her breast, fingers twitching as he imagined how it'd feel in his hand if it were mere inches higher.

"Coop?"

"Yeah?"

"I might be reading too much into this, but the answer is green."

He froze, heart pounding as he replayed what Tara had just said. "Uh… I— What?"

Fist tightening around the blanket, Tara refused to look at him. "Maybe you weren't trying to, or maybe all the mixed signals today were all in my imagination, but your hand keeps getting closer to my tit. So, if you want…green?" A broken laugh burst from her. "Hell, not just the tit—*anywhere* you want to put that hand! Go for it!"

"Wh—I was—Are you—" Gabe took a breath, struggling to get his brain ahead of his mouth. "Are you sure?"

She shot him a look over her shoulder. "I wouldn't have said anything if I wasn't sure."

His heart pounded, hope and dread singing through his veins. "I— Uh… I absolutely want to, but… My feelings haven't changed from last year. I— I can't do casual with you, Tara. I like you too much to pretend my heart isn't on the line."

Gabriel Cooper had never been so proud of himself, nor had he ever hated himself more. Everything he'd been dreaming about for months was within reach…and he had just successfully prioritized his needs over his wants for the first time in his life. *My therapist will either strangle me or give me a gold star.*

"Oh." Tara chewed her lip. "And if…" Her sigh rumbled with frustration. "What if it's not casual?"

With a pained groan, Gabe tightened his grip on her waist to keep his effervescent hope from spiraling skyward. "Don't play with me, Kitten."

"I'm not!" Tara's brow furrowed as she finally faced him. The blanket fell away, revealing the flush spreading down her chest and the brightness of her eyes. "I… I don't know exactly what I the fuck I'm doing, but my feelings are on the line, too. I— I want you…more than casually. Whatever the fuck that means." She looked away, jaw clenching. "And it's not like I was waiting around for you, but you said you wanted *more* with me. Then you started dating other people, and I thought you didn't…*want* me for—whatever the fuck *more* means—anymore." She huffed with an endearingly grouchy expression, her green eyes wide. "But then the flowers, and all the shit that Angie did today, and then you asked me out to lunch, and—" Tara furrowed her brow and let out a frustrated huff.

"I'm sorry." Unable to process any of the chaos churning in his mind, Gabe wrapped his arms around Tara's waist. Burying his face in her neck, he couldn't help but bask in the feeling of holding her so close. Nothing centered his racing thoughts as much as Tara in his arms, and his effervescent delirium at the turn this day had taken was paralyzing. He took a deep breath of the light lavender scent on her skin to steady his racing pulse, pausing himself until he could form concrete thoughts. "I didn't know— I thought you just wanted to be friends."

Tara scoffed, arms sliding up his chest to encircle his neck, erasing any space between them. "Because that's what you said *you* wanted! I'm not good with this feelings shit!"

Despite himself, Gabe laughed, their bodies melting closer together. "Me either."

"Shut up, yes you are."

"I'm really not. Otherwise I would have thrown myself at your feet and begged you—" Catching himself, Gabe shook his head. "No, that's an unhelpful thought. Forget I said that."

Tara pulled back. "I don't..."

It hurt to let her go, but Gabe gave Tara the distance she needed. Thankfully, it was only inches. "I know. Sorry. I can get too intense, and you probably don't want all that. And I don't want to ruin our friendship by being...me."

"It's not that I *don't* want all that. I just don't know if I can handle it," Tara murmured, fiddling with a hangnail. "I don't know how to do any of this, let alone intense. But intense sounds really nice."

"Then we take it slow." Gabe put his hand on hers, to keep her—and this chance—from slipping away. He couldn't afford to be that toxic, needy version of himself ever again, especially not with Tara. With the distance she was asking for, maybe Gabe stood a chance to ease into something healthy this time. "You're really important to me, Tara, as a friend or more. I don't want to lose you by pushing you into anything you're not ready for." He shifted, wordlessly inviting her back into his arms. "But if you want, I'd love the chance to find out how good we could be together."

"Okay. Same and shit." Tara fought a smile as she edged closer. "Does slow mean no sex?"

Considering he'd been hard since she'd first gotten comfortable under his arm—and given that he *frequently* got himself off to thoughts of her—Gabe hoped not. But he would do whatever it took to make Tara comfortable, to prove that they could be as perfect for each other as he'd been dreaming of. "If that's what you want."

"Fuck no, I'm so green!" With a laugh, Tara pulled the blanket all the way off him so she could swing a leg over his lap. She paused, hovering too far away. "But I don't want you to feel like I'm treating this casually, or like I'm using you, especially since I need space on the feelings front."

"It will be good for me, too. To take the feelings slow." Gabe traced down her jaw with his thumb, stopping when he reached her lips. "Can I kiss you here?"

"Okay, not that green." Tara huffed, a bitter smile twisting under this thumb. "Is that a problem?"

"Of course not." Gabe wrapped his hand around her neck to pull her closer, kissing her cheek, along her jaw and down her neck. "But just know that I really really want to if you ever change your mind."

"Coop, you still haven't answered." Tara gasped as his tongue traced the shell of her ear. "Is whatever this is happening or not?"

Catching her earlobe between his teeth, he whispered, "Green."

"Thank fuck!" Hand wound through his hair, Tara pulled it as she settled in his lap. Arching up to meet her, Gabe moaned as she rolled her hips against his cock, rocking against him until they were both gasping.

With anyone else, Gabe might have been embarrassed about the sounds she tore from him, but he was too busy pressing kisses down her neck to care. Within seconds, her hoodie and tank top flew somewhere else in the room, and he was sucking and licking and loving on the small breasts with dusky pink nipples that had haunted his dreams for years.

"Gabe?" Tara gasped.

"Mm?" he murmured around her nipple.

"We have an audience."

Hippo's tail thumped on the couch when he noticed them watching him back.

"Oh, that's weird." With an apologetic wince, Gabe pointed toward the kitchen. "Go lay down."

Hippo groaned, as if to say he was already laying on the couch.

"In the kitchen! Go to bed!"

With a loud grumble, his gray mass slid off the couch, slowly stretching as he left the room. Within moments, the pit bull sighed as he flopped into his bed in the kitchen.

Their eyes met as they both laughed. "Sorry about that."

Tara shook her head. "Don't be. At least he didn't try to get involved."

"Where were we?" Gabe murmured against her freckled chest. "Or do you want to take this slower? We can do whatever you— You have a new tattoo!" His hand had been covering it. He'd been so focused on getting his mouth on her, that Gabe hadn't noticed the elegant scriptwork and flower on her left ribcage, following the line of her breast. "'Suck it up, Buttercup'? When did you get this? Not that you tell me everything, but a tattoo seems like something you'd tell me about."

Tara's cheeks pinkened. "I went with Antonio when he got his tattoos to mark two years of sobriety." She looked away, biting her lip. "I kinda needed help keeping everything inside so I wouldn't fuck up the boundaries you asked for, and this," Tara laughed awkwardly as her finger traced the linework. "This helped remind me not to openly thirst over you. That I had to show up as your friend, like you asked. So telling you about it would have been counterproductive. I didn't think I'd ever have to explain this out loud, but especially not with you— Ugh, I should have lied!" She huffed. "Forget everything I just said. This is a memorial tattoo for Auntie Alitrice."

Gabe frowned; he'd been so blind to how much pain he'd caused her. He thought he'd been doing right by her by not projecting his feelings over their friendship. But instead he'd been—

"I can see you overthinking. Stop it." Tara pressed a finger to his nose, narrowing her eyes. "Things happened how they needed to happen, and now we're talking about what we want." She cupped his jaw. "And what I want is to fuck you, because I have been *dreaming* about having you again every day—sometimes several times a day—for months, and I'm so fucking tired of waiting."

Grin blooming with delight, Gabe pressed a kiss to her chest. "Several times a day? About me?"

"Don't judge me," Tara huffed, her smile wry.

"I would never." Gabe winked, his cock somehow getting harder at the vision of Tara, fucking herself to thoughts of him. "Because same."

Tara laughed. "Good. Then we can get naked?" At his nod, Tara climbed off him to peel the jeans from her legs. Unable to tear his eyes from her long legs and pert ass, he stripped his own clothes off and tried not to think too hard about his nudity. For whatever reason, Tara *wanted* him naked; he wouldn't—*couldn't*—hide himself from her. Even if it was daylight.

"Your body is such a fucking masterpiece." Tara eyed him appreciatively, tongue peeking out from between her lips. Gabe blushed, fighting between pride and self-consciousness, as her hands traced his hips and up his belly and chest, until she straddled him once more. Her cunt was wet and hot as she dragged it slowly up his cock.

Fingers digging into the meat of her thighs, Gabe buried his face in the crux of Tara's shoulder. Pressing kisses to her collarbone, he inhaled the lavender scent that clung to her skin. A bittersweet surge of emotions had him curling up around her to hold her tight. "Fuck, I missed you."

"I've been here the whole time, Coop." Tara's fingers traced the shell of his ear to his neck, along his shoulders, and down his arm. She guided his hand from her thigh to fit between her legs. "Show me what we've been missing."

He traced along the damp auburn curls, parting her already-soaked slit to sink two fingers knuckle-deep into her. Her whine sent a thrill down his spine; he'd dreamed of Tara's enthusiastic sounds, the way her cunt swallowed his fingers, the way she fucked him with her whole body. Wrapping his other arm around her hips, he hauled her closer to get a deeper angle. Pressing his thumb to her clit, his lips and tongue returned to her perfect tits. As much as he wanted to watch her face contort with pleasure, he wanted more to hear her every sound as she came undone.

Dreamlike bliss sprang from her fingers tugging through his hair. Her lovely moans filled the room with the most beautiful arias, her soft gasps delicate symphonies. And as Tara shuddered, rocking into his hand, the sharp cry of his name from her mouth struck Gabe's heart, like the universe was telling him he was right where he belonged.

Tara pulled his hand away and rested her forehead against his, panting. "Fuck, you're even better at that than I remember. *Please* tell me you have a condom handy!" Tara's hoarse demand brought him crashing back down to Earth.

"Shit, sorry. In the bedroom. I'll go get one." Gabe sat up.

Tara pushed him back down, her hands firmly planted on his chest. "You get tested lately? Because mine was good, and I'm on birth control... Unless you'd rather get a condom, that's cool too."

Tara must be trying to kill him. He took a deep breath, and then another. "To be clear, are you saying you're comfortable without one?

Because my last test was good, and I've been vaccinated against HPV and hepatitis. Not that I've slept with anyone else since we..." Gabe trailed off, not quite willing to admit she was the only person he'd had sex with since moving home. He didn't care to explain just how long his heart had been on the line.

"Wait, really?" Tara pulled back in confusion. "Why did the silver fox call you Daddy if you weren't fucking him?"

"I had the same question!" Gabe choked on his laugh. "He started up with that shit literally five minutes into dinner. For the record, I meant it when I said I liked you too much last year—I can't imagine being with anyone but you." He swallowed the lump threatening to form in his throat. "I thought you didn't want me, so I was pushing myself to move on."

"Who wouldn't want you?" Tara bit her lip, fighting a shy smile. "So, are we okay without a condom? I'm on birth control, so it's cool if your pull out game is a little weak."

"My pull out game is not *weak*," Gabe teased, sounding more confident than he was. He added, "Just maybe a little rusty."

The idea of fucking her raw filled him with as much insecurity and doubt as giddy anticipation. But he could always go down on her to finish her off, if he couldn't last long. Hell, he would eat her out regardless. He'd been dreaming of the sounds she made, how she tasted, the feel of her around his tongue for months.

"I trust you." Tara reached behind her to stroke his erection. At his nod, she slowly sank down onto him, snatching his heart and soul inside her cunt, along with his cock.

Gabe exhaled sharply through his nose, lip clenched between his teeth as he fought for control. The feeling of giving himself over to her completely had overwhelmed him the first time they'd hooked up, long ago in the bathroom of Confession. And again on her birthday last year. His heart had to slowly regrow both times she'd stolen it— *Stop. Not stolen, you gave that shit to her. You reverse-pickpocketed her.* Tara had run away each of their other encounters, completely unaware she'd ripped his heart out and taken it with her.

But this time, Tara knew him. She wanted him. She trusted him. And Gabe knew and wanted and trusted her. Maybe this time would be different. Better. Maybe this time, his heart would come out of this whole.

Tara's cool, dry lips brushed his throat. "You okay? Can I move?"

"One more moment," he admitted, struggling to breathe. "It's been a while. And you... Fuck, you feel amazing. I missed this, you have no idea how much."

"No, I definitely know what you mean." Her cunt clenched around him as Tara laughed, sending searing pleasure up his spine. She moaned so deep he could feel it in his toes. "Christ, I forgot how big you were."

Hands gripping her ass, Gabe barely overcame the urge to turn them over and fuck her senseless. He took one last deep breath. "Oh, fuck, okay, ready."

Tara's laugh sent pleasure rolling through him with every peal. Rising up and down excruciatingly slowly, she set a steady pace, hands splayed across his chest. Gabe roamed her body, tweaking her nipple with one hand, while the other pressed two fingers against her clit.

The hot pressure of her drove him wild, forcing Gabe to bite down on his lip hard enough to draw blood. The tremors of another orgasm shook her body, fluttering around him within seconds.

"Gabe, I hate to say it, but stop fingering me," Tara teased, pulling his hands away from her. "I'll get overstimulated before I get to ride you properly."

He grinned and licked a nipple that passed close to his mouth, permitting her to pin his arms above his head to the back of the sectional. Gabe breathed deep, forcing himself to think of anything but how wet Tara was, the sound of her groans and slap of her ass as she bounced on his cock. He had to last for however long Tara wanted. Her grip tightened around his wrists, her nails cutting into his skin like zip ties.

A whimpered, "you feel so *good*," made dread trickle down his spine like sweat, pooling in his stomach. He didn't have control over himself like this. But she'd be mad if he freed his hands. Would that be worse than if he came too soon, though? What would she do if— *Stop. This is Tara. Not Emily.*

Gabe winced, his stomach turning as he reminded himself he was safe. "Kitten, I'm starting to turn yellow."

"Oh, shit! Sorry!" Tara released his hands and scrambled to detangle from him.

"Oh, no, no, no!" He gripped her hips to pull her back down on his erection, biting his lip as the wet heat of her surrounded him again. "Not *that* yellow. Just, uhh... Being held down was bringing me somewhere I didn't want to be."

Her green eyes swam with guilt as she cupped his face. "Sorry, I didn't know! Are you okay? Do you want to slow down? Should we change position?"

Gabe kissed her palm, grateful that Tara simply accepted what he needed. "It's fine. I didn't know either. I think the position is good, just maybe..." He tapped her wrist gently before lacing their fingers together. Keeping one around her waist, he drew their arms back over his head. Already, the barest shift from control to affection eased his dread. Hopefully, his compromise wouldn't trigger her own issues with having her hands pinned down. "Is this okay? I won't stop you if you want to let go."

Tara nodded, squeezing his hand. "Color?"

"Green."

Tara rolled her hips slowly, gauging his reaction. With a nod of satisfaction at what she found there, she asked, "Can you choke me?"

"I like how you trust me to choke you, but not kiss you," Gabe hissed, squeezing her hand when she ground against him.

"Feeling like I could die is part of the fun," Tara teased. Each slow roll of her hips sent shock waves through him. "And I trust you not to kill me more than I trust my own brain not to panic. Hand around my throat? Hot, if it's someone I trust, like you. Hand around my wrist or a tongue in my mouth? Fight or flight. Probably fight."

With his free hand, Gabe gently gripped her throat. Her pulse fluttered under his thumb. "This good?"

"For now. I'll tell you when I want it harder." Her grin was wry as Tara moved faster, her free hand trailing down to circle her clit. She clenched around him, her gasps growing more frequent as pleasure contorted her face. He traced her pulse with his thumb, awed at the vision in front of him. Gabe had to clench her hand to keep from coming at the sight.

Perhaps they should be doing this slower, sweeter, making love instead of fucking. But Gabe had stifled his passionate feelings for her for so long, the relit embers needed only the slightest encouragement to grow to an inferno. The rock of her hips, almost violent, said that Tara felt the same. The clench of her cunt around him was driving both of them into a frenzy.

"Harder. Please," she begged, her voice strained.

Locking away the parts of him that wanted to fuck her ruthlessly until she screamed, the parts that wanted to kiss her senselessly deep in his heart—he squeezed his hand firmly around Tara's throat until she came with a silent cry, careful to keep pressure off her windpipe. The part of his brain that still worked did its best to remember the sight of her. But allowing himself to truly embrace that this was Tara coming on his cock was too risky.

Once her tremors stopped, he rubbed away any soreness he might have caused to her throat. "Was that okay?"

"Okay is an understatement!" Tara raised her eyebrows in disbelief. "How have you gone this long without needing to pull out?"

Gabe shrugged, choosing not to think too hard about how he'd learned to dissociate himself out of an orgasm. "What, done so soon? I can keep going if you want to keep using me."

"Dude, I'm not *using* you. You're not a sex toy. You're a part of this, too." Tara snorted, rising off of him just enough that his cock slipped out of her, her mouth trailing down his neck.

Reeling, Gabe resisted the urge to pull her back onto him. Tara always bombed his heart with the simplest, yet most meaningful affirmations, when he least expected it. Every doubt and insecurity that had drowned him for years was obliterated; the only survivor of her onslaught was the irrepressible hope that she might want him back.

Reaching a hand between them, Tara slowly stroked his cock. "Where do you want to finish—"

"On your ass."

"You answered that so quick!" Tara laughed, gesturing for him to make room for her to kneel on the lounge.

He shifted around her so she was under him, his mouth caressing every inch of freckled skin that came close. "I've thought about it constantly, Kitten. Every time I get off in the shower, before bed, all the time." Bracing a foot on the ground, Gabe knelt behind her, gripping her hip with one hand and using the other to stroke himself, sliding the head of his cock along her slit. "In my fantasies, I've come all over and inside you, but this ass haunts my dreams."

Grinning at him over her shoulder, Tara sank into a deep arch, wiggling her ass. "That makes me feel so much better about naming all of my toys after you."

With a relieved grin, Gabe abandoned his plan of jerking himself off and slipped back inside her cunt. Letting the needy, wanting part of himself back out was safer now. With Tara facing away from him, he wouldn't be tempted to kiss her.

Gabe wrapped his fingers through her hair and pulled her head back. Tara moaned in pleasure. Her fingertips dug marks into the upholstery, the sectional creaking with every snap of his hips. Her ass jiggled when his free hand struck her with a loud *crack*.

Staring in awe, he rubbed the handprint pinkening her skin. "Kitten, your ass is even more phenomenal than the last time I had you bent over like this."

Tara smiled over her shoulder, her green eyes half-closed in a daze. "Fun, isn't it? I've been eating three square meals a day for the first time in my life this past year, and I figured out it can jiggle a few months ago. I can't stop looking at it in the mirror."

Imagining Tara playing with herself in the mirror was definitely going to become a recurring fantasy. With a groan, he thrust harder, smacking and gripping the perfect globes of her ass, while Tara fingered herself. Her scream was muffled by a throw pillow when she came again. Her cunt pulsing around him made his orgasm finally win out. He waited as long as he dared, the tension creeping up his spine. Just as his body seized, Gabe pulled out, cum spurting between her ass cheeks.

The vision in front of him made him wish he could take a photo of the glory of Tara's asshole, covered in his cum. "Kitten, don't get up."

"Can't anyway," came her muffled reply. Instead she sagged into the pillows with a contented sigh.

With a smug grin, Gabe bent down to lick her clean; the saltiness from his own cum mingled with the clean sweat and sweet musk of her. Tara's surprised "fuck" made his heart skip a beat.

With two fingers in her cunt and his thumb on her clit, he brought her to orgasm once more, lapping her asshole with the flat of his tongue for the sheer pleasure of hearing her moan his name again. Satisfied only once she'd collapsed, boneless against the pillows, legs still twitching, he kissed his way up her spine. The journey ended with a chaste peck on the corner of her lips.

Tara stiffened.

"Sorry, too close to the mouth?" Gabe backed away.

"No! That was good!" she insisted, rolling onto her side to face him. But Tara still wasn't meeting his eyes. "Honestly, the whole thing, great. Phenomenal."

"But..." Gabe sat back. Resignation was a bitter pill after the high of finally having Tara in his arms.

"I'm feeling a lot right now. A little overwhelmed?" Tara finally looked at him. Her green eyes were swimming with anxiety, just like they had that first night at Confession. "I meant what I said earlier. This wasn't casual, and I want you for more than sex and friendship. I just..."

"Need time to think?" He wanted to draw her close again and keep her there. But Tara's deer-in-the-headlights expression told him that might not be the right move. If she wanted space, he would give her as much as she needed. After all, she'd given him far more time and space than anyone else would have. So much so that he hadn't even realized she was doing it for nine months.

Tara nodded in relief as she sat up. "I know we should talk about this..."

"We should, but it's okay if you need time to process." Gabe tried not to let his disappointment show, but knowing him, he looked positively dejected. "I could probably use some time myself. Pause?"

"Pause." Tara smiled softly as she tapped his nose, resting her forehead against his. "The fact that you understand me so well is terrifying."

"You don't know the half of it, Kitten." He pressed a kiss behind her jaw, imagining he was kissing her lips instead. Of all the people in Gabe's life who loved and cared for and worried about him, no one quite understood him the way Tara did. Everyone else pushed back, or asked endless questions, or took matters into their own hands. "Thank you for being honest with me about what you're feeling."

The smallest gesture shouldn't mean so much. But for Gabe, it was everything.

Wrapping her arms around his shoulders, Tara buried her face in his neck. "I hate to run out after that, but can you bring me home? Not personal, I'm just on edge."

Gabe hugged her back. "Yeah, of course. Want to drive?"

Tara laughed, her smile shining sunlight into his soul. "I can't believe I'm going to say this, but no. My head is in so many places, I might actually hit someone this time."

Gabe and Tara looked at each other a moment longer, before bursting into laughter. He could probably credit this lightness to endorphins, a chemical rush in his brain from finally having the person he'd been dreaming about for months in his arms again.

But this time felt different.

This time—even though Tara was yet again running, pulling her jeans back on and tossing him his boxers—Gabe trusted she wasn't running *from* him. Her feelings for him, perhaps, but not Gabe himself. Neither his gnawing insecurity, nor his relentless pessimism could convince him that he was delusional.

Today, he was...hopeful.

Friday, March Nineteenth

CHAPTER ELEVEN

LEE

FINDING JAZZ IN THE god-awful bar she'd chosen, a sketchy nightclub called Belly's, had taken far too long for Lee's comfort. Especially since he'd found her *alone* by the bar, no friend in sight. With a sigh of relief, Lee hugged his little sister. "Happy birthday, Jazzy!"

Belly's was popular among frat boys, with a convenient location downtown and a dingy dance floor downstairs. Too well-lit to be a decent basement club—which should have dark corners and intimate lighting—the lack of ambiance made Lee feel very exposed. But it was probably safer for the women clientele if they could see their drinks.

"You made it!" Jazz hugged him and the rest of their friends in turn—even Richard, who awkwardly patted her back, doing his best to avoid touching her bare skin. A feat easier said than done. Jazz was dressing too grown for Lee's comfort these days, wearing a tight-fitting magenta crop top and matching shorts. Lee repressed the brotherly urge to cover her with his jacket. "Why are all of you wet, though?"

"It started pouring on the way here," Sunny called over the music, looking around with a confused expression of distaste. "I hope you know I'd only come here for you."

The whole place smelled like stale PBR and cheap cologne. Already crowded with scrubby bros and packs of young women in minidresses at only ten on a Saturday evening, Belly's was oppressively loud. Lee had hoped that getting there early would mean the place was dead, so he wouldn't have to witness the heterosexual mating rituals sober, but no such luck. Confession was infinitely better.

"If it helps, your makeup held up really well in the rain," Jazz said to Sunny. Her smile was so easy and her posture so relaxed that Lee wondered if maybe her birthday dinner had been canceled, that she hadn't told their parents about him after all. He wouldn't blame her for changing her mind.

Sunny beamed. "It does help, thanks."

"Blanche couldn't get out of their session?" Jazz asked over the music, pouting.

Lee shook his head, hoping she wouldn't be too disappointed. "But they said to tell you happy birthday!"

Jazz merely grinned. "They're so sweet. We'll just have to have fun without them."

Lee frowned in confusion. Just like when everyone had admitted her tea was awful, Lee was surprised that she shrugged everything off so easily. The Jazz he'd grown up with would have pouted and been in a mood the rest of the night if something didn't go her way.

On her seventh birthday, Dad had gotten mad about her "attitude" the day before and refused to go out to eat, like they always did to celebrate. Jazz had cried and hid in her closet the whole day. Lee had asked to go for a walk and stolen a bag of Donettes from a convenience store, sneaking it past his parents. They'd sat in her closet together, feasting on the empty carbs their dad abhorred, until their mom had found them covered in powdered sugar.

The ass beating had been worth it. And at least Jazz had been spared, since Lee had been the "bad influence" on her.

Why exactly do I want to see them again? Despite the overwhelming bitterness Lee still carried, the closer they got to the wedding, the more his heart hurt that his parents wouldn't be there. They wouldn't see him succeed despite their best efforts to cut him down, nor have a chance to do better for one of the most important milestones of his life. His sister was forced to lie about her whereabouts just to be in his wedding party. Antonio was bringing so much love to his life, and Lee couldn't even give him shitty in-laws.

It was a strange place to be, to regret both the action and inaction. Would moving past his anger and hurt be worth it, especially when they didn't deserve it?

As if reading his mind, Jazz put her arm through his and pulled him aside. "I told them over dessert yesterday."

His chest tightened, anxiety burning under his skin. "You got dessert?" *Of all the questions to ask.*

Jazz laughed. "I told you, they're different people now. I can eat cake without you taking one for the team. I still feel guilty while I'm eating it, though," she tsked. "It's so annoying!"

Rubbing his hands against his thighs, Lee blurted out, "How'd they take it?"

"Dad still hasn't said a word to me. Which, honestly, that's cool." Jazz shrugged. "Mom asked to see you before I even suggested it. She's gonna try to convince Dad to keep an open mind at their next couple's therapy session. He's always more likely to listen with a man there to call him out on his passive-aggressive bullshit."

"They're in *couple's therapy*?!" The Leland and Althea who had raised him would *never* have gone to counseling. They would have prayed over the issue, until Althea grew resigned enough to fall in line. "What the fuck happened to them?"

Jazz made a face, sighing in exasperation. "Oh, I dunno, Dad unilaterally disowned you, and Mom's resented him ever since? His sister took your side and died before he could get his head out of his ass?" She shook her head. "Dad's pride has been his only support for over a decade. He won't need much convincing."

"We have completely different parents." Lee pulled her into a hug. Even if his confusing mess of conflicting feelings were irreconcilable, he appreciated Jazz risking her own neck to give him a path forward. "Thank you. Seriously."

"Buy me a drink, and we'll call it even."

"That's nowhere close to even, Jazz." But he dragged her to the bar anyway, where Antonio, Gabe, and Tara huddled in a pack. Hands wringing his hair, Gabe was doing his best to hide behind them, while Tara looked warily at the crowd of bros. They were leering at her from a distance too close for comfort.

Lee judged Jazz hard when, out of all the possibilities, she ordered a White Claw. But it was probably easier to cover than a cocktail would be. He ordered a couple of Modelos for him and Gabe, and sparkling water for Antonio and Tara. "Where'd Sunny and Richard go?"

"Sunny made him dance with her." Antonio took the sparkling water gratefully, but eyed the one in Tara's hand. "Why aren't you drinking? Are you pregnant?! We're gonna be uncles! Who's the father?"

Lee and Gabe both choked on their beer.

"What? No! Dude, why would you put that on me?" Tara shook her head vehemently. "It's Friday. I only drink on Saturdays."

"And special occasions!" Antonio gestured to Jazz. "Birthday party!"

Tara winced apologetically. "Jazz, no offense, I probably would have a drink if we were at Confession, but here? I'm good."

Jazz laughed. "None taken! I'd rather be at Confession, too. But Ed let it slip that we were going out for my birthday, and everyone in his frat house jumped on the plans and took over. I would never have come here if it were up to me."

"Who's Ed?" Lee asked, protectiveness prickling.

Jazz frowned. "My friend's boyfriend. And *my* friend, because I have friends now, and some of them are men, and you need to get over that."

"These *friends* just left you?" Lee crossed his arms.

Jazz rolled her eyes with a shake of her head. "No, they're dancing. I took a break because we've been drinking since noon." She shook her head. "I don't know how they do it. I'm not built for this."

As if called by her words, a tall white girl with brown curly hair and hoop earrings emerged from the crowd to pull Jazz to the dance floor. She wasn't quite as tall as Jazz, but few women reached six feet.

Jazz allowed herself to be pulled away, waving as she was led to the dance floor.

"Come on, Tara, be my beard! I'm supposed to act straight tonight, but I wanna dance!" Antonio begged as he dragged her after him.

Lee pouted as Tara mouthed for help over her shoulder. As much as he loved to feel up his fiancée on a dance floor, this wasn't the safest place for two queer Black men to be close. He knocked his bottle of Modelo against Gabe's. "Well, Gabe. It's just us. Cheers."

Gabe took a sip of his beer. "Can I ask you something?"

"Is it about Tara?" Lee teased. Gabe obviously had a thing for her, but Tara was an immovable fortress when it came to letting people in. For a while, he thought there might be something between them, but Tara seemed to have gotten over her initial attraction months ago. *Gabe is going to have to be patient as rocks to even have half a chance with her.*

Gabe didn't seem to pick up on Lee's ribbing. He frowned into his beer. "Does she go hot and cold on everyone, or just me?"

Lee followed Gabe's gaze; the familiar red frizz and brown curls of his best friend and his fiancée were barely visible in the crowd. He wasn't sure if Gabe was referring to something specific, but he knew Tara. "Everyone except me and Blanche. She likes to pretend she doesn't have feelings. So when she gets overwhelmed with any emotion—good or bad—she hides until she's successfully repressed them again."

"Relatable."

"Right?" Lee huffed out a laugh as he put the bottle to his lips. The fizzy beer gave him a moment to figure out what he wanted to say. "She got it in her head that she shouldn't need anyone for anything, let alone emotional support, so she doesn't trust anyone to be there when she *does* need someone." He paused, unsure how much he should say. "Blanche and I happened to be in the right place at a bad time when she didn't have anyone else to turn to. And we stuck around when the crisis was over, so she didn't push us away. Still doesn't."

Sunny had been a constant presence in Tara's life for years, but she'd struggled to prove she had Tara's back until about four years ago, when she'd punched some creep in the face who wouldn't leave Tara alone. Antonio and Richard got exceptions because they were—as far as Tara was concerned—extensions of Lee and Sunny.

They were the only people Tara had ever let in. Chas, Freddy, Walter, Wanda, Aunt Alitrice—all the people in Tara's life that she'd loved—she never really trusted that they loved her in return. Just Lee, Blanche, and, to a degree, Sunny.

Gabe ran his hand through his hair. "I felt like we were clicking last week. But then, silence. She won't even look at me or text me back. How am I supposed to know what I did wrong?"

"I wouldn't take it personally, Gabey." After a moment's hesitation, Lee rubbed his shoulder, trying to look as bro-ey as he could pull off. Normally, he and Gabe would already be snuggling for this conversation. "Look, even *I* don't know everything about her life from before we met, but change is hard for her. It threatens the little stability we've had since moving in with Blanche. If you're serious about being in her life, give her time and space. Like a cat, you gotta let her come to you. She'll run if you push her for more than she's ready for, so you need to be steady. Show her that you'll be there for her when shit gets hard *and* when it's easy."

Lee paused; he was making Tara sound a little insane. He should talk her up, instead of scaring Gabe off. They obviously weren't talking about friendship anymore. But Gabe was asking for his advice, so Lee decided this didn't count as meddling. "But she's the best person to have on your team. No one is more loyal and generous. Just be sure that's what you want because I will make your life miserable if you push her into something and then bail."

Gabe snorted. "I'm not going anywhere. I just hate feeling like I'm not enough. Or too much, or whatever."

"If it helps, everything is too much for Tara." Lee frowned, amending, "But also, *nothing* is too much once she decides she wants something."

Gabe took a sip of his beer, considering Lee's words for a long moment. "I have no idea what that means."

"You'll figure it out." Lee patted his shoulder again, biting back the urge to share more. Inserting himself into shit that wasn't his business would only piss Tara off, and he hated when his Buttercup was mad at him.

When Antonio and Tara finally emerged, they were both sweaty and laughing. "Okay, Lee, your turn!" Antonio put Tara's hand in his. "I need some water!"

"Can't I get a break too?" Tara laughed.

Lee grabbed her hands and pulled her back to the dance floor, relieved to end this guarded heart-to-heart. "Nope, Buttercup, dance with me first!"

The dance floor was crowded, the music even louder than by the bar. As Tara and he danced to a terrible remix of "Pony" ("This is my jam!" cried several girls who probably weren't even born when it came out), he called in her ear "Are you having fun?"

Tara grinned. "I am! It's been so long since I danced like this."

Lee pulled her close to stop her weird robot dance, before she accidentally sacked him in the balls. "Buttercup, that shit you're doing is not dancing. You're like Pinocchio on molly."

Tara flipped him off and flailed harder.

Lee laughed. Grouchy and obstinate as she could be, they always had fun together.

Too soon, Gabe cut in. "Tonio asked for you, said it's urgent," he called to Lee, pointing a thumb back toward the bar. With a shy smile to Tara, he added, "Sorry. Tonio told me to 'keep you occupied'."

"Fair warning, she's a terrible dancer." Lee grinned.

Tara smacked him.

Gabe grinned back, more at Tara than Lee. "I'll survive."

"Be nice, Buttercup," Lee called in her ear. Tara rolled her eyes.

As Lee made his way through the crowd, worry washed over him. *Did something happen?* Antonio shouldn't be alone if he was struggling with temptation. They always planned for it when they went anywhere besides Confession. Gabe wouldn't have left Antonio alone if that was the case, though; he was a key part of the plan.

Antonio beckoned him closer as Lee approached the bar. Leaning in close, he subtly touched Antonio's back. "What's wrong? You okay? Are you—"

Antonio shushed him with a gesture down the bar. "Look over that way without *looking* like you're looking."

Lee immediately craned his neck in the direction Antonio pointed, searching for some sign of a fight or drugs, something that Antonio would consider an emergency.

Instead, he saw Jazz and her friend—the *female* friend who had pulled her to dance earlier—leaning against the bar, tongues down each other's throats. Her friend—again, *female* friend—had her hand blatantly under Jazz's crop top.

And Jazz did not seem the least bit uncomfortable.

"Jesus, Tonio. I did not need to see that!" Lee covered his eyes, making gagging noises. "I need bleach for my eyes."

"Yeah, yeah, big brother, protective, I get it. But did *you* know she was, you know?" Antonio made a limp wrist gesture. "I thought she was straight! Do your *parents* know?"

Lee groaned, not wanting to consider the implications of the nightmare fuel he'd just witnessed. "I didn't know, but until she tells me, it's not my business. Can we just not mention it? Especially if we end up meeting with my parents?"

Jazz was an adult, and she could do and love whoever she wanted. But he didn't want Jazz getting the same parental treatment he had. He'd survived it, but it hadn't been easy. At least she had Lee for support if they made the same mistakes with her, but Lee would never forgive them. They'd already bought an air mattress, in case Jazz's conversation with their parents hadn't gone well; it'd still be there for her, no matter the reason.

Antonio elbowed him with a reproachful look. "Give me some credit, Lee. I wasn't going to meet your parents and be all 'Oh, nice to meet you Mr. and Mrs. Homophobe. By the way, did you know your daughter is also hella gay?'"

"Babe, you know I didn't mean it like that. She…needs them. They're paying for her school, and she still lives with them." Lee turned his back on where his baby sister was playing tonsil hockey with her friend to avoid catching another glimpse of the horror. "I'm not *that* surprised that she isn't straight, but she probably has her reasons for keeping it to herself."

"The septum ring should have been a clue." Antonio was not looking away at all. "But you can't not say *anything*. She probably wants your support."

With a firm touch to his jaw, Lee nudged Antonio's gaze away from his sister and back toward him. He put on his best imitation of Antonio's pout when he was jealous. Not that he actually thought Antonio was enjoying watching Jazz get felt up, but it was still a little weird for him to be staring in her direction that hard.

Swatting his hand away playfully, Antonio's hazel eyes smiled up at him. "Don't worry. I'm not watching the show your sister's putting on, just keeping an eye out for creeps. She's got guts. I mean, *we're* too paranoid to even dance, and we're getting married soon!"

The knot in his chest loosened at the warmth in Antonio's face. All of the worries weighing him down—for Jazz and his parents, for Blanche and Confession, for their wedding—were so manageable with Antonio's support and encouragement. No matter what happened, he and Antonio would figure it all out together. "I appreciate you."

Antonio's grin was as good as any kiss. "That's what future husbands are for, Angel."

Chapter Twelve

Richard

For as often as she drove him up the wall, Sunny was by far the best part of his life. Sure, she could be argumentative, snotty, and *so* chaotic, but he wouldn't have her any other way. Before her, his days had been reduced to a steady heartbeat, calm but predictable. Now, his heart raced.

Especially when he could hold her close on the dance floor, in a bar he would never have gone to on his own. She fit perfectly in his arms, the crook of her neck providing the escape he needed from the loud music and flashing lights. Even though the floor was sticky, and the crowd pressed against them, Sunny made all of the irritations in life easier to bear.

Squeezing her ass through her dress, Richard pulled her closer as the obnoxious crowd around them shouted the lyrics.

Sunny's teasing was barely audible over the thumping bassline. "You're handsy tonight, Dicky. You haven't been drinking, have you? You're the DD."

"Since when do you have a problem with me being handsy, Sunshine?" He kissed her in the spot she liked, just behind her jaw.

With a quiet laugh that he felt more than heard, Sunny smiled against his cheek. "Never. Touch my butt all you want."

"Ladies, got room for a couple more?" An unfamiliar voice called near them.

Sunny stiffened in Richard's arms with a scoff. "Oh balls, he's talking to us."

Richard's irritation flickered back in full force. *Here we go.* "Ignore him," he muttered, moving them through a gap in the crowd, hoping to disappear quietly in the chaos. Sunny's eyes narrowed, but she let him guide her away.

Dudebro was persistent as he grabbed Richard's hip. "Hey Blondie, hold up."

Pushing Sunny behind him, Richard shot him a glare, his skin already crawling from the unwanted touch. He was a head taller than Richard, twice as wide, and more than a little drunk. His friend next to him was a little shorter but broader, and swaying on his feet, even drunker than Dudebro. Both were wearing shirts with the University of Bellamy's otter mascot. They were large enough to possibly be college athletes. Not good odds. *Maybe I can talk our way out of this.* In the deepest voice he could muster, Richard said, "I think you're confused. Only one lady here and, as you can see, she's with me."

Dudebro looked confused. "Nah, no way in hell. You're too pretty to have a dick."

His friend laughed like he had told the funniest joke. Squeezing Sunny's hand to hopefully keep her calm, Richard fought the urge to force a polite smile, like his mother would have done. "Trust me, I'm a man. Now, I'd like to go back to dancing with my girlfriend."

Dudebro crossed his arms over his chest. "Prove it."

"Excuse me?" Richard's stomach clenched; he might not be able to talk their way out of this. He glanced around for any sign of Lee or Gabe in the crowd, who were big and masc enough for these guys to leave them alone. More of a lover than a fighter, Gabe could hold his own better than Richard. If Gabe's physique alone didn't scare them off, he'd mastered the art of deescalating (physically, if necessary) the fights that Antonio had gotten into with their bullies when they were kids. But all Richard saw were strangers. Even Antonio and Tara, who had been dancing nearby, had vanished.

"Yeah, dude, whip it out." Dudebro leered. "Let's see this dick of yours."

Richard balled his fists. That these two assholes had misgendered him was infuriating enough; that they would, in all likelihood, only take a "no" from a cis man made it so much worse. "I'm not go—"

"Hey asshole, leave us the fuck alone!"

Richard's hopes of talking their way out crumbled as Sunny cut in, her shout angry and piercing. *Fuck, I hope this doesn't turn physical. I'm so bad at fighting.*

Unimpressed, Dudebro simply leered back. "Oh shit, you talk like that in bed too? I was gonna go for Blondie here, but you can come too."

Adrenaline rooting him to the floor, Richard searched helplessly for Gabe. Or even Antonio.

Sunny had a different approach. "That Blondie is *mine,* you entitled asshat! Get fucked!"

Richard watched in horror as Dudebro reeled from her right hook. "Sunny, what the fuck!" He reached for Sunny's hand, desperate to drag her to safety.

But Sunny evaded him as easily as she ducked Dudebro's swing, landing another punch to his gut. To Richard's horror, the drunk friend was already shoving through the crowd to back his friend up. Occupied with Dudebro, Sunny couldn't see him lurching toward her.

Desperate to keep Sunny safe, Richard reached for her hand again, throwing himself at the drunk friend's fist. He collided with it cheek-first. *How did we end up here?*

The room spun, and yet his head was strangely clear. Held up by a group of young women, all of them asking if he was okay. Richard blinked, patting his cheek for signs of broken bones. His ears weren't ringing. He didn't have double vision. No nausea. He'd had worse blows to the head in soccer.

Wrenching herself free from Richard's grasp, Sunny threw herself at Dudebro. *What's the safeword for when we want to leave? Was it an animal?* Maybe that punch to the face was worse than he'd thought. *It might be too late for the safeword.*

As the crowd gathering around them cheered, the drunk friend picked himself up from the floor and lurched for Sunny again. Richard had no idea when the drunk friend had even fallen, or how. Panic rose up in his throat; he was out of options. He couldn't find Gabe. He couldn't get Sunny away. He couldn't keep either of them safe. *Fuck.*

Like Dumpster after the laser pen, Tara came flying out of the crowd, landing on the drunk friend's back seconds before he reached Sunny. She landed punch after punch, pummeling the guy's head until he collapsed. The circle of onlookers whooped.

Still frozen and dazed, Richard's rush of appreciation for Tara was only mildly tempered by the realization of a second assault charge he'd have to find a way out of.

Richard shook off the hands holding him upright. Dudebro's chin was dripping blood from a split lip. Scratch marks streaked red across his face. Just as Sunny landed a hard punch to his throat, Richard managed to get his arms around her waist. "Sunny, you won. Let's go!" Sunny didn't make it easy; she fought every step as Richard pulled her away. The crowd booing him didn't help.

Dudebro staggered after them, but he was stopped short by a muscular hand gripping the back of his neck. Gabe swept a leg under him and pushed Dudebro face-first to the floor. Richard smothered his burning envy at how easily Gabe handled the guy.

"About time you showed up," Richard said instead, as Sunny struggled against his grip on her waist. He was flooded with relief, but his stomach curdled with resentment for how weak he'd felt in the moment; he should feel grateful to have a giant best friend in times like this.

"Sorry. It took me a minute to figure out why Tara took off." Gabe picked up Tara around the waist from where she was kneeling on the drunk friend's chest. Despite the crowd's encouragement and Tara spitting insults at him, the drunk friend stayed down, still conscious but too dazed to fight back. Gabe hoisted Tara over his shoulder and patted her on the ass. "Come on, Kitten. You did good. Time to bounce before security shows up."

With the action over, the crowd returned to dancing, shouting along to whatever awful music the DJ was playing. Still shaking with adrenaline, Richard inspected Sunny as she kept yelling at Dudebro on the floor. At least she'd stopped fighting to break free from his grip around her waist. She seemed unharmed, other than some blood on her knuckle that might not be hers. Not even a hair had come loose from her ponytail.

"Help me get Sunny out of here, too," Richard said to Gabe, not commenting on his handsiness with Tara. Or the nickname. Or the hickey on his neck that was definitely not there when they'd arrived. Nor would he bring up that Tara didn't put up much of a fight against Gabe manhandling her into a fireman's carry. Not as much as Richard expected from her, anyway. The dreamy half-smile on her face as she hung over Gabe's shoulder really undermined her halfhearted protests. "I'll find a manager, do what I can."

Gabe nodded, looping his other arm around Sunny's waist to pull her away from cussing out Dudebro, who continued shouting back from where he lay on the floor, hand pressed to his eye. Richard followed in Gabe's wake, encouraging Sunny towards where Lee and Antonio waited.

"Time to go," Richard said once they found them.

Lee took one look at Sunny and Tara, both still held firmly by Gabe, and nodded in understanding. He turned to Antonio. "Can you tell Jazz that we're leaving? And that I love her very much no matter what. And I support her, and I'm here for her however she needs me."

Antonio nodded. "I'll be right behind you."

"I'll take Sunny," Lee offered. "You need two hands, or she'll try to run back the moment your guard's down."

"I don't need anyone to take me anywhere," Sunny spat, pushing against Gabe's arm to no avail.

Lee took her by one hand, leading her to the stairs with his other arm firmly around her waist. "Why don't you tell me what happened, Sunny?"

Grumbling under his breath as he followed, Richard was astounded at how everyone was taking this in stride. Like no one had committed assault. Sure, the two guys had been harassing them first, but still, the risk of legal trouble was too high. His stomach clenched. He and Phineas had worked hard to keep Gabe's name out of any public records, and here he was casually joining a bar fight! Yes, he did it to help Sunny, but he wouldn't need to risk getting booked if Sunny hadn't— Or if Richard had...

He shook his head; that train of thought was unproductive. *What's done is done.* At the top of the stairs, he asked the bouncer if he could talk to a manager.

With a shrug, the bouncer waved over an older heavyset man. Richard was surprised that no one had come to kick them out. Or questioned Gabe and Lee as they carried two women out of the bar against their will. *What kind of establishment is this?*

Skin too tight, Richard fiddled with his cuff, ensuring his watch was visible. Hopefully, the manager would pick up on the blatant social cue, instead of the tremor in Richard's hand. "We had a minor incident downstairs. A couple of gentlemen were harassing my girlfriend, and things got heated. If they ask to get the police involved to press charges, please give them my lawyer's card." Fighting the tremble of his hands, he reached into his wallet and passed over Phineas's business card with a hundred-dollar bill. "They will find it beneficial to discuss the situation with him first."

The manager shrugged, uncaring, but pocketed the cash and the card anyway.

Richard nodded politely and stepped out onto the street, immediately calmed by the chill and quiet. Freezing rain pelting his face, he hurried under the awning half a block away to join the others, still waiting for Antonio.

Aside from the thinly-veiled offer of hush money, there wasn't much else he could do, not until he knew for sure if anyone wanted to press charges. Richard hadn't seen any phone flashlights, but he'd have Antonio and Sunny check social media for any clear shots of Gabe's face later. Until then, he didn't have a way to find out who these guys were to dig up any dirt on them. Other than finding their nondescript faces within the U's athletics department photos, which was unlikely. Once again, spectacularly useless.

"Dicky, what's wrong with your face?" Sunny frowned as Richard wiped rain out of his eyes.

"What? Oh." Richard had forgotten about the hit that the drunk friend had landed. Now that he thought about it, his skin was hot and itchy. "I'm fine. No lasting harm done."

"You don't look fine, dude. He got you good," Tara said with a skeptical eyebrow raised.

"Oh, that fuckers getting it!"

"Sun, you already got him." Lee grabbed Sunny just as she charged. Pulling her into a bear hug, he murmured to her quietly as he rocked her back and forth. Sunny bit her lip, but she stopped fighting, eventually humming along with whatever song Lee was singing. Apparently it was "Umbrella," because Sunny started singing along loudly with the chorus.

Fighting a smile, Richard checked to make sure Gabe still had a hold on Tara. With his thumbs hooked in her belt loops, he kept a firm grip on her hips via her front pockets. She looked calmer—if a little cold and wet—leaning into the circle of Gabe's arms. Presumably, she was in no hurry to resume the fight. Gabe certainly didn't seem to mind hanging onto her either.

"You should take a photo, Richard," Gabe said. "For evidence. In case you need to prove self-defense."

Richard really didn't want to take a photo that showed how indecisive and panicked he'd been, but Gabe was right. He handed Tara his phone, who snapped a few pictures, far too close to his face. He pocketed it as she passed it back to him, not even checking the damage. He didn't really want to see himself if he looked "*pretty*" enough for straight men to hit on.

Luckily, Antonio ducked under the shelter with them seconds later, shaking the rain from his hair. "Everything smoothed over, Dicky?"

Richard shrugged. "As much as I could, given the circumstances." *I'll have to text Phin.* Phineas hated surprises like this. Even if he always handled them well.

"Did Jazz say anything?" Lee asked Antonio.

"Thanks for coming, and she'll text you. Then I added the other stuff, and she said 'duh' and went right back to business like I wasn't even there." Antonio grinned at Lee's groan. "So, on our way home, who wants to tell me what the fuck happened? Spare no details!"

They piled into Richard's Range Rover, Sunny taking control of the console. She turned the heat up full blast and put "Umbrella" on repeat.

Gabe managed to origami himself into the third row with Tara. He didn't put up much protest, unlike the way there, when he'd made Antonio climb in the back. But Tara hadn't been audibly shivering from the freezing rain then. As expected, Gabe had his arm around her, rubbing her shoulder.

Sunny regaled Antonio with her version of events as Richard drove across the river to Eastside. Hearing Sunny explain that she had acted in Richard's defense didn't sit right with him. Hands clammy and still shaking, Richard tapped the steering wheel, unsure why he felt the need to correct her. She had, undeniably, but he was upset that he'd needed rescue in the first place. He was always the cool head in a crisis, unless the crisis was his own.

He'd dealt with worse in his life than a couple of drunk creeps, but they'd always been Gabe's problems, or Phineas's, or Antonio's. Other than what his parents inevitably foisted on him, Richard had always intentionally avoided trouble. Before he moved for college, his mom had poured them both a bottle of wine and had a Talk. He had already heard the Talk before prom and several other occasions—always with wine involved, so Barbie never remembered. She shared with him her go-to manipulation tactics. How there was always a way to convince even the most stubborn, persistent men out of whatever ideas they had.

That saying no or getting angry would just make it worse. That sucking someone off was better than being raped and getting an abortion later.

And Barbie—disturbing as her advice was—had prepared his sheltered ass for the real world as much as she could. While not foolproof, he'd managed to talk, or sometimes buy, his way out of many bad situations. No nonconsensual blow jobs needed.

This was the first hit Richard had ever taken, aside from the occasional stray wine glass from his father's anger. Soccer, sure—he'd taken a cleat to the jaw, or an elbow to the nose, many times. He'd spit the blood out and keep playing. But an angry drunk attacking them was not something he ever wanted to experience again. His father had done that enough for one lifetime; Richard much preferred to lose a little dignity and money, especially if he could keep Sunny safe.

He dropped Lee and Antonio off first, then headed to Blanche's apartment a few streets over to drop off Tara. The side of his face throbbed noticeably at every stoplight.

"Hey, Tara?" He looked at her in the rearview mirror as she unbuckled. She had surprised him tonight, dropping in out of nowhere to help. "Thanks."

Tara shot him a wry smile. "Don't mention it. Try blocking with your hands next time."

Richard chuckled. "I'll keep that in mind."

To Richard's surprise, Tara kissed Sunny's cheek before she got out. "And thank *you* for giving me some excitement. Glad to know I can still take a motherfucker down, even if he was drunk off his ass."

Sunny laughed. "Please, he started it. No one can come for my Dicky without catching these hands."

"Bitch, you totally started it. But we also finished it, and that's what matters." Tara tapped Richard's shoulder and shut the door behind her, running up the steps to escape the rain.

Richard fought the urge to rub her touch away. Tara wasn't normally that affectionate with either of them. It was strange, but...nice. Even if Richard was a mess in a fight, it was reassuring that Sunny had someone at her back who could handle themself in a tight spot.

"Maybe we should remind everyone that as far as Phin is concerned, *they* started it, not us." Gabe moved to the middle row as Richard drove away. "I don't suppose you checked for cameras down there, did you?"

"No." Richard huffed, annoyed at himself that he hadn't asked the manager about that either. Another thing Phineas would have to follow up on. "I've been mentally drafting what I'm going to text him. He's going to be pissed if those guys actually turn up, but he's dealt with worse from us before. And these guys seemed to be college students, hopefully not well-connected ones whose parents would insist on filing charges."

The last thing Gabe needed was to end up in legal trouble, not when his ex's lawyers would use any excuse to get rid of the protection order. Emily claimed it was mere optics: a socialite heiress's ex, taking out a protection order against her. But if she'd just left Gabe alone, they wouldn't need—

"Who's Phin?" Sunny asked.

"What do you mean 'Who's Phin?'" Richard gaped as he headed to Gabe's house across the river. He'd mentioned Phineas before, many times. "In the context of this conversation, my lawyer. But also, our friend from undergrad? I've mentioned him before. Phin? Phineas Watkins?"

"Please, I would have remembered you mentioning the existence of another friend," Sunny teased. "Why don't you ever talk about him?"

"I do! You just don't listen to me," Richard teased back. He'd long given up on Sunny remembering anything without a visual aid; he'd have to text her a picture of Phineas. Or better yet, he should make him stop working long enough to introduce them in person.

"Agree to disagree." Sunny shrugged. "What do we need a lawyer for, anyway? We dipped before the cops showed up—we're good! You think this is our first rodeo?"

"Does this happen often?" Gabe asked. "Tag team bar fights?"

Sunny shook her head. "Not as often anymore since we only ever go to Confession these days, but that's how I finally won Tara over. Lee's too nice to be useful in a scrap. You should be glad Blanche wasn't here."

"Remind me to never piss off any of you," Gabe muttered. "Thanks for driving, Dicky." He clapped Richard on the shoulder as he got out.

As soon as they were alone, Sunny asked, "I'm in trouble, aren't I?"

Richard couldn't help but snort as he drove home. "Maybe, but I don't know what for. I don't like that you felt you had to defend me. And I would appreciate it if you'd let me talk us out of situations like that instead."

"I didn't think about it as defending you, to be honest. I'm a queer trans girl from Eastside. I was the only Thai kid in school, and I was too loud and too weird to have many friends. Even before I came out, I had a target on my back." She shrugged. "I know I'm not the most self-aware person, but I can tell when I can talk my way out of trouble, and when I can't. In a hopeless situation, all talking does is give people a chance to hit me first. Defending your honor sounds way more justifiable when I'm retelling the story," Sunny admitted with a smile. "I'm sorry for losing my temper, but I'd probably do it again. They deserved it."

Richard put his hand on her thigh; her skin felt warm through the fishnets beneath his palm. "It's not so much that you lost your temper. It felt...backward."

"What do you mean?" Sunny asked.

He sighed, not quite able to connect his vague ideas to explainable concepts. He needed more time to process a good answer. "I don't know how to describe it. Like, I was looking for escape routes and ways to talk him down, and you just punched him. Like when the seahorse broke, you were the one who took charge, while I fucking cried. Or how I feel like I have to nag before you clean up after yourself. I don't want to sound insecure or toxic, but... *I'm* supposed to do those things."

Sunny huffed, and in the dark, Richard couldn't tell if she was laughing or annoyed. "You're unhappy with how we were socialized to act a certain way, even though some of our behavior stems from our personalities, instead of gender norms. Is that what you mean?"

Richard nodded. "You made way more sense of it than I did."

Sunny hummed in acknowledgement, and they fell into silence broken only by the squeak of the windshield wipers and pattering of rain. He wasn't sure where to take the conversation from there. The problem had been acknowledged, but he couldn't think of a single solution for it.

Once they were home—and Dumpster was noisily eating, instead of loudly begging for food in her already-full bowl—Sunny pulled an ice pack from the freezer and the first aid kit from under the sink. "Come on, sit down. Let me get this cleaned up a little."

Richard sat at the small dining table he bought for the kitchen, so they could eat without Dumpster pawing at their food from the back of the couch. Sitting at an empty table with a first aid kit, instead of his and Sunny's takeout containers, was odd. He hissed as Sunny gently pressed a wet wipe to his face, wiping away the blood from a cut on his cheek. He hadn't even realized he was bleeding.

"This is probably poor timing, but can I ask if you'd be open to trying something?" Sunny asked as she dabbed the cut.

Richard snorted. "You can ask. I can't promise anything."

"Don't push me, Dicky. I'm trying to be serious and mature, kind of." She rolled her eyes. "What do you think about adding a more...formal kink arrangement to our relationship?"

"Where is this coming from?" Richard asked, insecurity twinging in his chest. He thought she'd been happy with their current love life. "Do we need to revisit the list?"

"No, our sex life is amazing! I just..." Sunny groaned. "I worry that we're not progressing fast enough. Because Lee and Antonio got engaged like, right away, and we've been together a year, and I'm not ready for all that yet, but *you* are."

"Just because Tonio and Lee are getting married quickly doesn't mean *we* need to," Richard paused, a curl of excitement glowing in his chest. They'd never talked this seriously about their future beyond agreeing they wanted one. Sunny had changed the subject anytime they'd come close before, and he was happy with how things were, so he hadn't pushed. "But if you *want* to get mar—"

"No!" Sunny interjected, flicking his injured cheek. Richard winced as her nail sliced along the cut. "I just said I'm not ready! I want to figure out how to be Wifey material and a good mother, and I want my surgery, and I want Luna to graduate first so I don't have to worry about her tuition payments, and I want to have a direction besides being stuck on the dev team forever!" Sunny huffed. "Besides, don't bring it up like *that*! I deserve more romance than a hypothetical question while I'm doing first aid. This is not where I thought the conversation would go!"

"Okay." Richard nodded, fighting a giddy smile; the turn in conversation had been delightful as far as he was concerned. Much better than a bar fight. He brought her hand with the wet wipe back to soothe the fresh sting in his cheek. "I only ask that you tell me when you're ready for me to bring *that* subject up again. And if money is a concern—"

"Do not make me flick you again," Sunny threatened, waving her finger at him. "I don't want your money, I am sharing what *I* want to accomplish before we revisit this topic. I am asking about *roleplaying* because, like," she huffed, "I want to figure out how to become the best me for our future, but also, I don't want to lose the me you fell in love with." Sunny's gaze fell, her brow creasing. "And this might help us do both, instead of me feeling guilty for acting bratty when you need me to be serious. And maybe roleplaying could help with some of our gender dynamic issues?" Sunny bit her lip. "'Cause, like, even if we can't control how we interact with the rest of the world, at least we can express ourselves with each other, you know?"

"Teeth," Richard said to delay responding to her question. Sunny pursed her lips to show she wasn't biting them with a guilty smile. "Good girl."

With a flustered groan, Sunny wrinkled her nose. "Eat a dick."

Richard laughed; he saw her blush with that nose wrinkle. They had been dancing around...*something* when they'd argued lately, even beyond what they already did. They probably should discuss the possibilities, before they followed through without getting on the same page. "I will always love you, even if you're brattier than Dumpster, but if being more serious is what you want to do, I support you." He paused, then added, "I'm just not sure how I feel about using roleplay to make me more secure in my masculinity."

She grinned over her shoulder as she put the wet wipe in the trash can. "Okay, well, full disclosure, this is mostly selfish. *I* want to roleplay your cute housewife, so I can have an outlet for the brattiness without pissing you off for real." She tossed her somehow-still-perfect ponytail over her shoulder. "But it might help with the other stuff, too."

Roleplaying didn't really sound up Richard's alley, but he would try it if Sunny wanted to, and this might cover other things they'd been interested in, but had been hesitant to try—like edging (which Sunny always shot down, but insisted it stay on the maybe list) and exhibitionism beyond the occasional hookup at Confession (which he *was* willing to do, if they could mitigate the risk). With their list, they'd already been kinkier than he had been with any partner. Even in Sunny's brattiest moments, she irritated him in the most delightful ways.

He huffed, frustrated that the words weren't coming, and forced them out anyway. "I want... I guess I keep falling into a caregiver role, and that doesn't suit me. That's more Gabe and his dad, so it's not as if being a caregiver can't be masculine, it just doesn't fit my personality. But I'm not sure how else to be. Would roleplaying help? I dunno." As Sunny opened the freezer behind him, Richard sighed. "It's not that I don't want to. Just...the moral aspect is concerning. A wealthy white man controlling and punishing his submissive Asian girlfriend? It sounds like a toxic parody of the worst stereotypes."

He gasped in pain when Sunny surprised him with an ice pack to his face. "Fuck, this is going to hurt tomorrow," he muttered.

"How the turn tables," Sunny laughed. "Dicky, you already spank me and tie me up on the regular. And you're very bossy. I know you're not fetishizing me, and you know I'm not *that* submissive." She circled him to straddle his lap, curling around him as she held the ice pack to his cheek. Her voice dropped to a whisper as she leaned, "Picture it: me, in a little vintage dress, serving you a martini when you get home from work? Your good little wife blowing you on the couch, while you read a book?"

Richard allowed himself to get lost in the vision of Sunny's head between his legs as he read her favorite erotica aloud. Maybe she'd be wearing a cute dress that concealed the remote control plug. Or maybe she'd look better in nothing but an apron and lingerie as he bent her over the couch. *Could I get her to clean her hair out of the drain with this?*

"That's what I thought," Sunny teased, her lovely eyes searching his face. Richard cleared his throat, trying to hide whatever it was she saw. "Maybe we can talk to Blanche? They have a standing offer to help us negotiate a dom/sub agreement. Black Hawk overemphasized how important communicating everything first is—they even recommended Blanche's page to me." Her brow furrowed. "It was such a strange coincidence."

"Is that so?" Richard bristled at the idea of Sunny sharing her desires with Blanche, or her "gamer friend", before she'd even told him. But he quickly stamped it out. She was right to get advice. Gabe was still recovering from having his boundaries blown away by his exes in his previous relationships.

Richard's curiosity in any formal D/s arrangement had vanished after seeing what it had done to his best friend. But that was before Antonio had met Lee, and brought Blanche—the professional dominatrix with a hobby of psychoanalyzing people—into his inner circle. If anyone could keep Richard and Sunny from going the way Gabe and his exes did, it'd be Blanche. Maybe this could be good for them.

He sighed. "I'm not saying yes yet, but we can talk to Blanche."

Sunny squealed, kissing him on his uninjured cheek before pulling out her phone. Her face fell, eyes scanning the screen as she scrolled furiously. "Shit."

Concern flared through him. "What is it?"

Sunny frowned. "Walter died."

"Who?"

"The guy who ran the hippie hideaway." Sunny handed him the phone. "*Bellamy Icon Walter Johannson Dead in Police Custody*" read the headline on the screen. Under it was a picture of a weathered old man in a top hat and pea coat, smiling next to a woman in a beret while they stood in front of a bus painted with flowers.

Richard, Gabe, Phineas, and Antonio had all been living in New York when the shantytown had been razed, but they'd heard various and contradicting retellings of the situation and subsequent riots. The incident had put the whole metro on edge and landed Bellamy in national headlines.

Taking her phone back to read the article, Sunny's dark eyes flashed. Her jaw clenched, and her nostrils flared as she scrolled through the comments.

"Sunny?" Richard had never seen her this angry, even in the middle of the fight they'd just been in. That itch to fix everything for her burned in his chest, even though he didn't understand her distress for this stranger she'd never mentioned before. Even if Sunny didn't want his help, or his money, or a proposal quite yet, he'd do what he could to make things easier for her. "Can I help? I can call—"

"No." Sunny shook her head as if clearing her thoughts. "Fuck. I have to call Tara."

SATURDAY, MARCH TWENTIETH

Chapter Thirteen

Tara

"This is bullshit," Sunny muttered, her voice dark, an edge to her tone that Tara rarely heard.

Jaw clenched and fists balled at her side, Tara wasn't sure what exactly Sunny was referring to, but she agreed. This "vigil" was bullshit. The island where she'd spent most of her childhood was crowded with people she didn't know. Their long shadows, stretching from the sinking sun, engulfed the space around them. It made the crowd seem bigger than it should. The sacred ground, where Walter had founded a community of lost souls for his beloved Wanda, was swarmed with strangers from a city Tara barely recognized anymore.

A vigil in honor of Walter had been thrown together overnight by a hodgepodge of community organizations; the whole of the Bellamy metro area had gathered in the park. Anarchists and punks mingled with pastors and preachers. Former hippies turned college professors stood next to youth activists. Elderly Black folks born and raised in Eastside mixed with the "young professionals" looking for roommates in the luxury condos that kept popping up overnight. A circle of misfits played guitar and drums, sang and prayed and cried. It would be idyllic, a sign of a united city.

That is, if any of them had actually come to honor Walter, instead of putting on a performance to further their own causes.

As soon as Sunny had called her last night, Tara knew she had to go to the island to pay her respects. Walter had been there for her every time she'd needed him; she had to show up for him. Lee, Blanche, and Sunny had wanted to come, too. Sunny had never known Walter like they did, but she knew what he meant to them. Tara was grateful for all three of them. *I wouldn't get through this alone.*

It just so happened that everyone else in Bellamy had the same idea. Sunny had found out about the vigil before they'd left home, so they'd decided to wait until close to sundown to attend instead. A decision Tara was regretting; the crowd of strangers on the island she'd once called home left her unsettled.

She used to feel safe here. Before it was razed to the ground.

Her nerves were frayed, her self-control on edge. Being *here* around this many people would have had her on her last nerve already. Everything was only made worse after a long night of confusing feelings and a bar brawl.

"Seriously?" Blanche scoffed, making Tara jump. Their phone lit up with an incoming call. "Stop calling me! I told him I'm not available." They turned off their phone instead of answering it.

"What's up?" Lee asked.

"You already know." They shot him a baleful look as they tucked their phone into their coat pocket, nodding for everyone to keep walking. Tara's stomach tightened as they passed through the crowd. Blanche's patron would take their absence personally, but they deserved tonight to themself. Walter had been their friend too; if not for him, Blanche might not have lived long enough to meet Lee or Tara at all.

Tara doubted even a fraction of these people had ever looked Walter in the eye. Their gaze would slide over him as if he wasn't there. Just as they'd done to Tara when she was a kid, and her mother, and all of the other people in their camp. Not having a residential address turned people invisible to those who did. Even emergency shelters and soup kitchens were ignored, the buildings invisible to those who never worried about having food to eat.

And Walter had been the best person. All the mourners who'd ignored him in life had missed out on his easy smile and wild stories and generous heart. On his love for the world, for every lost soul who made their way to his camp, and most of all, his love for Wanda.

The fact that she'd never see him again seemed impossible to process. When she'd learned of Wanda's passing a couple of years ago, Tara had buried that grief under time and a long absence. But she'd seen Walter a *week* ago. While he hadn't been looking his best, he had been alive.

And now, he wasn't.

Tears springing to her eyes, Tara swallowed hard to stay in control, even as her thoughts raced. Blanche led the way to the far side of the island, trying to find a quiet spot amidst the hubbub.

When Tara was growing up, Wanda and Walter were her only example of what love should be. They were each other's family, taking care of each other, and keeping each other safe. Through all of their adventures and hardships, they'd brought each other joy and lightness and love. And now Walter was finally with Wanda again, in whatever afterlife might exist for the invisible people who loved the world. If such a place even existed.

As the group found a quiet spot along the riverbank, still within earshot of the preacher on the microphone leading a prayer, Lee squeezed her hand. Tara squeezed back, shooting him a grateful smile. Breathing deep and leaning into Lee's comfort next to her, she forced herself to stay alert. More and more people were streaming over the footbridges to the island. Tara did her best to fight her anxiety that her exit route was blocked; she needed to stick it out for Walter.

When she'd lived here, Tara had to cross a makeshift pallet-and-rope bridge that broke every spring, when the ice went out on the river. The whole camp would move to the mounds, until the spring floods died down. Though Tara had rarely overwintered in the camp; her mom hadn't cared about much, but Anne had hated the cold even more than Tara did. They'd started off every winter season by moving into some run-down studio or trailer. In good years, they managed to stay through spring.

The footbridges the East Bellamy City Council had built were much sturdier, large enough for an ambulance or a food truck to get to the park. Funny how the city couldn't be bothered with bridges when people actually lived there. They'd only been built to make it easier to evict them.

Folks came through the crowd, distributing red carnations—like the one Tara had given Walter a mere week ago—and tapers with paper cups around the bottom to catch the wax. Others walked around to light the candles as the light turned rosy from the sunset. Tara and Lee took a flower each, Sunny a candle. Blanche passed on all of it with a polite wave of their hand.

Tara questioned if giving the crowd fire was a good idea. The few people she recognized were the activists who had promised Walter and Wanda they'd protect the camp from eviction. Promised to hold the line against the deputies sent to clear it. Instead, they'd burned the camp down in their enthusiasm, doing more harm than a mere eviction would have that night. *The audacity to even be here.*

And with Walter dying in police custody for "trespassing" (daring to take refuge in the entryway of a hotel, amid torrential freezing rain) the mood of the crowd was restless. Walter had lived a good life. He'd died from heart failure, and he'd likely have passed regardless. Yeah, fuck the assholes who ignored the medical emergency in the holding cell, who let him die. Walter never trusted them either. But he wouldn't have wanted to be a martyr for someone else's cause.

He was an old hippie. A pacifist. Walter had often regaled the camp with stories about his anti-war civil disobedience when he was young. Then Wanda would chime in and tell him he was too old for that shit now. He'd laugh and agree; he just missed the "good drugs and kumbaya shit." He would have appreciated the candles and the singing, and smiled at everyone who came. And then he would have disappeared quietly into the night once the speeches started.

The pastor with the microphone, who Tara recognized from the Baptist church over Eastside, finished his story about how Walter had always played harmonica when they shared meals. Walter had liked him. Volunteers from their church had always brought food leftover from funerals and cookouts to the camp, and they made sure to spend time talking with everyone.

The next speaker would have pissed Walter off. She was some "advocate for the homeless" from Saint Mary's, going on about treating every one of God's Children with dignity and respect. Protecting the innocent souls from hurt to cradle, against the bosom of God.

Tara rolled her eyes at Lee.

He smirked, shaking his head. "This lady is so full of shit."

"Fuck Saint Mary's," Tara agreed. Walter hadn't trusted them a lick. They never did anything worth a damn for anyone. They'd send volunteers to the camp to convince them to come to the shelter to get prayed over and have a hot meal. Instead, they'd be preyed on. Like Tara had been, when she was foolish enough to go there.

Tara breathed, centering herself by taking Lee's hand. His palms sweaty, he laced his fingers through hers. St. Mary's had brought them together, so in a way, Tara was grateful. Without Lee and his reassuring hand always ready to hold hers, who knows how she'd keep calm in a moment like this, surrounded by strangers blocking her exit? But that church could burn to the ground, and she'd rejoice.

Someone handed the mic to a young white man, but he opted to use a bullhorn to loudly announce he was the leader of some organization with an innocuous name: Equitable Community Housing Organization.

"ECHO?" Blanche muttered. "The irony."

True to Blanche's expectations, he started shouting catchy phrases, the chants co-opted from other movements.

The crowd ate it up. Tara couldn't blame them, even as it brought her hackles up. Nothing had gotten better after the riot; just quibbling and finger-pointing between politicians about why dozens of people had been violently arrested for the crime of...existing? Rent had skyrocketed, and there was never enough housing. Even the overpriced luxury condos that spread like a rash had waitlists.

The trio of local and state governments in the Bellamy metro couldn't coordinate their own councils and representatives, let alone work across state lines to address any metro-wide issues. The police from all three counties abused their power, eroding what little trust people had in their local government. Especially over Eastside. People were sick of their shit.

Walter was a convenient face for a variety of causes to use, including this ECHO character. The young man's point was lost in his delivery—he was angry and frustrated, and he wanted everyone there to be angry and frustrated with him. And that honored Walter, somehow. They would create change, somehow.

The "somehow" was unspoken, undefined. It always was. Not that Tara had any idea how either. That was something for people with more time, money, and education to figure out. Tara could barely stand quietly in this crowd without the support of her family.

Her breath shaky, she looked to Blanche, who nodded. "Time to go," they said.

Time to fade quietly out of sight, like Walter would right about now. Time to stay out of trouble, to leave before the crowd got worse. She tugged Lee's hand, nodding for him to follow.

Standing between them, Sunny hadn't gotten the memo as she shouted along. Tara and Blanche exchanged an exasperated smile. Sunny always was the optimist, the dreamer, the activist of their group. As much as a socially awkward nerd, who got overwhelmed by crowds, could be an activist.

After a few polite attempts to get her attention, Blanche lost their patience and gripped her jaw, murmuring in her ear. With a self-conscious smile, Sunny nodded and grabbed Blanche's and Lee's hands as Blanche led them back toward the footbridge.

Bright flashes of blue and red lights stopped them in their tracks. *Fuck.*

In the parking lot across the bridge, buses awaited behind a line of cops in riot gear, who shouted orders to disperse.

"Disperse where?" Tara asked, her voice breaking as her throat tightened. Her exit route off the island was more than blocked; it was dangerous.

"That bastard," Blanche muttered, their face tight.

"You think this is Covey's doing?" Lee asked, his face ashen.

"Doesn't matter." They shook their head. "This was a foolish place for a crowd."

Like unlucky penguins pushed into the ocean, a few brave souls tried to walk past the police line with their hands up, only to get zip-tied and loaded onto buses. A couple of people jumped into the offshoot of the Mississippi in an attempt to swim back to Eastside. Tara wished them luck. The current was strong there, especially this time of year. The water was fast and freezing, and fallen trees lurked just under the surface.

Lee's eyes were wide behind his glasses. Beads of sweat dotted his lip and his palm grew clammy against hers. Blanche looked nervous, too; the tendon in their jaw flickered.

Only Sunny hadn't realized the severity of the situation, glaring angrily at the riot police. "What the fuck is this shit?"

"Not good," Tara muttered, her stomach sinking. Four queer people, three of them people of color, two of them trans. And Tara was the one who had dragged them here.

Lee tugged on her hand, gesturing in the direction they'd come from. "Bridge?"

Tara nodded, grateful he'd kept his head enough to remember their escape route from the night of the riots. The bridge to Downtown was anchored by a pylon on the northern end of the island, with an ancient service ladder built into the far side. As a kid, Tara had played there often.

A young white man with dreadlocks passed, shouting at everyone to form a chain, as if he were a war general. He grabbed Tara's wrist, dragging her from Lee's grip, their hands slipping apart.

Fuck fuck fuck. Tara threw herself against him, desperate to get back to Lee. But she couldn't get the right angle to wrench her wrist free as he pulled her along. Blood pounded in her ears as she lost sight of her friends.

She had to get away. *Run run run.*

Whatever it took, she had to get back to Lee. Fear rose up like bile at the feeling of his hand around her wrist like a vise—

"Get your fucking hands off her!"

Releasing Tara's wrist, the man pressed a hand to his jaw. He cussed at Sunny, who cussed at him back, threatening to punch him again. Tara ran back to Lee, breathing in the solace of his hug. He murmured halfhearted reassurances, his voice quaking.

Blanche was at her elbow a second later, their arm firmly around Sunny's, who shook out her fist with a wince. "I need you to keep your head, Tara. Can you do that?"

Tara nodded, forcing herself to breathe deep. Getting them all to safety was the only thing that mattered. They reformed their line—Sunny at the back this time, still cussing out the asshole who'd grabbed Tara—as they headed to the pylon.

Screams erupted behind them. Tara's heart pounded in her throat. The crowd pushed with them, away from the lights, spreading panic and confusion.

"What the fuck?" Blanche snapped. Nostrils flaring, they stood on their tiptoes to peer over the crowd in search of the cause for chaos. "Are they seriously gassing people? Tara, I packed some scarves in the bag. They were supposed to be in case anyone got cold—not fucking tear gas!"

Tara let go of Lee's hand to dig through his backpack, passing flannel scarves out to Blanche, Sunny, and Lee. Blanche tied the last one around Tara's mouth and nose as people pushed past. Waves of peppery, acidic air rolled off of them.

"I swear you can see the future, Blanche," Sunny said, her voice muffled.

Blanche snorted derisively. "If I could, we wouldn't be here, Babygirl. I only have the common sense to bring extra layers when it's forty degrees."

Hands linked, they pushed through the panicked crowd toward the bridge. Around them, people ran directionless, coughing and crying. Others who had avoided the direct impact, like Tara and their group, covered their mouths as they poured water over people's eyes. Strangely calm amid the chaos, Tara was tempted to tell people to follow them, but her friends took priority. She wouldn't want to draw attention to their escape route and end up in more trouble. The lucky ones would find a hiding spot and lie low until the buses were full.

As they made their way through the crowd, toward the small ravine that led down to freedom, a mop of hair with uneven bangs caught Tara's eyes. The slight figure retched into a shrub.

Tara cursed under her breath. "Hold on a second."

"Tara, we don't have a second," Blanche warned.

She pulled her hands from Lee and Blanche's. "Then give me a bottle of water. I'll catch up."

Blanche looked at her solemnly, passing a bottle from Lee's backpack. "I hope you know what you're doing."

Tara shook her head. "I never do. We'll catch up to you."

"*We*? Who is *we*? Tara, this isn't the time to pick up strays!"

But Tara was already dashing away, trusting Lee to lead them. Kneeling beside the kid, she blinked, her eyes burning. "Tilt your head to the side. I'm gonna rinse your eyes, then we can get out of here."

"Who the fuck are you?" Syl squinted through streaming snot and tears.

Tara snorted, amused that he was still suspicious of anyone trying to help at a time like this. She lowered the scarf around her face, coughing as her throat burned from the chemicals singeing the air. "It's Tara. I sat in on the flower class with you."

"Oh. Coop's girl? What the fuck are you doing here?" Tara was glad the others hadn't heard that. They didn't have time for *that* conversation, nor did she know exactly what she was to Gabe. Not that it was Syl's business, anyway.

"I should ask you the same thing." Tara poured the water over his eyes and handed him the scarf Blanche had tied around her face. "Are you here alone?"

He wiped his face dry before messily tying it around his head. "My brother's here, but they already got him. He told me to get somewhere safe, but where the fuck am I going to go?"

Tara jerked her head in the direction of the bridge. "I know a way. Come on."

Syl followed her. "I don't have to swim, do I?"

"No, but I hope you're not scared of heights." She slid down the short slope to the pylon's footing, turning to help him down as she coughed into her elbow. Her throat itched whenever Syl got too close. The scarf was tied haphazardly around his face, hair poking out around his ears. The lock of hair he'd cut in class was stuck upright. "Watch your step."

Under the slope of the bridge, Tara crouched along the edge of the river. Carefully, she avoided the pitted patches of concrete where metal rebar, hidden by graffiti, might trip her. An ice floe bobbed along in the current, swollen from last night's rain. The rapidly fading light from sunset made the shadow of the bridge even dimmer.

"Is this safe? I can't swim." Syl's voice shook.

Tara shrugged, not trusting her balance to look back at him. "Me either, so don't fall in."

With a sigh of relief, she emerged on the other side to Lee's visible relief.

"She's here!" he called up. Sunny's legs disappeared over the top, and Blanche was about halfway up. "Who's this?" He nodded to Syl, scrambling out from the bridge behind her.

"Lee, Syl," Tara introduced quickly. "Can you climb that?"

Syl looked up and shrugged. "Do I have a choice? How'd you know this was here?"

"Questions later. Climb now."

The kid nodded, wiping his hands on his jeans before quickly climbing up.

Tara turned to Lee. "You next."

Lee shook his head. "No, I'll go last."

Tara frowned; she would slow Lee down. "No, *I'll* go last. I'll be right behind you."

With a glare, Lee reached up the ladder and started climbing. "Fine, but only because I don't want to waste time arguing."

"You'd lose anyway!" she called after him, waiting until he was at least a body length ahead of her, before she put her foot on the first rung. Her gut twisted. She hated heights. Tara tucked the red carnation in the buttonhole of her peacoat, the way Walter had, so she wouldn't accidentally drop it.

Focusing on her breathing, Tara kept her eyes trained upward. One hand and foot in front of the other, she maintained three points of contact as her head swam. "Save the meltdown for when you're safe," she muttered to herself. "Shoulda stayed home today."

Exhaling with every rung, Tara imagined what she'd eat after this instead. Or how Gabe would react when she told him this story. Or how he'd comforted her last night, under the guise of holding her back or warming her up, until the worst of the sadistic adrenaline she always got in a fight had passed. Thinking of Gabe's comforting hug was infinitely preferable to being aware that she was thirty feet in the air, with only rusty iron rungs to keep her from falling.

Before she knew it, Lee and Sunny were helping her over the railing. As soon as Tara's feet touched the sidewalk, Lee pulled her into a tight hug. A strange mix of relief and sadness washed over her. Her chest grew heavy as her panicked, shallow breaths slowed. Now that she was relatively safe on solid footing, her fear abated, and the grief flooded back in.

"They've got Eastside locked down," Blanche said, nodding toward the east end of the bridge. Cars were completely blocked from leaving, and traffic going in was frozen. Some were turning around to go outbound against the gridlock on the shoulder. "We should probably go Downtown until shit dies down."

"So, we kick it at the museum?" Lee suggested. "If we go to Confession, I'll end up working."

"There is usually a taco truck at the museum," Tara supplied.

They all laughed.

"There's Tara. Always thinking about food," Sunny teased.

Arms crossed, Blanche turned to Syl. "Look, kid. I don't know who you are, but I'm not getting charged with taking a minor across state lines. *We're* going to the art museum." They uncrossed their arms to gesture across the river. "If you happen to also go that way, completely separate from us, there'll be tacos if you're hungry."

"And you scolded me about strays." Tara grinned.

A siren blared past them, followed by a city bus full of people. Blanche frowned. "Why would they take folks arrested over Eastside to the Iowa side for processing? Fucking Bellamy can't even arrest people right. This is all wrong."

They ignored the strange looks from the people stopped in their cars as Tara's family crossed the bridge. Not many pedestrians used it, let alone with this much police activity. Most crossed the river via the old train bridge that connected to the riverwalk. The narrow sidewalks on this bridge were full of cracks, debris, and patches of rebar poking through, barely visible in the shadows cast by the sparse streetlights. Like most things in Bellamy, even the bridges slipped through the cracks. *Small wonder people are pissed off. Nothing at that fucking vigil was about Walter.*

That made her even sadder. He shouldn't be a symbol of the city's problems. He was the best part of Bellamy. He was the love and life and community and history. Tara had been hoping to spend the vigil reflecting on all of those things Walter meant to her.

Instead, everyone had only proven that for most of Bellamy, Walter was the rebar showing through Bellamy's cracks. Every badly done speech brought her right back to that terrifying night—trying to keep her and Lee safe, to not fall off the damn bridge, to repress her panic attack until she could scramble together some semblance of safety. Even the tear gas burning the air reminded her of waking up to the smell of smoke.

Like they had that night, her palms smelled like iron no matter how much she wiped them on her joggers.

On the other side of the river, they settled into the same secluded spot in the museum's amphitheater where she'd last seen Walter. Out of sight from the street, they could watch the situation unfold across the river in safety. There were several discreet escape routes if anyone questioned them.

Blanche collapsed against the oversized concrete steps. "I'm too old for this shit."

"At least we all got out." Lee set the backpack next to them. "None of us got arrested."

"Just my brother." Syl stood awkwardly far from them. "I hope he's okay."

Blanche patted the concrete next to them; Syl sat down. "He will be. I can't imagine any charges against a peaceful gathering would stick, and they must know that if they're taking people to Iowa for processing. This is fishy."

"Lee, want to help me get tacos for everyone?" Sunny asked, surprising Tara—and Lee, from his bemused nod. Sunny wasn't usually considerate unless she had an ulterior motive, but Tara couldn't imagine what that might be.

The evening light grew dimmer, highlighting the red and blue lights still flashing across the river. Shivering as Lee left her side to help Sunny, Tara wondered how long they could stay here. Museum security would move them along once they closed for the night. Maybe they could find a coffee shop to keep warm, if the fuckshit over Eastside didn't calm down—

"Man, I never thought Coop could bag a girl as cool as you." Syl broke the silence with the one topic Tara had been trying not to overthink.

With a huff, Tara shot a glare at Blanche, daring them to say something. But Blanche merely raised an eyebrow. At least Lee and Sunny hadn't heard that. "We gotta get you home, Syl."

"Yeah, my aunt is gonna be pissed! She told us not to go." Syl wrapped his arms around himself, reminding Tara how young he was.

Sunny and Lee soon returned, passing out tacos, bottles of soda, and wet wipes. Tara scrubbed at her palms to get that iron smell from her hands before unwrapping the first one.

With a contented sigh, Tara inhaled the perfectly seasoned chicken tinga, the lime juice brightening the flavors on her tongue. She hadn't realized how hungry she was. "The last time I saw Walter was here, just last week."

"I'd see him around Confession sometimes. He'd be busking with that old harmonica he had. He always asked me to tell you hi." Lee snorted. "I mean, he told me to tell my old lady hi. You'd think he would have gotten the hint since I was always at a gay bar, but I never corrected him."

Tara chuckled softly. "He knew. I told him you were getting married last week. He said congratulations."

Lee's smile twisted, and he twirled the carnation he'd been handed at the vigil.

There'd been no point correcting Walter before last week. When they were younger, Tara always assumed she and Lee would be together forever, platonic soulmates. It was safer if they pretended anyway. She supposed they still would be, just not exactly how she'd imagined. He had Antonio to grow old with now. Her gut twisted in a confusing lurch of envy; she didn't have anyone like that for herself. But maybe Gabe...

"To Walter." Blanche raised their soda. "Protector of the vulnerable. Defender of peace. Lover of Wanda. Let's remember him for being the sweet ol' hippie he was."

"To Walter!" they echoed, raising their bottles in toast.

Tara smiled. This was the kind of vigil Walter would have enjoyed.

CHAPTER FOURTEEN

GABE

Deep within the admin wing of the MAI, Gabe tucked the progress report he'd finally finished into the corresponding folder. Leaning back in the chair of the desk he'd borrowed, he rubbed his eyes. The light filtering in from the sculpture garden was barely enough to see by; he probably should have turned the overhead lights on when the sun set. But he could have sworn he'd only needed one more minute.

Getting up to turn on the light switch would have been too tempting to walk right out the door, and he'd already put this off to the last minute. There were better things to do on a Saturday evening than writing reports, tracking expenses, and submitting check requests for a volunteer gig. *Who am I kidding?* His Saturday nights were normally spent hunched over his computer, playing the same games he'd played hundreds of times. And since Tara still hadn't answered his texts in over a week, he'd probably end up there again tonight. *This is positively exciting by comparison.*

He was supposed to get all of the paperwork done last weekend, after the flower class. But then he'd found Tara outside, and he'd been living in a constant state of confusion and insecurity since.

Gabe dropped the expense report and check requests in the admin's to-do file. The checks for the upcoming class—and to reimburse Angie for the flowers—would have to wait until the next pay period. He felt a little guilty for making Angie wait for reimbursement just because he'd been confused and sad all week, but she'd caused it by meddling.

Tara's mixed signals had become painfully bewildering. She'd told him she might have some feelings for him, turned his entire existence upside down, and then ghosted him for a week straight. His conversation with Lee hadn't clarified a damn thing, and his attempt to check in with her directly had, well...

The loud music, being pressed together in a crowd of dancers—their "talk" had lasted all of two seconds, before they were practically dry humping on the dance floor like high schoolers. All thoughts had left his brain the second she'd turned her green eyes up at him with a smirk, to drag him closer by his belt loops. Gabe had left Belly's more confused than ever, with a hickey and an adrenaline high that still hadn't settled.

He flipped his phone over, making sure there were no new texts since the one last one he'd sent her this morning. With a groan, he ran his fingers along his scalp to soothe the frustration. She wanted him, but for what? Had she meant it, when she'd said that last weekend wasn't just casual? He didn't want to think she'd lied to him, but then why hadn't she texted? It all brought him right back to what the flowers might mean—

The door to the office opened and shut quickly, followed by an uncomfortably familiar giggle that morphed into a gasp.

Of all the fucking days. Gabe let out a disgusted groan. "Can you two get a room?"

The light flicked on. His parents looked at him in shock. John had Miriam pressed against the door, her dress hiked up her thigh. Thankfully, Gabe didn't see anything but a flash of his mom's knee as his parents stepped apart.

"Gabriel Fucking Cooper! You scared the shit out of me," his mom scolded. "Why are you sitting in the dark?"

"Why are you going at it in public like horny teenagers, without checking that you're alone first?" he shot back.

Miriam straightened her dress and wiped her lipstick off of his dad's face. She turned to him with an innocent smile. "We're here to say hi to you! There was a gallery opening tonight."

"Don't pretend you knew I was here." Gabe crossed his arms. "It's a miracle I don't have a sibling."

John shrugged unapologetically, fixing his wife's hair.

"So, Gabey, how are you?" Miriam asked serenely, still pretending her son hadn't caught them about to bone in public.

"I'm fine. How are you?" If his mom wanted to pretend this was a planned social visit, he could play along.

She raised an eyebrow. "It's Saturday night, Gabey Baby, and you're sitting alone in a dark office, presumably doing that late expense report. So how are you? Really?"

Gabe ignored her. If she didn't want to answer his question, he wouldn't answer hers. "The kids really enjoyed Angie's class. And I lined up a graphic designer since our pottery class fell through." It felt excruciatingly wrong to reduce Tara to her mere occupation, but he wasn't about to share anything more than that with his parents.

"Speaking of Angie, how was your date?" Miriam asked with a probing look. "Are you going to see her again?"

Gabe sighed with a slow shake of his head. "Angie and I aren't going to work out, Ma."

"Why not? She's lovely!"

"She's Tonio's cousin, for one!" Gabe snorted. "And we didn't connect that way. Yes, I kept an open mind about it."

Miriam shrugged. "That's all I ask. Do you want me to set up a date with someone else?"

Gabe pressed on, avoiding her question. "She's going to do the flowers for Tonio's wedding. On that note, I don't suppose Cooper Winery would want to gift wine for the meal service?"

His mom brightened; she could never resist talking shop. "Oh, of course! It's at that Confession place a few blocks down, right? I'll get in touch with them to arrange it." She turned to John as she pulled her phone out of her purse to set a reminder for herself. "You know, this might be a good opportunity for a new venue. We should see if they're open to a tasting."

Gabe cleared his throat to preemptively supply the insider information his mom would ask for. "Chas is the co-owner and manager you should talk to. She uses any pronouns, but Tonio told me to adjust based on how she's presenting. She goes to church with Tonio's mom. She's married with four young kids and is currently expecting. Chas is emceeing the reception, if you need face time to close a deal. Oh, and do *not* flirt with her husband."

"Great information. Thank you, Gabey." Miriam nodded approvingly as she took notes on her phone. "So, back to the question you avoided. Do you want me to set you up with someone else?"

He sighed, "Ma, come on."

"What? I want to see you happy. You look so sad all the time." She tilted her head as she examined him. "Even now, you got the sad hound dog eyes. Have you been having trouble sleeping?"

Gabe couldn't help but let out a sarcastic laugh. "Yeah, because relationships are usually such a joy for me. Where do you think these eye bags come from? Happiness?"

Miriam's expression softened. "You said this was something you wanted."

John touched Miriam lightly on the arm. "What your mother means is that we want what's best for you. And being alone isn't making you any happier. For a while, being alone was better for you. You healed enough to stand on your own two feet. But you can't keep isolating yourself forever. If you're not ready, you don't have to jump into any relationships, but at least start putting yourself out there. Meet more people. You'll grow stronger with more support in your life, more people to grow with you."

"I know," Gabe said softly, touched that his dad had basically given a speech for his well-being. John was usually the quiet parent. Soft-spoken and reserved, as if he'd run out of words if he used too many at once. As much as he longed to reassure them, Gabe couldn't explain that he *had* someone he wanted to grow with. At least not before he gave Tara the time and space she needed to figure out what she wanted.

Gabe stood, gathering his belongings. "I don't think I'm as ready for dating again as I hoped, but when I am, I'll manage my dating life myself. Either way, I won't isolate myself as much, okay?" He forced a smile as he pulled his coat on. "I'll get out of your hair. Let you guys get back to fucking in peace if I haven't totally killed the mood."

He made a show of shutting off the light as he left. John laughed as Gabe closed the door behind him. They'd never had any shame. As a kid, he'd been embarrassed to have such amorous parents. But now, he was more envious than anything.

Fiddling with the office keys, Gabe headed to the security desk to return them before the guards started their rounds to close down the museum for the night. The atrium—normally lively with people playing on the musical tiles in the floor, filling the air with chaotic, dissonant melodies—was hushed as a crowd looked out the window across the river.

"Just a heads-up, my parents are uh...*using* the office," he told the security guard, Sammy, as he checked the key back in.

Sammy laughed knowingly. "I'll do my rounds over there later then. Your mom got her key?"

"She should." Gabe nodded toward the crowd pressing against the window. "What's going on over there?"

Sammy shook his head with a sigh. "You know that old guy Walter? The poor guy's heart gave out when he was in jail last night. They were having a vigil for him across the way, where his camp used to be, but the cops came, and they're rounding everyone up."

"What for?" Gabe's first thought was if his parents knew their oldest friend had died. But if their public tryst was anything to go by, they did. Everyone grieved in different ways, and his mom... Well, there'd been a reason he was born less than a year after her mother had passed. Miriam would always put on a brave face; only her husband was permitted to witness the grief and anxiety she kept locked up. Only John could make her tea, roll her a joint, and do whatever it took to remind Miriam that she was alive, and she wouldn't despair forever.

Gabe's second thought was if Tara knew. Even if she hadn't texted him, he should reach out to make sure she was okay.

Sammy shrugged. "Why do they ever do anything? The right person must have complained. I got a couple folks posted to keep an eye out, but looks like the trouble's staying over Eastside."

"Shit." Gabe shook his head. If Tara did know Walter had passed, maybe she'd gotten caught up in it. He glanced at his phone, but there was still no word from her.

Sammy waved as he put Gabe's key back in the lockbox. "Get home safe, now."

"You too." Lost in thought (Should he let Tara know, or check in on her? Could he ask how to support her, without causing her to feel pressured into "*more*" than she was ready for?), Gabe headed to the staff exit. He pushed the door open, welcoming the cool, damp air of the tunnel. His footsteps splashed in the puddles, where last night's rain had flooded the sidewalk. As he stepped into the amphitheater toward the employee parking, he found himself looking at Tara. Her face was a mirror of his, jaw hanging open in surprise. Why was she here? Or Lee, Blanche, Sunny, and...

"Syl? What are *you* doing here?" They all looked exhausted and cold, huddled together with scarves bundled around them. Their noses and eyes were red, faces wan as they looked back at him with their own confused expressions.

"Oh, hey Coop!" Syl waved, rubbing his red-rimmed eyes and blinking furiously as the boy squinted up at him. "You got a car, right? Think you can give me a ride home? I really need a shower. I'm so itchy!"

"We'll have to go through Wisconsin, I think," Blanche said, gathering up their belongings and stuffing everything into a backpack. "The bridge is still shut down."

"We can't all fit in Gabe's car, though," Sunny pointed out. "We have one too many."

"Tara can sit on my lap 'til we drop Syl off," Lee said. "Then she can take his spot up front."

"Does it count as transporting a minor across state lines if we're bringing him home?" Blanche mused. "Given the circumstances, Gabe would take the fall, and I doubt they'd pull over a station wagon."

"We can put you in the dog crate." Tara elbowed Syl.

"Come on, I'm not a dog!" Syl elbowed her back. "*You* go in the dog crate!"

Gabe blinked. None of this was making sense yet.

"I love that confused expression of his." Blanche looked at Gabe fondly, hand pressed to their chest. Tara shushed them.

Gabe rubbed his forehead, trying to put the scene in front of him together. He'd never been the cleverest person, but he hated how often Blanche pointed it out.

Lee took pity on him. "We got caught up in the fuckshit across the river. We were waiting here until it died down, but it's been an hour, and they're still going."

"If you were *there*, how'd you get *here*?" Gabe scratched his head.

"We climbed the bridge. It was so badass!" Syl grinned. "Why is your girl so much cooler than you, Coop?"

Tara elbowed Syl, but she didn't correct him. Behind her, Blanche clapped a hand over Sunny's mouth. Lee just smirked.

It took everything to keep his brain from getting stuck on *that*. "You climbed the bridge?"

"Yeah. After I got tear-gassed." Syl's nonchalant tone trembled with a manic quiver.

"What the fuck." Gabe ran a hand through his hair, wishing he could scratch his brain instead of merely his scalp.

"So, can we get a ride home?" Tara asked. "Syl is going to his aunt's, and the rest of us are about to get trashed at our apartment, if you want to join us."

"Can I come?" Syl asked eagerly.

"No. You're fourteen. And you need to let your auntie know your brother got arrested," Tara reminded him.

"Bernie got arrested?" Gabe asked. Syl's brother had done the program the first year Gabe ran it. He was as much of a class clown as Syl.

Syl frowned. His mask slipped again, revealing the scared kid underneath. "Yeah. He just turned eighteen, too. Shit sucks."

With a shake of his head, Gabe turned to the parking lot. "Okay, skoden." No point in wasting time. He hoped Phineas would be sober enough for a phone call when he got home; knowing Phin, he was either still at work or already shitfaced.

"Can I drive?" Tara asked, falling into step beside him.

"No." With a grin, Gabe fought the urge to take her hand as her fingers brushed against his.

"Why not?"

"Because then *Syl* would have to lap it, and with you in the driver's seat, he might not make it home," Gabe teased quietly. "You okay?"

Tara nodded, sliding her ice-cold hand into his. "Surprisingly, yeah. I am."

Cheeks heating as the warmth in his chest spread, Gabe laced his fingers through hers.

CHAPTER FIFTEEN

BLANCHE

"Lee, you prefer a sativa, don't you?" Blanche asked, opening their weed box.

Sitting on the floor next to Sunny, Lee wedged the top of his beer bottle on the corner of the coffee table. He smacked down to open it. "No, yeah, I'll pass out in five minutes with that shit you smoke." His smile was tired, but genuine, as he sagged back against the couch, looking as exhausted as Blanche felt.

Blanche forced a smile back. Anything other than Northern Lights would make them think too much about topics they'd rather avoid, but they could be a good host for Lee's sake. They dug around the box, squinting at the labels on the jars. "Any objections to Super Silver Haze?"

Sunny took the fizzy drink Tara handed her. "I don't smoke enough to have an opinion."

"Sounds fine to me," Tara said, setting a stack of glass tumblers on the coffee table. "Gabe, we have beer, whiskey, or I can make another kiddie cocktail for you."

"Excuse me, this better *not be* a kiddie cocktail. I asked for vodka!" Sunny eyed the grenadine lurking at the bottom of her glass. "There's no cherries, either."

"We don't have cherries, and if you drank it before complaining, *Karen*, you'd taste the vodka!" Tara rolled her eyes. "So, beer, whiskey, or a *big kids* cocktail?"

Gabe—squeezed into the far end of the otherwise empty sofa—shrugged. "Whatever you're having is cool."

Tara held up a bottle of Black Label as she cracked open the cap. "Neat okay?"

He nodded. "Whatever you're having, Tara."

"You're allowed to be inconvenient, Coop," Tara grumbled, pouring a generous splash of scotch into three tumblers. "I just made Sunny a fucking Shirley Temple that's half vodka, so you can have a damn ice cube if you want."

Lee caught Blanche's eye and mouthed, *Coop?*

Blanche gave the tiniest shrug as Tara handed them their drink. Tara normally wasn't one to give nicknames. Everyone was "dude." Except for Sunny, who was usually "bitch," because "dude" was dysphoric for her.

As Tara edged between Gabe and the coffee table to sit down, Sunny fluffed her hair so it fanned across the seat with a smirk. Lee groaned as he stretched, resting his elbow on the cushion. The couch was small; Lee's well-timed stretch and Sunny's hair forced Tara to sit closer to Gabe.

Blanche dug around under the chair for a bong large enough for the group to hide their amusement. *So much for no meddling.* They pulled out one that had been plain glass, but Daisy had borrowed paint from Wanda and covered it in—of course—daisies. Each flower had a smiley face in the middle.

As complicated as Blanche's feelings were for Daisy, they still loved her. Missed her dearly. And after months of sharing their story with therapist after therapist, talking about her was getting easier. Even with their friends. Normally, the story would stay inside their head. But they were talking about Walter today, and the weed was already out. "Daisy painted this for my birthday one year, when we were staying in Walter's camp."

They ignored the way everyone froze and turned to look at them, focusing on packing the bowl.

Blanche and Daisy had stayed at the camp off and on over the years. Freddy always kept his pullout couch available for them, but Daisy's stepdad would come there looking for her; they'd snuck out Freddy's fire escape more than once. Walter and Wanda had always let them hide out at the camp, until Freddy gave them the all clear.

The stalking had declined as Daisy grew older, but she'd always looked over her shoulder for him until the end. Guilt still ate at Blanche's heart.

After a lifetime of thinking her stepdad would kill her, it ended up being Blanche's client who'd murdered her.

Squeezing their eyes shut, Blanche lit the bong, breathing deeply to capture the smoke in their lungs. That train of thought was too intense when they weren't even high yet. When the burn became unbearable, they exhaled slowly. Everyone looked at Blanche with wide, expectant eyes. Except Sunny, who reached for the bong.

"It's sweet that you still have it after all this time." Sunny coughed as she exhaled.

Blanche scoffed, relieved that Sunny hadn't joined in the trepidatious stares from everyone else. "All this time? I'm not *that* old."

"What happened to 'I'm too old for this shit' from earlier today?" Sunny teased, turning on the Wii. She passed out controllers to everyone but Blanche. "Okay, time for y'all to get your ass beat."

Gabe downed his whiskey with a wince. "It's on."

Sipping their own, Blanche stayed where they were, draped over the chair facing the couch so the TV was behind them. The Wii had been a gift from their patron when Blanche had first moved in; a housewarming gift for Blanche's two "kids" (the fully grown Tara and Lee), back when Covey was still pretending to be a decent person. While video games entertained their ducklings, the real show was watching them play it.

Lee laughed, passing the bong up to Tara. "Gabey, I love you, but I've played enough with you to know that Sunny is going to kick your ass. You're fighting me for third place."

Everyone laughed, even Gabe.

"True. I identify as a gamer, but not a good one." Gabe leaned over to take the hit Tara offered. His hands lingered over hers as she held the bong for him.

Blanche sipped their whiskey and pretended not to notice.

"Holy fuck." Gabe blinked rapidly as he exhaled, blowing the smoke away from Tara's face as he grinned at her. "I should have gone home. That shit's going to fuck me up."

"Too late now, Coop. You're already here," Tara teased, passing the bong back to Blanche and refilling their tumblers. She settled even closer to Gabe on the couch, who shifted over so slightly, until they were practically snuggling.

And to think, mere hours ago, Blanche had been bracing to spend the night in the same jail where they'd spent the worst days of their life. Covey had to have been behind it; why else would they come down so hard on a peaceful vigil, if they weren't even going to arrest people properly? Only someone with enough power and pettiness could have wrought such a demonstration.

Before Lee had taken charge, Blanche had been resigned, looking around the crowd for the kindest, calmest woman they could find, so Tara would have someone to help her through her inevitable panic attack when she was in the women's holding cell alone. Legally, Sunny should be placed with Tara, but Blanche didn't trust—

Blanche shook their head, taking another hit. *This is why I don't smoke sativa. Why am I allowing myself to overthink?*

They shouldn't be thinking about what might have gone wrong. They'd pulled together and helped each other out, kept their heads. Their family had gone there together, and they'd all gotten out. What mattered now was that they were home safe—canoodling, getting shit-faced, and playing video games. Together and safe, minus that stray kid that Tara had picked up along the way.

That Syl was funny, though. For only having met Tara once before, even he could see she was Gabe's through and through. *Interesting that Tara never corrected him.*

"Anyone got any good jokes?" Gabe asked, a grin on his face.

"What? One toke and you're making jokes now?" Lee teased, focused on the TV. "And here I always thought you were the serious one."

Gabe laughed. "Oh, I got one: What's Mario's favorite pair of pants?"

"Denim denim denim," Sunny sang, never taking her eyes from the screen. "Heard that one in elementary school."

"What happened to Mario's car?" Gabe scowled, leaning against Tara as if to help steer better. Tara leaned back against him, fighting a smile.

"It was Toad." Sunny shrugged. "You seriously don't have anything better?"

"What's a rogue's favorite drink?"

Sunny laughed. "Subtle-tea. That's a good one."

"What the fuck? Stop taking all of my punch lines!" Gabe groaned.

"Okay, okay, I have one," Sunny giggled as she came in first. Tara crossed the finish line shortly after, a scowl on her face. "A warrior, a druid, and a paladin walk into a bar. Bartender asks if they want a drink. Paladin replies—"

"No thanks, we're already tanked," Gabe interrupted, followed by a frustrated whine as Lee narrowly beat him to third place. "Someone is stealing all of my jokes!"

"Maybe it's a sign to stop telling nerdy-ass jokes," Lee teased. "Maybe you *should* come out with Phin and I sometimes. This is embarrassing for you."

"I'm not even high," Gabe sighed. "It's just been a while since I've smoked anything. My dad's been experimenting with indica edibles so my mom doesn't have to go outside to smoke in the winter, so lately that's all I've had."

"That's kinda sweet. I thought your parents would be drinkers, not stoners." Tara was practically tucked under his arm at this point. "What with owning a vineyard and shit."

"Well, Tonio and I drank a lot in high school, too. Ask Angie about the time she bullied me and Tonio into drinking a bottle of tequila with her."

"Maybe I will." Tara grinned. "I do have her number."

"Do you?" Gabe's mouth twisted. Until he noticed that Tara had her phone out. Then he panicked. "No, Tara! That was rhetorical! Oh, no. Please, do not text her! Why are you like this?" He grabbed his own phone, grumbling under his breath. "Now I have to threaten her with extortion. Come on! She's probably going to tell you too!"

"Who's Angie?" Sunny asked.

Blanche had been wondering the same thing.

"Oh look, you were paying attention," Tara teased. "Tonio's cousin."

Lee cocked his head in confusion. "I'm sorry, how do either of you know *that* Angie?"

Gabe and Tara exchanged a look, and then another. "She's the florist cousin," Tara finally said. "We got a quote from her."

Lee accepted her nonanswer with a shrug.

Blanche kept quiet, observing as always over the rim of their whiskey. It was reassuring to see Gabe so surprisingly goofy. For someone as sensitive and earnest as he was, his sarcastic humor could be bitter. Tara needed more fun, too. With a satisfied nod, Blanche sent the bong around to the others again, then refilled everyone's drinks as they played another round.

As soon as Gabe crossed the finish line long after Lee, Blanche held up their whiskey. "I propose a toast. To our family, for working together to get ourselves out of that shitshow of a vigil. And that includes you, Gabe. You were part of the adventure, you're part of the family."

Gabe reddened. "To family." He held up his glass.

Though their voices were tired, everyone echoed the sentiment and fondly clinked glasses. Hiding their giddy smile in their drink, Blanche pretended not to notice how sweetly Tara and Gabe looked at each other over the rims of their glasses.

"Speaking of family, Buttercup, are you free over the next few weeks? I want you to come with me to something, but I'm not sure when or where it is yet. Or if it'll happen at all." Lee asked, reaching up behind him to pat her leg. Instead, he touched Gabe's. "Oh damn, that's not you. Sorry, Gabe."

Gabe laughed. "Touch my leg all you want, Lee."

Tara grabbed Lee's hand from Gabe's thigh. "If you're asking me to come with you to meet your parents, the answer is no."

Lee pouted, leaning back to look up at her. "How did you know?"

"Jazz mentioned it when she was here a couple days ago, and since she survived to celebrate her birthday yesterday, I assume they're open to it." Tara kissed Lee's forehead. "Your parents want to meet you and your fiancée. Not you, your fiancée, and your codependent bestie who wants to beat the shit out of your dad. This is something in the Lee and Tonio bubble, just like how today was in the Lee and Tara bubble."

"Ugh, fine!" Lee pouted. "You're right. You always are."

"And don't you forget it." Tara grinned. "Besides, I'll be here when it's over to let you bitch every mean thought you pretend not to have."

She pulled Gabe's arm around her before drawing down the knit blanket from the back of the couch. Gabe's eyes widened, but he shifted ever so slightly to hold her beneath it with a soft smile. She leaned on his chest as she got herself comfortable, and stayed there. Again, Blanche sipped their whiskey, pretending not to notice, while delight hummed through their chest. Their affection had ramped up far beyond platonic since their last casual get-together.

"Can we play now?" Sunny asked, tapping her nails on her glass.

As their ducklings teased and bickered over their game, Blanche let their head fall back over the arm of the chair. *So, Lee is reconnecting with his parents.* That was something, that his parents wanted him in their life again—or at least were willing to meet him. That was more than Blanche ever thought was possible.

Blanche's own Papa and Mama—or anyone else in the Family—had never found them. Even after they'd reached adulthood, Blanche had never reached out. They never knew if their parents had bothered looking for them, or if they were glad to have their changeling disappear.

If they had ever planned to tell Blanche who their birth parents might have been, or if they really did plan to "correct" their body like they'd threatened to. There were some questions it was better to not know the answers.

But from what Lee had said of his parents, they were far worse than neglectful. What had caused them to change their hearts? Did they love and miss him and regret their actions, or was this a salve for their own conscience, a chance to get him back under their control? Would Lee—with his anxiety and abandonment issues—recognize the difference?

At least he'd have Antonio, with his effervescent love, by his side to help him through it. And Jazz, never afraid to speak her mind, would be there to smooth things over. And he had Tara, Blanche, and Sunny to support him afterward. Their family would be there for him always, whatever happened with his parents.

"I'm hungry," Tara complained, eyes on the TV. Gabe had wrapped his arm around her waist to reach the other end of the controller. He'd turned to cradle her more comfortably, tucking a leg under her and resting his chin on the top of her head.

"Bitch, how many damn tacos did you eat?" Sunny teased. "And you're still hungry?"

"That was hours ago." Tara pouted. "I'm hungry again. We should have gotten a pizza on the way home."

"I can order some," Gabe offered. "What kind does everyone like?"

Lee turned to warn him about the dangers of asking that question; instead, he froze as he noticed how close they were. "I—Uh...I don't usually ask. Just order a supreme." He whirled back around to look at Blanche, mouthing, *Oh my God, they're cuddling!*

Blanche blinked slowly at him, keeping their expression neutral. Hopefully, he took that to mean *Don't say anything. Sunny will ruin the moment.* Tara and Gabe looked adorable. It'd be a shame to interrupt them.

Lee thankfully merely bit back a grin, turning back to the game. "How'd I end up fourth?"

"Because you couldn't keep your eyes off me," Gabe teased.

"I want chicken, jalapeno, and pineapple," Sunny belatedly announced. "It's my favorite."

Lee made a face. "That's why I usually don't ask."

To Tara's ire (softer than usual, courtesy of Gabe's presence), Sunny easily won two more games before the pizza came. Blanche gave her a warning glare when Tara sat down practically in Gabe's lap to eat. The best chance she'd ever had at experiencing romance shouldn't be the butt of a joke from the tactless Sunny. Teasing her would only set her back.

Sunny rolled her eyes, but thankfully kept quiet. It probably helped that Gabe had ordered a small chicken, jalapeno, and pineapple pizza for her.

"What did you order for you?" Tara asked.

"Pizza?" Gabe looked at her like she had two heads. "What else would I— Oh, yeah, you're right. This doesn't fit my mac—"

"Coop, if you talk about your macros one more time, I'm never going to eat a vegetable ever again," Tara said. "Eat the damn pizza."

"Like you eat vegetables in the first place." Gabe laughed and started in on a slice.

As the night wound down, Richard showed up to pick up Sunny, offering the other two a ride. Based on the empty bottle of Black Label, and their depleted stash of Super Silver Haze, it was probably for the best that Richard drove everyone home.

Gabe, however, declined, insisting he was good to drive. Blanche suspected Tara might want an overnight guest, so they didn't push it. However, as soon as everyone else left, silence fell over the three of them. Gabe quickly stood and shuffled to the door, anxiously fluffing his hair. "I should— I should go."

Blanche stayed silent—pretending to check their phone to give them privacy—as Tara followed him to the door. "Are you sure? You can wait here a little longer if you need more time to sober up."

You can stay the night in Tara's room.

"I'm okay to drive. I just don't want to overstay my welcome."

Blanche raised an eyebrow. *Not possible. If she wakes up with you next to her, she'll be on cloud nine.*

Tara hummed disapprovingly. "You sure?"

"Yeah, I just—I should go let Hippo out."

"Text me when you make it home?"

Gabe snorted. "Will you text me back if I do?"

"Ugh, yeah. Sorry, I've been meaning to, but—" Tara grumbled. "I will do that. Sorry if I say the wrong thing."

After a few moments of quiet, punctuated only by a contented sigh from Tara, Gabe left with a heartfelt goodbye that included Blanche too.

"Don't start." Tara flopped on the couch and pulled the blanket over her head.

"Wasn't going to." Blanche tapped the bowl into the ashtray. "Anything you want to talk about from today, babes?"

Tara shook her head with a sigh. "No, today was fucked up."

"It was, but at least we made it home."

"*We* did. Sucks that everyone else didn't."

"Nothing we can do about it." Someone more forgiving of the world than Blanche could care about everyone else. No one in this city—not even the do-gooders who pretended to give a shit—gave a damn about people like them. Barely anyone gave a damn about Walter, and yet they'd turned out in droves to *honor* him. "Everyone I care about is safe at home tonight."

"Yeah, it's not like we can afford to bail hundreds of people out of jail."

They sat quietly, drinking the rest of the scotch and polishing off the pizza, until Tara's phone buzzed. She smiled at the text—presumably from Gabe, telling her he'd made it home. Tara wouldn't smile if it was from Sunny, nor would she bite her lip while she texted Lee.

"You can go to bed now, Tara. Sweet dreams," Blanche teased, actually turning on their phone for the first time since the vigil. Their subscribers would want some interaction on a Saturday night. Among the dozens of SubParty notifications was a single text from Covey.

> I hope an evening in jail will remind you who's in charge here.

That bastard. Blanche's stomach churned, their skin burning. All of the pleasant nostalgia, peace, and delight burnt to a crisp as rage coursed through them. They threw the phone onto the coffee table, too angry to care that it bounced off and slid under the couch.

This was the last straw.

All evening, they'd suspected he'd been behind the show of force. But for him to actually admit that he'd tried to get Blanche arrested, risking hundreds of others in the process? He'd put the nail in the coffin of whatever empathy and affection Blanche might have had left.

While Covey had thrown them off by buying a stake of Confession, Blanche had not been without their own plans. They'd been putting everything into their SubParty channel, spending the last nine months saving up the fortune needed to break the contract, without risking their own ten percent of Confession. Covey's insidious power move, inserting himself into their family's nightclub, had only made Blanche work harder than ever.

They had hoped for more time, for enough patience, to save up the funds needed to buy a small fixer upper for themself and Tara to live in, break the contract, *and* get that bastard out of Confession. Thanks to their family's support of their SubParty—Tara, Lee, and Sunny handling all of the technological necessities that so easily overwhelmed them, Gabe's secret donations—Blanche could maybe afford two of the three. But Covey had just made Blanche's choice for them; his time was up. Maybe Blanche could finally break free, without risking a roof over Tara's head. After all, Gabe had a lot of space for just himself and Hippo.

Blanche rose, retrieving their phone from under the couch. Ignoring all of the messages from Covey and their subscribers, they pulled up a new email to that Phineas character. The smile that stretched across Blanche's face was cold as they typed.

Maybe tomorrow would be a little less fucked up.

Chapter Sixteen

Gabe

Gabe should not have driven home. But he'd made it in one piece, without fucking anything up with Tara. He had successfully parked in the garage, chugged a quart of water while Hippo was doing his business, and sent a couple texts. The first to Phineas, asking if he was still up, and the second to Tara. That one took much longer to craft, because he was still a little high and overthinking every word to make sure he wasn't being too much, or not enough, or—

His phone lit up with an incoming call, brightening the otherwise dark living room where Gabe laid stretched out on the couch. Hippo lay sprawled across his legs.

"Cooper, are you coming on to me?" Phineas asked in lieu of a hello when Gabe answered.

Stretching out on the couch and rubbing his stomach under his shirt, Gabe laughed too loudly. Hippo's ears perked up, but within seconds, he was snoring against Gabe's thigh. "This isn't a booty call, Phin. I was genuinely wondering if you were up when I sent that text."

"Sure, that's what you always said back in undergrad when you couldn't sleep, and yet we'd end up sucking each other off anyway."

Gabe laughed again. "You were a fun roommate."

"You're giggly today," Phineas's voice was skeptical. "Are you good?"

"I might be drunk. Or high. Or both."

"Oh? What were *you* up to?"

"Just hung out with some friends." He'd been at Blanche's apartment for far longer than he'd thought he would. But it'd been fun. He couldn't remember the last time he'd had so much fun, without Antonio pushing him out of his comfort zone.

"Where was my invite?"

Gabe winced at the insecurity behind Phineas's teasing. "It was a spur-of-the-moment kind of thing." That wasn't a lie, per se, but Gabe was still torn on never inviting Phineas to anything. Antonio wanted to keep Phineas away from his social life, even if Lee and Phineas were close friends. Gabe was reluctant to push that boundary, though he felt guilty for excluding a friend, albeit a flaky workaholic who never showed up anyway. "Hey, can you do me a favor?"

"Oh, so this *is* a work call." Phineas sounded disappointed.

Gabe winced again. "Yeah, sorry. Charge me extra. You know the shit that happened at the vigil tonight? Think you can coordinate a donation for bail? Anonymously, of course."

Phineas laughed. "Richard already beat you to the bail money."

"What, *all* of it?"

"You know Richard. He doesn't half-ass shit." The clacking of a keyboard tapped in the background. "But I got an email about an hour ago, asking for lawyers to volunteer legal aid to the people who got arrested. I offered to help pro bono for the people processed in Iowa, since I don't practice in Illinois. Donations to help cover any retainer fees would probably go a long way, since most people were processed in Eastside. They must not care to actually prosecute anyone, because these cases will probably be tossed anyway, even if they hadn't brought detainees across state lines."

Phineas's legal chatter went right over Gabe's head. "Whatever's needed, go for it on my behalf." It shouldn't surprise him that Richard had already covered the bail. Sunny had called him once they were safely in Blanche's apartment; she'd had to reassure him about eighty times that she was safe and unharmed. He'd still insisted on driving her home; he'd taken it personally that she hadn't asked him to pick them up from the museum.

He'll get over it. Richard wasn't truly pissed, just a control freak with a savior complex.

At least Richard had someone else to worry over, besides Gabe. Richard thought he was so subtle, but he let his anxiety for his friends—and now Sunny—get out of hand sometimes. He was a worrywart. Always had been. Though he'd gotten Gabe, Antonio, and Phineas all out of trouble more times than Gabe cared to admit, often without a word of acknowledgment.

"There's no chance your mom was at the vigil, was she?" Phineas asked. "I figure this is coming out of the trust."

"Yeah, it is. But no, I ran into her and Dad at the museum for a gallery opening while all that was going down."

"You went to a gallery opening, and you're calling me drunk and high at this time of night? You, the shut-in who never goes—" Phin gasped. "Were you on a *date*?"

Gabe sighed. "Not you, too, Phin. Just send me the details when you have them so I can wire the money." He fiddled with his hair. "And if you come across Bernard Parker, can you make sure he's got a good lawyer? He's a good kid. Just turned eighteen. No record as far as I know, and I'd like to keep it that way. Anonymously, of course."

"Give me some credit, Cooper. I know better than to put your name on anything that might end up public," Phineas said. "Anything else?"

"I don't think so?"

"Good." Gabe heard a laptop snap shut as Phineas sighed. "I got all that over to the people who can do something about it, but that's all the work I can handle at the moment. I'd need an upper if you had more. I drank more than I thought I did."

"That makes two of us." Considering the couch was swaying under him, Gabe *really* should not have driven, but he couldn't stay at that apartment once Lee and Sunny had left. As incredibly tempting as the idea of spending the night was, he couldn't be this inebriated around Tara. He'd do something stupid, like spilling his feelings—or worse, try to kiss her. Both would fuck up whatever chance he had.

Besides, he'd made it home safely. It was fine. Everything was fine. "Did *you* have a date? Do you have company or something? I can let you go."

Phineas laughed sardonically. "No, just drinking by myself. Wallowing in self-pity. What else is new?"

The only thing new there was Phineas admitting it. "You wanna talk about it?"

Phineas always drank away his problems, snorted or swallowed whatever it took to pretend he was functional. He threw himself into work to prove he was fine, insisting he didn't have time to go to rehab. Or see a therapist. Or go to the gym. Or eat right. Or spend time with friends. Or any good habits really.

But Gabe couldn't force him to do anything. As far as Gabe knew, Phineas never took anything as addictive as Antonio had, but his habits to avoid burnout weren't healthy. It was impossible not to worry about him, but Gabe had tried to make peace with his friend's choices.

"When do you tell people you're queer?" Phineas asked. "Like, when you're dating. Do you tell them before you meet them? Date three? Before you fuck 'em? *After* you fuck 'em?"

"I don't know if you want dating advice from me, Phin," Gabe reminded him. "I literally had my mom setting me up on blind dates, and my track record with relationships is shit."

"Yeah, that's true, but I'm asking anyway. You probably don't get stood up like I did tonight. Or ghosted the second you start opening up to someone. And you're queer like me. Only better, because you...are you."

Gabe laughed at that. "I'm not better. You know what a mess I am."

"But like, even before all that shit happened, it was never an issue for you. Like, people just accept that part of you and still love you." Phineas's voice sounded strained.

Gabe doubted if anyone ever really loved him, at least romantically. Antonio, Richard, and Phineas certainly hadn't, nor had he truly had romantic feelings for them. And if any of his exes had loved him, they'd had a really fucked up way of showing it. But he'd never hidden himself the way Phineas did.

Even as a kid, knowing he'd be bullied for it, Gabe had been proud of his queerness. He was already bullied for being Native, but not *really* Native; for being Jewish, but never Jewish *enough*; or for being a nerd, or fat, or sensitive—what was one more target on his back? His parents had never made it an issue in the way that Phineas's would, if he ever did come out.

"That's because it's not part of me, Phin. I'm just me, and I happen to be queer." Gabe ran a hand over his face, scratching the stubble along his jaw. "I guess if it's not obvious from my personality, it comes up when the dating history conversation happens? I don't make a big deal of it. I just mention my previous partners, and people figure it out."

"Ugh, you make it sound so easy," Phineas groaned. "Like, I'm trying to be more open about it, right? I used to not tell anyone until we were getting serious, but that backfired every time. So I started telling people sooner, and now they either don't give me a chance, or they just want a threesome."

"Phineas Watkins, are *you* complaining about a threesome?" Gabe teased. Phineas had invited him to many threesomes, sex parties, and orgies over the years. He'd joined fairly often when he was younger. He was a horny ass nerd; why wouldn't he go to a sex party? But he'd met Isa at one of those parties, and that had ended that phase of his life. He missed when sex could simply be fun, and not an overwhelming, life-altering revelation. At least with Tara, he had both. He hadn't had fun with sex since he and Isa had first started dating.

"Fuck! What happened to me?" Phineas laughed. "I just feel very...objectified. Which sounds hypocritical as hell coming from me. I know it does! But, like, remember that Signe, the one I was seeing last year? Who came to the charity auction thing?"

Gabe barely remembered her. None of Phineas's girlfriends lasted long enough to be memorable. "Sure."

"She was the first woman I've told who seemed really supportive. But then she kept asking when we would hang out with Lee again. Like *all* the time. Turns out she had, like, some DP Blacked Raw fantasy shit. She didn't want *me*." Phineas's voice cracked, and he laughed to cover it. "She wanted two Black guys to fuck her, and somehow I'd be the ticket to whatever fucked-up racist shit she wanted, especially after I introduced her to Lee. And like, I get it. Lee's hot. He's a damn good lay. Hung as hell!"

Gabe blinked, chest tightening as his brain struggled to process *that* statement.

"But like damn, I'm not a piece of meat, you know? I'm a person with feelings. I want someone to like me for me. Not because I have hot friends," Phineas scoffed. "As if my friends are just waiting to have a threesome with me! Not like Lee would ever cheat on Tonio—let alone with a woman. Once I told her that, she started demanding I find another guy. Apparently that's all she wanted, because she ghosted me after I refused. Which sucks! But also, bullet dodged!"

Gabe's jaw clenched, trying to keep his cool. *I'm too fucked up for all of this. Of all days for Phineas to actually talk about his feelings.* "You know Lee's a good lay, *how*, exactly?"

Phineas groaned. "Can you pretend you didn't hear that?"

"No." Gabe's protectiveness for Antonio grew as Phineas didn't deny anything.

"Fuck, you sound mad. It's not a big deal, I swear! I may or may not have hooked up with Lee a *long* time ago, *before* he met Antonio. It was a onetime thing. And Antonio knows it happened and already threatened me to never make a pass at Lee—which I wouldn't anyway because I'm not a complete asshole. So yeah, like, not a big deal. But I asked him not to tell anyone, and here I am running *my* fucking mouth."

Gabe pinched his nose. Phineas was talking *so* fast, but at least he was saying the right things. "In that case, I didn't hear anything." It wasn't Gabe's business what Lee got up to before Antonio. Antonio had more than his fair share of "before" fun too, including with Phineas. "Why did you tell him not to tell anyone?"

"Honestly?" Phineas paused, "I panicked. You know how I always jump to the worst possible conclusion? Within half a second of seeing him open the door at your house that first time Antonio brought him over, I managed to convince myself that he'd tell my parents. It all flashed before my eyes before we even said hello. There'd be a smear campaign during the next election, and Councilman Watkins's disappointment of a son would be in the headlines, causing the scandal that ended his career. But that's so fucking irrational!

"There's no chance Lee would ever meet my dad, let alone be all 'Hey Councilman Watkins, your son did a line of coke off my massive dick before I fucked him so good he cried, and then I was really nice to him about it afterward, and he *still* ghosted me.' I'm just so fucking paranoid that my dad's going to find out, because he doesn't deserve to know the real me. It just freaked me out when someone I hooked up with opened your front door, you know? My worlds collided!"

Gabe scratched Hippo's ears, struggling to get the image of Phineas snorting coke off Lee's dick out of his head.

"Sorry, that was TMI, wasn't it?"

"That's fine, Phin," Gabe chuckled, barely following anything flying out of Phineas's mouth. Phineas was rarely this open about his feelings, but perhaps that meant he'd be more open to suggestions.

Besides, Gabe didn't really have anything else to do besides mope about where he and Tara stood, or didn't stand. Or overthink the stupid shit that must have left his mouth tonight around her and everyone she loved most. *If only I could remember what I fucking said.* He really should not have driven home. His hand slid across his belly. Or he could jerk off to thoughts of her— *No, wait until you're off the phone.*

"Why don't you date guys? Like actually date them, not just hook up with them?" Gabe asked.

Phineas laughed, sounding slightly unhinged even through the phone. "Oh, Gabriel. You're so naive. So innocent. You think I haven't *tried*? There is no dating in hookup culture. Or maybe I'm not boyfriend material," Phineas sighed. "Just because you fall in love at first sight and woo people with your brooding mysterious, sensitive act and pretty eyes, doesn't mean I can."

"I don't *woo* people. At least not intentionally." If he did, maybe things would be different with Tara, and he'd know where he stood with her. Instead of pining over her and overthinking every hidden signal he was probably imagining.

Although his sexuality had been a nonissue with her, just like hers was with him.

When Gabe had tried to flirt with the butch redhead with the perky ass and long legs at Confession ("tried" because he looked back at every moment of those fumbling attempts to be charming with hot shame), he'd fully expected to get outright rejected. Despite his cringeworthy one-liners, he'd had her pressed against the bathroom door within minutes. And fallen in love before he was even truly ready to leave the safety of his house. *Stop, you were not in love with her. You became obsessed with a stranger.*

It'd been for the best though. He would never have found the drive to heal without meeting her. And now... Well, now he *was* in love with her. The real Tara, this time.

Gabe sighed, trying to find something that might be reassuring. "Maybe try dating other queer people? You know, bi or pan people? They'd at least get the sexuality issue, so you can focus on other ways to fuck it up."

Phineas barked out a laugh. "Thanks, Cooper. But like, where do I find people like that?"

"In the wild. You'll have to stop working long enough to meet them," Gabe teased.

"Fuck. I'm going to be single forever," Phineas laughed. "Know any single queer people who might want to date me?"

Angie and Phineas would probably get along, but Antonio would not be happy if Phineas got with any of his relatives. Setting Phineas up with Antonio's cousin would blow right past all of Antonio's carefully managed boundaries, which would last as long as it took for Phineas to get his shit together.

"I mean, Blanche is single-ish as far as I know," Gabe laughed. Phineas needed therapy, not a dominatrix with a big heart and a penchant for fixing damaged people to avoid healing themself. "But that'd be a bad idea for several reasons," he added, in case Phineas took him seriously.

"Who?" Phineas asked.

Gabe blinked. "Blanche? Blanche Van Horne?"

"It's not ringing a bell," Phineas said, then whistled. "But damn, I just googled her, and oh my god, I'm in love."

"No, you're not! That's your client, dumbass!" Gabe groaned. "At least they *said* they were working with you. My friend who needed help with the contract?"

"Wait, that's *Chad*? We've just been emailing because I've been helping them off the clock. They are *not* what I thought Chad would look like." Phineas cleared his throat. "Oh man, okay, be professional, Phin. Any other single queer people you know who *aren't* a conflict of interest?"

Just Tara. "Nope. I'll talk you up if I meet any though."

"Bullshit, you'll fall in love with them first," Phineas teased.

I already have. "Not if I can help it. That's why I'm in therapy. Have you considered therapy, Phin?" Gabe teased back.

"What's that? You're breaking up. I can't hear a word you're saying."

Gabe laughed. "Good night, Phin. Thank you."

"You too, man. Thanks. For real, I love you."

"Love ya too." Gabe ended the call and wiggled out from underneath Hippo. His buddy grumbled, but settled back to sleep when Gabe tucked him in with a throw blanket.

Dancing on the way to his bedroom, Gabe lost the battle against his thoughts of Tara, already half hard. Rubbing one out, without the guilt that he was jerking off to someone who only saw him as a friend, was a nice change. Tara wanted him, too, so much so that she pretended all of her toys were him. Gabe grinned as he bumped into his doorframe.

Even during his past week of insecurity, he never felt that burning shame, or the abject self-loathing, that he'd felt after her birthday outing the year before. The limerence that had plagued him most of his adult life had finally eased, thanks to the EMDR treatment that built on his previous efforts. He'd maintained his routines, without a debilitating spell of depression, for over nine months. His therapist was lowering his

SSRIs with the goal of weaning him off of them completely, when Gabe had expected to take them for the rest of his life.

It was...nice. Happiness was relentlessly hopeful. Loving without pain was so freeing.

For so long, he'd convinced himself his feelings for Tara were the same delusional obsession he'd had since that first night. But at some point in the last nine months, things had shifted. Mellowed. Perhaps as he'd processed the cause of his obsessive tendencies, his feelings for Tara had grown roots in reality, instead of delusion. Instead of struggling to reconcile the Kitten in his head with the Tara who wouldn't look him in the eyes, he had connected with the real Tara. Developed a friendship with the person, not the fantasy. He'd gotten a handle on his mood swings and insecurity, yet his feelings for her were stronger than ever.

With a groan, Gabe collapsed into bed, burying his foolish grin into the pillows. Every time he thought of her, or let himself sit with his feelings, he ended up with this dazed expression. But alone in the privacy of his bed, he couldn't bring himself to fight it.

The peek into her life tonight had been cathartic, seeing her at ease and laughing with the people Tara loved most—even after the emotionally fraught day she'd had. It would have been nice if she'd reached out to him for support, but he understood why she'd turned to her family. Gabe was honored to be a part of the evening at all. His mind was a little fuzzy on the details, but he'd enjoyed every second. She'd talked a lot, more than she usually did around him.

Gabe had talked a lot too. He hadn't smoked that much in years, rarely drank as much as he did tonight. He vaguely remembered Lee and Sunny, teasing him for how messed up he'd gotten after one hit.

Ugh, and I drove home?

Hand sliding across the waistband of his sweatpants, Gabe replayed what little he remembered. How Tara hadn't corrected Syl when he said she was his girl. How she'd helped Syl in the first place, when she barely knew him. How Tara had been so carefree and touchy all evening. The happy hums she'd made when she ate the pizza he ordered for her. The red heart emoji she'd sent with the "ty again for ur help today. And the pizza. Im glad you were there" text after he let her know he'd made it home safely. Red had to be a good sign, right? A yellow or blue heart would have hinted at friendship, but red meant romance.

Or at least passion? Or both?

Both, hopefully. Having her in his arms half the night had been sweet, domestic, and an appetizer, his body craving her closer all evening. Gabe pulled his clothes off and, with a pump of lotion, took his growing erection in hand.

Stroking slowly, he lost himself in thought of how fucking delightful Tara's body felt cradled against him. How she'd looked softly at him with those green eyes whenever he spoke. What might have happened if he'd stayed, slept in Tara's room with her and got to see all those toys she had named after him, and use them together. If he got to devour and worship her slowly, softly. Now that the initial relieved, desperate fucking was out of the way, they would take their time, savor each touch. Let each kiss linger, until they couldn't take the anticipation anymore.

With a groan, Gabe remembered all the ways Tara let him worship her a mere week ago. How she'd given him a spark of hope that one day, he might be loved better than he deserved.

Sunday, April Fourth

Chapter Seventeen

Sunny

"So gracious of you to bless us with your presence, Sunny," her mother teased, elbow-deep in dishes as Sunny walked in. "If I'd known you'd be home tonight, I would have waited to eat."

"Mae!" Sunny groaned. "I'm always here for dinner on Sundays."

She'd lingered a little longer at Richard's than usual (surprisingly, they'd lost track of time reading in bed, instead of anything sexy), but she wasn't late enough to miss *dinner*. Not even a sweet, peaceful day with Richard could keep her from Mae's cooking—partly because Richard needed the alone time to psych himself up for the workweek.

"Luna had to go to campus to work on a group project tonight." Birdie rinsed a pot. "She texted you that we were having dinner early, but said you weren't coming."

"She didn't say anything about dinner." Sunny checked her phone. Luna's texts were bare bones, so her sister was probably lying about this group project. Good for her. "She just asked when I'd be home. And I told her I'd come home when I felt like it."

Birdie snorted. "Well, there's a container for you in the fridge."

"Good, I'm starving!" Yanking it open, Sunny found a reused take-out container, stuffed with noodles, shrimp, and veggies. Maybe she had stayed later than she thought; their usual Sunday brunch order typically kept her full until dinner. But their lovely day had been perfect. Waking

Richard up with her hand between his legs, eating the feast he'd bought her, curled up in his arms as he read to her—

Birdie turned off the water. "So when do I get to meet Richard's parents?"

The first bite of noodles was halfway to her mouth when Sunny froze. The very idea shattered her afterglow, almost enough to make her lose her appetite. "Uh...never?"

Birdie raised an eyebrow. "His parents would let you propose without meeting us? Will the first time we meet be the wedding?"

"Whoa, Mae, slow down." Sunny took a bite in an attempt to ignore her sudden queasiness. Breathing through the tightness of her chest, she untangled all the assumptions her mother had just made one at a time. Maybe Richard had been right. Maybe they were backward, but it wasn't their doing. "Um, question: What the fuck?"

"Sunny, language!" Birdie tsked. "And don't talk with food in your mouth."

Rolling her eyes, Sunny swallowed before she said, "First of all, I highly doubt Richard would want his parents at the wedding." She feigned gagging. "Second, why would I ask his parents' permission? And why am *I* proposing to *him* in this fantasy land you live in?" Sunny wrinkled her nose; that would leave them both feeling Icky, and Sunny deserved to be wooed, at minimum. "And finally, Mae, what wedding? We aren't even seriously talking about marriage yet!"

"Why not? You've been together for over a year, and you practically live at his place as it is. And he's older than you, so his fertile window is—"

"Mae!" Sunny groaned. "Please stop. I'm not ready."

Birdie tsked. "You really should lock that down. Richard's a catch."

"I'm aware of that, Mae," Sunny huffed. "If you must know, a big reason why I don't want to get married is because I'm not...me, yet. Physically, I mean. Emotionally, too but that's blurrier than surgery. Richard knows that and supports me. So unless you're offering to cover the cost of a vaginoplasty and take care of the bills for two months while I recover, you're gonna have to wait a little longer for babies."

Birdie narrowed her eyes as she opened the dishwasher, putting the clean dishes on the rack to dry. "How much is it?"

"The surgeon said I should save up forty grand. Minimum."

Birdie wheezed in protest. "Why so expensive? It's much cheaper in Thailand—do it there! You could finally meet your grandparents!"

Sunny sucked her teeth. "If I do that, I won't have income while I'm recovering, or a job when I get back. To qualify for medical leave, I have to bend over backward and sacrifice a virgin, since this is an 'elective' procedure." Sunny picked at her shrimp. "You think I haven't researched this or something? If I could have gotten this done when I was eighteen, I would have, but the stars refuse to align. Trust me, I wish they'd hurry up!"

Shutting the dishwasher, her mother crossed her arms and leaned against the counter. "How much have you saved so far?"

Sunny winced, catching herself as she started to chew on her lip. "Like, six grand."

Birdie tsked. "Sunny, you're hiding that much money from me?"

Sunny huffed. "I know, I'm such a bad child for having a savings account. However will you live with the shame?" She tsked, imitating her mae. "Besides, I've been saving for eight years. Six stacks is not exactly a fortune."

"Don't give me that attitude. We need to make these decisions as a family." Birdie cleared her throat, saying archly, "I still haven't forgotten when I came home to find you passed out on painkillers, with huge breasts that hadn't been there the night before! You don't have to do all of this in secret."

Sunny laughed, not feeling an ounce of remorse. "Yeah, I probably could have let you know I was doing that. I figured you'd try to talk me out of spending that much money."

"True, I was not happy about that." Birdie sighed. "I'll contribute five thousand."

Sunny perked up. "Twenty? We can go fifty-fifty?"

Birdie scowled. "Risky move, negotiating a gift."

"Richard's clock is ticking, Mae." Sunny gagged. "Please never make me say that again!"

Her mother pursed her lips. "Ten, but we'll have to tighten our budget."

"Deal." Sunny held out her hand. Birdie shook it. "Pleasure doing business with you. Also, don't bring this conversation up to Richard. He keeps trying to give me money."

Birdie rubbed her forehead with a sigh. "And you aren't taking it, why?"

"Because!" Sunny pursed her lips. "I feel like I have to do this on my own, you know? It's one thing for him to buy me gifts and stuff, but this is something that I want to do myself."

"So you don't want my contribution then?" Birdie teased.

"That's different! You're my mother." Sunny twirled the last of her noodles around her fork. "I just... If Richard and I do get married, I want to be wholly me when we become us. Having him paying for this feels like I can't be me without him, like he's a cheat code. Does that make sense?"

"Not to me, but I can tell it's important to you." Birdie took Sunny's empty take-out container to wash it. "You should go look for a part-time job."

"Why?"

"Forty grand doesn't grow on trees!"

"Yeah, sure. I'll look for a part-time job." Sunny wrapped her arms around her mae, grateful Birdie was supportive, even if she didn't quite understand. Maybe instead of a second job, Sunny could get back to working on her apps again. She smiled, excited for a savings goal that was now far more achievable with her mae's help. "Thanks for dinner, Mae. And everything."

Safe in the privacy of her room—at least until her little sister came home—Sunny opened her tablet, halfheartedly considering setting up freelance gigs like Tara did. Richard had been happily taking up a lot of her free time; app making had fallen by the wayside. She'd been stuck on the early stages of a kanban style self-help app for months.

A message waiting from Black Hawk distracted her from any thoughts of a side hustle.

Black_Hawk_Up88: Where are you? You missed me getting completely obliterated in League tonight.

SunnywithOmeatballs: Sorry, got waylaid by my mother asking when I'm going to get married and give her grandbabies.

Black_Hawk_Up88: I swear your mom is worse than mine when it comes to that kind of stuff.

Black_Hawk_Up88: Can I process something with you, stranger on the internet who gives me advice?

Sunny winced. Her mae had just agreed to basically accelerate her future goals. Maybe if she'd stood up for herself and cleared the air with her mother years ago, instead of talking shit about her to her online friend, she wouldn't need her family to sacrifice their comforts for her sake now. She sighed. Responsible Sunny would probably not disparage her mother to strangers on the internet.

Sunnywith0meatballs: She's getting better about it. And of course! Give me the TMI!

Black_Hawk_Up88: So you remember that one person?

Sunnywith0meatballs: The life-changing, mind-blowing sex that fucked you up, but that you don't regret at all even though you're kind of friends now?

Sunnywith0meatballs: Let me guess, you did it again?

Black_Hawk_Up88: ...Yeah.

Sunnywith0meatballs: How was it? Any regrets this time? Catch feelings mid-nut again?

Black_Hawk_Up88: It was...everything! And no regrets! Feelings have already been caught long ago, so I didn't get as emotionally fucked up this time.

Sunnywith0meatballs: Great! So...what do you need to process?

Black_Hawk_Up88: I know I kinda talked shit when you asked how to take a relationship to the next step, but my question is worse. How do healthy relationships start?

Sunnywith0meatballs: Oh, I dunno dude. I didn't even realize my partner and I were dating until after we'd been in an exclusive relationship for several months. I thought we were just fucking until he gave me a spare key and a diamond bracelet.

Black_Hawk_Up88: That's not really reassuring considering you're the only one I can come to for advice on this besides my therapist.

Sunnywith0meatballs: You've been in relationships before. How did you and E get together?

Black_Hawk_Up88: Not healthy ones. E basically told me that she was going to fix me, and suddenly we were living together. And J said we were gonna fix each other, and we ended up making each other worse.

Sunnywith0meatballs: Dude...

Black_Hawk_Up88: I know.

Sunnywith0meatballs: So don't tell this new person that you're going to fix her (she/her pronouns?). That seems like a good start.

> **Black_Hawk_Up88**: I think she would literally fight me if I told
> her that, so yeah, wasn't going to do that anyway.

Sunny grinned, proud she'd finally weaseled something out of her online BFF. Black Hawk was a straight man. Not that it was surprising—*A straight man on the internet? Shocker!*—but he'd previously only referred to any partners with gender-neutral pronouns.

> **SunnywithOmeatballs**: What do you usually do together?
> **Black_Hawk_Up88**: Hang out at my house. Watch a show or play
> a game, usually around our friends. We've been texting a bit and
> stuff, too.
> **SunnywithOmeatballs**: Stuff = mind-blowing, life-changing sex?
> **Black_Hawk_Up88**: ...yes, but just once a few weeks ago. I don't
> want to rush into anything because honestly I'm VERY happy
> with the recent developments, but also this isn't just casual sex for
> me. I think she knows that, but I'm scared to push her because I
> don't want to lose her as a friend, either.
> **SunnywithOmeatballs**: Maybe ask her to hang out outside of your
> normal routine where you don't do "stuff" at your house. Show
> her that being with you is more than just sex.
> **Black_Hawk_Up88**: So...I should ask her on a date? Like a real
> date, not just food and hanging out?
> **SunnywithOmeatballs**: Sure?
> **Black_Hawk_Up88**: Cool. What do normal people do on dates?
> **SunnywithOmeatballs**: You've never been on a date?
> **Black_Hawk_Up88**: This is going to sound really bad, but like I
> said, everyone else I've been with, we just happened, so the only
> Dates I've been on are blind dates that my mom set up for me.
> **SunnywithOmeatballs**: Lmao that does sound bad, but I get it. I
> have a friend IRL doing that.
> **Black_Hawk_Up88**: Oh good, so I am normal.
> **SunnywithOmeatballs**: I wouldn't go that far.
> **Black_Hawk_Up88**: Anyway, Mom always picks fancy places,
> but I don't think that's the right move here. She's more of a 'hang
> out in sweatpants' kind of a person.
> **SunnywithOmeatballs**: What does she do for fun? Any shared
> hobbies?
> **Black_Hawk_Up88**: We're both into photography?

> **Sunnywith0meatballs**: Take nudes of each other.
> **Black_Hawk_Up88**: How about literally anything else?
> **Sunnywith0meatballs**: Maybe go for a walk or hike or something to take pictures?
> **Black_Hawk_Up88**: That could work...
> **Sunnywith0meatballs**: I'm a genius.
> **Black_Hawk_Up88**: You might be because she's down. We are now going on a walk next weekend.
> **Sunnywith0meatballs**: Yay! I get full credit when you get married one day.
> **Black_Hawk_Up88**: Oh, let's not jump to that conclusion!
> **Black_Hawk_Up88**: But... IF that happens, you can have partial credit. As long as I get partial credit for yours. I gave you shitty advice about serious relationships, remember.
> **Sunnywith0meatballs**: Bitch please! I'm taking this relationship to the altar all on my own!

All on her own, minus her mother's contributions, Blanche's contract, and...well, Richard.

Sunny laughed, reminding herself not to chew on her lip. Maybe it was silly of her to deny Richard's help so often. He was proud of the mysterious network he kept up his sleeve, like this lawyer friend, and all of the money he wanted to throw at her. But he was always so helpful and generous. Sunny wanted to do that for him, too.

In her own way.

Saturday, April Tenth

Chapter Eighteen

Crouching, Tara snapped a close-up of Hippo sniffing a bright red tulip. The overcast skies made the lighting perfect, and the fresh layer of snow made the bright flowers and colorful sculptures around them pop. Gabe's invitation for an afternoon spent taking pictures at the MAI had been unexpected, but the day was perfect for it. "You brought Hippo to class this morning? I thought dogs weren't allowed in the museum."

Behind her, Gabe chuckled. "Technically, they're not, but my mom's on the board, so..."

"Nepotism means you're above the rules, huh?" Tara teased over her shoulder.

"Exactly. Though I wouldn't have brought him to class if he wasn't an angel." Gabe grinned, holding out a hand to help her up.

Tara didn't need help, but she took it anyway. His fingers tapped the inside of her wrist, silently asking for permission to take her hand. Fighting a smile, she opened her fingers around his. With the chill of spring hanging in the air, and the afternoon sun hidden behind clouds that promised more snow, his touch was pleasantly warm. "Is he coming with us to the bachelor weekend, too?"

"Surprisingly my mom has no influence over the resort, so we'll follow the 'no pets' rule." Gabe laughed. "Besides, he has some separation anxiety, so leaving him alone in a strange cabin while we're out at the bar wouldn't be good."

Tara raised an eyebrow. "*Hippo* has separation anxiety?"

Gabe scoffed in mock offense. "Okay, *I* have separation anxiety. He's staying with my parents that weekend, where he'll be comfortable and spoiled, won't you, Buddy?"

Hippo jumped up on Gabe, tail wagging.

Tara snapped a picture right as a beam of sunlight broke through the clouds and reflected off the mirrored sculpture behind them, casting them in a silhouette. She checked how it came out on the screen. "Can I add this to my portfolio? It turned out better than I expected."

Gabe looked over her shoulder. "Can you see my face in it?"

"No, it's shadowed." Tara smirked. "Is this an insecurity thing again? You want me to tell you how pretty you are?"

"Please don't." Gabe winced. "More of a privacy concern. I try to keep myself off the internet."

Tara raised a skeptical eyebrow. "Between Tonio and Sunny constantly posting on Instagram, good luck."

He shrugged. "And yet, have they ever posted a picture of me?"

Tara considered it. "No. How? Every time we hang out, they tag me in a dozen posts each."

Gabe shrugged again. "Richard managed to train Tonio—and presumably Sunny—to keep me off of their posts. Tonio will sometimes text me pictures, so I know I'm in them, but he doesn't post them."

"That's so impressive." Tara slid her hand back into his, unprompted. "Don't tell them this, but I like that they take so many. Pictures make good memories more…permanent. So every shitty candid that they post is nice, like a reminder of how happy we were at that moment." She laughed awkwardly. "Sorry, that sounds so corny. My memory isn't as bad as Tonio's, but it's not great, and pictures help."

Rule Ten (take pictures, and back them up) was her final rule—added after she'd left behind the old photos of her parents and the new ones she'd taken of Aunt Alitrice. She could barely remember what Lee's aunt looked like, let alone her parents. Half-tempted to tell Gabe that, she thought better of it; she already felt weird about opening up this much. He'd asked her to come for a walk, not for Tara to dump all of her regrets on him.

"That's not corny." Gabe squeezed her hand. "But feel free to be corny around me, because I guarantee I'm worse."

Tara chuckled. "You really are. I still like you, though."

"Good." Gabe opened his mouth to say something else but seemed to think better of it.

"How was your class this morning?" Tara asked to fill the silence, squinting at a strange sculpture of what was probably supposed to be a person. But the cast iron dripped down from their outstretched limbs, creating an uncanny, melted cryptid.

"Refreshingly uneventful after the public humiliation of Angie's class." Gabe huffed a laugh. "Syl was so well-behaved that he fell asleep. Though I have to admit, I was expecting a choreographer to teach more dancing than movement theory, so I don't blame him."

"Oh god, I never thought I might bore them," Tara groaned. "Now I have something else to worry about in a couple weeks."

"Trust me, you won't bore them." Gabe gestured to the sculpture with their joined hands. "So, smash or pass?"

Tara burst into laughter. "Pass!"

"What, you're too good for melted metal that vaguely resembles a person?"

Tara looked at him incredulously. "Dude, are you saying you would smash *that*?"

Gabe shrugged with a grin. "I'm not saying I wouldn't."

"What about that one?" Tara gestured to a human figure made of marshmallow-looking concrete forms. "Smash or pass?"

"Oh, smash, easy!"

"I never realized how freaky you are," Tara laughed.

"You're just realizing this now?" Gabe looped an arm around her waist and pulled her close, speaking quietly in her ear. "Kitten, you literally spat my own cum into my mouth, and I practically came a second time. You haven't noticed because you're almost as bad as I am."

Tara leaned into him, stretching tall to fuse closer with his solid frame. "True. I still think about that time you ate my ass when you didn't even know my name."

"What about the wall?" Gabe pointed to a wavy blue metal wall, dotted with unevenly sized scattered holes.

Since he was still holding her tight against his chest, Tara wrapped her arm around his. "I'm not sure how I might fuck a wall."

"I was imagining a glory hole situation."

"With *you* on the other side? Hell yeah!" Tara lifted the camera. "Go on, let's see it. What are my options?"

Gabe groaned. "I should have known this would happen." With a reluctant sigh, he handed her the leash. Aligning his body with the holes, he poked his cringing face out of the largest one his tall frame could reach. "This isn't going on the internet, right?"

"No, this is for me. Now stop pouting. I'm not torturing you."

"Kitten, just know I would not do this for anyone else." Gabe grimaced in an approximation of a smile.

"You can do better than that, Coop. What's the face you'd make if your melted cryptid fuck buddy wanted a turn?" Tara teased. She managed to snap one good shot of Gabe laughing, before Hippo pulled her toward Gabe. Tail wagging, he begged Gabe to play through the holes.

"Much better." Tara rose up on her tiptoes to kiss the corner of Gabe's mouth through the wall, before she could question if she should. They were just on a walk. Even though she really wanted this to be more than just a walk. This easy, comfortable, fun conversation, the charged flirting—this was what she'd imagined dating Gabe would be like. And she was loving every second. "Thank you. For the good memory."

Gabe's eyes flicked to her lips, a blush darkening his olive skin. "Tara, can I— Can we..." He sighed and stepped back. "Are you hungry?"

Inexplicable disappointment flooding through her, Tara stepped back with a tight smile. "Always. But you don't have to buy me food. We're just on a walk, right?"

With a laugh that sounded more like a frustrated groan, Gabe stepped around the wall between them. "Tara, if it wasn't blatantly obvious, I asked you to come on a walk as a date. So if you're hungry, it'd be a dick move not to take you to lunch. Even if you don't want this to be a date, as your... *friend*, I will always buy you food when you're hungry."

Relief and anxiety swirled in her chest, along with a pang of annoyance at his emphasis on "friend". Breathing became harder than it should have been. "I want it to be. A date, I mean. I don't know... I'm still not sure what—"

"Pause, Tara." Gabe poked her nose with a quiet sigh, taking the leash back. "I'm not pushing you to talk about what we're doing if you're not ready. First and foremost, we're friends, right? I don't want to lose that. Yes, I want more, but I want you to be sure that's what you want, too." He tapped her nose again. "Play."

Tara hugged him, relieved she didn't have to force the words out, when she barely understood what they might be. "Can we get tacos then?"

"Yes, Kitten, we can get tacos." Gabe kissed her temple, arm over her shoulder as they walked back toward the museum.

Tara kept her own arm around his hips. She'd been overthinking for weeks, yet she was still no closer to reconciling her conflicting feelings. She wanted him. She wanted to be with him. Gabe was so well suited to her, it was terrifying. He was sweet and patient, adoring and understanding. His life was so...stable. A charming house that he'd never have to leave, a cute dog to care for, seemingly limitless savings, loyal friends, and parents who supported him—Gabe was everything she'd ever longed for. He made her feel so wanted and cared for, no matter how much she tried to keep him at arm's length.

Losing him would devastate her.

Rule Eight (keep the circle small) existed to keep Tara's heart in one piece when everyone eventually left. Her dad was the first. Her mom's endless cycle of boyfriends never stuck around. And her mom had left so many times, until she finally made Tara leave instead. If Tara kept her distance from people, they couldn't hurt her when they left too. No one but Lee and Blanche—not even Sunny or Walter or Wanda or Alitrice—had ever truly been a part of her inner circle.

Was it worth opening herself up to so much pain, to let Gabe truly love her? These last boundaries caging her heart were her only protection. As much as she tried to keep him compartmentalized away, he'd become ingrained in her life. At least in this limbo, she might still keep his friendship when something eventually went wrong.

"I ruined it, didn't I?" Gabe asked, wiping his fingers with a napkin. He'd eaten approximately four bites of steak and onions from his tacos, before pushing the tray away. "You got quiet."

Tara frowned. The mostly empty tortillas he'd left behind were a personal insult. "No, you didn't ruin anything. I'm just thinking."

"Don't hurt yourself."

"Shut up, Coop!" Tara laughed. "Are you going to eat that?"

"You want cold tortillas?" Gabe looked at her skeptically.

Tara set her chin. "As a rule, I don't waste food unless it'll make me sick."

"Well, if it's a rule..." Gabe pushed the tinfoil-littered tray to her.

"Rule Five, specifically."

"Wait, the rules are numbered?" Gabe asked in fascination. "How many are there? What are they?"

"Don't push it, Coop." Tara stuffed the tortillas in her mouth to keep from spilling all of the answers. Telling Gabe all of her rules would mean letting him in too deep to ever let him go, and she couldn't make that leap, not yet. Maybe not ever.

Swallowing her anxiety along with the tortillas, Tara finally muttered, "There's ten-ish, but I'm not listing them for you."

GABE

"I LIKE HOW YOU gave me your weighted blanket, and then bought another one," Tara teased, stealing his spot on the couch as she turned on yet another cooking show. With a grin, she patted the chaise between her legs in invitation.

"This is a *couch* weighted blanket. I don't know why I never had one before, honestly." Flashing an apologetic smile, Gabe instead lifted her legs over his as he leaned against her shoulder, spreading the heavy lap blanket over them. "This comfortable?"

He should feel a little guilty—and he did, he felt *a lot* guilty—for being happy that Blanche's patron had come over unexpectedly. He would have been satisfied with their walk and lunch. But spending the afternoon with Tara in the museum (where his mom thankfully wasn't), then getting takeout for dinner, and coming home to split a bottle of wine and watch a show together?

It felt so incredibly...perfect. Real. Right.

Tara wrapped her arms around his shoulders, kissing his temple as she adjusted to get more comfortable. "Yeah, it's cool. If you don't want to be between my legs, I guess, anyway."

Gabe chuckled. "Kitten, there's nowhere else I'd rather be. I figured this would be more comfortable for watching a movie. Or, more likely, a cooking show."

"Oh, are we actually gonna watch it?" Tara laughed. "I figured this was an excuse for foreplay."

"Why would we need an excuse for foreplay?" Gabe pinched her thigh, delighted by her gasp. "But no, I didn't invite you over to watch a movie as a pretense for fooling around. I thought... I want you to know that this isn't just sex for me. I want to actually talk and spend time together."

Tara's eyes went wide. "What do you want to talk about?"

"Nothing." Gabe grinned at her confused expression. "Everything. Whatever we happen to feel like talking about."

Tara's brow furrowed. "How is that different from normal?"

"It doesn't have to be anything special, is what I'm trying to say. We've become close friends over the past year, but I've been holding back so I wouldn't make you uncomfortable. Considering I had no idea you even wanted me anymore until last month, I'd hazard a guess that you have, too." Gabe raised an eyebrow, until Tara nodded with a bashful smile.

"I've gotten really good at holding back." She frowned, her nose wrinkling. "I hate it."

"Me too," Gabe murmured. "But today, we didn't hold back as much, and we had a good time. I want us to connect like that because," he huffed, struggling to find the right words to convey his meaning. To overcome his reluctance to dredge up his insecurities, with someone who'd unintentionally been stirring them up. "In my past relationships, everything turned serious and intense so fast, and I don't want to do that with you. If we do decide to be more than friends, I don't want to lose the fun we have together." He took her hand, bringing it close to kiss her palm. "If we had gotten together sooner, I would have dragged you down into a horny, toxic mess, and that would be a disaster for both of us."

"Sounds kinda fun, though," Tara teased.

Gabe huffed. "It's addictive, not sure I'd call it fun."

"Since you want to talk about everything and nothing," Tara hesitated. "Why do you always funnel Lee and Antonio money for their wedding through Blanche's channel, instead of giving it to them directly? I doubt they'd turn it down."

Gabe winced, but he'd been the one to open the doors to this. "Because my mom is going to be at the wedding, and the terms of my trust fund are that she cannot benefit from it. I pay out of pocket, and then get reimbursed from the executor after I prove my mom did not benefit in any way. So, I can pay Blanche ten grand every month without issue, but I can't gift Antonio money for his wedding, because I'd have to provide the guest list to show my mom isn't on it. The flowers are coming from my own personal money, so I don't have to jump through hoops."

"Why not just give you the money?" Tara asked, running a hand through his hair. He leaned into her touch, ignoring the tugs when her fingers caught in his curls.

"To make it hard for me to use. I only got an inheritance so my grandpa could save face. He didn't actually want me to have anything, but I shamed him into it." Gabe laughed, deciding this was as good a time as any to share a story he didn't often talk about. "You know how Richard and I pretended to date when we were in undergrad? We did that because his dad has always been weirdly obsessed with my mom. She was supposed to be Dick's ticket into an old money family, but then she ran off with my dad. Once Dick heard my mom was pregnant, he settled for Richard's mom instead. So *Richard* was supposed to then be Dick's ticket into an old money legacy through me, except I'd never met any of my mom's family.

"So basically, Dick finds out I was going to Yale too, and makes it his business to show up to every alumni event he can, on the off chance that my mom's dad would be there, so he could start network-ing *before* Richard and I got engaged." Gabe scoffed. "Which was never gonna happen, but I pretended to be a good future son-in-law for Richard's sake. And lo and behold, at one of these hoity-toity events that Richard and I both hated, guess who showed up, but my mom's dad? Dick was so over the moon that he dragged Richard and I over. So I met my waste of space grandfather for the first time, when he was surrounded by his fellow old rich men. I basically peer pressured him into publicly acknowledging me as his grandson."

Gabe snorted. "I have no shame that I milked the shit out of the interaction. I hated him for what he put my parents through. That was *before* my head injury, so I was a bit quicker on my feet. Over the course of one conversation, I managed to coerce him into paying my tuition, connecting me with his accountant to set up the trust fund, and giving me the watch right off his wrist." Gabe tugged his sleeve back, where the old silver timepiece still ticked away. A reminder that at one point, Gabriel Cooper had been clever and assertive and spiteful, instead of the sad doormat he'd become. "He probably meant to cut me off after that, but he had a heart attack and died the next week." He laughed. "And I don't even feel bad for it. I will happily redistribute his estate purely out of spite on my mom's behalf." He paused, looking up at Tara. "Sorry, I'm rambling. You probably didn't want the whole story."

With a soft look as she gently stroked his hair, Tara shook her head. "I like hearing your stories. Your voice is nice."

"Did you ever know your grandparents?" Gabe asked, forcing an air of nonchalance over the question. Other than the one time she'd shared that she'd lost contact with her parents, Tara had never revealed much about her family. Gabe was a sponge, thirsty and desperate for as much as he could learn. Two years ago, he'd committed to memory everything he'd learned about his Kitten—her birthday, her favorite drink, how she responded to his touch, how she didn't want to kiss him—and slowly compiled a mental encyclopedia about the Tara he'd come to know. But everything about her life before she met Lee was blank.

"Just Walter and Wanda, and I wasn't actually related to them." Tara's smile faded briefly, but she forced it back on. "Tell me another story?"

After a moment in which he considered asking a different, perhaps easier question, Gabe nodded. "What do you want to hear?" If Lee hadn't learned everything after a decade of her friendship, Gabe wouldn't earn Tara's confidence in a single day.

They were so similar, he and Tara. He hated talking about himself too, hated exposing himself to ridicule and judgment. To prove that she could be open with him, Gabe would have to open up to her in a way he'd never opened up with anyone—not even with Antonio, or Richard, or his therapist. He would tell her as many stories as it took.

Tara settled around him, resting her cheek on his hair with a contented sigh. "A happy memory?"

Burying his smile in her neck, the cooking show forgotten in the background, Gabe told her about meeting Antonio in middle school. About all the trouble Gabe was happy to get into, for the first real friend he had. How the Floreses had met the Coopers, and decided they belonged in their family.

About the first time his dad had brought him along to a powwow when he was fifteen, and how he'd felt like an imposter, because everyone else seemed to know who they belonged to. He'd eventually let go of his bitter armor and started listening. He'd connected his roots to his dad's legacy as a boarding school kid and activist. He'd learned how to introduce himself, so people wouldn't give him that skeptical look, reserved for people who claimed their great-great-grandmother was a Cherokee princess. He'd come to understand that the skepticism had been in his head the whole time, and that "All my relations" included him too.

Gabe was in the middle of telling her about when his mom taught him the secret family recipe for cheesecake, when he realized Tara was asleep. Her chest rose deep and even, her leg twitching like Hippo's when he was dreaming.

With a smile, Gabe quieted and settled against her. Full of food and wine, and love, he joined her in sleep under the blanket.

TARA

"KITTEN," A DEEP VOICE murmured, soft lips pressing down her jaw. "I'm sorry to wake you up, but Blanche called you, and texted me after."

Tara grumbled, fighting to stay asleep. She was comfortable, warm and heavy, where she was... Wait, where was she?

She stiffened, realizing she wasn't at home, she didn't know where her bag— Gabe's lips on her collarbone, the oak and vanilla scent of him, made her exhale slowly in relief. She was at his house, they'd had a...date. She blinked in the dark room. The TV screen was on, asking if they were still watching. She took another calming breath before asking, "What time is it?"

"Late. Almost ten." Gabe's hand slid up her thigh to her hip, squeezing gently. "They asked when you'd be home, and if they should wait up for you."

"What did you say?" Tara hissed as Gabe's teeth scraped her throat, heat pulsing under her skin.

His grip on her hip tightened and flexed, slowly easing back to cup her ass. "Nothing, I haven't answered. What should I tell them?"

With a slow grin, Tara stretched, thrilled at the hard cock under her thigh. Gabe's breath shuddered against her neck when she rubbed against it. "What happened to today not being about sex?"

"Who said that?" Gabe teased, nipping her earlobe. He rolled over to press her into the couch. "What fool would suggest not fucking you?"

"Yeah, that was definitely you," Tara teased, arching her back as he sucked behind her jaw. "You wanted us to talk about everything and nothing."

"That sounds like Gabe from a few hours ago. *This* Gabe just had the best nap of his life and dreamed of eating this pussy." Gabe slid a hand around her thigh to cup her between her thighs, fingers pressing right over her clit. Even through her joggers, his touch sent shock waves through Tara's body. He grinned down at her as curses flew from her lips. Her thighs squeezed his hand to trap it where she needed it. Where she'd been craving his touch for hours, weeks, months. "And then your phone was in your pocket. I almost came when Blanche called you."

Tara laughed, delighted by his dimples. They were still visible even in the dim of the room. She took a quiet breath before she killed the mood. "I should go home though."

Unphased, Gabe nodded, still massaging her pussy through her clothes. "I figured. Can I go down on you before you go?"

With a whine, Tara melted into the couch. "What happened to avoiding being horny and toxic?"

"We can be horny and *fun*." Gabe kissed her cheek, lips dragging down her jaw and throat. "I'd love it if we could be horny and fun. But if you don't want to—"

"I didn't say that!" Tara said in a rush, laughing with Gabe. "Just making sure that's what *you* want. I've been fully down to fool around this whole time."

"Honestly, I would have woken you up with my mouth on your clit, but I wasn't sure if you'd like that." Gabe looked at her with a silent question.

"Probably not," Tara winced apologetically. It was always a toss-up if waking up would be pleasant or panicked. "Sorry."

"Don't apologize." Gabe shook his head. "For the record, I do *not* like that either. Had an ex who did that without asking too many times."

"Want me to fuck them up?" Tara asked, keeping her tone light and teasing; Gabe had already seen enough of her bloodlust at Belly's. If she ever met one of these nameless exes who'd hurt him, she'd probably end up in jail.

Gabe laughed. "No! I don't want anything to do with him ever again. Stay away from New York, please. That's where all the bad exes live. I am safe in Bellamy, here with you." His hand slid up her belly as he kissed down her body, pushing her shirt up to suck on her tits.

With a quiet cry, Tara buried her fingers in his hair, arching into his mouth. All thoughts about potential assault charges against the people who had dared hurt her friend—no, her...lover, she supposed—were wiped from her mind as Gabe moaned around her nipple. His fingers worked under the waistband of her joggers. Tara eagerly lifted her hips to help him toss them aside.

Hippo, who had been snoring on the end of the couch, yawned. Tara and Gabe froze. The massive dog groaned as he stretched to slide off the couch. Lumbering by slowly with quiet grumbles, he headed to the kitchen.

"I forgot he was in here," Tara whispered, fighting a laugh at Hippo's dramatics. A giggle escaped her as Hippo flopped down in the kitchen with a heavy sigh.

"I feel bad." Gabe pressed his lips together, his dimples deepening as he tried to hide his grin. "Maybe we should fool around in the bedroom."

"But he already left, so..." With a smirk, Tara hooked her bare leg around his hip. "Show me what you were dreaming about, Coop."

"Fuck," Gabe groaned, his strong hands gripping her thighs to draw her knees over his shoulders. Kissing the soft skin of her inner thighs, he stretched out over the chaise. "I have a question for you, this time." He nipped hard at the crease of her hip, grinning at Tara's yelp. "Tell me about these sex toys you named after me. I want to hear all about how you use them."

Tara huffed, her laugh catching as his tongue circled her cunt. Now *this* question, she was happy to answer. "It took a lot of trial and error, but I finally found a dildo that was both big enough and felt *almost* as good as you did that first night." Her thumb traced his temple, her hand framing the dark eyes looking up at her in devotion, as Gabe buried his face between her legs. His nose nudged her clit, stubble scraping her inner thighs. She hissed as his tongue delved deep into her cunt. "It was never as good as the real you, though."

Hips rolling against the foot of the chaise, Gabe hummed, prompting her to keep going. But the vibration of his deep voice made her arch, dragging his tongue from her hole to her clit.

Rising up on her elbows, Tara panted. "I have this other toy I got after you ate me out in Lee and Antonio's bathroom." She groaned as Gabe sucked on her clit, biting her lip at the amused glint in his eye. "It's got this g spot vibe and clit suction that can make me cum in seconds, over and over again. Just like you." She arched her back at Gabe's self-satisfied hum against her clit. Sweat broke out down her spine. "Fuck, I'm close."

"Keep talking, Kitten," Gabe said, muffled by her cunt. "Fuck, you're so sexy right now."

Tara fought for control of her voice through the pleasure singing in her veins. Tension coiled in her belly as her thighs tensed. "Sometimes, it makes me come so hard I squirt, like I did that time I sat on your face. Remember that? Your hair was soaked."

Gabe groaned, gripping her hips hard enough to bruise as he pulled her tight against his mouth. Tara's thighs squeezed around his head as she came with a cry of his name. The upholstery scraped her back where her shirt rode up as she arched.

"As if I could ever forget that, Kitten," Gabe's deep voice was raspy as he kissed her thigh, giving Tara a much-needed moment to catch her breath. "I think about that night constantly." He dragged his tongue up her slit. "You taste amazing."

"I have one more," Tara said with a smile. "One I got for us to use together, in case you ever wanted to make another risky bet with me."

Gabe groaned, his head dropping to her thigh. "Kitten, you didn't."

Tara laughed, thrilled he already knew where she was going. "I did."

"Tell me about it. Have you used it?" Gabe asked, those full lips dragging across her thigh, until they were back on her clit where they belonged. Two fingers slid inside her, curling over and over again.

Swallowing her moan, Tara stroked his cheek, fingers lingering on the shell of his ear. "All the time. I had to see what it might feel like. It's got two ends, one for me, one for you. I stroke myself off, imagining how you'd look riding me. How eager you'd be for me to fuck you from behind, the sounds you'd make when I have you bent over for me." She smiled as Gabe growled against her clit, his body writhing against the chaise. "You like that, Gabe? Are you thinking about how it'd feel to have me inside you?"

Her foot drew a line down his spine, toe digging into the meat of his ass, as her other leg curled around his head. She rutted against his face, thrilling in his enthusiasm as he grunted with every thrust of his fingers inside her. "I think about eating this ass constantly, stroking you off when I have you spread open for me. How you'd be begging for me to fuck you—" She cried out as Gabe whined against her clit; his shuddered sob brought her right back over the edge. "Fuck. God, how are you so good at eating me out?"

Instead of responding, Gabe groaned, hiding his face against her thigh. "What, what's wrong?"

"I just came," he muttered. "I was gonna get off on your tits this time. Dammit."

Tara bit her lip, holding in a delighted laugh. "You really do want me to peg you, don't you?"

Gabe shot her a glare, but his dimples never faded. "You're not the only one with toys and an imagination, Kitten."

"Oh?" Tara grinned eagerly. "Tell me yours."

"I'd rather show you." Gabe kissed up her belly, ravishing her tits again before he pressed a kiss to her sternum. His coffee-brown eyes had that puppy dog expression that tugged at her heart. "You're welcome to stay as long as you want, but I imagine you want to go home tonight?"

Tara nodded, a pang of disappointment dimming her afterglow. Part of her wanted to stay longer, for Gabe to drag her to the bedroom and show her all the filthy things he'd imagined. For this day to never end.

But... Blanche was waiting up for her (probably a mess, despite their message of "just curious"). Her duffel bag was there, and, well... She wasn't ready to stay the way Gabe really meant. He might be talking about tonight, but they both knew he wanted her to stay for good.

Already, it was so hard to leave when she should. With his big, cute house, and his big, cute dog, this giant, beautiful soul overwhelmed her every defense.

How much harder would it become if she let herself stay? How much more would her heart hurt if she let her guard down? Rule Seven—don't get attached—was barely clinging to life, as Gabe continued to permeate her bedrock. But that rule kept her safe, kept Tara whole when everyone left her. Her heart was still so fragile after being caged within her walls for so long; she had to keep some distance, for her sake.

And Gabe's.

Tara forced a smile. "Can I drive?"

Sunday, April Eleventh

Chapter Nineteen

Lee

"Breathe, Angel." Antonio caught Lee's hand to stop its incessant path up and down his thigh. Squeezing his fingers, he smiled up at fiancée encouragingly. "You have me here for support. We're in public. Everything will be okay. You're a strong, independent woman."

Despite Antonio's attempt to make him laugh, Lee only managed a weak smile. Inside, he was a wreck. Nausea ate at his stomach. His attempt at a smile probably did nothing to mask his anxiety. Sweat kept beading on his nose, sliding his glasses down every few seconds.

They were waiting at a diner, one that Lee hadn't been to in over a decade, because it was where his family had always eaten after church. After ten years of silence, Jazz had somehow convinced their parents to come to lunch, to meet their hellbound homosexual son and his fiancée. Alone at a six-top table as families around them downed hash browns and pancakes, Lee and Antonio fidgeted in anticipation, waiting quietly for the Joneses to arrive. If they hadn't changed their minds.

"Thank you," Lee murmured.

"For what, Angel?"

"Being here. I couldn't do this without you."

Lee hadn't been able to sleep in days; the nightmares had been relentless. Yet Antonio had been there every minute, holding him until he fell back asleep. He'd listened patiently to Lee's indecisive wavering about if he wanted to do this up until they'd walked through the door, and quietly supported him in whatever Lee decided. Even though he knew Antonio didn't understand why he needed to do this at all.

"You could and you would, but you're welcome. There's nowhere else I'd rather be." Antonio winked.

"I can think of *many* places I'd rather be." Lee snorted. He still found it hard to believe that Antonio wanted to marry into his nightmare of a family, when Antonio's was a dream. His phone buzzed in his pocket with a text from Jazz; they were here. "Well, no getting out of this now."

Antonio gave him a quick kiss on the cheek. Lee tightened his hand before Antonio's could slip away. They had talked about keeping affection to a minimum, but Lee needed Antonio's comfort. Even if they were in public, even if it might make his parents uncomfortable. If the smallest affection ruined their chances of reconciliation, better to sabotage things before they placed their orders.

He and Antonio stood up to greet Jazz with a comforting hug. She was dressed modestly in a baggy sweater and khakis, her hair wrapped in a scarf; they must have come right from church. Seeing her dressed so conservatively again was disconcerting, a reminder that the Jazz he knew was not the Jazz his parents did. It was one thing to hear her complain about it, and another to see Jazz looking like their daughter, instead of his sister. Lee let the hug linger, nervous to turn and face his past.

"If this goes south, I'm coming home with you," Jazz teased quietly.

"Love the confidence, Jazz." Lee squared his shoulders and took a calming breath, before taking in the sight of his parents.

Hanging back behind his little sister, Althea and Leland Sr. stared back at him in silence. They were smaller than he remembered. He had grown taller than his dad at some point, and his mom barely came up to Jazz's chin. They looked...older.

Of course, they looked older. They should. They *were* older. They were nearly fifty now. He'd never thought of them as anything but frozen in time.

His mom looked much the same, dressed in a modest blouse and long skirt, like she always had. Her hair was wrapped in plain white silk; she'd worn it to church like that his whole life. Althea looked softer, more tired than he remembered, with a few lines around her eyes that hadn't been there before.

His dad, on the other hand, seemed deflated. The intimidating muscle mass when Lee was a kid had become a paunchy gut and rounded shoulders. His clothes were unchanged, gray slacks and a starched button-down, albeit looser fitting than they used to be.

Lee bit his lip, unsure what to say. He had imagined how this conversation would go a thousand different ways; every time he'd figured the first words would come naturally. He'd practiced the important things, not the hello. Faced with the reality of his parents actually here with him, his voice failed him.

He wanted to leave. He wanted to hug them and cry, and yell, and give them the silent treatment, while asking ten million questions all at once. But Lee was frozen.

His mom broke first.

"Oh, my baby!" Althea cried as she threw herself at him, wrapping her arms around his shoulders for the first time in over a decade. He hugged her back automatically, overcome with emotions that caught in his throat because his mom was hugging him. The mother he'd written off in his heart was clinging to his shoulders, like Lee might disappear if she let go. He was suddenly a kid again, and yet... Althea Jones had never been so affectionate when he was younger.

Althea sobbed, shaking; the emotion in her voice blurred his vision. For once, Lee couldn't find it in himself to care that he was tearing up in public.

"I've thought about you every day. I was so worried," his mom whispered into his shoulder. Her thin arms were a tight band around him.

Lee's temper spiked, burning hot under his skin. *Not worried enough to call me or bother looking for me.* He swallowed it down. There would be time for that later. They could have a happy moment, before the hard conversations began.

Pulling away, his mother searched his face. Her dark brown eyes, the same ones as Jazz, were wet with tears. "I'm so sorry, Lee. I don't know how to tell you how sorry I am."

"I'm sorry, too." His dad finally spoke. The deep voice that haunted his nightmares was incongruous with those words. His father had never *apologized* before. For anything. Leland's head bowed, not meeting Lee's eyes. "Your mother and I fought so much after... She wanted to bring you home, and I was too proud, too stubborn to admit I was wrong."

What had happened to them? His mom had been the picture of obedience, submitting to her husband's will and following wherever he led. They'd been the couple that their pastor had extolled as the standard for their congregation. That she had argued against his decision was monumental. It was one thing for Jazz to tell him that, but to see how bowed Leland Senior had become, to hear the difference in his father's voice...

Maybe this was going to be worth it.

Lee found his voice. "I'm not ready to forgive anything yet, but I'm glad that you're here now." He let out a tiny sigh of relief as he held out his hand. At least something he'd rehearsed had actually come out the way he'd planned.

Leland looked up then, and Lee was met with a mirror of own face, aged another twenty-two years. No matter how long his hair grew or thick his beard became, Lee could never escape his dad's face in every reflection and picture. Even their glasses were the same shape, his father's tortoiseshell where Lee's were clear.

Leland took Lee's hand, but there was no formal shake. Instead, his estranged father pulled him into a hug.

First an apology, now a hug? Lee stiffened, unsure of how he was supposed to act. He had no memories of his dad hugging him. *Is he going to tell me he loves me next? The trifecta of firsts from Dad?*

"I love you so much, son," Leland said, as if reading Lee's bitter thoughts. "I'm sorry I never said it before. I'm sorry that I ever gave you cause to doubt it."

Bitterness surged in Lee's stomach, but again, he did his best to swallow it. He didn't believe his dad, not even for a second. A parent who loved their child would never have done what Leland Senior did to him.

But that was a conversation for another time. For now, he could only accept that, in this moment, his dad might truly be a changed man. That time had softened Leland's memories of how he'd treated his son. This might all be an act, but only time would tell, and Lee had come here hoping to make peace, or at least find closure.

Tentatively, Lee patted his dad's shoulder.

"Oh my god, Jazz, you can't cry. You're going to make me cry," Antonio whispered, clinging to her arm as the two of them wiped tears from their eyes.

Lee stepped back from his parents to return to Antonio's side, taking his hand. "This is my fiancée, Antonio."

Leland's eyes darted to their joined hands; Lee laced their fingers together and held on tight. He pulled himself to his full height, and Antonio drew his shoulders back, exuding so much confidence that no one would think he was six inches shorter than everyone else in this tense circle. Lee smiled, beyond caring if they made his parents uncomfortable. They *should* be uncomfortable. This was his life. If they wanted to be in it, they could deal with him holding his fiancée's hand.

Althea spoke first again. "I'm so glad you're in his life, Antonio."

Antonio's hazel eyes blinked in confusion at her odd statement, but he smiled tightly. "Me too. Lee's amazing, and I'm so lucky I get to love him." The unspoken "because you didn't" hung in the air.

Lee's heart swelled with appreciation. Eventually, they'd have to have some tough conversations, but he'd been waiting his whole life for any warmth from his parents like this. He half-wished that he'd insisted Tara be here, but if all kept going well, there'd be time to introduce both of his families in the future.

As they sat down, the server came over to take their orders. Feeling like a rebellious child, Lee ordered the farmers breakfast with extra bacon, like he'd always wanted to get after church, even though Leland had never allowed them to eat pork. Though he didn't say anything, Leland's frown was disapproving. Antonio and the server negotiated back and forth, until they finally figured out something on the menu he could eat.

"So what all did Jazz tell you?" Lee asked after the server left, unsure of how to start the conversation they needed to have. He didn't trust himself to say the right things. Everything was too raw to do anything except listen.

"Just that she'd been in contact with you, and that you were getting married soon," Althea said, affectionately tucking one of Jazz's locs back under her scarf. Jazz forced a smile, but Lee could see the tension in his sister's eyes. "She had nothing but nice things to say about Antonio. I still can't believe she kept something like this from us, but I was so relieved to hear you were happy. I'd been keeping you in my prayers every night."

Lee shot a glance at his sister, the picture of modesty in khakis and a burgundy cardigan. *Jazz keeps a lot of things from you.* The hidden septum ring was only the tip of the iceberg. Jazz smiled at him, a faint warning in her look.

"Where did you go?" Althea asked. "After Alitrice passed?"

"You mean after Dad evicted me and Tara?" Lee muttered. He couldn't help himself—sure, he was cautiously optimistic, but that didn't mean his parents shouldn't feel guilty. "We stayed in a tent in the old encampment until the riot, then our friend Blanche got an apartment for all three of us. We stayed there together until I moved in with Antonio last year."

"Is Tara the redhead girl?" Althea asked, her hands clasped in front of her heart. "I saved her things when we were packing up Alitrice's belongings. Yours, too."

Excitement bloomed in Lee's chest. Most of their belongings had been clothes and replaceable stuff. But the photos Tara had been forced to leave behind were the only memories of her parents that she had. "She'd appreciate that. But fair warning, don't expect her to be grateful."

"She might fight you," Antonio added, clearly directed to his dad. "She's very protective of Lee. We all are."

Leland nodded, resigned. "It's what I deserve. I saw her name all over Ali's documents, mentioned in the letters she wrote to me that I never opened, on the records from the hospital. Some stranger—a teenage girl—was there for her when I was too cowardly to be."

"Tara went with her to every chemo treatment. Learned how to take care of her when we couldn't afford a hospice nurse anymore." Lee didn't know how he would have handled his aunt's slow decline to cancer, without Tara's resilience and support. Or her iron stomach. Prone to sympathetic vomiting, Lee had quickly excused himself many times whenever the feeding tube backed up, leaving Tara to clean up before he made the situation worse. She'd kept them all going, even when all three of them had lost hope, because Tara didn't need hope to persist.

Meanwhile, his dad had abandoned his only sister in her final days, all because Auntie Alitrice had taken her gay nephew in.

Grief clouded Leland's face. Lee had never expected his dad to be so open. The only emotions he'd ever shown were anger, disappointment, and pride. "I'm sorry. I was so stuck in my ways. Ali's death hit me harder than I thought possible. You know I didn't even know she was sick? She'd reached out so many times, and I ignored her out of wounded pride." He cleared his throat, but his voice was still haggard. "Getting your voicemail that she'd passed brought up all of the shame and regret I'd been telling myself wasn't there. And I acted without thinking. Your mother made me go to a counselor, and I'm glad she did. I'd probably still be a stubborn, weak, shell of a man if it wasn't for you, dear." His dad smiled at Althea, kissing her hand.

Another sight Lee had never seen. Affection, love, emotions? *Who is this man?*

Antonio slid him an envelope under the table. His eyes asked an unspoken question.

Lee nodded. "Here. It's an invitation to our wedding." He slid the envelope across the table to them. "Fair warning, we're getting married at the gay bar where we work, so if that's a problem, don't come."

He tried to sound more confident than he felt. Part of him was sure that they'd reject the invitation, reject him. But if they wanted to be in his life, they'd have to accept that he was an out and proud gay man. They'd have to accept that Confession was important to him. Because he strangely, inexplicably, desperately *needed* them to come to his wedding.

Althea took the invitation gently, admiring the photo of them openly happy, loving and affectionate. When he'd taken it, Lee never would have imagined that his parents might see it. "We wouldn't miss it, would we?"

Lee checked for his father's reaction, half expecting him to say something negative about the photo, or the venue, or him.

Instead, Leland wilted at something in his glance. "I'm honored to be even invited."

Holding off on any sigh of relief, Lee refused to consider it a victory yet. Too many questions still plagued his heart. Would they want to meet him if he wasn't getting married? Did they actually want to be in his life, or did they only want to soothe their guilt? *How can I be so relieved and angry at the same time?*

"So what do you do for work?" Althea asked. "Did you meet there?"

"Yup! Lee's the audio tech, and I'm a drag queen," Antonio said confidently, challenging his parents to say something.

Lee bit back a smile. He let his parents squirm a little before adding, "You're also a choir teacher, but yes, we met at Confession."

"They made an album together too," Jazz added. "It's really good. Tonio sings. Lee produced it."

"Oh? You make music? I'd love to hear it!?" Althea said, too enthusiastically.

Antonio choked on his water. Avoiding eye contact with his parents, Lee glared at Jazz, who grinned back at him innocently. He hadn't been planning to tell his parents about the album; it wasn't exactly family-friendly. Carlita Asada had really leaned into the campy meat jokes in even the tamest of her songs. "Uh, you might not like how secular it is. Some of the lyrics are a little R-rated," Lee finally managed to say, adding, "Jazz can explain the slang for you, if you do listen to it."

His sister's innocent smile fell into a glare of her own.

"So, you teach?" Althea changed the subject quickly.

"Yup, middle school choir!" Antonio nodded enthusiastically, seemingly as grateful as Lee to change topics. "Teaching is so rewarding, and yet so humbling."

"Are you guys going to have kids of your own?" Althea asked bluntly.

"Oh, no!" Lee and Antonio said in unified horror. Anger surged hot in him again at her audacity. *Damn, ten years without a word, and she wants to play grandma?* He and Antonio had been on the same page from the beginning, but Althea had a lot to make up for before asking questions like that.

Luckily, Antonio spoke more diplomatically than Lee could at the moment. "Don't get me wrong, kids are great, but I have enough cousins and nieces and nephews to keep us busy. We don't really see that for ourselves."

Althea looked a little disappointed. "I'll just wait patiently for grandkids then." She smiled knowingly at Jazz; her return smile looked more like a wince.

After what Lee had seen at her birthday party, Althea would be waiting a *long* time. Accidents seemed unlikely. Sure, Jazz might be bi, but Lee doubted it. Now that he was forced to acknowledge the signs, his sister was undoubtedly a lesbian. Divine justice for his parents' behavior, if such a thing existed.

To Lee's surprise, their meal continued somewhat comfortably. He expected it to be awkward, with more arguments or tense silences than polite conversation.

And it *was* awkward. There were plenty of tense silences and sarcastic comments that escaped Lee, whenever his parents said something that struck a nerve. Jazz wasn't herself, and Antonio was being far more polite than Lee had expected. Lee resented that all three of them felt forced to keep a civil mask on. How Jazz did this constantly was beyond him. But Leland and Althea did their best, taking any biting remarks with humility and apologies. It only made Lee burn from annoyance that they wouldn't have an honest discussion. Instead he squirmed from discomfort, because his parents had never apologized before, and he didn't know how to respond.

As they talked, the knot in his chest began to relax. He may not be ready to forgive them yet, but he wanted to move past that. Lee's heart grew ever so slightly more whole, in this moment with his parents. His...family?

The word felt wrong. Tara, Blanche, and Sunny were his real family.

But, as awkward and tense as they were, his parents were too, undeniably. Jazz and Antonio might bridge the two groups, but reconciling those opposite experiences would take much longer than a meal. Or even a wedding.

If there was one thing Lee believed, it was that family were the people who showed up and stuck around. Today, his parents had showed up for him.

Maybe they would stick around for him, too.

LEE LET OUT A loud, pained groan as Antonio worked out a knot in his back with his elbow, as he lay stretched out in bed. "This is what you get when you hold your shoulders up around your ears like that for hours. Couldn't you feel how tense you were?" Antonio teased.

The second they were safe at home, Lee had sat on the couch, numb and silent. Antonio had brought him tea and sat with him. After the gnawing conflict in his gut had given way to hunger, Antonio made dinner and ran a hot shower for him. Lee had dragged him into the shower with him, holding Antonio close until the water ran cold.

While lunch with his parents had gone better than expected, Lee still felt exhausted and drained. Even though he'd done nothing but sit all afternoon, he only wanted to collapse into bed and rest.

"I love you, Tonio," he sighed as Antonio pressed against another knot in his neck. The vanilla and lavender scented oil perfumed the room with each glide of Antonio's strong hands against his skin. "You're so good to me."

"I am, aren't I?" Antonio agreed with a kiss to his temple.

"So humble, too," Lee teased. "Seriously, thank you. Today never would have happened without you."

"Do you want to talk about it?" Antonio straddled Lee's hips for better leverage, his elbow digging into Lee's shoulder.

The tension in his muscles and his heart unwound under Antonio's hands, his constant supportive presence, and the weight of him perched on Lee's ass. The skin-to-skin contact was desperately needed. Clothes could wait until morning. "It was harder than I thought. And easier.

They've changed so much since I was fifteen. They're not the same people anymore."

"And neither are you." Antonio stretched out over Lee's back, setting against him. He smiled; Antonio's dick was hard against his lower back, as was Lee's against the mattress, but neither of them did anything about it. There was no rush, no desperate need, just quiet intimacy. Antonio's rich voice spoke softly into Lee's ear, "You're not the scared kid who got kicked out anymore. You're a wonderful, kind, proud, strong man. Who is incredibly hot."

Lee laughed. "I'm glad you still think I'm hot. You got a peek at what I'll look like in the future."

"Not to make it weird, because I don't like your dad, but he is very easy on the eyes. He looks just like you used to when we first met." Antonio kissed his cheek. "I have a lot to look forward to."

"Yeah, no, you made it weird, Tonio." Lee grinned, rubbing a thumb over Antonio's arm, comforted by his weight pressing him down. "I'm glad it's over. The Band-Aid has been ripped off. I just wish Aunt Alitrice was here. She always wanted him to see sense."

"I wish I could have met her. She sounds like an amazing person."

"I wish you could have too. She would have thought you were crazy, but she would have loved you more for it." Lee had often gotten the impression his aunt liked Tara more than him. Tara was so unapologetic, even back then. Auntie Alitrice had taken Lee in, even though she never really approved of his sexuality. Perhaps she was hopeful that he'd get together with Tara; Aunt Ali had never had any concerns about them sharing a bed.

Or perhaps she'd hoped Tara's personality would rub off on him. Auntie Alitrice had always thought Lee was too serious, too nice, somehow making "nice" sound like a bad thing. She'd scold Lee that he was too dithering and needed to stand up for himself. He'd timidly agree with her that yes, he did need to stand up for himself, which only pissed her off more.

Lee sighed. "But at least you got to meet my parents. Yours are way nicer." With Antonio's family, Lee experienced the love he'd never felt. Until today, anyway. But it had still felt conditional, like his parents had forced themselves into that diner, just to say the right things to ease their conscience.

"It's not a competition, Angel. Yours are important too. They made you who you are, and I am grateful for that, no matter how painfully awkward today was." Antonio kissed his neck.

"Do you think they'll get along with everyone at the wedding? Can I hire Gabe to be my parents' security guard?" Reaching behind him, Lee tangled his fingers in Antonio's curls, rubbing his scalp.

Antonio sighed softly into Lee's ear. "Everyone is mature enough not to make a scene at our wedding. Besides, I doubt Gabe would stop Tara if she was really determined."

"Hey, Tonio?"

"Yes, my love?" Antonio kissed his neck.

"Can I roll over? I didn't think I'd be up for it tonight, but can we fool around before we go to sleep? I can feel how hard your dick is, and I want to do something nice for you, too."

Antonio laughed. "Sorry, I was trying to behave. But the sounds you make when I give you a back rub always get me hard." He lifted himself off of Lee long enough for Lee to roll over underneath him, before straddling Lee's torso and kissing him deeply.

Lee dug his fingers into Antonio's scalp as their lips pressed together in a steady rhythm, devouring each other. Worn and spent from the day, Antonio's soft, loving kiss revived him with eager anticipation. Lee pulled Antonio tighter, relishing in the hardness between them.

"Let me take care of you, Angel," Antonio murmured huskily into Lee's ear, working his mouth down Lee's jawline. "Just relax." He sucked softly on Lee's neck as he reached between them. The smell of vanilla and lavender made him sigh contentedly as Antonio wrapped an oiled hand around both of them, pumping slowly around their erections. The warm oil slicked his grip.

Lee moaned, thrusting against Antonio, who could always read him so well. Tonight wasn't a night for fucking; Lee needed to feel intimacy, to be touched, to feel pleasure. Bucking into the strong hand stroking them together, he murmured into their kiss, "Tonio, please. Don't stop. I'm close."

"I wouldn't dream of stopping, Angel," Antonio panted, nibbling on his earlobe as he adjusted his grip, tightening the strokes around the head.

"I love you!" Lee's body tensed before finally releasing into Antonio's hand.

"You should say that every time you come for me." Antonio kissed him with a smile, stroking himself off to finish with a soft whine.

Lee looked at him sleepily, his thoughts hazy with affection as Antonio wiped them both clean with the tissues next to the bed.

"Go to sleep, Angel," Antonio whispered, pulling the blankets over them.

"I love you." Lee drifted off to sleep to the sound of Antonio's whispered, "I love you, too" against his chest, feeling safe, and cherished, and whole.

Saturday, April Twenty-Fourth

CHAPTER TWENTY

As the kids filed into the classroom, Tara elbowed him. "You're going to give yourself split ends." She'd dressed up, somewhat. Dressed up as far as Tara went, anyway, in an oversized mint green sweater (Lee's, probably) and leggings. "Why are you more nervous than me?"

Having completed the only setup he could help with (showing Tara what button to hit to share her laptop screen), Gabe unclenched his hand from the end of his braid, fighting the urge to reach for her. Instead he sat on the head table, hands tucked under his thighs. "There is a very good chance that I *am* more nervous than you."

Tara arched an eyebrow as she pulled up various programs and her presentation. "I think I can handle it."

"Oh, I know you can. You'll probably bully them back if they give you a hard time."

Tara snorted. "Only if they deserve it."

Gabe didn't know why *he* was nervous; *Tara* was the one teaching. And yet, anticipation gnawed at his stomach. He chalked the nerves up to having a new volunteer he hadn't worked with before. But in truth, this program—which had started out as a temporary favor to his mother—had become one of the few joys in Gabe's newly rebuilt life.

This class was the one place where Gabe felt like he made a meaningful impact. He got to help young artists experience new things, encourage their passions. Being "Coop" to a dozen students every year was the most useful he'd ever been to anyone. Tara teaching this class felt like when she'd met Hippo for the first time; he had needed them to love each other as much as he loved both of them. Tara and this group of teenagers had to get along.

"Ready when you are, Coop," Tara murmured as the last trio of teens wandered in with a handful of vending machine snacks. She leaned on the table next to him, sipping the coffee he'd brought her when he'd picked her up.

Delight rippled through him whenever she used the nickname the kids had given him. Mostly because she'd given him a pet name—one that fit her personality, the way calling her Kitten fit his. At least she hadn't picked up his childhood nickname of "Gabey Baby" from Antonio the way Lee had.

Gabe nodded, clearing his throat. "Good morning everyone. You remember Ms. Sanderson, who sat in with us last month, right? She's graciously agreed to come back to teach you all about graphic design today. Let's give her a warm welcome."

"Hi, Tara!" Syl called.

Gabe gave him the best imitation of the Look his mom had used on him as a kid. "Syl, remember our etiquette class?"

His mom always gave that class at the beginning of every cohort, teaching everyone the "performance art" of etiquette as a way to set the standards for expected classroom behavior. The program director before Gabe had been bullied to tears (by Syl's brother) and quit; Miriam Cooper had stepped in to ensure there'd be no more volunteers lost to poor teenage judgment. She always threw a luncheon afterward in the banquet room, inviting the kids' parents, guardians, or trusted adults to dine with them. And since Gabe hadn't been harassed to the point of quitting quite yet, it seemed to be working. Or perhaps Gabe's tolerance for being bullied was higher than those who'd come before him.

Syl rolled his eyes. "Hi, Ms. Sanderson!" There was nothing quite so biting as teenage sarcasm.

Tara laughed. "Please, for the love of God, do *not* call me Ms. Sanderson. Tara is fine."

Syl looked at Gabe with an "I told you so" smirk.

"Go sit down, Coop. This is my class." Tara shooed him away.

Fighting a smile, Gabe sat at his usual back corner table.

At the front of the classroom, Tara shifted her weight from leg to leg. "Hi. Uh... So, I work as a Graphic Designer, mostly focusing on small business marketing. I create logos and brochures for new and growing companies." She gestured to the screen behind her. It displayed the logo to her own company before switching to the next slide, with a list of various graphic design-related degrees. "The cool thing about working in Graphic Design is that the credentials you need can be minimal. For the type of freelance work I do, an Associates is all I need, so that's where I stopped. But you can find decent commissions without formal credentials, or you can go on to a four-year degree or even grad school if you want to keep learning, or if the work you want to do requires more education."

Tara cleared her throat, as if realizing she was talking too fast. "Most big companies like degrees if you want a steady desk job, but you don't have to get a bachelor's or master's to be successful in graphic design." Tara clicked on the next slide about the benefits of working in graphic design. "I like graphic design because it's flexible and combines creativity and business skills. I can manage my own schedule and what projects I take on. Basically, it's my favorite way to make money."

On cue, an animated dollar sign floated up onto the screen. Tara turned to the class with an expectant, cheesy grin.

The class groaned at the corny graphic.

"I take back what I said about you being too cool for Coop," Syl sneered. "You're as much of a nerd as he is."

Unsure how to take that, Gabe simply shrugged when Syl shot a smirk back at him. Tara was much cooler than him, but she had a dorky side, too.

Unabashed, Tara pulled up a different program on the computer. "The tablets in front of you should already have this app installed. This is one of my favorite programs to use. It's customizable, user-friendly, and most importantly, free! You can pay for more features if you want, but the free account has everything you should need to get started with the basics."

She held up a piece of paper. "Also on your tables is a spec sheet that I created for a pretend company. This is what a client would send you when they're commissioning a graphic designer. Let's walk through what's on here, then I'll give you a crash course on the app. You'll have the rest of the time to work on a logo for this company, while I keep talking about the business stuff and answering questions. You'll have time to show off what you come up with at the end, but you don't have to share unless you want to. Sound good?"

The class nodded, already busy reading the spec sheets in front of them. Tara walked through the different notes she usually got from clients, highlighting a few requirements to watch out for. For someone who didn't do a lot of public speaking, Tara found her stride quickly. The earlier signs of her nerves vanished as Tara led the class like a natural, holding their attention and engaging them in turn.

Gabe sat quietly, arms crossed as he leaned back in his chair. The kids played around with the tablets as Tara walked them through different free or low-cost websites, where they could find commissions or manage their portfolios; she made sure to emphasize that they could be used for any creative medium, not only graphic design. They asked questions as she taught them ways to save money on printing costs, and the most reliable sites to buy refurbished technology and download free software.

Lily raised her hand, shyly. "Can we see your portfolio?" The youngest of the group, Gabe had a soft spot for her. Quiet and timid, she rarely spoke up in class.

Gabe hoped Tara would say yes; he hadn't found an excuse to see her work other than for the wedding, and the editing she did for Blanche, which was not exactly appropriate for the present audience.

Tara nodded, pulling up her website. "I focus on digital stuff, not physical mediums. Nothing wrong with painting or fiber arts or anything, but a laptop is easier to pack if you move around a lot, and it can be backed up in the cloud in case someone steals your shi—stuff."

She grinned apologetically at Gabe as the class laughed. Tara pulled up the graphic design page first, showing them how potential clients could view her work by product, or by industry. "So here are the brochures I've done, for example. Or you could change the view to see the products I've created for restaurants."

"Can we see your photography?" Lily asked.

Tara nodded, clicking through the menu. "I haven't done as much professional photography as Coop has, so I've filled in some gaps with photos I've taken for fun."

Gabe fought the urge to clarify his paid work was all nepotism, filling in for events at his parents' wedding venue, or for people in his mom's network who needed headshots. It wouldn't be a good example for the kids to minimize his work, even if he felt the comparison was undue. Tara's portfolio wasn't meager by any means, between the photos she'd taken of Antonio and Lee for their engagement, several shots of Confession's shows, and some—thankfully tame—photos of Blanche.

Syl whistled. "Damn Coop, you look good there!"

The class laughed. Gabe's cheeks burned when he found the photo of Hippo and him from two weeks ago. Tara had asked if she could use it, but being confronted with himself on screen, even with his features in shadow, was strange. She always managed to capture him in a way that hid all of his flaws. "Syl, watch your language, please."

Syl ignored him. "So how'd you get into all this shit anyway?"

Tara grinned. "I happened to sign up for an art program at MAI when I was getting my GED at the Eastside Community Center."

"No shit, for real?" Syl asked. "That's this program!"

Tara laughed. "Yup!"

"No wonder you're talking about free shit and getting your laptop lifted, if you lived over Eastside. Is that how you knew about the bridge, too?" Syl asked. "Did you stay at the camp?"

Gabe tensed, ready to change the subject. But Tara casually hopped up on the table, her legs swinging as she leaned back on her hands. "Yeah, from time to time. *All* my shit got dumped when they evicted it, including my old laptop. Had to take out a loan for a new one when I started at BCC. A harsh lesson in backing my shit up, so learn from my mistake."

"So you like, do okay for yourself?" Syl asked. "Like you make a living doing this?"

"I keep a few different gigs going at a time, but yeah." Tara nodded. "I eat every day. I paid my student loans off. I don't have my own place or anything, but I haven't moved in *five* years!"

The class oohed as if she had won the lottery. Bewildered as Gabe was by the shift in mood, the kids clearly resonated with Tara better than any other teacher they'd had. His mind churned with the humbling realization of just how out of touch he was with their experiences.

"Did you grow up in Eastside?" Lily asked.

Tara nodded. "Yeah, we stayed in the area. Mostly lived in my mom's car when I was young, but after it got stolen, we bounced between public housing, different shelters, and the encampment. My friend's aunt let me stay with her for a few years after we got banned from Saint Mary's, though, so that was cool."

"How did you get banned from Saint Mary's?!" Syl asked, incredulous. "It's a church shelter. I didn't know they could ban people from a *church*."

Tara snorted. "They can, and they did. It isn't safe anyway." She looked distant for a second, but before Gabe could say anything, she forced a smile. "Enough about me though, let's see what you all came up with! Who wants to go first?"

Syl's hand shot up, eager to show off. Tara critiqued his logo encouragingly, asking the other kids what they thought of it, what Syl liked most about it, or if he would change anything if he had more time. Every kid volunteered to share, even the shy ones like Lily.

Gabe sat quietly, mulling over his conflicting feelings, even as they gave him heartburn. It should have been obvious in hindsight how much the kids would resonate with someone who had experienced the same things they were. That Tara had opened up to them was astounding. She'd shared so much about herself, so much more of her history than he'd never dared to ask. Her quirks (her rules about food, her anxiety about money, her aversion to change) made so much more sense. That she'd trusted the class—trusted *him*—with these hidden parts of herself filled him with warmth, even as he wondered what else she might not yet trust him with.

"Coop, can she come back?" Syl asked him quietly, plugging in his tablet on the cart. The two-hour lesson had flown by.

"Yeah, if she wants to." Gabe nodded with a glance at Tara, who was showing Lily more of her portfolio.

"She will." Syl smirked. "Lucky for you. It was embarrassing for you to only ever bring your mom to class."

Gabe shot him a look but didn't say anything. Syl would ignore him anyway.

After the kids had filed out to catch the bus back to the community center, he and Tara pushed the technology carts back to the office.

"Thank you for today. You were amazing."

Tara blushed. "I was so nervous, and I blabbed a lot. I overshared way too much."

"No, you were great. They liked you," Gabe insisted, unlocking the storage closet and plugging in the carts to charge. "Honestly, I've never seen them so enthusiastic. Or heard Lily talk so much. I can't believe I'd never thought to invite alums from the program. I feel like an idiot for not looking for more artists from Eastside before."

Tara grinned. "Yeah, check your privilege, dude."

He shook his head with a snort. "What I'm trying to say is, they got a lot out of your class—*you* teaching them in particular."

Tara looked at her feet. "Honestly? So did I. I wasn't really planning on sharing that much, but I would have loved to hear that shit can turn out okay when I was them," Tara said softly. "No one really gets what it's like to live like that. Except Blanche and Lee, but even they had a stable home when they were young. My stability fits in a duffel bag."

Unsure how to respond, Gabe handed her an envelope from the admins desk. "Here, this is yours."

She pulled out the check with a frown. "Gabe, I can't take this."

He frowned back. "Why not?"

Tara huffed. "I share a little bit about my past, and suddenly you're throwing money at me? I don't need charity."

Gabe bit back his frustration at her habit of jumping to conclusions without giving him the chance to explain himself. Even now, he could see her gearing up for an argument. He touched her nose instead. "Pause, please? Tara, it's not charity. It's the normal stipend we give to all of our guest teachers. We pay experts for their time." He paused, giving her a moment to consider his words. "If you want to donate it back to the program, you certainly can, but accounting wrote this check for you last week. It has nothing to do with anything I learned about you today." Gabe touched her nose again. "Play."

Seemingly mollified, Tara stuffed the check back in the envelope and into her tote bag. "Fine, but this is really high for two hours of talking."

"It's not. Trust me." Gabe sat on the edge of the desk, eye level with her. Resisting the temptation to draw her close, Gabe tucked his hands under his thighs. "I was serious about how I've never seen the class open up like they did today. The kids like you. Syl even asked if you'd come back."

Tara stepped in between his legs, resting her head on his shoulder as she hugged him. "I'd like to come back. For free next time, though. It feels fucking weird to get paid for shit like this."

"I'd like that too." With a quiet sigh of relief, Gabe held her tight, hoping no employees would walk in. "Can I make you dinner tonight?"

She snorted. "Is this something else you do for all of the guest teachers? Did I steal Angie's thank you lunch?"

He huffed out a laugh; her obtuseness would be frustrating on anyone but Tara. "No. If it wasn't abundantly clear by now, I am asking you on a date." He tightened his grip around her waist, murmuring, "Spend the day with me, Kitten, let me make you dinner, and spend as much of the night with me as you want. And if you don't want it to be a date, well, consider it an early birthday present from a friend."

Her green eyes blinked up at him from his shoulder. "You remember everything."

"Just the important things, Kitten," he murmured into her hair, kissing her temple before he could overthink it.

"I need to set up the recording equipment for Blanche's session, but lucky for you, I need to be out of the house after that. So a dinner date sounds perfect."

"Can I help? I don't have any plans," Gabe offered, hoping he wasn't coming across as too clingy. But if Tara was willing to give him any of her time and attention, Gabe would cherish every minute between now and whenever she left tonight. Or perhaps tomorrow? "Other than grocery shopping," he blurted out. "I don't have any ingredients."

Tara's sweet smile laid all his worries to rest. "Let's make a day of it, then."

Chapter Twenty-One

Blanche

Figuring out how to sit in their own chair in their own home had never been so difficult. Blanche hovered, debating if they should sit like Real Blanche, draped over the arms; or like Work Blanche, sitting up straight with their feet flat on the floor. Eventually, because it was probably not reassuring to their newest clients that they were standing there staring at the chair, Blanche decided to sit cross-legged. "Did you fill out the forms I sent you?"

Huddled together on the couch, Richard and Sunny nodded, looking as tense as Blanche felt. Even though Blanche wasn't going to play with them, so there was really no reason for all three of them to feel like they were waiting for a root canal. Blanche's role was simply to facilitate negotiations, and use Richard and Sunny to record a tutorial. Richard passed them a checklist from his jacket pocket that listed their preferences, boundaries, and other information Blanche would put into their contract.

As uncomfortable as it was to have their real-life friends bleeding into their work life, Blanche was positively ecstatic that Sunny had asked them to help negotiate a roleplaying agreement. Sunny deserved to explore this side of her. And Richard, as stoic as he could be, would make a great dom: he maintained an inhuman level of self-control, and he was attuned to Sunny's whims and needs better than Sunny herself, in some ways.

Blanche skimmed the checklists, noting where they aligned and a few places where they didn't. Their boundaries and preferences were similar—always a good sign—though Sunny's pain appetite seemed significantly larger than Richard's willingness to inflict it. They looked up with what they hoped was a confident smile. "So, tell me about why you want to do this. What have you been feeling, or missing, that you think adding a dom/sub dynamic will help with?"

"Well!" Sunny flipped her hair over her shoulder, which immediately got Work Blanche's hackles up. Real Blanche didn't fight it; gauging how bratty Sunny might be would be helpful today. "We've been finding ourselves in patterns that feel wrong for us. Like, the social dysphoria has been real lately, and we end up crossing boundaries without checking in with each other. This seems like a fun and productive way to hash it out."

Blanche raised an eyebrow. It could be fun and productive. Or it could be a way to avoid their problems. "Can you give me an example?"

"Richard has a hard time communicating what he wants, and even when he gets fed up, he's too sweet." Sunny held up a finger as Richard opened his mouth. Work Blanche raised an eyebrow; Richard would definitely need to become a decent brat tamer. "I am a total snot to him sometimes, and he just accepts that!"

"Oh no, I'm too considerate." A smirk played at Richard's lips, even as a blush crept up his neck.

"Sarcasm isn't becoming, Dicky. I'm just saying, you can be more demanding. That's why I want us to have the space to do this!" Sunny rolled her eyes. Work Blanche added another strike to her brat meter. "Because I know I piss you off! I like annoying you, and you like being annoyed, but I feel bad because you just take it most of the time. This will give us space to have fun, without getting in the way of our real relationship!"

Blanche chose not to quibble about Sunny's use of "real," because their new dynamic would be just as real as the rest of their relationship. Instead, they noted that this separation seemed important to her. "And you, Richard?"

Richard's cheeks turned bright red. "I just want Sunny to clean her hair out of the shower. Well, I want her to listen when I ask her to do things the first time, so I don't feel like a nag. Because I *do* tell you what I want. *You* just don't listen." He shot her a look.

Sunny grinned back at him smugly.

Work Blanche added a tally to Sunny's punishments that they wouldn't be doling out themself. *Richard has the patience of a saint if he's lasted this long.* Real Blanche pushed aside their fondness for their friends, forcing Work Blanche to the surface to distill their desires and needs into something measurable and compatible. "So during this roleplaying, you want Richard to take more control, but in a way where he communicates what he wants clearly and assertively?"

"Well, I want that all the time, but yeah." Sunny nodded. "During the roleplay, I want him to follow through with consequences when I don't listen. Because I fully plan on not listening."

Blanche muffled a laugh. "And Richard, you want Sunny to listen and be more cooperative?"

Richard nodded. "More or less. Maybe more cooperative *outside* of the scene, because she's right that we tend to argue unnecessarily, and we usually resolve it with sex, which is perhaps not the most sustainable arrangement."

"Any hesitations or concerns that either of you are having?"

Richard chuckled dryly. "Just the moral repugnancy of being a privileged white man, who punishes his submissive Asian girlfriend if she doesn't clean the house well enough."

Sunny huffed. "We love each other and respect each other, and you *like* the idea of me cleaning your house in a cute little outfit, you *like* the idea of me blowing you under your desk while you're working, you *like* the idea of funishing me when I'm a snot. I want all of those things and more!" She crossed her arms. "This isn't a dynamic that we're adopting over our whole relationship. We're establishing a time and place to play around with it. And you *know* just because I want to act like a cute housewife doesn't mean I'm suddenly going to be submissive all the time. We're making space to explore what *we* want as individuals and as a couple."

Blanche snapped their fingers. "Tell him, Babygirl! Dominance and submission are all about exploring new ways to be intimate, of creating new ways to trust and communicate. The dominant is in control, but in a healthy partnership, the submissive holds all the power. Sure, some parts of your dynamics may be rooted in how you've been socialized to interact, but that can also be a way to break free of those norms."

Sunny nodded, taking Richard's hand. "I didn't punch that douchebag because you needed defending. I punched that douchebag because he was annoying and a threat that needed to be dealt with. That's my personality, not any vestigial sexist chivalry." She bit her lip and let out a quiet huff. "I worry that you're letting some unspoken expectations for how you should behave control your actions. Like, I have to be responsible all of the time because my family needs me to. With you, I can let go of all of that and just be me. And I want you to trust me like that too. Be the version of Richard that you keep hidden inside all of the time."

Blanche sipped their tea, waiting for Richard as he searched for his response.

Richard pulled her hand into his lap. "I do hold myself back. And I like taking care of you. I like that you treat me with the respect and trust that I wish the rest of the world did. And I like how you see right through my bullshit and call me out on it. As much as it pisses me off." He smiled at her fondly.

"You just hate admitting I'm right." Sunny kissed his cheek. "And I don't want to push you into anything that you're not comfortable with. Black Hawk had bad experiences being pushed into things he didn't consent to, and I don't want us to be like that. But I wouldn't be pushing so hard if I didn't think you wanted this too."

Blanche's brow furrowed. Black Hawk something or other sounded like the name on Gabe's account. The one he used to funnel money from his trust to help Blanche save up to get out of their contract, for Lee to save money for the wedding, and to Tara— Well, that reason had stayed unspoken, but Blanche paid her the bonuses all the same. Why would Sunny be referring to Gabe by his username?

Richard shot Sunny a look. "How is your *friend* anyway?"

Sunny smirked. "You're not jealous, are you?"

Oh, Sunny didn't know? Blanche bit back a laugh.

"What reason would I have to be jealous? You don't even know his real name." Richard shot back. "Although, I would prefer it if you didn't share details about our sex life with strangers on the internet."

"Dicky, we're literally about to record a scene and post it online." Sunny gave him a bemused smile. "We're way past moderate exhibitionism, and you're worried about a stranger having details about our sex life?"

"It's not really a scene," Blanche clarified. "More educational content."

"Can we not tell this particular stranger?" Richard pleaded.

"He's a subscriber to Blanche's channel, Dicky. He's probably gonna see it," Sunny teased. "But don't worry. He has no idea who I am IRL, and we're gonna have masks. He doesn't even know I know Blanche."

The lines between Work and Real life had bled into each other more than Blanche cared to admit. They'd never expected moving their work online would mean that their ducklings needed to support them so much, or for so long. But the more Tara and Lee helped, the more they learned, and the less confident Blanche became that they'd ever be able to do this without them. Which was not promising, considering their ducklings were increasingly busy with their lives. But Blanche had to trust their friends to support them, just like they'd trusted Blanche all these years. Vulnerability took strength, or whatever the fuck their therapist had been harping on.

Sunny's phone chimed. "Oh speak of the blue moon! He just messaged me." Sunny laughed. "Ooh, he asked the person he's been talking to on another date, and now he's panicking because he invited her over for dinner, but he doesn't know what to make."

"Risotto," Richard answered, too quickly for Sunny's Black Hawk to be anyone but Gabe.

"Isn't risotto hard as shit to make?" Sunny asked. "Are you trying to make him look bad?"

He shook his head. "Trust me, risotto."

Sunny made a face. "You've never made *me* risotto."

"I can't cook it, but *Gabe* has a good recipe." Richard looked expectantly at Sunny.

She shrugged. "I don't know what Gabe has to do with it, but fine, I'll recommend risotto."

Blanche raised an eyebrow in a silent question to Richard. Coincidentally, Gabe had invited Tara over for dinner tonight.

Richard nodded and made an exasperated gesture to Sunny, who typed away on her phone.

"Oh, he says thanks for the idea. I guess he does know how to make it."

Blanche hid their grin behind the checklist, pretending to read the notes they'd been scribbling in the margin. "So, housewife roleplay sounds like a good fit, at least at the beginning. Maybe start with one evening after work. Take it in stages to get a feel for how the scene flows. So, Sunny, you wear a cute outfit for him and clean the house or whatever he asks. Richard, boss her around, make her do whatever you fantasize about, tell her what a good little wife she's being. Then bring her pleasure and pain into it. Reward her if she's good, punish her if she's been bratty, just give her feedback as you go.

"For example, make her count out loud how many funishments she's earned. Warn her if she's getting close to a real punishment, that sort of thing." Blanche tapped the papers against the coffee table. "As you get more into it, you can incorporate the funishments into the scene. But since you're just starting off, I'd cordon it off into its own phase, until you're both more comfortable in your roles. Ease into the headspaces and see how it goes. Always discuss the scene first and take care of each other afterward. Cuddle, kiss, tell each other how much you love each other, that sort of thing. Does that sound like a good place to start?"

With nods of approval from Richard and Sunny, Blanche opened their laptop to fill in their standard contract, index fingers pecking away at the keyboard one at a time.

"Oh my god, Blanche, just tell me what to type." Sunny pulled the laptop from them, exasperated. "We're going to be here all day with your chicken pecking. I wanna get to the fun part!"

BLANCHE SQUINTED AT THE camera, then at the laptop, and back at the camera, checking everything was recording. They didn't want to take any chances, so they triple-checked every time. Tara always teased them for how much time Blanche spent on it, threatening to make a compilation video of Blanche squinting at the camera. Blanche took the teasing in stride, playing it up to give Tara more content in case she did. "This seems on."

"Want me to check?" Sunny offered, tying a red lace mask behind her high ponytail. Her short black dress would cover everything that Sunny wanted to be covered, but revealed everything she was comfortable with to the internet.

"Please." Blanche stepped aside, pulling on a velvet dressing gown. They had acquired a wide variety of outfits for roleplaying, finding a niche with roleplaying authority figures, much like the priest they played for their patron. When the scenes were sexual, they'd disrobe to reveal something a bit more racy underneath (lately, something sponsored by fetishwear sites). But this wasn't their conventional recording; coaching Richard and Sunny would be positively tame. They could almost be Real Blanche, and wasn't that a thought?

Blanche hoped the more educational twist to their normal content would go over well with their audience. They were growing weary of the usual Judge or Professor shtick. Maybe if this was successful, they could move more into domming couples who wanted to play together. Then they could skip the Viagra that gave them migraines, except on the rare occasion Real Blanche truly wanted to.

Richard bent down next to Sunny to inspect the laptop, looking classy as usual—barely revealing his neck with his top button undone under his slim-line black suit. His black leather mask made him look somehow more imposing and serious than usual.

"I think we're good," Sunny said, looking more at Richard than the technology. "The mics are good, and all three cameras are feeding."

"Thank you, Babygirl. Go kneel on your mark, hands behind your back. Tits up, now!" Blanche gestured to a spot of tape on the floor. "Richard, sit in that chair behind her and try to look relaxed. Manspread more than usual."

Blanche turned to the camera, pulling their Work Blanche persona on with their "Professor" glasses, letting the dominant performer wash over them fully. Wearing Work Blanche without digging into their anger was almost unnerving. Blanche was not normally a soft domme, but then again, they normally didn't play with their friends. Today was mere instruction.

They looked into the camera with their best flirty smile. "I have a special treat for my lovely subscribers today. Many have asked how to do scenes yourselves at home, or how to introduce kink to your partners. I am joined by two baby kinksters, just starting their dom/sub partnership, to show you how you can get started with impact play and knotwork, getting into a roleplaying headspace, and the basics of navigating through scenes. As always, we already discussed the scene and tools we're playing with, our boundaries and safewords, and all of us have consented freely without influence or coercion." Blanche pointed to the air next to them as they spoke. Tara would fill in the words on the screen.

I really need to pay her and Lee more. Beyond Gabe's financial support, a good chunk of the comments and tips were because of the snarky captions, or sound effects, that Tara and Lee were adding. Blanche's CPA often scolded them for not paying better wages, but Tara argued every time Blanche gave her a bonus. Lee, thankfully, did not, but that could change after the wedding.

"These lovelies came to me for help to establish healthy boundaries and ideas for how they can use kink to improve their relationship in and out of the bedroom. It's such a wonderful idea, I've added a virtual session with you and your partner, or partners, to help negotiate a contract to my tip menu. This is, of course, in addition to the checklists and blank contracts that are always available for free here." Blanche pointed again to the air in front of them. Tara would put a link in the general vicinity or at least in the caption. "Before we get to all of the fun toys I'm going to show you today, let me introduce our players. Bunny here," Blanche gestured to Sunny kneeling patiently behind them, "has some bratty tendencies and bad habits. Mr. Robot wants to train her into a good little wife, but he will respect my authority today. Isn't that right?"

"Yes, Professor," both Sunny and Richard replied.

Blanche grinned as Richard muttered "Mr. Robot?" under his breath. "In addition to better communication issues, adding BDSM to a relationship can deepen trust and emotional intimacy, bring you higher energy and lighter emotions, and better understanding of each other's moods. Especially body language." Blanche winked. "For subs, you might also grow in mindfulness and focus, and improve impulse control if you have bad habits you want to break. For doms, your concentration, goal setting, self-awareness, and risk management are all skills you'll practice through dominating a partner. I'll link the research for the mental and physical benefits below."

It was a nice change—to wink at and flirt with the camera. Being angry and controlling all the time was exhausting. Especially since many clients were actually decent people these days, and Blanche actually liked them (other than one major red flag they couldn't escape because he paid the rent).

"BDSM partnerships are about trust. You need to support one another, and be there for each other, take care of each other. Trust in each other and yourselves to know your limits and communicate them. Dom/sub relationships aren't necessarily sexual; it's about one person freely handing someone else control, and that person guiding them to be their ideal self."

Blanche beckoned to Richard, who rose and stood on the mark next to them. They guided him through finding a tone of voice specifically for directing Sunny, hand signals they could use, and how to safely use cuffs and ropes to bind her.

Moving under a different camera, Blanche demonstrated a close-up of the handcuff knot (not that Richard needed the instruction, based on how deft his knotwork was). Sunny played up the brattiness a few times, and without prompting, Richard threatened to gag her if she kept interrupting. Sunny eagerly shut her mouth. They walked them through the different types of floggers, paddles, and crops, along with the best techniques for each one.

"Dicky, I love this," Sunny sighed dreamily, when Richard checked in as he practiced on her butt and thighs with a flogger, tickling her more than anything. Her skin was already bright red from the paddle.

Blanche made a mental note to have Tara edit his name out. Again. And to remind Sunny to find a different nickname for scenes. And for Richard to train her to use it. Outside of a full-time dynamic, they would need a sense of separation. The nicknames would help keep the scenes from leaking by accident. Or on purpose, at their discretion. Blanche would remind them later; Sunny was halfway to subspace, so there was no point in talking about it now.

Blanche turned to Richard, who stood straight with a crooked smile on his face, and asked, "And what are you feeling right now?"

"Honored that she trusts me with herself like this. Proud that I'm the one who gets to make her happy," Richard said softly, love clear in his voice.

Work Blanche was losing the battle to stay present against Real Blanche's delight for their friends. *Time to wrap this up. This seems like a cute spot to end.*

"Let's give these lovebirds some alone time to continue playing and do their aftercare in private, shall we? Let your imagination take over what happens next, my lovely subscribers. I hope you enjoyed today's tutorial, and let me know if you want me to make more content like this." Blanche smiled serenely at the camera again. "Remember, kink is about more than sex or control. Like any relationship, there's a give and take of power, rooted in trust and awareness. You must know yourself, trust yourself, so you can give all of you to someone else. Until next time!"

After a brief pause, Blanche turned off the cameras and microphones. "I will leave the two of you alone to play. I'll come back with some aftercare stuff in, let's say, thirty minutes? Sunny, remember the walls are thin."

Sunny hummed, still tied to the bench with a dreamy smile.

Grabbing the laptop, Blanche closed the door behind them. They settled their headphones over their ears (assuming Sunny would disregard their reminder) and set about copying the footage onto Tara's external hard drive. Blanche might still feel like a dinosaur around technology, but Tara had managed to teach them how to back up files at least.

While the data loaded and water boiled in the kettle, Blanche measured out the loose-leaf tea from Jazz to drink after sessions. After the first few days of gagging on the soapy smell and bitter grassy flavor, Blanche didn't mind the taste now. And they hadn't experienced a bad drop in weeks, only minor headaches after sessions. It was strange, not constantly worrying about the sudden rushes of guilt and self-loathing that came with the migraines. Normally, they were overwhelmed into a catatonia eased only by weed.

As the tea steeped, and the Smashing Pumpkins floated through the headphones, Blanche paced behind the couch, feeling odd about not lighting a preroll. But the tea was soothing, and the scene had barely required Work Blanche at all.

Checking that they still had plenty of time, Blanche gathered the candy, aloe, and a fuzzy blanket they'd guessed Sunny would like. Strange to think how far Sunny had come from the socially awkward, shy girl Blanche had met years ago. She'd taken control of her life and transformed into a confident, assertive young woman. Just as Blanche knew she would, with the right person to encourage her.

Their stomach twisted, souring at the reminder that they hadn't been able to help Sunny as much as Richard could. While Blanche was proud of her, the reminder that Blanche was stuck—still drowning in painful memories, still dependent on their asshole of a patron, still unsure of who they were without Daisy—left a bitter taste in their mouth.

But, if Blanche could be honest with themself, were they really stuck?

They took a long sip and let the earthy tea wash away their sourness. Blanche had come a long way, too—despite their many unsuccessful attempts at therapy thus far, and this Phineas character pointing out that even if they broke the contract, Covey would still have a stake in Confession. Maybe all the time and emotional energy they'd spent on this internet stuff would pay off, and they could help more couples like Richard and Sunny.

They paused. Maybe they could somehow get their patron into a similar agreement with his wife. Mrs. Covey had made a mess of her attempt to get him to leave Blanche before, but perhaps with a united front, and her cooperation to get Covey out of Confession... Things with Tara and Gabe were going well; risking the roof over their head for Confession's sake didn't sound as risky as it should.

Still nursing their tea, Blanche pulled out their phone to text Mrs. Covey.

I have an idea.

CHAPTER TWENTY-TWO

TARA

TARA COULDN'T RECALL THE last time she had this much fun doing such normal shit. After she and Gabe had made preparing Blanche's set into a game, they'd gone grocery shopping. Gabe had talked shit about Tara for not knowing what half the ingredients were. Tara had talked shit right back for shopping at a bougie-ass store that charged ten bucks for a tiny box of crackers that tasted like paper, and teased him even harder when Gabe admitted he never looked at the prices.

They'd gone for a walk with Hippo after, strolling around a nearby park. Anytime Gabe didn't need two hands for Hippo, one of his found hers. It was incredibly domestic. Comfortable. So easy that Tara had to remind herself not to get complacent as she turned on her favorite playlist on Gabe's phone, while he hung up Hippo's leash. The ingredients for their dinner were scattered across the kitchen island, a mess of fresh ingredients and dried goods Tara had only seen on cooking shows. All of it a visual reminder that she had no idea what she was doing here.

She should feel uncomfortable. From starting off the day talking about Saint Mary's (a place she usually tried to drive out of her mind) to giving a presentation about her "career" like a professional (she usually worked in bed), the day had been full of things that should have been hard. She should want to escape into her bed and wrap herself in the weighted blanket Gabe had given her. But she'd enjoyed every moment.

All day, her hard feelings had stayed in check more easily than she'd ever expected.

"So, this might be a little presumptuous, but I got stuff for cheesecake." Gabe scooped Hippo's food into the bowl and set it in front of him.

Tara's mouth fell open in delight. "What's presumptuous about that? I love cheesecake."

He hesitated. "It needs time to set."

"Yeah, I'm not great with delayed gratification, but cheesecake is worth it." Tara shrugged.

Gabe ran a hand through his hair, fingers catching in a snarl. "Like, overnight."

"Oh." Tara blinked. The quietest whisper of dread curled in her stomach.

Hippo scarfing down his food filled the uneasy silence.

Gabe gently worked the snarl out of his curls, shifting his weight back and forth on his feet. "I meant what I said earlier, you tell me when you want to go home. If that's before the cheesecake is ready, bring it home with you. But you're welcome to stay as long as you like."

"I didn't bring anything to stay overnight." Tara fiddled with a hangnail. Her duffel bag was under her bed at Blanche's apartment. But maybe one night wouldn't matter. She'd stopped bringing it with her everywhere after the first year at Blanche's, and it'd been fine. Her bag would still be safe for one night, just like it had been every night for the last six years. Blanche's apartment would still be home tomorrow. But Tara's stomach turned. "Can I think about it?"

"Of course. I didn't mean to—"

"You're not pressuring me, Coop." Tara shook her head with a smile, sliding her arms around his waist. "Just...let's play it by ear. I appreciate you making me cheesecake either way."

"Oh, *I'm* not making it." Gabe kissed her forehead. "*We're* making it. Together."

Tara hummed skeptically. As much as she loved cooking shows, being faced with confusing ingredients and a recipe she couldn't decipher made her skin prickle with shame.

One dimple appeared as Gabe snorted. "Stop overthinking. You're gonna start by smashing graham crackers with a rolling pin."

"Hell yeah!" Tara laughed in relief. "That I can do."

Gabe instructed her on what he called the "foolproof" steps as they worked, like mixing the graham cracker crumbs with butter, or pouring the ingredients he measured into the mixer. Tara tried to pay attention to Gabe reciting the ingredients and measurements from memory. But his outbursts of singing along to the pop music—and his carefree dancing—were more than a little distracting.

Gabe turned off the mixer. "You have to close your eyes for this part."

"Why?" Tara asked suspiciously as she carefully molded tinfoil around the pan.

"This is the step that sets the Cooper family recipe apart from the rest." Gabe pulled an immersion blender from the cabinet.

She laughed. "Dude, I don't remember anything you've told me. Like, I cracked eggs, but I could not tell you how many. Your secret is safe with me."

"All the same, eyes closed. Better yet, turn around." Gabe spun her around with firm hands on her shoulders and a kiss on the back of her neck. "No peeking."

"How do you keep this all in your head?" Tara covered her eyes with her hands as he fussed behind her, opening containers and unscrewing what sounded like a glass jar with a metal lid. "Don't most people need to write all this down?"

"You know how I mentioned my parents were busy a lot when I was a kid? Well, Tonio told my parents about my self-harm when we were teenagers, and it was kind of a wake-up call to my parents that maybe they should be more present. That started what felt like forced quality time then, which at first, I resented. But it was actually really good for us as a family. Like, my dad started taking me with him to the vineyard and powwows and stuff, and we volunteered at the art museum as a family, which is how my mom ended up on the board." Gabe chuckled softly as the spatula scraped against the mixing bowl. "Cooking was how my mom and I connected when she wasn't at the vineyard. She learned how to cook and bake from her nanny growing up."

"I thought this was the Cooper secret family recipe, handed down from generation to generation, not from the nanny," Tara teased. She tried not to think too hard about how different Gabe's childhood was from her own—let alone his mother's, who had been well-off enough to have a nanny. Tara's bonding activity with her mother had been packing her abscesses. Lee had only learned about her self-harm after Auntie

Alitrice's death, once Tara had stopped. No one had noticed the lines on her hips when they were newly made.

Gabe chuckled. "Well, I am only the second generation of Cooper, so technically, it has passed from generation to generation. Neither of my parents wanted to keep their last name when they got married, so they picked a new one."

"Why not?" Tara sniffed, eyes still closed, as the scent of almonds reached her.

"Neither of them really identified with their last names. Dad's was changed by the government to erase his tribal connections, and Mom's parents only remembered she existed when it made them look good. So, basically, her nanny was her family." Gabe paused, then added, "Sorry. It's about to get loud."

The immersion blender buzzed behind her, suctioning and slurping whatever Gabe was blending. When it finally shut off, Gabe banged it against the mixing bowl.

"Okay, you can look now."

Tara turned to find Gabe rinsing the blender under the sink. Before he could wash the tall measuring cup he'd used to blend the secret ingredients, she swiped a taste with two fingers. The creamy tang had that grounding note that was so familiar, but she still couldn't identify it. "Wait, this is the flavor I always ask about! You've never told me what it is!"

Gabe nodded, smirking as his eyes flicked to her mouth; she was still sucking on her fingers. "Yeah, kind of the point of a secret ingredient."

With a huff of annoyance, Tara held the mixing bowl so Gabe could pour the batter into the pan. He put her in charge of setting the timer once the pan was in the oven, and poured her a glass of wine to keep her busy while he did the dishes. Perched on the counter of the island, she sipped the dry white wine.

"For dinner, I'm making chicken with marsala risotto."

"Sounds fancy."

Gabe shrugged. "It's more fussy than fancy."

"My idea of fancy is baking the chicken nuggets instead of microwaving them."

With a snort, Gabe flicked water at her before drying his hands. "Do none of you know how to cook?"

Tara shook her head. "Sunny tried to teach me how to make a stir-fry once, but she's not very good at cooking either, and it burned while we were arguing, so we ordered pizza. Lee has learned some since moving in with Tonio. Or at least he can reheat whatever food they have."

"Half of what they eat is made by Tonio's stepdad, and the other half is made by me." Gabe snorted, lifting her off the counter by the hips. He kissed her cheek and turned to wipe down the surface. "Sorry, I need the space to mise en place."

Tara flushed hot as she caught herself against the edge, dizzy from his casual affection and manhandling. "Which means..."

"Mise en place is to prepare everything you'll need in arm's reach, before you start cooking. Risotto requires a lot of attention at the stove, so dicing and measuring everything ahead of time is less stressful," Gabe explained as he changed the music. The upbeat top-forty pop was replaced with mid-2000s R&B.

"Having everything in a packet is even less stressful."

"How's your knife handling skills?" Gabe asked, pulling a massive wooden cutting board out from under the counter.

"Is that a euphemism?" She winked.

Gabe laughed. "That bad, huh?"

Tara shrugged. "One time I saw a video about adding green onion and shit to ramen. When I tried to do it, the cutting board went flying and the knife barely missed my foot."

Gabe raised his eyebrows. "Okay, yeah, that's bad. Here, I'll show you." Effortlessly, he cut an onion in half, peeling it and slicing it over and over nearly to the root in tiny cuts. "The outer layers come off easier after you cut it, and the root will hold it together while you dice it. Hold it by your fingertips and move your fingers back as you cut, so you keep control without accidentally cutting yourself." His fingers and knife flew, turning a whole onion into tiny cubes within seconds. "Here, your turn." Gabe handed Tara the knife and retrieved a towel full of mushrooms he'd washed earlier. "These need to be cut into thin slices."

She attempted to slice the mushroom cap evenly, but ended up with a mess of different angles and thicknesses.

"Here, hold it like this." Gabe pushed her pointer finger around the handle, instead of over the top of the blade. He handed her another mushroom and moved behind her, placing his hands over hers. "Steady the end of the knife on the cutting board."

"Oh, I see what's happening," Tara teased, leaning into the heat of his body. "This is an elaborate scheme to get in my pants."

"Is it working?" Gabe asked quietly. The resonance of his deep voice, so close to her ear, flooded through her.

"Yes," Tara replied honestly.

"Good to know. Although I was only intending to show you basic kitchen safety." Gabe planted a kiss behind her ear. "Knife handling is very important, Kitten."

She shivered. Before she could suggest maybe dinner could wait, he stepped away to clip some herbs from the pots lining the patio door. Tara shook herself, focusing on cutting the mushrooms, not her fingers. Once the mushrooms were neat in their designated bowl, Tara slowly minced fresh rosemary, sage, and garlic as Gabe worked around her. The knife in her hand and her movements were awkward. But Gabe's teaching style of letting her be awkward without comment (other than the occasional flirting) put her more at ease than Sunny's impatient teasing.

The aroma of herbs and onion, mushroom and chicken soon filled her nose. Hippo wandered over from his bed, begging politely. Tara knew better by now not to give him anything; Hippo, much like herself, was relentless in his pursuit of snacks.

Tara kept telling herself this was too easy; something would go wrong, or they'd argue. But the conversation flowed as smoothly as the silences. The teasing stayed lighthearted, veering safely away from difficult topics. They still had the same affectionate chemistry, shameless innuendo, and heated glances as always, but it stayed light. Fun.

As he turned off the stove, Gabe enthusiastically burst into off-key singing at Ashanti's part of "Always on Time." Dragging Tara around the kitchen as he danced, his hands stayed firmly on her hips. Laughter rang out as she gave up trying to keep up with him. He picked her up instead, spinning them around.

"It's a good thing you're a better cook than you are a singer," Tara teased as she sat down with her plate, trying to catch her breath. She couldn't keep the smile off her face. For as much shit as she'd talked about Lee and Sunny being lovedrunk fools, the happiness they'd found in their partners had made her burn with envy and longing.

And now, here was Gabe, more carefree than ever, and Tara felt lighter than she ever had. Feeling this happy should be dangerous, but Tara couldn't bear to dim it. Not yet.

"Agreed. Tonio was always the singer." With a grin, Gabe flicked off the overhead light, plunging the room into the dim light of dusk. "But at least I can dance."

"Angie did mention you were always a good dancer." Tara's eyes followed him as he lit the candles in the center of the table.

"Oh no, have you two been talking about me?" Gabe winced, refilling her wineglass before finally sitting down next to her. "What did she say? Anything bad?"

"She texted me a couple of stories in between flower updates," Tara smirked. "I'm supposed to ask about ice cream sundaes."

"Please, don't ask." His brown eyes begged.

"Come on, Coop. Let's hear it." Tara sipped from her half-full glass, rolling the dry smooth burn of the white wine over her palate.

"Angie has a death wish." He groaned. "So, you know how in high school, Tonio and I..."

Tara nodded. "'Glorified fuck buddies' is how Tonio put it."

"Right. I made a—in hindsight, very cringe—joke about my dick being his dessert once at one of his sister's birthdays. He got this idea to steal the toppings from the ice cream sundae bar. Chocolate syrup, whipped cream, sprinkles, cherries—all this messy, sticky stuff. And I was game, until he started covering *all* of me in this, not just my dick." Gabe shook his head and gestured to his chest. "You think I'm hairy now? This is carefully groomed. I was much hairier back then."

Tara laughed, too enthralled with his story to split her attention with the food in front of her. "You're not *that* hairy."

"That's because I wax regularly." Gabe took a bite of his risotto. "Long story short, I tried to sneak—in the middle of a birthday party, remember—to the bathroom to wash all that shit off me, because Tonio decided he'd rather *not* eat my chest hair. And I ran smack into Angie, tripped and fell on *top* of her, covering her with chocolate syrup and whipped cream and sprinkles, all while completely naked."

Shaking with laughter, Tara wiped her eyes. "I need to thank her!"

"Please don't encourage her." Gabe shook his head. "That's the last time I ever made that joke—I don't want a repeat of picking sprinkles out of my pubes."

"So what you're saying is if I want to play with food, *I'm* dessert."

"Exactly." Gabe's embarrassed grin turned flirtatious.

"What a shame. I like food." Tara winked as she finally took a bite of the risotto. She moaned as she savored the herby, umami richness. "This is delicious! Sometimes, it's like my only skill is eating. Because I have no idea how you made something so heavenly as this, and I was here."

"That's not true, and you know it." Gabe looked at her softly as she shoveled the risotto in her mouth. "You were great at teaching the class today. And I was really impressed with your portfolio—you're talented."

"I wasn't looking for validation, but thank you." She nudged his foot. "You know, I earned more today in a few hours than I do from a lot of my commissions, and it didn't feel like work."

Gabe frowned as he hooked his feet around her ankle. "Not to tell you how to run your business, but I'd raise your commission prices. You should be paid significantly more for your quality of work."

Tara shrugged, a little embarrassed. But thankfully with no traces of the fear that normally accompanied their conversations about money. She swallowed. "I don't want to turn down work. A small customer now might be a bigger project later."

"Again, your business, your decision. But you have years of experience and a solid portfolio that you didn't have when you started out. You don't want to be a broke ass forever." Gabe's voice was teasing, but his brown eyes were thoughtful.

"Hey, I'm not a broke ass anymore!" Tara said smugly around a mouthful of risotto. "You've seen how good my ass looks now that I'm eating regularly."

"That isn't exactly a sign of luxury, Kitten." Thankfully, Gabe only teased her. Instead of giving her the pity she expected, his confused face was a mix of affection, and mild disgust for her poor table manners.

"Whatever, Investment Banker. Maybe you should be a life coach instead." Tara laughed, covering her full mouth when she spoke this time, for the sake of Gabe's snobbery. "Whatever happened to the guy who called me a fucking bitch two years ago?"

They both winced, but Gabe spoke before Tara could walk back her careless words.

"That guy called his therapist the next morning. He's had a lot of breakthroughs since then," Gabe said, softly adding, "But for what it's worth, I am sorry. I've never really handled rejection well, but especially then, I had no business setting myself up for it. I took it too personally when you turned me down, but you were honest and up-front with me. Not many people have given me that much consideration." He looked down at his plate, stirring the risotto he had barely eaten.

Tara took a slow sip of her wine, before admitting, "It wasn't personal. I was starting to dissociate and felt a panic attack coming on. Flight instinct kicked in." At his sympathetic look, she quickly added, "Not that I would have given you a chance anyway." She looked down at her own plate, mostly empty but for a few mushrooms she couldn't bring herself to eat.

Gabe slid his plate in front of her and speared the mushrooms for himself.

She shot him a grin and shoveled a forkful of his risotto in her mouth. "Honestly, it wasn't until after Lee met Tonio that I even considered trying to give *anyone* a chance. I thought I'd be fine alone with Lee forever, until I saw how happy he was with Tonio."

"To growth, then." Gabe raised his glass.

Tara clinked her glass against his. His soft brown eyes stayed on hers as they sipped their wine.

Jeremih's "Birthday Sex" effectively shattered the tension. They both laughed awkwardly as Tara scraped the last of the risotto off Gabe's plate.

"On that note, happy early birthday. And since your cheesecake won't be ready until the morning, allow me to make up for my poor planning. Let me take care of you tonight." Gabe took her hand and kissed her fingers gently.

As his lips captured her fingertips, Tara's heart quivered and heat flooded between her thighs. "Are you volunteering to be dessert again?"

Gabe laughed. "Not literally."

"Shame, but since I can't have cheesecake..." She shrugged with a smile. "Should we clean up first?"

He shook his head. "*I'll* clean up first, Kitten. Not you. It's your almost-birthday dinner."

"You already made me cook, I can help clean up." Tara picked up their empty plates, but Gabe stopped her with a look and took the dishes from her.

"How about you take the wine into the bedroom, and I'll join you shortly?" He kissed her cheek, murmuring in that deep timbre, "Think about everything you want me to do to you while you wait."

She bolted out of her chair with a grin, grabbing the wineglasses and the half-empty bottle. "Hurry, or I'll start without you."

With his laughter and promising smirk behind her, Tara practically skipped down the hallway. Visions flowed through her mind of him fucking her mouth, of a dildo in her ass (or maybe his) while she rode him, of him slowly fucking her while they passionately kissed—

The last fantasy stopped her with a chill. It was terrifying how much she wanted to kiss him like that. Not a mere cowardly peck while he slept, like she had dared to do a year ago.

She wanted to give him all of her, to claim him in return. To feel his cum drip out of her cunt. To leave marks all over his body, and hold his hand in front of their friends while he called her Kitten. To sit in his lap and kiss him slowly. Tara never thought she'd want that with anyone, but with Gabe? She wanted it—wanted *him*—desperately.

Yet the idea of any tongue forcing its way into her mouth still sent a trickle of cold fear down her spine. The memory of blood and screaming and the sickening thud—Tara shuddered, forcing that memory away. She wasn't ready. Not just for the kiss, either. Gabe would probably tell her it was totally fine if she never kissed him. The fear of letting someone else know her vulnerabilities—seeing her at her weakest as only Lee had—was paralyzing.

Tara's gut twisted. A sweetheart like Gabe deserved someone who could give him their whole selves. Someone who could be what he needed and kiss him freely. Not someone who let fear control them. Tara couldn't even *talk* about her past, couldn't even spend the night, couldn't even kiss him. How could she ever be enough for Gabe?

As she set the wine on the bedside table, Tara breathed deeply, putting those fears and doubts away. For now, she would enjoy what they had: the chance to be close with him in ways she had never expected she could with anyone. They both wanted this, and he was giving her space to figure out what she could give. Gabe hadn't run out of patience with her yet. Hopefully, she could eventually meet him halfway, and he would still want her. However long that took.

Undressing slowly, Tara did her best to process the flurry of confused feelings before Gabe joined her. With a sigh, she reluctantly closed the box in her mind that contained all of the soft feelings she had for Gabe, along with her fear and hurt. Fantasizing about him was safe, so she did that. This time she dreamed of all the sounds Gabe would make, if he didn't hold himself back this time.

CHAPTER TWENTY-THREE

GABE

Gabe froze, arrested by the sight of Tara spread out across his bed. Her chest was flushed and heaving, slim fingers slipping past the auburn curls between her thighs. Leaning against the door, he closed it quietly behind him, adjusting his hardening cock. Blood thrumming under his skin, he committed the sight of her back arched and eyes screwed shut to memory, before clearing his throat. "You actually started without me."

"You took too long." With a grin, Tara parted her legs, making him salivate for her wet cunt spread open for him. "Get over here, gorgeous."

Ignoring the flush of warmth from the compliment, Gabe crawled over her, licking a stripe up her neck. He murmured low into her ear, "I'm yours. How do you want me?"

Tara hissed as he dragged a hand down her hip to draw her legs around his waist, kissing her down her neck. "I want you to fuck my mouth—and before you get all weird about it, yes, that means I want you choking me with your dick and coming down my throat."

Gabe snorted as his tongue circled her nipple; of course she knew what he'd been about to say.

Tara's legs tightened around him as her back arched. "And then you're going to eat me out until you're ready to fuck me again. I want it slow and sweet for as long as you possibly can."

Gabe groaned against her freckled skin. He'd fuck her for the rest of their lives if she let him. "Condom or no?"

Her chuckle was sardonic. "If I say no, are you going to do that thing where you're not really with me?"

Confused, Gabe pulled back. "What do you mean?"

Her green eyes didn't quite meet his as Tara's fingers traced his ear. "Last time, it's like you weren't here until after I finished. I don't know if you were trying not to come or what, but I want you fully present this time. Not avoiding eye contact and quiet."

"Sorry, I didn't think it was noticeable. I can be more present." Gabe kissed her wrist. "But for the record, getting a blow job before you come at all feels wrong."

"Hey, it's my almost-birthday," Tara laughed, her pink nipples shaking with her. "I want to suck you off. Now get naked!"

Gabe kissed down her body before climbing off the bed, relishing how comfortable he was with her. A year ago, he couldn't bear to have anyone—especially her—see him naked. Now he stripped his clothes off, enjoying the burn of her gaze on his back as he tossed them onto the chair.

When he turned around, Tara was kneeling on the edge of the bed. Her lips were parted in a hungry gaze as she touched herself. He stood in front of her and waited, fighting his self-consciousness as she openly admired him. No matter how much he worked out, or how many compliments his friends gave him, even Tara's obvious appreciation couldn't quell his insecurity. When Gabe looked in the mirror, he still saw the hurt, angry boy who was the butt of every joke. Still heard his ex's sigh of disappointment when he didn't measure up to her standards.

Tara pulled him back to the present as she rose up on her knees to suck his neck. Wrapping his arms around her waist to pull her tight against him, Gabe sighed contentedly. He closed his eyes, while she nibbled and licked and sucked the sensitive skin below his jaw. Tara could leave hickeys all over; he'd proudly wear every mark.

Her green eyes sparkled with amusement as she traced his lips with fingers that were still wet from her cunt. He sucked them into his mouth with a groan. The taste, the smell of her, drove him wild. His cock twitched against her, aching for more than her hip. Gabe craved to be devoured by her, to feast upon her in return, until they were consumed in each other completely.

Hands tightening around her waist, he moaned around her fingers again as she took his cock in hand, stroking it slowly. His urge to take control, to touch her in return, was only overcome by how heavenly her tight grip felt around his shaft. Her mouth trailed down his chest to lap at his nipple, teasing him with each lick.

Gabe fisted her hair to hold her there a moment longer, earning him a hum of approval against his sensitive skin. Her lips seared a line down his stomach; he had to clench to stifle the urge to buck his hips. The sight of her so close to his dick made him dizzy. Gabe was so hard it hurt.

Tara scooted back on the bed, bringing her head down until she was at eye level with his cock. Her hand wrapped around the root, she looked up at him with those stunning eyes before she kissed the tip.

Gabe's grip returned to her hair, fighting for some semblance of self-control. Eyes bright with desire, Tara swirled her tongue around the head as curses left his lips. His voice cut off in a strangled moan when she swallowed him down as far as she could. "I'm not going to last if you keep that up."

"Good," she said, muffled around the head of his cock. His stomach clenched as wet heat swallowed the sensitive tip. Her lips met her hand, pumping in time. Her throat constricted around him as she choked, her green eyes watering until she was forced to pull back to catch her breath. "You're not supposed to last. Just enjoy this."

Gabe groaned as she sucked him hard again. He lost control of his hips, yanking her hair tight as he bucked into her mouth. "Shit, sorry."

She moaned in response, giving him a single tap to his inner thigh. *Green.*

"Are you sure?" Gabe's voice came out more like a whimper.

With a baleful look, Tara pulled away. "What part of 'I want to choke on your dick' and 'just enjoy this' was unclear?"

Gabe swallowed hard, his self-control cracking. He always tried so hard to not hurt people, to please them exactly how they wanted, and here she was, *asking* him to lose control. "Fine, but tap twice if I get too rough. Your mouth feels fucking amazing, Kitten. I don't know if I can hold back."

Tara wet her fingers with spit. "Good! Don't. I get off on feeling like I might die, remember?"

With a reluctant grumble that quickly devolved into a string of unintelligible curses, Gabe fucked her mouth as he held her hair tight, careful not to push too far. At least until Tara's hand slid around to his ass, encouraging him to thrust harder. He snapped his hips with more force than he'd dared in years, holding her tight against him until she gagged, sure that would be the end of it.

But when he let her up, Tara was laughing deliriously, eyelashes damp. Drool dripped from her smile before she sucked him greedily again.

With a feverish laugh that devolved into encouraging babble, Gabe stopped holding back, fucking her throat in earnest. When her fingers trailed up to his asshole, he spread his legs, groaning her name as she rubbed circles around the sensitive nerves. Her thumb pressed upward into his perineum.

The sensation was too much. White-hot pleasure surged through him, his love for her overwhelming. He came with a shout of her name, instead of a warning. Tara gagged as he shot down her throat, but she took it all with enthusiasm. Moans escaped her smile, along with a drip of cum down her chin.

Wiping her lips, Tara sat back on her heels to lick his cum from her hand. Where he expected a scowl of displeasure—or worse—there was only a contented smile on her face.

Muscles giving out, Gabe collapsed next to the bed, resting his head on her knee. "Sorry, Kitten."

"Don't be." Tara stroked his hair. "I liked it."

"Fine, but I could have warned you before I came." He smiled up at her, reaching up to wipe a spot she'd missed on her lip. "Though I don't understand why you like that."

"Yes, you do." She kissed the pad of his thumb before sucking it into her mouth. "Because you get off on getting people off, just like I do." Tara spread her legs open in invitation. "But unlike me, you're not good about letting them return the favor."

With an exasperated laugh, Gabe dragged her closer by the hips. Tara wrapped her legs around his shoulders, leaning back on her elbow to suck on her fingers. She sighed contentedly as he kissed his way down her thighs.

He pressed a kiss to her auburn curls, already soaking wet, and inhaled. The sweet musk of her made his mouth water. With a contented sigh, Gabe dragged his tongue up her slit. She tasted as divine as she smelled.

Tara moaned as she buried her fingers in his hair. He went slowly, kissing every inch of her pussy before curling his tongue inside. The sounds she made—the whines, and breathy moans, and gasps of his name—had haunted his dreams.

"You're such a tease, Gabe," she scolded. "You haven't even touched my clit."

He buried his nose against her in reply, tongue-deep inside her cunt. Hand tight in his hair, Tara ground against his face, her heels kneading into his back. Breathing was a challenge, but making her come apart was more important.

Eventually, his need for air won out, and he replaced his tongue with his fingers. The flat of his tongue worshiped her clit before he gently sucked on it. Quicker than he expected, Tara bucked against him, crying out. With a firm hand spread over her belly, he held her down through her orgasm, determined to make her come as long and hard as he could. He kept the pressure on her clit until her legs stopped twitching around his ears.

With a smug grin, Gabe sat back. Wiping his face on her thigh, he lifted her limp thigh over his head. "On your stomach."

"I thought I was in charge," Tara panted. She rolled over with a grunt anyway, spreading her legs for him as she sagged against the duvet. Hands sliding up her legs, Gabe admired her adorable ass, tracing the smoky wisps of ink embedded into the scars that sliced across her hips and thighs. The new curves made his heart melt and knees weak. Her gorgeous pussy glistened, soaked with her. At the thought of sliding into her, bent over the bed like this, his gradually hardening cock twitched to life.

Gabe dove back in, sucking hard at her clit before kissing his way up to swirl his tongue around her perfect asshole. Her muffled groans, how her body responded so enthusiastically—everything about her was addictive. Gabe's fingers thrust into her cunt eagerly, dreaming of how she'd feel around his cock. He palmed his cock until he was fully erect again, moaning into her ass as his thumb circled her clit. Tara tightened around his fingers, crying out as she shuddered through another orgasm.

Picking Tara up, Gabe tossed her further up the bed so she was cradled in the pillows. With Tara laughing in delight, Gabe attacked her neck to keep from kissing her. Licking and biting, he slid his erection against her cunt. Tara moaned and wrapped her legs and arms around him, grinding against him.

Her wet heat was as tempting as always. It'd be so easy to slide in, to fuck her hard and fast and desperate. Just as easy as it would be to kiss her, to tell her he loved her.

But Tara wasn't ready for any of that yet. Especially not in a moment of heated frenzy, with Gabe on the verge of losing himself. Tara wanted slow, and sweet, and cautious. Instead, Gabe tried to calm down, to be *good*, biting her collarbone to alleviate his ardor. Tara cried out, gouging scratch marks into his shoulders. He shuddered in pleasure at the pain, tension shooting up his spine.

"Gabe, fuck soft and sweet—I changed my mind. I need you to fuck me hard. Please!" Tara whined desperately, arching her back and rolling her hips until his tip found her hole.

With a relieved moan, Gabe snapped into her roughly. She yelped, but Gabe didn't stop; he knew her well enough by now to recognize it as a sound of pleasure. He pounded into her relentlessly, desperately, practically gnawing on the crux of her neck to keep his mouth a safe distance from hers, half mad with desperation. He needed to feel her come while he was buried in her.

"Gabe, please, I'm so close," Tara begged, punctuated by moans with every thrust. Her fingers slid into his hair, fingernails scraping his scalp.

"Fuck, Kitten," he panted against her collarbone. *Be good. Be good. Be good.*

The sharp tugs on his hair sent shock waves down his spine. Tension grew in his lower back, as his orgasm crept ever closer. But he couldn't come, not until she went first. *Be good, be good, be good.* His desperation waned, overtaken by fear of disappointing her.

Shifting his weight up on his elbow to wriggle a hand in between them, Gabe rubbed frantic circles around her clit. She cried out, sinking her teeth into his neck as she pulled his head back. The pull on his scalp, the scrape of her teeth on his skin, the fluttering of her cunt around his cock, sent him over the edge.

"Come for me, please! Please, please, please," he begged as he came undone, pleasure crashing over him, drowning him in bliss.

His rapture was short-lived, doused in icy cold fear and burnt to a crisp by shame. Anguish and guilt oozed from his heart as he helplessly filled her.

She came seconds later, her cunt clamping around his still-pulsing cock as she sobbed her pleasure against his neck. Limbs curled around him tightly, Tara convulsed beneath him.

Gabe barely noticed, too caught up in his own sense of failure.

"I'm sorry. I'm so sorry. I wasn't good." Gabe collapsed against her in a panic. He had failed. He'd come without permission. Shuddering a sob into her neck, he begged for forgiveness, knowing he wouldn't get it. Mistakes were always punished. "I'll do better next time. I promise! Please don't punish me," his voice broke.

"Whoa, what's happening?" Hands stroked his hair. "Gabe, you were so good! Everything is okay." The tears leaking from the corner of his eyes were wiped away by cool fingers. "Breathe, Gabe. You're safe. You're at home. I'm here with you. Can you look at me? You're with Tara. This is your bed."

Green eyes swam in front of him and freckled skin surrounded him, pulling him into a hug. *Get a hold of yourself. You're safe. This is Tara.*

Detangling himself from her, Gabe scrambled to the foot of the bed. Hot shame coursed through him, turning to ice in his veins. Partly from the relentless sense of failure, partly from falling apart so utterly helplessly in front of *Tara*.

Skin crawling, Gabe shivered, wrapping his arms around himself. One hand found the end of his hair, yanking desperately, needing the pain in his scalp to ease the storm in his head. To remind him he was alive and real, and not in a waking nightmare.

He'd been trying so hard. It'd been so long since he'd broken down like this, let the panic and guilt and fear take over. For it to happen at a time like this... "I'm sorry," he whispered, his voice raspy.

Tara sat up, patting the bed next to her and beckoning him to lie down. "Get back here. You're not pulling away after that."

"Fuck, this is humiliating." His emotions were going haywire, his heart thumping so hard in his chest he could hear the blood in his ears. He wished he was strong enough to not need her touch, but he was all over the place, and being held by her would help. Crawling back to Tara's side, Gabe curled around her, resting his head against her chest as Tara wrapped her arms around him. She was so warm. Clinging to her like she was the only flame left in the world, Gabe shivered. "I'm sorry."

"You have nothing to apologize for." Tara stroked his hair gently. "Do you want to talk about it?"

"Not really," Gabe admitted. "But I should."

"You don't have to," Tara said. Her voice was airy, the way it got when she was doing her breathing exercises. Gabe slowed his breath to match the slow rise and fall of her chest.

"I kind of do." His thumb traced the ink lining her hip as his body warmed and his heart rate steadied. He hated talking about his time in New York. But knowing might help her to understand what being with him meant. Better to learn now if she couldn't handle it. After a few quiet breaths in time with Tara's, he said, "So, you know already that my exes kinda fucked me up, but I've downplayed it. Avoided talking about it so I don't freak people out. And it's a long, sad story, so I understand if you don't want to hear it all."

"I want to hear everything you want to share," Tara murmured. Her cool fingers through his hair soothed the inferno in his head.

"If you're sure," Gabe sighed into her chest, already ashamed of how weak he'd been. How fragile he still was. But if he could tell his therapist, he could tell Tara. Finding his heartbeat to keep calm, he took a deep breath and told the story he'd only told Joy before. "My first serious relationship was with a woman I met in grad school. I hooked up with Isabella at a party, and we just clicked. Everything was good, we were in love. I wanted to spend the rest of my life with her. And after the initial honeymoon period calmed down, Isa said she wanted me to dominate her. I was a horny fool—still am—so I was down, but I had no idea what I was doing. And she kept pushing me to do things I didn't want, like, extreme CNC and rape fantasies and shit."

Gabe shook his head, stomach churning with regret that he hadn't told Isa no. That they hadn't eased into it, so he'd have a better understanding of how to do it safely. But Isa hadn't wanted to be eased into it; she didn't want to feel safe. Even back then, he'd been a fucking doormat—he never imagined anyone would want a fat, ugly, nerd like everyone said he was. Who was *he* to say no to someone like Isa?

"And after I finally gave in, she said *I* took it too far, that *I* was too much. And she left me. I didn't understand, because I'd done everything she asked, even though I didn't want to. She never used the safeword, never called red, wouldn't let me come near her for aftercare. I still feel horrible. She had *nightmares* about me." He had nightmares about her sometimes too. The look of terror on her face, when she saw the monster he'd become for her.

Gabe felt a kiss on his forehead, and the relief of it brought tears to his eyes. If Tara still wanted him after telling her that, maybe he'd get through this with his heart in one piece. He took a breath before he continued, "So I met up with another dom I knew—Derek—to help me understand what I should have done. Instead of helping me, he basically coerced me into a slave dynamic. Told me I was a horrible person and needed to be controlled, taught a lesson. He did the same things to me that I'd done to her—the things I never wanted to do in the first place! Anytime I said the safeword, he told me I was a weak piece of shit and kept going. And I thought I deserved it, so I stayed with him for months.

I woke up in the hospital one day with a head injury and never heard from him again."

Tara's arms tightened around him. In hindsight, Gabe suspected Richard had somehow paid Derek off to leave Gabe alone. When he'd come to, Richard had been at his bedside to explain that Derek had said Gabe fell and took off. The concussion and cracked skull had left him infuriatingly foggy—he still struggled to process shit sometimes, all these years later. The only reason he'd scraped through his MBA was because Richard had helped him. Hell, Richard had stuck around for a second degree, just to make sure Gabe had support when he'd needed an extra year to finish.

"I now know, after a lot of therapy—and honestly, watching Blanche's content—that neither were healthy relationships. We didn't negotiate anything. We didn't communicate. I was coerced into a lot of things I wasn't comfortable with. As messed up as things ended up with Isa, I can rationalize how it ended, because we both had no idea what we were doing. I was the dom. I should have stood up to her or checked in. But Derek? He knew what he was doing. He broke me down. Told me I deserved it."

"No one deserves that, Gabe." Tara held him tight, stroking his hair.

"At the time, I thought I did." A part of him still did. "And unfortunately, so did Justin, my next partner. At first, he was wonderful and understood me, because he had his own issues he was dealing with. I thought I'd found someone to love me again, someone who would heal with me. But he couldn't handle it, being with someone struggling with sexual trauma. Not when he was dealing with his own.

"Turns out relationships can't be built around fixing each other. Lesson learned!" Gabe laughed mirthlessly. "It got toxic and codependent. He treated me like *I* was the one who caused his trauma, instead of the one trying to help him. But I stayed until he finally left me. He just disappeared one day, all of his stuff gone, his key on the counter."

"He was so fucking wrong to project that on you," Tara murmured into his hair, holding him close.

Gabe nodded, proud that he could believe that these days. "That's why I needed space from you last year. I was starting to feel that same toxic insecurity and obsession for you that I used to feel for him. I couldn't go there again." He shook his head. "Anyway, that's just the context before I tell you about the real story, because all of that? That all took place over the three years I was in grad school."

He felt Tara's head jerk back in surprise, but he didn't dare look up from the safety of her sternum. "That's the *context*?" she asked, incredulous.

Gabe snorted. "Right?"

"Holy shit, Gabe," Tara rested her cheek on his hair. "You don't have to share if this is too hard to talk about."

He looked up at her with what he hoped was a reassuring smile. "Tara, if I don't get it out now, I don't think I ever will. And I want you to understand this about me. Because the last one is a fucking doozy." At her nod, Gabe let out a mirthless laugh and tucked himself back around her. "My last ex—Emily—told me she wanted to fix me. And I was a stupid piece of shit who didn't learn my lesson from Justin. I still thought love was the answer to everything, and here was this beautiful woman, showing up like an angel to help me heal. She made me tell her everything, about how my parents weren't around that much, how I'd been bullied, about Isa and Derek and Justin, even if I would break down just *thinking* about it."

Gabe's jaw tightened, anger surging at the memories. At Emily, and himself for not seeing the truth. "And then she used it all against me. She'd have me make her food and not let me eat it. She'd make me fuck her, but not let me come. She'd make me buy her gifts and pay her bills, but I couldn't spend my own money or use my time how I wanted. If I hadn't lost enough weight that week, I was supposed to kneel by the door, while she went out with our friends." He snorted. "I wasn't that good, though. I'd play video games while she was gone, and I doubt she knew. She would have gotten rid of my PC if she had.

"But I trusted her completely, thinking it was part of healing and growing up and improving my life. And it wasn't all bad. She had me eating healthy, going to the gym, getting promotions at work. She was my whole world. I did *everything* for her! Five fucking years of my life, I spent under her control!" His anger had scarred over the years, but that sharp bitterness at what she'd done, and what he'd put up with, surged back. As if talking about it made the wound fresh—

Stop, you've forgiven yourself so many times. You're moving on. Em is in the past. His breath turned shaky as his anger leached out of him. "Looking back, I realize how broken I was. She made me cut off contact with everyone outside of work. Convinced me that no one cared about me but her. I stopped talking to my parents, Phin, and Tonio. And look what happened to him—I almost lost my best friend because of her."

Gabe's voice cracked. "I wasn't there for him when he was struggling, when he needed me! I fucking kicked him out of my life for caring about me."

Gabe paused, getting control of his breathing to fight the cold numbness spreading through him. It still hurt to remember he'd abandoned his friends and family for a life of abuse. But it hurt less now. His poor therapist was a miracle worker, helping him process his trauma like it was a to-do list. He clung to Tara harder, grateful for her warmth.

"But then she left. I still don't know why. Her note just said she was giving up on me, and I needed to leave. Richard might have paid her off or something, but that doesn't make sense because she had more money than either of us. But he was the only one who still saw me because we worked together, who saw what I became with her. It had to be him, but I don't know how he did it.

"The day she disappeared, my parents showed up to move me back to Bellamy in my dad's old pickup." He huffed a laugh. "Still can't believe that fucking thing made it to Manhattan and back. Richard coordinated with work to relocate us to the offices here, while I took a leave of absence to go to inpatient therapy." Gabe's throat tightened. "He's always been there—visiting me in the clinic, showing me around the new office we were working in, and asking how my therapy was going. He brought Phineas, who I hadn't talked to in *years*, not since I met Justin, along one day to help with a protection order after Emily showed up at the vineyard looking for me. They helped set up an LLC, so my name wouldn't show up on the property records for this house or my car, and set up some communications system to intercept her, so I don't have to know if she tries to contact me. I don't know how I can ever make it up to either of them."

Gabe laughed weakly. "And then Tonio showed up six months later, when I was back in inpatient after I couldn't handle living by myself. He was going to rehab in the same clinic. He just hugged me like I hadn't fucking abandoned him and said we should get jello sometime or some shit like that. I owe all of them everything."

Tara kissed his forehead, wiping away his tears. "I'm glad they were there for you. I had no idea you'd been through so much."

"No one does, not really. I hate talking about it." Gabe held her closer, hoping she wouldn't judge his clinginess, but he needed affection right now. "But all of that was to explain the breakdown and why I... Well, why I'm me. I wasn't allowed to come until she gave me permission. I would have had to lay facedown in a cold shower for however long she wanted. One time I was sure I'd drown, because she wouldn't let me lift my head off the floor when the drain clogged." He shuddered. "The fucked up part was I would have gladly drowned myself. She never had to raise a hand against me. She was so deep in my head, I punished myself to make her proud. Guess my therapist still has a few more years of steady income from me."

His attempt at a joke fell flat even to his own ears.

"No one should ever be punished for feeling good. If you want to do something, do it. If you want to come, come," Tara murmured into his hair. "And if it's any consolation, I came *because* you did."

"Surprisingly, it does help a little." He pressed a kiss to her sternum. "And now you know what I meant when I said I was barely hanging onto myself last year. I've healed a lot, but I still have a long way to go."

"Thank you for trusting me with it. Is it fucked up that it makes me feel a little better, knowing I'm not the only one with issues?" Tara snorted, still running her hand through his hair. "You seem so in control of yourself all of the time, I feel like a fucking mess compared to you."

"Yeah, that is fucked up, Kitten. But I get it." He laughed with her, surprised he could smile so soon after reliving his lowest moments. "Thank you for listening, and caring. You're the first person I've told this to besides my therapist. I haven't even told Tonio any of this, just that she messed me up. Richard and Phin only know enough to legally protect me.

"My parents have a better sense of what she did. They were the ones who showed up to bring me home. They saw the schedules, the reminders, the devices, everything. They didn't ask though. Mom just took photos for evidence, while Dad packed up my stuff. And they brought me home, wedged in the cab between them like I was a kid again. And to think Em convinced me that they didn't care about me." Gabe shook his head, jaw tightening at the rift she'd wedged between him and his parents, who had done nothing but their best for him his whole life.

"They love you. They were there for you when you needed it. That's beautiful." Tara's voice quavered as she spoke. "And now you have all of us there for you too. Lee, Blanche, Sunny. And me. We all care for you. *I* care for you. You're stuck with us." She hugged him tighter, as he tried to ignore how loud his heart was singing. She asked softly, "Is there a reason you still follow her rules?"

"What do you mean?"

Her fingers traced his jaw. "You make food, but barely eat it. You work out every day—and you're fucking gorgeous—but you don't let anyone compliment you. You are generous with your friends, but not with yourself. When do you get to enjoy anything?"

His heart sank as he mulled over her question. Gabe hadn't put that together before. Tara wasn't wrong. His therapist had mentioned his body image issues and obsession with his diet, but Gabe didn't think it was a priority compared to everything else. He hadn't considered that it might be related. He swallowed hard, eyes burning. The way Tara saw through him was heart-wrenching. Terrifying. Validating. Exhilarating. "Didn't realize I did. Something else to bring up to my therapist, I guess."

"Good. You deserve to enjoy life. Your food is fucking bomb. Your body looks like a god. And you should enjoy sex without worrying about how long you can last." Tara shrugged. "Not that I'm complaining about your stamina, but if you want to come, you should come. That's the point of sex. There's always round two. Or three. Or seven."

Gabe snorted. "My wax lady says I have a dad bod. She means it as a compliment, but it's not super validating. I like being called a god better."

He kissed her sternum again, his heart pounding in his chest. "I really care about you, Kitten. I have issues I'm still working through, but I've made good progress over the past year, and I trust myself to stand on my own. I adore you, and I've never been as happy as I am with you." He looked up, searching her face. Her eyes were damp, or maybe his were teary; everything was watery. "What I'm trying to say is I want us to... I guess— I want *us*. If you want that."

"Oh, Gabe. You're wonderful. I want that too, but..." Tara paused, shoulders curling in around herself. "I'm not ready yet. I am terrified that I could want anyone as badly as I want you, but I'm not there, not yet. And I'm not sure I ever will be."

His heart cracked. *I was too much again*. He turned to look away.

Tara grabbed his jaw, forcing his gaze back on her. Her green eyes stared into his heart. "I need you to understand that it's because of me and my fucking issues, not you. My trust issues run deep. Me not being ready is not a reflection on you, or anything you just shared. Do you believe me?"

Tara's words were as earnest as her compliments. He felt the truth in them. Gabe nodded. "I do. Sorry to bring it up, especially now when I already feel like I've been hit by a bus." He leaned up to kiss her jaw.

Cradling her face in his hands, he traced her freckles with his thumb. "Would it be too clingy to ask you to stay? For the night I mean. You don't have to, but I'd like it if you would."

Tara's eyes widened just long enough to make his needy heart drop, but she nodded. "Um... Can you be here for me in the morning? I might have a panic attack from waking up in a strange place, but I want to stay."

Gabe nodded. "I won't go anywhere, Kitten." He never wanted to leave her side. He could live in this limbo with her forever, wait years for her to be open to the idea of them, as long as he had hope. And Tara was still in his arms, still in his bed, still wanted him. How could he not hope?

Tara smiled shyly. "Can we maybe take a shower? A hot one, I mean. I'm not complaining, but I'm uh...oozing? I've never been creampied before, and I'm into it, but I'm worried about your sheets."

Feeling the stickiness on his thigh from between her legs, Gabe groaned with dawning awareness. "I didn't pull out!"

"Birth control, remember?" Tara tsked. "I just said I'm not complaining. It was hot."

"It's not that." Gabe fought a laugh, feeling ridiculous that after everything—the emotional conversations they'd had today, the sweet domesticity of their afternoon, the passion and intensity they'd just shared—he was most dismayed by this one small regret. "I wanted to put it on your tits."

Tara burst into giggles, and Gabe lost his fight against the bubbling in his chest. Laughing with her filled him with relief and gratitude that she was still here, still caring for him, instead of running like she often did when they veered into heavy moments. Still giggling, Tara kissed his cheek. "We have all night. Save it for round two."

Sunday, April Twenty-Fifth

CHAPTER TWENTY-FOUR

TARA

Waking up was far more comfortable than usual. Tara was warm. Heavy. Surrounded by soft blankets that smelled so wonderful that she woke with a smile. The idea of leaving the fluffy duvet enveloping her made her want to go back to sleep. She burrowed into the blankets, eyes refusing to open in hopes of staying safe and warm forever.

Normally, she woke up too cold, curled up in a fetal position on her twin bed, one hand wrapped around the strap of her duffle bag. But today? She stretched, the thick duvet never-ending, and her hand—

Her hand was empty.

My bed isn't this big. Tara's brain struggled to make sense of her surroundings. *This isn't my quilt.* Blinking, she pulled the duvet back. Light streamed through the sheer curtains of the picture window, painting the sage green walls in sunshine.

Her heart froze. *Where am I?* Her mind raced, struggling to remember before fear stalled her thoughts. *Where's my bag?*

Scrambling over to the edge, Tara patted the floor under the bed, feeling for the worn leather strap that should be there. Looking for any familiarity in her surroundings, something to anchor her head.

But she was alone. With no signs of where she was, none of her few possessions. Her breathing grew rapid as her ears rang. *I need to get out of here.*

Jumping from the bed, Tara pulled on a navy sweater draped over a chair to cover her nakedness. Her phone was missing. Her clothes were missing. She rushed out of the hallway to find a way out. *Run run run.* Familiar keys were lying on the kitchen table; she snatched them up with a clatter.

"Oh, Kitten, you're up. Are you hungry?" a deep voice said cheerily from the stove.

Gabe. Tara barely registered his existence. She needed to find her bag.

Tara opened her mouth helplessly to ask him for help—to tell him they needed to run, that they weren't safe, to say something, *anything*—unsure if she was even forming words over the roar of *run run run*. The only sound was someone crying.

Everything was so far away.

Without her bag, Tara was small and alone and scared. Without her bag, she was no one. She needed to find herself. She needed to run, to get somewhere safe, find her bag.

She couldn't wait—not for Gabe to understand, not even to find her shoes. As if underwater, someone called her name as she fled barefoot to the garage.

BLINKING, TARA STOOD IN front of the door to safety, unsure how she got there. The damn crying sound had overwhelmed her the whole way home. Over and over, Tara knocked, praying Blanche would let her in. That Blanche hadn't left her, wouldn't scream at her to get lost. She didn't know where her keys were. But she couldn't go back. If she could get past this door, she'd find her bag. She'd be safe again. She'd be Tara again.

Tying their robe around them, Blanche opened the door. Taking in her appearance at a glance, they pulled her into their arms. "Oh, babes, get in here. You must be freezing."

Was she? Tara didn't know. Hands steered her to a couch.

"Sit down."

Tara sat. A blanket was tucked around her. The crying broke into loud sobs.

Blanche's face swam in her vision. "Tara, listen to me. You're having a panic attack. You are safe at home. Your bag is safe in your room. I'm going to take care of you. What you're feeling is going to pass, the fear is temporary." Hands gripped her own. "Can you breathe for me? Remember your meditation? Inhale to the count of five."

Tara nodded. *I'm safe. Blanche is here.* Her breath was shaky and shallow *1, 2, 3, 4, 5.*

"That's good, Tara. Keep breathing."

Exhale, 4, 3, 2, 1.

"What can you see?"

As she blinked, Blanche's worried face came into focus. Light filtered through the plants hanging in the window. A blue glow came from the coffee table. "I see you. I see plants. I see a laptop."

"Good. Breathe for me. In through the nose—what do you smell?"

Inhale, 2, 3, 4, 5.

Tara struggled to place the scents of the room but managed to connect some with her memories. The pungent, grassy odor was Blanche's tea. Rose from Blanche's lotion that reminded them of their grandma. Vanilla and oak clung to the sweater she wore. Burying her face in the soft fabric, she inhaled Gabe's comforting scent. The sobbing sound got quieter.

"Tara, can you tell me?"

Tara swallowed, her mouth dry. "I smell your tea. And your lotion. And Gabe."

"I thought that sweater looked familiar. Well, it covered everything it needed to. Keep breathing, babes. Tell me what you feel."

Tara inhaled. Her face was damp; she was the one who'd been crying. The knitted yarn wrapped around her bare legs was soft and warm. "I feel the blanket. I feel...cold."

"I bet. It's freezing, and you're half-naked." A warm mug was pressed into her hands. "Drink this. What do you taste?"

Tara took a tentative sip and gagged. "Oh, this tastes awful! Like dirt and soap. What is this shit?"

Blanche laughed. "The tea blend that Jazzy made. It grows on you after a while."

Tara took another sip. Still dank, but she could identify the soapy taste as lavender. She took another, focusing on identifying all of the awful flavors.

"It's been a long time since you've had a panic attack, especially one that bad. Do you want to talk about what happened?" Blanche asked. "Did you stay at Gabe's?"

The memories rushed back with clarity as her panic waned. Tara groaned. "Fuck. I did stay at Gabe's. I didn't know where I was when I woke up."

"Was he there?"

Tara shook her head. She had woken up alone. But she had seen him, though, hadn't she? In the kitchen, when she'd taken the car keys. "He was, but he wasn't in the room when I woke up. I was already in deep by the time I saw him."

"And he didn't come after you?" Blanche's voice sharpened. "How did you get home?"

"Oh, god! Fuck!" Tara set the tea down and buried her head in her hands, piecing together the few scraps of awareness she could. "He *couldn't* come after me because I stole his fucking car, Blanche. I stole his car and his shirt, and he was making fucking breakfast for us. We were going to have cheesecake." A broken sob escaped her.

"Oh, Tara." Blanche sat next to her on the couch and pulled her into a hug.

"Why am I so fucked up, Blanche? Why do I have to ruin everything?" Her eyes welled up with tears. She blinked them away, sniffling.

"Babes, you didn't ruin anything." Blanche kissed the top of her head as they rocked her gently. "I'm sure if you drove back right now and explained to him what happened, he'd still feed you breakfast and cheesecake."

"He would! In a heartbeat." Tara's heart ached as her chest heaved. "I can't do this to him. He needs someone who doesn't panic, and steal his car, and constantly push him away. He deserves someone who's not fucking scared to kiss him!"

She couldn't keep hurting him. Especially not after everything he'd said last night, what he'd told her. Gabe needed someone stable to be there for him, to love him the way he deserved. And Tara could never be that person. Not when she couldn't even be that for herself.

"Let it out, Babes." Blanche stroked her hair as she cried. "You don't need to decide anything right now, okay? Just feel your feelings."

There was no decision to make. As he'd said, relationships weren't for fixing each other, and Tara was beyond broken. But she let Blanche hold her as her body resynced with her brain. "Is that the footage from your shoot yesterday?" Tara asked, pointing at the laptop with her chin.

"Don't worry about that today. Do you want me to drive Gabe's car back to him?"

Tara shook her head. "No, I'll do it after I've had time to think. I owe him an explanation, but I need to take my mind off of things for a while. I'll just check on my bag, grab my blanket, and work on this for a while. It'll be a good distraction." She smiled at Blanche, doing her best to look strong to ease the worry in their eyes. "Thank you for taking care of me. I don't know where I'd be without you."

"Right back at you, babes. I'm here for you, and you're here for me." Blanche kissed the top of her head, before standing up. "How's this? I'll bring you the bag and your heavy-ass blanket, then I'll text Gabe so he knows you're okay. You drink the rest of that tea and relax. Will you be okay if I take off? I'm meeting with my patron's wife soon. We're exploring options for how to get Confession out of Covey's portfolio."

"Of course! That's more important! I'll be fine." Tara forced a smile, settling herself into the couch. Touching the worn leather straps of the duffel bag Blanche had handed her, to reassure herself that she was real and safe, Tara tucked it under her legs and wrapped herself within the weighted blanket. She let herself zone out and get wrapped up in editing the footage, like it was any other day.

Blanche's words at the outro brought tears to Tara's eyes. *I'm so stupid. It's not that deep.* But it felt like Blanche was speaking right to her: "You must know yourself, trust yourself, so you can give all of you to someone else."

Tara couldn't bring *any* of that to a relationship. She didn't trust herself, and she barely knew who she was. She didn't even know what she was feeling half the time. How could she let someone as wonderful as Gabe into her fucked-up mess of a life, when she didn't even let herself in?

A knock on the door made her heart sink. Hours had passed—the edits were almost done, and the sun had passed behind the building across the street—but Tara was not yet ready to face reality.

Setting the laptop down, Tara padded barefoot to the door. The weighted blanket dragged on the floor behind her. Tara opened it and walked back to the couch without looking, burying herself and her duffel bag under the blanket again.

Gabe set a plastic bag and a round storage container on the coffee table. "Here, your clothes and phone and stuff. And your cheesecake."

"Thanks." Too ashamed to meet his eyes, Tara fussed with a loose thread on the blanket.

The chair creaked as he sat down. "Do you want to talk about it?"

"Panic attack," Tara shrugged. "Sorry for stealing your car."

"That's what Uber is for." Gabe took a long, deep breath. "I'm sorry for not being there when you woke up like I promised. Safe to say that I underestimated what you meant. I'll do better in the future."

Tara frowned. "You didn't do anything wrong. I'm the problem. Not you."

Worry furrowed Gabe's brow as his fingers clawed the ends of his hair. "Kitten, you had a panic attack. It happens. Obviously, you saw how I got last night. I'm sorry I wasn't there for you, like you were for me."

"Stop apologizing for shit." *Why isn't he mad at me?* Anger flared through her; how could Gabe be so patient and understanding, when Tara had just shown him her worst? "I stole your fucking car! You love your car!"

"I love—" Gabe huffed, looking away. "It's just a car, Tara!"

"It's not just the car, Gabe!" Her heart broke, but it needed to be said. He needed to hear it, but she hated that he was making her be the one to say it. If she didn't, she would hurt him like everyone else had. "We have to end this. I'm not good for you."

His eyes narrowed, and the hurt in Gabe's glare stabbed her in the chest. "I'm perfectly capable of deciding who is good for me or not."

Gabe's anger strengthened Tara's resolve. "And I can choose not to hurt you. So thank you for the cheesecake. And for bringing me my stuff. And for the wonderful day yesterday. And *everything*." Her voice broke. "But we can't do this anymore."

"Why?"

The anger within that single word sent a shock wave of anxiety through her, but she shoved it away. *Good. Get mad at me. Make this easier.* It was for the best, no matter how she loathed herself for hurting them both.

"Can't we talk about this?" he pleaded desperately, his voice wavering.

Gabe deserved an explanation. He'd done that for her, when he'd ended things last year. But Tara couldn't bring herself to explain why. Sweet, sensible, understanding Gabe would find a reason why he wanted her to hurt him.

Tara couldn't give in. She never imagined her rule to keep her circle small would be used to protect someone else from her. Tears streamed cold down her cheeks as her breath shook, but her voice remained steady. "Your keys are by the door. I'll get your shirt back to you."

"Keep it." Gabe stood, keys jangling as he picked them up. He paused in the doorway, opening and closing his mouth as if searching for what he wanted to say.

Part of her wanted him to argue with her, tell her all of the reasons she was wrong. To pause her, give them a chance to cool off, so he could give a rational explanation to convince her to give in. To let him love her into whatever happily ever after he'd envisioned for them.

But she'd still be Tara. And she would drag his dreams down into the nightmare that her whole life had been.

Instead, Gabe's jaw set as he gave her one last resigned look. "Goodbye, Tara."

The door slammed behind him, and Tara was left alone. Her only comforts were Gabe's lingering scent on his sweater, and the heavy embrace of the blanket he'd given her.

Wednesday, April Twenty-Eighth

CHAPTER TWENTY-FIVE

SUNNY

SUNNY PULLED DUMPSTER OFF of her keyboard and deposited the orange cat back in her lap to type a greeting to Black_Hawk. Undeterred, her beloved cat nipped her fingers.

With a yelp, Sunny jerked away. "Fucking brat, that hurt! Do you want me to move my computer back to Mae's? Because that's what will happen if you keep that up!"

As Sunny tentatively tried to type again, Dumpster's sharp teeth gouged her thumb. Sunny hissed in pain. "Dicky, can you take Dumpster? She's being a fucking brat!"

Richard wandered in a moment later, looking delightful in his sweatpants and glasses, blond hair rumpled.

Seeing him so relaxed, sleepy-eyed with all of his tattoos on display, made Sunny melt. "Sorry, did I interrupt your nap?"

Rubbing his eyes, Richard shook his head. "No, just got up to see where you were. Dumpster taking after you again?"

Sunny held up her thumb to show him the fang-shaped welts. "No, she's taking after you this time. She bit me."

Richard snorted and kissed her thumb. "You never complain when I do it." He looked at her screen. "Talking to your 'friend' again?"

Sunny replied primly, "There's no need to be condescending about someone I've known for years." If she had to guess, Richard was jealous. But he had nothing to worry about from the complete stranger on the internet. The snobby tone he used whenever Black_Hawk came up in conversation was still annoying though.

Richard carried Dumpster to the guest bed, cuddling her against his chest. The cat turned into an angel, purring softly as she kneaded the tattooed deer on his torso. "I think she just wanted pets."

Sunny huffed. "She's supposed to be *my* cat."

"You should feed her, then." Richard's grin was smug.

Stealing glances at the adorable sight of her boyfriend and their cat cuddling, she turned her attention back to her computer. She wanted to thank Black_Hawk for the advice he'd given her, even if he would never know she was starring in the next video that would be uploaded to Blanche's channel.

Blanche's playroom had been exhilarating—especially once the cameras were off—but she was even more excited to get into playing within the privacy of their home. Their Friday evening scenes would start later this week. Sunny had sent dozens of links to Richard, who'd (as usual) ordered everything she wanted.

> **Sunnywith0meatballs**: Sorry in advance for the sex-life talk, but my partner and I watched a bunch of Blanche Van Horne's stuff and had our first scene last weekend!
>
> **Black_Hawk_Up88**: Congrats! How was it? No TMI.
>
> **Sunnywith0meatballs**: 10/10. I can't wait to do more.
>
> **Black_Hawk_Up88**: Glad it worked out. Just keep up the communication.
>
> **Sunnywith0meatballs**: Absolutely. We're already communicating better, and it's only been a few days. I feel like I'm listening to my body in ways I've never experienced before. But that just might be the bruises.
>
> **Black_Hawk_Up88**: lol try calendula
>
> **Sunnywith0meatballs**: I'll add it to the shopping list. I hope we never have to have another argument about my hair in the shower drain again. Figuring it out this way is way more fun.
>
> **Black_Hawk_Up88**: My friend has that problem with his girlfriend too lol

Sunny laughed. "Black Hawk has a friend with the same 'hair in the drain' problem as us."

Richard coughed, startling Dumpster, who flattened her ears and bit his hand. "You told him about *that*?!"

Sunny shrugged. "What? It's no big deal."

"Sunshine." Richard let an edge of warning in his voice. He was less stern than how Blanche had trained him, but with just as much promise.

She smiled innocently at him, even as her pulse quickened. "Fine. I'll change the subject."

Sunnywith0meatballs: I think that's a great plan. But my SO says I'm not allowed to share any more personal details with you. Lol

Black_Hawk_Up88: Lol, it wasn't even that bad. But I get it.

Sunnywith0meatballs: Exactly what I said! Like, I barely know anything about your SO either!

Black_Hawk_Up88: Hmgojirojiosjiseohisehr What SO? :'(

Sunnywith0meatballs: Wait, what happened to the mind-blowing life-changing sex person you've been talking to? The one you were doing the Pause thing with? Didn't you just make dinner for her???

Black_Hawk_Up88: Uhggorioejfiomoishoie Yes, but that kind of ended before it even could begin. Like, at best it was off and on, but it was off most of the time. And now it's off off.

Sunnywith0meatballs: <.< Haven't you been sleeping with her for like 2 years now? I'd say that was definitely On. Even if it was a situationship.

"*Two* years?" Richard asked, reading over her shoulder with Dumpster curled up in his arms like a fluffy baby; it made her look deceptively sweet. "That long?"

Sunny glared at him. "Excuse me, eavesdropping!"

Richard ignored her, his brow furrowing. "I didn't know he'd been seeing her for *two* years!"

Still confused why Richard was so invested in this stranger's love life, Sunny shrugged. "Yeah, it was around when Lee and Antonio met."

He snorted. "I like how you can remember *that* but remember next to nothing about Gabe."

"I know everything about Gabe that I need to know. It might surprise you, but I can listen perfectly well, Dicky." Sunny turned back to her screen. "Gabe has nothing to do with this, anyway."

Black_Hawk_Up88: >.< It's confusing for me too. Especially since I have to spend a lot of time with them coming up. Even after that, we will probably have to be "friends" for the rest of our lives. Don't get me wrong, I am and want to be her friend, and I think she wants to be mine. But it hurts to shift back to a place where I don't think either of us want to be. But what-the-fuck-ever. What do I know?

Black_Hawk_Up88: I just feel like I'm being tested by the universe to make sure my therapy is working. Which it is—like I haven't missed work all week or skipped our game nights. So that's cool. Yay being a functioning adult despite my mental illness. But also, overall, the whole situation is very very uncool.

Sunnywith0meatballs: I'm sorry. Being Off and On is hard. Do you think you'll work it out with them? Get back On?

Black_Hawk_Up88: I want to, but maybe I shouldn't? Like maybe this is a sign that I'm not ready. Like maybe I still have work to do before I'm ready for a relationship. There's that whole thing of loving yourself before you can love someone else.

Sunnywith0meatballs: I think that's a load of shit.

Black_Hawk_Up88: Lmao ok???

Sunnywith0meatballs: Caveat that this is advice from someone who has never felt very comfortable with myself. You might not ever love yourself, or even if you do, you might not even realize you do because it doesn't happen the way you think it should. You can work on learning to love yourself while you're with someone. Sometimes it even helps. It has for me, anyway.

Black_Hawk_Up88: Wouldn't that lead to codependency?

Sunnywith0meatballs: Not if you stay self-aware and communicate, like you're always telling me to do. A partner can be supportive and helpful without doing the work for you or making your self-worth reliant on the relationship. You can lean on someone without using them as a crutch.

Black_Hawk_Up88: Fuck, you sound like my therapist.

Sunnywith0meatballs: Thanks, I think. Lol. My fingers are crossed for your situationship. I'm sure you will work it out if you two decide to try again. Hopefully, it stays On next time.

Black_Hawk_Up88: Thanks, but I don't think she wants to work it out. The ball is in her court either way, tho.

> **Sunnywith0meatballs**: Sounds like you need to meet her where she's at. Trying to force something that she's not ready for won't work out. But also, she needs to meet you where *you're* at. If she wants you, great. But don't put in all the effort if she isn't willing to. I'd get used to being "just friends" sooner rather than later because letting that shit linger is going to hurt. Protect your heart, you know?
> **Black_Hawk_Up88**: Good advice. Thanks, friend.

"That *is* good advice," Richard said, still peering over her shoulder. Clutching Dumpster against his chest, he leaned closer to squint at the screen. "Where did you pull that from?"

"Do you mind?" She pushed his face away playfully, reluctant to admit that her emotionally mature advice had come from Jazz. "We're talking about his problems now, nothing personal about us. Stop creeping."

Richard straightened his glasses, shooting her that crooked smile that always melted her heart. "He needs to hear it from someone. Especially if this has been going on for two years. I can't figure out the timeline."

"I swear, I'm going to move this computer back to Mae's." She turned back to her screen in a huff, but even to her, it sounded like an empty threat. The desk in the guest room was so much more comfortable than her cramped computer cart at her mother's. Richard had even gotten her a mini fridge.

Richard kissed the top of her head. "But then how will Dumpster and I annoy you?"

LEE

"KNOCK KNOCK!" LEE UNLOCKED the door to Blanche's apartment and let himself in, balancing several boxes on one arm. "Happy birthday, Buttercup! Hey, Blanche! I come bearing gifts. First, pizza!" He let Tara take the still-warm box, awkwardly stacked on a case of beer. After two years of rarely eating anything with real meat or cheese due to Antonio's weak-ass stomach, Lee was practically salivating over the large supreme he'd carried upstairs.

Covered head to toe in her baggiest sweatpants and hoodie, Tara opened it with a smile. She pulled out a slice as she carried it to the coffee table. "You always know the fastest way to my heart."

"Second, it's not Saturday, but it *is* a special occasion, so I figured beer would be a slightly more amenable bend to your rules." He put a twelve-pack of Modelo in the fridge and at Tara's nod, grabbed three for them. Lee held up a banker box, tucked under his arm. "And third, a present of sorts."

Tara looked up at him suspiciously. "What kind of present? You didn't buy me anything, did you? The pizza and the beer are already enough."

"No, I didn't spend any money. But fair warning, it will be emotional." He set the box next to the pizza and passed the beers to Blanche, who had grabbed the bottle opener. Tara would like what was inside, but she'd need to psych herself up for it first.

"Well, good thing I've been drinking Jazz's tea every day then. I'm as emotionally stable as a rock." Tara asserted confidently, pulling her hood over her frizzy hair and tightening the cord so only her curls and nose were visible.

Blanche met Lee's eyes with a warning look as they passed him a beer. He knew that look. That was a "Tara's emotionally constipated and pretending she has no feelings again" look. A familiar place for Tara, albeit not one she'd been in often since he'd first started dating Antonio.

Instead of asking what had got Tara so not-upset, because she hadn't mentioned anything to him (or shit-talking her for drinking the nasty swill his sister had concocted), Lee simply said, "Glad to hear it, Buttercup."

Tara bit into her pizza with enthusiasm. She made no move to open the box yet, but considering the look from Blanche, it was probably for the best. He sat next to her and tucked in, moaning at the rush that could only come from real cheese, the salty umami of the sausage that lentils and walnuts could never truly replicate.

Tara's phone buzzed; she snatched it up. Face crumpling, she fell into Blanche's already open and waiting arms with a sniffle. "He wished me happy birthday. What do I say?"

Stomach dropping, Lee raised his eyebrows as Blanche grimaced over Tara's head. Had Tara been crying like this a lot? Sure Lee'd been a little obsessive over the wedding, but he would have made time for Tara if he'd known she was upset. Why hadn't Blanche told him? Why hadn't Tara?

"You don't have to say anything right away, Babes. Let's eat our pizza and tell Lee what happened," Blanche suggested patiently. "Leave him on read for now."

Tara groaned. "Gabe and I got in a fight."

"Tara." Blanche shot her a warning look.

"Fine." Tara sat up and grabbed another slice. "I was really heartless and unfair to Gabe, and now I feel like shit. Because he's been really sweet and patient and trusted me, and I fucking ruin everything." Tara practically snarled as she bit into her pizza.

This was more of the Tara that Lee knew, angry and eating. Not crying over a text message from a friend, wishing her happy birthday. Sure, Tara was a crier, but not over shit like that. Her tears were more for hard feelings and shit— *Oh. Oh! Gabe is hard feelings now!? When did that happen?*

Biting back all his invasive questions, Lee rubbed her back. At least it sounded like Gabe hadn't done anything wrong; he didn't *actually* want to make Gabe's life miserable like he'd threatened to do. "Gabe will come around if you talk it out. He's an understanding person."

Tara sipped her beer. "I know. It's not fair."

Lee burned with curiosity. Was Gabe in his feelings, too? He'd had a thing for Tara for a while, despite his claims otherwise. Had Antonio talked to him at all? "Can I know what happened?"

Tara shook her head. "There's no point in talking about it. I won't let it impact anything, okay? The bachelor party will still be amazing, and the wedding will be perfect. I will get my shit together and pretend we're friends, and everything will be fine."

"Buttercup, don't worry about me or Tonio or the wedding, just let yourself feel your feelings for once." Lee leaned in to blanket Tara in a hug. Maybe he had been too caught up in wedding stress if Tara thought he would put the wedding before her well-being. "I mean, don't cause a scene if you can help it. But even if you do, you're still *my* friend. Tonio's too. And Gabe's. We get past shit, whatever it is, okay? We're all here for you."

"You know what would be good right now, Tara?" Blanche asked.

"A birthday joint?" Tara asked hopefully.

Blanche laughed. "That too. But I was thinking there's a cheesecake in the fridge that you miraculously haven't touched."

Tara groaned, sliding off the couch. "Fine. Let's fucking eat the fucking cheesecake that Gabe made for my fucking birthday before I fucked everything up." She stalked out of the room, slamming the utensil drawer with a clatter and yanking open the fridge door. The condiment jars rattled as the fridge door banged against the cabinets.

With a glance, Lee silently asked Blanche for the details. Blanche shrugged as they leaned over to their stash box, hidden under the couch, and rolled a joint. If they knew anything, they wouldn't tell him until Tara was ready.

Lee sipped his beer, confused. He wished Antonio was here so they could debrief later, but he was busy with parent-teacher conferences. Maybe it was for the best; Antonio would push for answers, and Tara would get stubborn. Lee would get more information with patience.

Setting the cheesecake on the coffee table, Tara handed out forks. "Come on. This is going to be fucking delicious, and I'm going to hate myself even more afterward."

Blanche passed her the joint, allowing her to do the honors of taking the first hit.

Tara coughed as she inhaled and passed it back to Blanche. "I love you guys," she snapped.

"One puff, and you're already sappy," Blanche teased, passing it to Lee.

He inhaled, letting the smoke linger in his lungs, hoping it would settle the anxiety burning his skin. Lee smoked so rarely these days; living with a fiancée in recovery had him a lot more straight edge than he'd been living here. He pulled out his phone.

I'd rather have you skunky and in my bed than have you shack up with that Jezebel!!!

Again, kidding. Love Tara.

Except I would rather have you home with me.

Your fussy ass made me shower three times before you let me into bed after the vigil. Also, she's upset about something that happened with Gabe. I'm trying to get more details, and I think she'll tell me more when it's just us in bed. That was when we always had our heart-to-hearts.

Parent incoming. One sec.

Tara stabbed the cheesecake, right in the middle, and scooped up a bite. She groaned, sounding more aroused than upset. Until she muttered, "Why does he have to be such a good cook? I hate this."

A pang of guilt seized Lee's gut. He and Antonio had always thought Tara and Gabe would be good together. Hell, they'd basically been encouraging them for the past year and a half. He hadn't expected that Tara would end up *this* in her feelings. Knowing Gabe's sensitive ass, he was in the same boat.

Lee had been so hopeful that maybe something would finally happen when that Syl kid had called her "Coop's girl," and neither had corrected him. But now she was crying over text messages and mad about cheesecake.

Maybe Lee had pushed her too far, too fast.

His phone buzzed.

I support you 100% Angel. Get the tea.

Tell her I said happy birthday!

Lee put his phone away. "Buttercup, do you remember the advice you gave me when I first met Tonio?"

Tara shook her head, sucking on her fork.

"You told me that if I want to do something, I should just do it. Keep it simple, no overthinking it—just do it. You were talking about deleting Grindr, but I've kept that mentality this whole time with Tonio. With everything really. It was the best advice I think anyone's ever given me, because I would never have let myself be this happy without it." He curled a leg under himself to face her. "And even if you're not ready to talk about it, figure out what you want and trust yourself to go for it."

"If you want to come, come," Tara muttered to herself, taking another bite of the cheesecake. "Oh no, am I worse than Gabe?" She whined around her fork. "Ugh, I *am* worse than Gabe!"

Blanche put their arm around her, taking the joint from her for a deep pull. "Babes, if you both want it enough, you'll find a way to make it happen together."

Tara stabbed the cheesecake again, pouting as she ate. "But what I want is terrifying. It'll fuck *him* up too, not just me. I can't do that to him."

Lee had seen Tara in a full spectrum of negative moods over the years, most of them scared. This was something new. Lots of things terrified Tara; this wasn't terror. His chest tightened, a mix of excitement and dread making it hard to breathe. He shouldn't jump to conclusions. Even if the conclusion that Tara had fallen for Gabe was very easy to jump to at the moment. More of a small hop, really.

Blanche grabbed a fork and took a bite of the cheesecake, nibbling on the crust. "Both you and Gabe are so resilient. You will figure things out together, so you learn not to hurt each other. As friends or otherwise. You will find a way to grow and heal together *and* individually." They took another bite. "And I say 'you will' instead of 'you can' because you *have* to. For my sake. This cheesecake is fucking delicious."

Lee aimed for a spot slathered in chocolate sauce. Leaning back against his friends, he moaned at the rich, dairy delight overwhelming his taste buds. "Damn, this shit is really good. I don't suppose you can get the recipe out of him?"

Tara shook her head, snagging the joint from Blanche. "I helped make it, but he made me close my eyes when he added a secret ingredient. He says it's a family recipe."

"Damn, that's adorable as hell, Buttercup. You fucked up," Lee teased.

Tara laughed, smoke billowing from her lips. It sounded like a sob, except she was smiling. "I did. And I'm going to keep fucking up." Her smile faded.

Lee took another bite before saying, "You know I tried to break up with Tonio once?"

Blanche and Tara both whirled to face him. "What? Why?"

"It was before we moved in together." Lee scooped up more of the chocolate sauce, licking his fork to chase the rich flavor. "I told myself that it was because he wasn't serious about us. But really, I was scared that he didn't really love me and that moving in together would make him resent me. I thought I would hold him back, and he'd be better off without me."

"Wow, that's bullshit, dude. He's been crazy about you since day one. And you both work so perfectly, it's uncanny." Tara took a huge bite, not bothering to chew before she asked, "What did he do?"

"Told me to shut the fuck up, and that he'd elope with me if it'd make me believe that he was serious about us." Lee laughed. "And that I need to trust him to know what's best for him, instead of making that decision for him. So I did, and it's worked out so far."

"Ugh. That's so cute. Why do I hate it?" Tara groaned.

"Hmm... Maybe because you're making that same decision for Gabe?" Blanche suggested, breaking off more of the crust.

"Shh..." Tara stuck the joint back in Blanche's mouth. They took it with a laugh. "And it's not the same. Lee and Antonio were together. Gabe and I are...*friends*. We're always going to be friends. And that's that."

The mood grew more peaceful as they talked and ate after that. Lee was starting to feel more than a little fucked up from the beer, and smoking so much of Blanche's indica, when Tara announced, "I should text him back."

Lee exchanged another look with Blanche. "What are you going to text him, Buttercup?"

She smirked and stabbed her fork into the cheesecake. "A picture of this fucking cheesecake. It'll piss him off that we ate it like this."

The prized dessert was a mess. A gaping hole in the middle had formed where Tara had eaten the center, fork marks gouged across the top from Lee scraping away the chocolate drizzle, and Blanche had methodically carved out the crust all the way around.

"Are you trying to piss him off?" Blanche asked.

"No. Yes. Kinda?" Tara huffed, scratching her head. "It'd be helpful if he hated me. But I also want to apologize. And this is proof that I'm a mess, and he needs to remember that so we can figure out how to be...*friends*. If he still wants to be, anyway."

Lee didn't follow her logic, but he was also high and on his fourth beer. It probably made sense. "Can we proofread it before you send it?"

Tara nodded as she took out her camera to snap a picture. After typing and deleting and typing some more, she passed it to him. Blinking past his dry eyes, Lee squinted at her phone.

Happy Birthday, Tara.

> Thanks for the cheesecake. Ur too nice. Sorry Im a fucking monster. I hope we can be friends.

Below the image of the mangled cheesecake, a message popped up in reply.

> If that's what you want, I'd be honored to be your friend.

> Even if you eat cheesecake like a fucking psychopath.

"Tara, you already sent it," Lee laughed. "Here, he answered. He even double-texted."

"*Friend*. Fuck me!" Tara threw her head back, laughter and exasperation fighting for control. "Why does this hurt so much? I thought I was too hurt to hurt more."

Blanche hugged her. "Life hurts, and time heals, babes. You were hurt, but you learned and healed and grew from it. And you'll get hurt again, and you'll heal and grow from that too. It's a painful process that never stops and never really gets easier. At least it hasn't for me yet."

"I don't know if this will make you hurt less," Lee paused, then shrugged, "but you're already emotionally all over the place, so fuck it." He set the banker's box in Tara's lap. The thing had been tempting him since Sunday brunch. His mom had expected Lee to go through it with her; Lee had come down a bit harshly, insisting he open it with Tara. "Here, this belongs to you. Some of it's mine, but I thought we should go through it together."

Tara lifted the lid off with a gasp, pulling out the stack of pictures she'd left behind at Aunt Alitrice's house when they'd been evicted. Lee hadn't dared to look in the box himself, but now he dove into clothes and CDs he hadn't seen in years.

Riffling through the photos, Tara looked at him with eyes that sparkled with tears. "How did you get these?"

Lee smiled, his own eyes burning from more than the weed. "My mom saved them."

Tara held up a photo of her as a toddler. A slender blond woman in a blue sundress, and a tall man with curly red hair and tattoos covering his thin chest, stood on either side of her, holding her tiny hands. "I'd forgotten what they looked like. How could I forget what my *parents* fucking looked like? They look like me. We look so...normal. Happy."

Blanche leaned in, resting their head on Tara's shoulder. "They do look like you, babes. It must be nice to get some memories back of your family."

Tara wiped her tears away. "Is it nice? It hurts to see these. It's a relief to remember, but it hurts too. Why does everything have to fucking hurt?"

With a sigh, Lee leaned on her other side, flipping through a notebook he'd filled with half-written songs when he'd thought his calling might be songwriting. It was a good thing he'd discovered music production, to put it kindly. "Seeing my parents again hurts too. I didn't think it'd be easy, but it's so much harder than I expected. I'm angry with them, and I'm angry with myself for wanting them in my life again. And they're so different than they used to be. None of us are the same people."

Tossing the notebook on the table, Lee took a swig of beer to ease the resentment bubbling in his gut. "It's so confusing. Like, can I be angry at them if they say they're sorry, if they've changed? But I *need* to be angry and hurt and resentful before I can forgive them. Because I've been carrying all that shit around for a decade, and it's their fault! But they just keep fucking apologizing." Lee scoffed, annoyed at the situation he'd put himself in a mere two months before the wedding. As if he hadn't been stressed out enough without voluntarily dredging up his childhood trauma. "I've gotten heartburn and a damn headache all three times I've seen them."

Blanche rubbed his shoulders. "We heal and we grow. I just wish growing didn't hurt so damn much."

Tara put her head on his. "And you have Tonio to help you."

"I do. He's my rock." Lee hugged Blanche and Tara tight, who hugged him back. "And you guys are my real family, way more than my parents ever will be."

"Still, I'm glad one of us at least reconnected with their parents," Blanche said. "Not that I want to reconnect with my adopted parents. Biological, maybe, but no way to find out who they were without contacting the adopted ones. Or doing one of those DNA test things, but fuck that. That shit's the Feds."

Tara and Lee laughed.

They smiled, thumb rubbing against Lee's elbow. "I'm proud of you, you know. Both of you. When we met, I had no idea who I was without Daisy. She was the only person who was truly mine, and I was hers, and even though our relationship was toxic as hell, I was so devastated to lose her. And then, you two came along and gave me a purpose again. And I'm so proud you've grown and healed into such resilient, happy, and wonderful people. Even if that means you don't need me anymore." They snorted.

"Thanks to you," Lee murmured, hesitant to speak; Blanche talking about Daisy had always been a warning sign that they were on the edge of a drop. In the early years, Blanche would go catatonic for days, unable to get out of bed or feed themself. With time and weed, their drops had shortened to mere hours of quiet dissociation. But now? Blanche seemed fine, like it cost them nothing to talk about her. "We did—and do—need you."

"But you did this all on your own, because I certainly didn't teach you that. If you had learned the lessons I had, you'd still be stuck." Blanche sighed. "I'm getting there, finally, thanks to the two of you."

"Sounds like therapy is going well?" Lee asked gently.

"Oh, no, it's shit. The one I've been seeing can suck an egg." They laughed. "I've been on the waitlist for six months for this other therapist though, and they just reached out to see if I'm still interested in an appointment, so I'm breaking up with Judge Judy any day now."

"I want someone to call mine," Tara said softly. "Of course, I have you guys, but I want someone to be *mine* like you have Tonio. Like Walter and Wanda were for each other. I want shit like this." She flicked a photo of her mom, smiling and holding a baby Tara on a swing set. "My mom looks so happy here. I *never* saw her smile like this. I don't remember stuff like swing sets, or my dad holding my hand. I don't remember him at all. I just remember Mom dopesick and screaming at me to get lost." She shook the photo again. "I want to know what a family like this feels like, instead of the bad memories. You know?"

"If you're talking about having kids, then no, can't relate." Lee teased, but his heart went out to her all the same. He'd been struggling with the same things for the past year. Longer, really. His real family was enough, and yet he'd also needed to reconnect—or find closure—with his parents. Like how he'd longed for the romantic love he'd found in Antonio, even though his codependency with Tara was in some ways closer to a marriage than a friendship. "But I get it. I didn't know what I was missing before Tonio. It's different from what we have. The three of us might grow apart, even if that doesn't change our love for each other. And Antonio and I will grow together."

"So, Tara, in this hypothetical family of yours, is someone like Gabe in it?" Blanche smirked.

Tara grumbled something that sounded like a reluctant yes, though she refused to look at anything other than the box. "Remember this shirt?" She tossed a ball of white cotton fabric at Lee.

Lee held out the wrinkled white tee, taking the hint to change the subject. Even though that muttered agreement had piqued his curiosity and ignited his hope that, maybe, everything would work out better than Tara expected. "Oh my god! The deep V-neck! Why did I buy this? I was *way* too insecure to show that much skin. It's practically see-through!" He clutched it to his chest, inebriation overcoming his reservations. "You think I could pull this off now?"

Their whooping chorus of encouragement brought a grin to Lee's face. He might regret this in the morning, when he saw the pictures Tara would inevitably take. But right now, there was nothing Lee would rather be doing than reliving the teenage years he and Tara had lost.

Chapter Twenty-Six

Antonio

Antonio slid open the patio door to Gabe's dining room and quietly stepped inside. "Not Gon' Cry" by Mary J Blige played on the speakers throughout the house, cloaked in darkness but for the porch light that had lit up when Antonio parked out front.

"Oh my god." A laugh escaped him before he could muffle it. "It really is that bad."

He half expected Gabe to tell him to shut the fuck up. Or at least Hippo to greet him. But no one answered. Flicking on lights as he went, Antonio poked his head around the living room and kitchen, but found no sign of either of them. There was only uncharacteristic clutter Gabe had left behind: half-empty glasses littering the coffee table, lonely socks on the floor, and dog hair dust bunnies along the kitchen cabinets. Uncertainty crept up Antonio's spine.

Lee had only shared that Tara and Gabe had had a falling out, and Tara blamed herself. Antonio doubted he'd get more from Gabe, but he'd try his hardest. When Gabe was in a mood—Hell, even when he was happy—he wasn't the most forthcoming person.

Antonio checked Gabe's bedroom and en suite, but the unmade bed was empty. Clothes were scattered everywhere. Mildewy towels littered the bathroom floor. He listened, but could only hear music. The guest rooms upstairs were empty, as usual.

It's no wonder he adopted Hippo, living in this house all by himself. Why does he have four extra bedrooms? Antonio checked the garage. His car was there, and Hippo's leash hung on the hook, so they weren't on a walk.

As he passed by the door to the basement, a faint ringing caught his ear. *I should have known. The fucking pinball machine.* Gabe had always gone to arcades after a bad day at school. Why would he be any different as an adult?

As the only two queer students of color at Driftwood Academy, they'd really only had each other for support against constant harassment. Antonio had dealt with the slurs and deportation jokes by throwing himself into theater and choir, where he'd managed to find friends—well, a group of people who didn't bully him.

Gabe, on the other hand, could never harden his sensitive heart against the "Chief Fatass" nickname, the cruel questions if he would have worn a yellow star or a pink triangle during the Holocaust, or the stupid war cries that followed him in the hallways. Antonio had done his best to defend him, but as a scrawny target, Gabe ended up having to rescue Tonio more often than not. The few friends Gabe gamed with were just as bullied as he was.

After school, Gabe would play pinball at the nearby arcade alone, until Antonio was done with rehearsal. Then they'd go to Gabe's house to smoke weed and listen to music, or get drunk and fool around, until Miriam drove Antonio home after dinner. Neither of them had the best coping mechanisms; their parents weren't around enough to notice their self-destructive tendencies.

From his spot on the futon, Hippo wagged his tail in greeting as Antonio descended the steps. The partially finished basement was decorated like Gabe's parents' basement in their old house. The same futon, area rug, posters on the walls, and the same fucking pinball machine.

In front of the ringing, flashing arcade game stood Gabe, naked but for boxers slung low on his hips. Antonio's mouth fell open; it'd been years since he'd seen Gabe wearing so little. He'd always been attractive, but Gabe had never been *this* built—his broad shoulders and back rippled with muscle, and his thighs were tree trunks.

A guilty demon scolded him halfheartedly for ogling anyone besides Lee, but Antonio easily ignored it. Lee would be staring too. *Our eyes are our own, and our hearts and holes are each other's.* He dragged his eyes away from his best friend's ass all the same, noting that Gabe's normally lush hair was a tangled, frizzy disaster.

With a worried sigh, Antonio sat on the futon and pet Hippo instead. Two empty bottles of wine sat on the coffee table. Based on Gabe's offbeat swaying, they were probably both from tonight.

Gabe still hadn't noticed him when the song changed from Lauren Hill's "Ex-Factor" to Boyz II Men's "End of the Road."

Antonio bit back a pitying laugh as Gabe sang along. *He never could sing tenor.* "You're a little flat, Gabey."

Gabe jumped, barely catching a mostly-empty wineglass before it fell off the pinball machine. "Fucking hell, Tonio! How long have you been here?"

Antonio couldn't help but smile. "I came in halfway through Miss Mary J Blige. You wanna talk about why you're listening to my mom's divorce playlist?"

Gabe emptied the rest of his glass. "What's there to talk about?"

Antonio looked skeptically at him. "Oh, I don't know. The fact that you're listening to breakup jams in your underwear? The fact that your hair looks like you haven't touched it in days? The two empty bottles of wine on a Wednesday? Don't you work tomorrow?"

"I fucking hate my job." Gabe combed his fingers through his hair in a failed attempt to make it more presentable.

"That don't explain shit, babe!" Antonio crossed his legs. "Since when do you spend your weeknights wine drunk and singing R&B?"

Gabe shrugged. "What else would I be doing?"

"Oh, I dunno. Going to the gym? Eating rabbit food? Playing video games?"

Another shrug. Instead of answering, Gabe flumped down next to Antonio on the futon, picking up a bottle of wine to see if it had anything left.

"How about I get you some water instead?" Antonio took both empty bottles. Maybe a slightly more sober Gabe would be more open to talking. Unlikely. But right now, Drunk Gabe wasn't giving him anything. "Have you eaten? I can bring you something from upstairs."

Gabe nodded, crossing his arms in agitation. "Yes. I do want some food. Some good fucking food that *I* cooked!" He turned to Antonio, overly serious the way only a drunk person could be. "There's spinach puffs in the freezer. Can you please put one—no, two!—in the toaster oven for ten minutes at three-fifty?"

Antonio bolted upstairs, before Gabe could change his mind and ask for celery or some shit. He popped the spinach puffs into the toaster oven and rinsed out the bottles of wine, refilling one with water. Hopefully, Gabe wouldn't fight it if it was in a wineglass.

> Sooooo is it cool if I platonically sleep with Gabe tonight?

> Also platonically shower with him. His hair is in desperate need of some pampering.

> Yes, I know I'm a hypocrite.

> But you were right. This is bad. He's drunk, mostly naked, and singing Boyz II Men.

> I trust you implicitly, my love. As long as you only wash his hair and nothing else. (…and tell me how he looks naked.)

> Angel, you're not allowed to think of Gabe naked.

> But! You would really appreciate the view, let me tell you!

> Don't worry. My eyes are my own, but my heart is yours.

> And my holes.

> You don't need to add the bit about the holes every time. It's implied. Do you want to see what Tara's platonically sleeping with tonight?

ARE YOU ABOUT TO SEND ME A DICK PIC????

Pleaseeeee??? You never send me nudes.

We live together! You see me nude every day.

Antonio gasped in delight as a picture of Lee in a skintight t-shirt, reclining on the couch with a joint dangling from his lips, popped up on his phone screen. The thin white fabric dipped low enough that the swell of Lee's belly was visible above the collar, exposing his coils of chest hair and drool-worthy pecs.

Oh my god I love thatttttttijrgiodrgono

The deep V looks so good on youuuuuuu <3

Please bring that to the bachelor weekend.

I'm saying yes now, but I reserve the right to change my mind when I'm sober.

When Antonio came back downstairs, spinach puffs in hand, Gabe was already swirling a full glass of wine. Another bottle was open in front of him.

"Where the fuck did you get that?" With an exasperated huff, Antonio worked the cork back into the bottle. The smell was fortunately unpleasant to his nose. Gabe was in no shape to support him if he had been tempted. Neither was Lee by the sound of it. That meant Richard was next, and he was the *worst* person to call for sobriety support. "Please drink water. You're going to hate yourself tomorrow if you don't."

Gabe sighed loudly. "I already hate myself. At least I'll feel something with a hangover."

With a sighed "oh my god," under his breath, Antonio rubbed his forehead. Gabe was usually the emotional support friend. Richard, Phineas, and Antonio were not particularly good at the whole compassionate listening thing. Not like Gabe was. Especially when Gabe got into his emo-ass moods like this. He was so intense. A dramatic motherfucker, through and through.

Lee was so much easier to handle when he was upset. Lee was sweet, cooperative, and appreciative. Gabe was like talking to a surly wall. But Gabe had babysat him through much worse than this; Antonio could return the favor.

"Gabey, you might not like yourself very much right now, but you don't hate yourself. And you're feeling a lot already, aren't you?"

Gabe nodded and swallowed hard. "Shit sucks."

"Do you want to talk about it?"

Gabe shook his head emphatically. "No. I'm saving it all up for Joy tomorrow."

Antonio considered pushing, but decided against it. "I don't think feelings need to be rationed, but I'm glad you're talking to our therapist."

He had seen Gabe in all sorts of moods before, but this was a perplexing level of despondency. When Antonio had moved to New York a month after Justin had vanished—the latest of a string of bad relationships, according to Richard—Gabe's shame and self-disgust had been visceral. And when they'd reconnected in rehab—after that *bitch* ruined his life—Gabe had been detached, empty.

This Gabe in front of him today was not empty, nor self-loathing. Yes, he was resentful and hurt, but he merely seemed...dejected. The last time Gabe had been like this was after they'd broken up back in high school. But that had lasted all of half an hour before Gabe was over it. From what Lee had told him, this might have been going on for days.

Antonio handed the spinach puffs to Gabe; maybe the food would help his mood. Ignoring the fork and napkin Antonio had considerately brought downstairs, Gabe picked the tart off the plate and bit into it grumpily.

"Ow, that's hot." Gabe puffed around the bite, closing his eyes with a groan. "But it's so good."

Antonio stifled a laugh. "You're turning into Tara."

Gabe's face crumpled, his lips and chin trembling. He set the half-eaten pastry down.

Antonio's heart sank, cursing himself for never thinking before he spoke. But before Antonio could apologize, Gabe's phone vibrated. He snatched it off the coffee table with a disappointed frown.

"Who are you texting?" Antonio asked.

"It's just Phin. He wants to know if Joy's clinic is taking new clients."

Antonio gasped, his heart leaping. "I never thought this day would come!" He looked over his shoulder as Gabe copied the link to their therapist's website. His chest bubbled with hope. Maybe with some therapy—and hopefully Phineas sobering up a bit—they could finally reconnect. Even if Phineas had always been more of Gabe's friend, Antonio still loved him. He just couldn't be around someone whose vices reminded him too much of Old Antonio's.

Gabe put the phone down.

"What?" Antonio smacked his shoulder. "Gabey, you're just gonna send the link? You're not going to ask if he's okay, or tell him you're proud of him or anything? We've been after him for *years* to figure his shit out. This is a huge step!"

Gabe scowled, but picked up the phone again. Typing away, he hid the phone from Antonio's view. "This is why I don't like company."

Antonio scowled back. "Sure, your best friend comes to check on you to make sure you're alive, and *I'm* the bad guy here? Why do you have us over constantly for wedding planning stuff, if you don't secretly like company?"

Gabe laid down to rest his head on Antonio's lap. "I don't want to talk about it."

Antonio rubbed his shoulder. Several bruises covered Gabe's neck and collarbone; they'd been blocked by his hair before. He poked a particularly dark one under Gabe's jaw.

"Ow, Tonio! What the fuck?" Gabe swatted his hand.

"I should ask you the same thing. Or maybe *'who'* the fuck would be more appropriate." Antonio prodded another one. "These are some serious love bites, Gabey."

Grumbling, Gabe moved to get up, but Antonio held him down. "I know. I know. You don't want to talk about it. Just stay put. I'll stop asking." He rubbed Gabe's shoulders, massaging the impressive muscles, comprised of what felt like one giant knot. Antonio got to work, digging his thumbs into every tight spot he found. For someone so health focused, Gabe really could bear to stretch more. Not even Lee, a literal bundle of anxiety that grew tighter and tighter as their wedding drew nearer, was this bad.

"Do you remember when we broke up?" Antonio asked. If those hickies came from Tara, and then they had a falling out...small wonder Gabe was a mess.

Gabe chuckled. "You mean the time I surprised you with tickets to MCR, and you dumped me before the show and *still* made me pay for dinner?"

Not Antonio's finest moment, in hindsight. "Yes. And do you remember why?"

"Because you thought Mikey Way would want to fuck some barely-legal twink?"

Antonio swatted his shoulder. "That was *one* reason, but not the one I'm talking about."

"Because you didn't have feelings for me." Gabe's voice was husky.

"And because *you* also didn't have feelings for *me*. When we were together, it was exactly the same as when we were friends. We only put a label on us because everyone else thought we should be boyfriends. Why wouldn't two queer best friends who fool around regularly end up together? That was the *only* reason you asked me to be in a relationship. And the *only* reason I said yes. But we never had romantic feelings for each other."

Gabe rolled on his back to look up at Antonio. "Yeah, but I didn't know that then. It still hurt like hell to get broken up with—in the middle of what is still the *best* date I've ever planned, might I add."

"That's because you're a fucking people pleaser, Gabe. You'll bend over backward to avoid being rejected. Learn to set some fucking boundaries," Antonio laughed, running his fingers through Gabe's chest hair like they were young again. "And besides, you were hurt for all of thirty minutes until we got to the concert, and then we had a great fucking time. As friends."

A smile crept across Gabe's face. "The breakup sex after the show helped."

"Only happened because Mikey didn't invite me backstage," Antonio laughed. "But you know what I mean, Gabey. Our friendship is more important than any hurt feelings. We help each other through shit." He touched Gabe's cheek gently. "Look what happened when we weren't there for each other. I was waking up in my own vomit every day, and I barely remember anything I did in New York. Shit, I *still* barely remember anything that happens *now*. And you ended up—well, you know..." Antonio waved a hand. Gabe didn't need him to go into detail on his own trauma. Not that he'd ever given Antonio many details in the first place.

"I'm sorry I wasn't there for you when you needed me," Gabe murmured.

Antonio bent down to kiss Gabe's forehead. "And I'm sorry I couldn't keep my mouth shut when you needed me to stop fighting for you. But we agreed to stick together when we reconnected. And we're going to get you through whatever shit's got you so eaten up, okay? I'm here for you. Even if you won't tell me what it is."

"Thanks, Tonio." Gabe's brown eyes watered. He sniffled.

"You know what you need?" Antonio reached for Gabe's phone, unlocking it to reveal a text chat with someone saved as *Kitten* in his phone. *Oh no, I'm snooping... Total accident.*

Gabe had drafted a text message: I'm sorry for pushing too hard. I'm sorry I wasn't there when you needed me. I'm sorry I wasn't enough. Please give me the chance to do better. I—

The draft cut off there, as if Gabe hadn't finished typing it. Or he had typed a lot more, and deleted it. "Are you planning to send this melodramatic text to uh... Kitten?" Tempting as it was to scroll up in the conversation, Antonio held back. Not snooping *and* not talking shit about the corny pet name attached to Tara's number? He deserved a gold star for this.

Gabe shook his head, tears rolling down his temples as he stared at the ceiling. "Delete it. I'm done bending over backward for people who don't want me. I can't do that to myself again."

With a nod, Antonio erased the rest of the message and found Gabe's music app. "As I was saying, no disrespect to my mom's divorce playlist, but we need something livelier."

As the first chords of "I'm Not Okay (Trust Me)" played on the speakers, Gabe finally smiled, dimples appearing for the first time since Antonio had arrived. "Are you fucking kidding me?"

"Nope! Come on!" Jumping onto the couch, Antonio strummed along on his air bass. At Antonio's urging, Gabe got up to join him, eventually whaling on his air guitar. Just like old times.

Antonio screamed along to the lyrics with Gabe, jumping wildly like they had when they were sixteen. Hippo barked and bounded around them. When they were kids, he and Gabe had always had each other's backs through everything. Gabe was closer to him than a brother; Antonio would be with him through this too. *Even if I couldn't figure out exactly what happened, I'm glad I came here.*

Friday, April Thirtieth

Chapter Twenty-Seven

RICHARD

THE CHAIR NEXT TO Richard scraped against the break room floor, drawing his attention from his book. Gabe sat heavily with an exhale, opening his container of fruit without a word.

"Gabe."

"Hey."

Richard waited, but Gabe stayed silent, spreading peanut butter on his banana. *Still not ready to talk, then.* Gabe had been in one of his moods all week, but at least he was still coming to work. The circles under his eyes hinted his insomnia was getting worse. "Did you have a session with Joy yesterday?"

Gabe nodded.

"Good." Turning back to his book, Richard took a bite of the chicken salad he'd brought. Gabe would open up about his breakup with Tara when he was ready.

Hopefully, this was a bump in the road, instead of an indication of how things would be with Tara in the future—assuming they could get their heads out of their asses to make that future happen. He didn't really want to step in; Richard liked Tara far more than anyone else Gabe had fallen in love with.

If worse came to worst, he had money. Tara was proud; she'd probably dig her heels, until he found her price. Justin had done the same when Richard had finally convinced him that he and Gabe would be better off without each other. A year's rent for a brownstone in Brooklyn, and a few introductions to art gallery owners, was a pittance for Gabe's well-being. Though Richard had regretted that decision later, because it led Gabe right to Emily. Interfering with Justin had left Richard indecisive, unsure if he should involve himself in Gabe's love life so much, even if it was for his own good. The result had left Gabe in Emily's clutches for far longer than he should have been.

Blackmailing Tara, in some technically legal way, into disappearing from Gabe's life would be significantly harder than it had been with Emily or Derek—Tara was embedded in Gabe's support system, his life really. Sunny and Lee would never give up their friendship with her, nor would Antonio.

Richard could only find one potential crime that Tara might want to stay buried as leverage, but Tara and Lee had been minors at the time; the blackmail wouldn't be very effective. Besides, if the police reports were anything to go by, the guy had deserved it. Tara and Lee hadn't even been booked.

Tara and Gabe would just have to figure something out. As friends, or otherwise. After all, Richard could only protect Gabe from everything but himself. *I still don't understand the timeline.*

"Gabe! Can we join you?" Three of Gabe's friends strolled up to their table with their salads. Maybe-Beth, along with a woman whose name he should know, and a third he'd never seen before in his life, didn't wait for an answer; they descended around the table unprompted.

Richard did his best to tune out their chatter as Maybe-Beth sat next to him without acknowledgement, which was fine. He didn't work directly with any of them; there was no reason to become acquainted, beyond their distant connection via Gabe.

"You okay, Gabe? You're so quiet today!" Maybe-Beth asked.

"Just tired." Gabe forced an unconvincing smile.

Richard's phone vibrated in his pocket. He pulled it out, and opened it to a photo of the black lace teddy and thigh-high stockings he'd left spread out on his bed.

I assume this is for me to wear tonight?

Why aren't you at work?

I took a half day.

Again, why?

Since you're making me clean, I thought I'd get the unsexy parts of cleaning done before you get here. There's nothing sexy about cleaning the cat box or scrubbing a toilet.

I wasn't going to make you clean the cat box during the scene.

I notice you didn't say anything about the toilet, which is why I took a half day! I'm going to clean so all I have left to do is vacuum and dust by the time you get home because I figure I can make those sexy.

You're always sexy. And you do not have to take a half day for our scenes. You want me to be your Dom, so trust me. I'm not going to force you to do anything you don't want, and that includes scrubbing toilets.

The scene hasn't started yet—don't tell me what to do.

BTW is this how you want me to greet you at the door?

Richard coughed and immediately hid his phone under the table, cheeks burning at Sunny's selfie—in his bed, posing in the teddy and thigh highs.

> Sunshine, I want you to greet me at the door in a pretty dress, high heels, and your favorite jewelry. And when I tear your pretty dress off you, you better look exactly like that under it.

> Yes, Mr. Carter.

> You're not going to actually tear my dress though, are you?

> If I do, I promise to replace it with something higher quality.

> You're such a snob.

> You like it.

"Are you seriously texting a girl with Gabe right next to you?" Maybe-Beth hissed.

Snatching his phone to his chest, Richard glared at her. "I fail to see what business it is of yours who I text on my lunch break."

Maybe-Beth scoffed. "Gabe's been sad all week, and now I see why! He deserves so much better than you!"

Richard sputtered. "That's not why— I'm not— We're not..."

"How dare you?" The woman whose name he should know chimed in, sneering at Richard. "How do you sleep at night, knowing you're cheating on the sweetest man on Earth?"

"Quite well, considering I'm not cheating on anyone!" Richard looked helplessly at Gabe. "Tell them, please! This has gone on long enough!"

Gabe sighed. "We're not together. We're just...friends." His eyes filled with tears as he let out a shuddering breath.

"Jesus Christ, Cooper," Richard huffed.

"He was perfectly happy last week! And you're already talking to someone new?" Maybe-Beth shook her head. "You're heartless! I expected better of someone like *you*."

That *you* dripped with transphobia. Richard's nostrils flared as he struggled to keep his composure. "Not that it's *any* of your business, but I am texting the woman I've been in a committed relationship with for over a year!"

"So? Just because Gabe's your side piece doesn't mean you didn't break his heart!" The third woman chimed in. "You're a *manager*! You should be fired for exploiting—"

"That's enough!" Richard slammed his book shut as his temper snapped, resentment flaring when he noticed his bookmark was still on the table. "Gabe is my best friend, not my side piece, or my secret lover, or any of the bullshit rumors you've drummed up with your gossiping! I have never had any improper relationships with anyone at this company, and you would do well to check your assumptions before you start making serious accusations.

"If you kept your nose out of our personal lives, instead of spreading unfounded gossip, then the sweetest man on Earth wouldn't be crying in the break room right now! If anyone is disgusting and heartless, it's all of you! I'm not going to sit here and take your disrespect, when I've been supporting him through a hard time the way he wants to be supported."

"I'm not going through a hard time. I'm fine!" Gabe stabbed an apple slice.

"Cooper," Richard snapped, practically a snarl. "Go home."

"No! I'm fine!" Gabe's jaw set. "I don't need to go home."

Richard sighed, softening his voice. "Gabe, you don't have to push yourself. You've been here every day this week—that's great progress, and you should be proud of that. But it's Friday, and you're exhausted and upset. You have nothing to prove to anyone, not even yourself." Richard stood and pulled Gabe into a hug. "I'll talk to Leigh Anne and bring your stuff over tomorrow. Go home. Get some rest."

Gabe clung to Richard, shuddering. "Fine." His voice was muffled by Richard's chest.

Richard glared at the trio of women gaping at him. "Can he have some privacy?"

"No, I'll go." Gabe stood, wiping his eyes. "Thanks, Richard."

Richard waited until the elevator doors closed behind Gabe, before he rounded silently back to Gabe's "friends", who only saw their Gay Work Bestie and his shitty boyfriend. With louder and more exaggerated gestures than truly necessary, he gathered up Gabe's belongings, before stalking back to his office to call Gabe's boss.

"Leigh Anne speaking, how can I help you?" a chipper Southern drawl answered.

"It's Richard Carter."

"Oh. *You*. What do you want?"

There was that *you* again. Richard rolled his eyes. Leigh Anne was a self-righteous cunt on a good day. "I'm calling to let you know that Gabe fell ill on his lunch break and will be unavailable the rest of the day."

"Like Hell, he will! He's been dragging his feet all week—"

"Because he's been sick!" Richard snapped. "I already sent him home."

Leigh Anne scoffed. "It'll have to come out of his vacation days."

"It will not. Might I remind you that your direct report has a documented medical accommodation?" Richard snapped. "Do you often violate federal law and company policy where Gabe is concerned?"

"Are you threatening me?" Leigh Anne's voice rose. "Over a made-up health condition? Did he serve in the military? I don't think so!"

"It's a fair question, since you seem to be seriously misinformed about PTSD. Do you always make Gabe use vacation days for his protected medical time away?"

"That is none of your business. Might I remind *you* that Gabe is my employee, not yours! I can manage him how I see fit."

"The EEOC and Department of Labor would disagree. And yes, that is a threat. Have a great weekend, Leigh Anne." Richard slammed his desk phone down before she could answer.

RICHARD SHUT THE DOOR to his apartment with a sigh and toed off his shoes. He'd spent over an hour in Jaida's office to file a report against Leigh Anne. And then another hour on hold with another HR rep to document his side of his outburst at Gabe's fan club, just in case anyone decided to report him for creating a hostile work environment. He'd been at the firm long enough to know it wouldn't take much. At least Jaida had recused herself from documenting the report against her friends, rightfully so.

That venom-laced *you* that Bella—whose name, he had learned for the sake of the HR call, was not Beth—still rang in his mind. That *you* usually preceded a complaint about him for correcting someone for using the wrong pronouns, or using the bathroom. He'd spent a lot of time on hold for HR.

"Welcome home, Mr. Carter." Sunny—reminiscent of a '50s pin-up in a red dress with a plunging neckline, and a hemline that barely brushed the lace that capped her stockings—greeted him with a kiss on the cheek.

With a heavy sigh, Richard grabbed her wrist and pinned her against the door to kiss her deeply, losing himself in Sunny's comforting familiarity. The sweet taste of her mouth and the softness of her hair between his fingers... He kissed her once more for good measure before he pulled away. "Sorry, I'm late."

Sunny panted in his arms, eyes closed. "Hmm."

"How was your day, Mrs. Carter?" Richard prompted with a soft smile. The housewife roleplay still felt uncomfortable—especially since he fully planned on taking her last name when they actually got married. But for now, pretending he was happily married to Sunny was the best way he could ease himself into Sunny's desires. And frankly, he needed the escape after today.

She blinked as if remembering where she was. "Peachy. How was yours, Mr. Carter?"

"Long and hard." He smirked. "But I'm glad I'm home."

"Me too." She kissed his cheek again. "I have a couple chores to finish up. Why don't you relax on the couch, and I'll make you a drink to keep you company until I'm done?"

"Hurry, Mrs. Carter." Richard let his hand trail up her thigh under the dress. "I want to do more than kiss you before dinner."

"And I want something else other than your day to be long and hard." Sunny threw a wink over her shoulder as she spun out of his arms.

Richard snorted, blissfully following her to sprawl on the couch. Maybe Sunny was right—maybe this was what they needed to deal with life. Here with him, Sunny could be a woman whose biggest worry was vacuuming. Here with her, Richard could be a man who could keep the people he loved safe from the world. So when Sunny pressed a cocktail into his hand, he rewarded her with another kiss and a pinch to her ass.

RICHARD MUFFLED HIS COUGH as the second dirty martini burned down his throat. He wasn't a big drinker. The first had been a lot already; Sunny had made him another without prompting.

He set the drink down and tried to focus on his book, instead of the toys hidden beneath his clothing, as he surreptitiously watched Sunny dance around the house with the feather duster. She noticed him watching and danced a little sexier. Soon enough, the dust distracted her, and Sunny forgot she was roleplaying again.

Richard could barely concentrate on his book. Her cute dress showed off her curves, making her legs go on forever. And her heels made her already bountiful ass even more smackable. And her lips, decorated in a dark glossy red—utterly kissable.

How drunk am I?

"Are you just going to stare at me, Dicky, or are you going to lift your legs so I can vacuum under you?"

He blinked. Sunny stared at him expectantly, waiting for him to move.

Shit. Pay attention. Instead, Richard raised an expectant eyebrow back at her. He hoped he looked intimidating enough to pull it off. Throwing their planned scene out to fuck her now sounded like a good idea. But he was trying to stay in the role, and she'd just used the wrong name. Again. Not that he was particularly fond of the nicknames she'd chosen.

Sunny rolled her eyes. "Sorry, Mr. Carter. Can you please lift your legs so I can vacuum?"

"How many is that?" Richard had lost count of how often she'd used the wrong name; she was so pretty.

"Seven." She scowled, with a hint of smile in her dark eyes. Her makeup was beautiful. She was beautiful. "Mr. Carter," she added in a hurry.

Richard bit back his smile as he put his legs up on the coffee table. He sipped the martini again—wincing as it burned down his throat—and turned back to his book. But just like every other attempt, he couldn't help but watch as she put the vacuum away, untying her frilly to hang it up in the hall closet.

His heart thumped when Sunny removed the scarf around her hair and shook it free. Her hair was so beautiful, sleek and black and thick. He loved burying his fingers in it. Loved the cute whines she made when he pulled it.

"You missed a spot," he teased. Richard didn't even look. The room was perfect. He didn't fucking care how well she cleaned.

"What?" She whirled as she looked around. "Where? Is it the bookshelf? Did I miss something when I was dusting?" Sunny looked back at him in frustration. "Seriously, Dicky. Where?"

Richard smiled and tapped his cheek. "Right here."

Sunny laughed. "You're such an ass."

He set the book down as she kissed him on the cheek. He needed the space to pull her into his lap. "That's two more, by the way. You're at nine."

Sunny straddled him with a pout. "How'd I get to nine, Mr. Carter?"

"One for the attitude, one for the name." He tightened his grip on her hips, heart pounding. He was trying really hard to be in control, but Richard just wanted to kiss her and hear her moan. "Let's see if you can make it up to me."

"What would you like me to do, Mr. Carter?" Sunny asked with a shy smile.

"As you're told." He couldn't keep the smirk off his face as she bit her lip. "Kiss me with that pretty mouth, then show me what else it can do."

"Yes, Mr. Carter." Her voice turned breathy as she leaned in.

His stomach tensed as those pouty glossy lips captured his own. He loved kissing Sunny; she threw herself into everything. He wove a hand into that lovely hair, tightening his grip to feel one of those lovely whines in his mouth.

Moving down her jaw to kiss her neck, Richard sucked hard enough to earn a moan. He loved the sounds she made. In the year they'd been together, Richard had learned to play Sunny like an instrument. A pull to her hair caused a whine. Sucking her neck made her moan. A gentle bite to her nipples, or a hard slap on the ass, earned a squeak. Every sound was music.

Sunny gasped. "As much as I love this, I'm supposed to make you feel good."

"In a minute." Richard pinched a nipple through her dress in reprimand, smiling at her adorable squeak. His pleasure could wait; he wanted to kiss her more first.

Sunny surprised him, ducking her own head to suck behind his jaw. Her nails scraped across his scalp to comb through his hair.

"Mrs. Carter." He held back a groan as she sucked on his earlobe. "What do you think you're doing?"

Sunny smiled against his neck, her murmur a tickle against his skin. "As I'm told, Mr. Carter. Showing you what this pretty mouth can do."

Richard couldn't stifle his laugh. She had kept her tone sweet, but the snotty attitude still shone through. "On your knees, Mrs. Carter."

She gave him one last kiss before climbing off his lap to unzip his slacks. The strap he'd put on earlier sprang out. She grabbed it eagerly.

"No hands," Richard reminded her. "Hands stay behind your back today. Tapping me is the safeword when you can't speak. Understood?"

Sunny nodded eagerly. "Yes, Mr. Carter." She clasped her hands behind her back with a smile. Her dark eyes blinked slowly, tongue sweeping across her lips.

"That's my girl." Pulling her hair back into his fist, he gently pressed the tip into her mouth. Gripping her tight, he let her set the pace. Richard wished he could actually feel her mouth on it, but the visual was half the pleasure. He felt every tug of her lips all along and inside of him.

With a click of the remote, he turned the vibration to the lowest setting. The silicone humming against his clit made him hiss. Richard wanted this to last, though the buzzing spreading through him dashed those hopes. There was no way he was making it through the scene without becoming overstimulated.

Even the lowest setting, combined with Sunny's eager slurps around the strap, made his hips jerk uncontrollably. Sunny gagged as he unexpectedly shoved further into her mouth. Her lovely eyes flicked up at him dreamily. Normally, he'd hold back, no matter how many times she'd told him to be rougher.

That's the point of the scene, isn't it? To let myself enjoy this? Richard gave in, her smiling dark eyes never leaving him as he fucked her mouth. Tension climbed from every nerve ending as the toy vibrated against and within him. Tears streamed from Sunny's eyes, her mascara was running, but her hands stayed clasped behind her back. He tugged her hair sharply, pulling a loud whine from her. Pleasure tore through him at the sound. His legs cramped and his back arched as he came with a quiet moan.

Panting heavily, he turned off the vibration, already too overstimulated to even try for another. He pulled Sunny off the strap.

"Done already, Mr. Carter?" Sunny asked innocently, her voice raspy. A long line of drool connected her lips to him. "You don't want another?"

He wiped a thumb across her lower lip to clear away the spit. "Not yet. You doing okay?"

She nodded eagerly, mouth chasing his thumb. "Yes, Mr. Carter."

"Good." He bent down to kiss her just once; he couldn't resist her lipstick-smeared mouth. "Get up. Bend over the couch. Don't touch yourself, just hold your dress up so I get a good look at that ass of yours."

She nodded, letting go of her hands behind her back. "Yes, sir."

Richard helped her to her feet, then picked up a riding crop from the coffee table that Sunny had asked him to buy. A leather heart decorated the end; hopefully, it'd leave heart-shaped marks on her ass.

She threw a teasing smile over her shoulder as Sunny eagerly bent over the arm of the couch. The gem on her butt plug peeked out from around the thong of her teddy.

"Count for me." He swung the crop safely away from her, getting a feel for how it moved and felt in his hand.

"Yes, sir."

Smack.

"One," Sunny squeaked out.

On her left ass cheek was a perfect rosy heart. And it had come with a squeak. Richard couldn't keep the grin off his face. He'd never imagined that he'd like causing her pain as much as he did, but his guilt was soothed by how much she adored it.

He swung again, aiming for the same spot on the other side.

Another squeak. "Two."

Dragging the riding crop up her thigh and over the curve of her ass, Richard lined it up with the first mark. *Smack.*

"Three. You can hit harder than that, Mr. Carter."

Richard shook his head. "I'm trying to aim."

"Aim harder," came a snotty reply. "Sir."

He snorted but put a warning edge to his voice. "That's ten for the attitude. Do I need to gag you, or will you be good?"

"No, Mr. Carter. I'll be good."

Smack. Richard put more weight behind this blow. To his satisfaction, it still landed in the right spot on her right cheek. And, to his delight, Sunny squealed even louder.

"Four."

Dragging it across her inner thighs, he tickled her with the crop, before lining it up below the first mark. Again, he did his best to use as much force as he could, without ruining his work.

"Five," she squealed.

By the tenth and final strike, Richard decided he liked this riding crop very much. "How are you, my dear?"

Sunny sighed, "Absolutely lovely."

Richard pulled his phone out of his pocket to take a picture. She'd enjoy seeing this later.

"Are you done already, Mr. Carter?" Sunny pouted over her shoulder.

He raised an eyebrow. "Is that a problem? I can leave you here waiting, while I get myself off without you."

She shook her head. "No, Mr. Carter. Please fuck me."

"That's exactly what I'd hoped you'd say. You've been so good today, Mrs. Carter." He lubed up his strap and stood behind her, pulling the thong of the teddy to the side. "Hold this for me." He waited until she curled her fingers around the fabric before he eased the plug out of her. Happy sighs and moans erupted from underneath him as he slowly pushed the strap into her.

Turning on the vibration again, he gripped Sunny's hips and fucked her far too slowly for either of their tastes; he wanted to hear her beg. Rolling his hips, he watched the strap slide in and out, stretching her open, while the buzzing sent pleasure running through his body.

"Please, Mr. Carter." Her adorable, breathy voice was barely audible as she whined.

"Please what?"

"Can you please fuck me harder?"

"Hmm. I don't think you want it enough." He bent over and gathered her hair again, dragging her head back. She whined as he licked her neck. "Beg like you mean it, Mrs. Carter."

"Fuck!" She moaned as he slowed his hips further. "Harder! Please, Mr. Carter. Please touch me. I can't fucking take it. You feel so good. I need you to touch me."

He smiled. She was so cute. He should make her beg more, but his hand was already working between her and the arm of the couch. "That's more like it, Sunshine."

He fucked her hard, his hips snapping, as he cupped her clit with one hand, rubbing gently in time with his faster thrusts. His own orgasm crept up again from the vibrations and her moans.

Yanking her head back, he sucked on her neck. Sunny was panting, begging him for *more, please* and *don't stop*. Her pretty sounds and the relentless buzzing finally pushed him over the edge. Richard bit her neck hard as his orgasm overwhelmed him, a soft moan escaping him

She cried out as she came a few moments later. *God, she's perfect.* He loved that sound, even when he wasn't shuddering from the aftershocks of his orgasm.

"You okay, Mrs. Carter?" he panted. He turned off the toy before it threatened to overstimulate him again.

"Fucking peachy, Mr. Carter. No sarcasm."

Richard laughed as he eased out of her and pulled the toy out of himself. He tossed it on the towel with the butt plug, covering them so Dumpster wouldn't be tempted to investigate. They'd get washed after Sunny was taken care of. "What do you want for aftercare, Sunshine? Do you need aloe?"

"You didn't hit me hard enough for aloe," Sunny teased as she stood up, stretching. "I want us naked and making out in bed."

Richard snorted. He'd been holding back; he needed to test everything out first. Ease into this to make sure they didn't rush too far, too fast. Taking Sunny's hand, Richard laced their fingers together as he led her to the bedroom, opening the door to the guest room on the way.

Dumpster tore past them, eager to escape from her prison. She zoomed down the hall like a tiny orange tornado, disappearing under the couch.

Unzipping Sunny's dress, Richard kissed her neck and shoulders as he slid it down her body, blatantly admiring her in the lace teddy. He hung her dress up before undressing himself.

"So, my love, did you enjoy that?" He kissed her as he crawled into bed next to her, unlacing the teddy to strip it slowly from her body, rubbing to soothe where the elastic had pinched her skin.

She nodded. "I did. Thank you, Dicky. It was fun."

"What would you change for next time? I want it to be perfect for you."

Sunny smiled, almost shyly. "I want us naked. You promised to tear my dress off, and I missed you touching me."

He touched her now, palming her beautiful tits as he kissed her neck. "Nakeder it is."

"Also, what was with those weak-ass hits?"

Richard laughed. "I got a little distracted by how cute your ass was with the heart shape." He grabbed his phone from the nightstand to show her the picture.

Sunny squealed in delight. "Okay, I forgive you. That's so fucking cute. Can you send this to me?"

He texted it to her. She rewarded him with a slow, sweet kiss.

"Thanks, Dicky. How was that for you? Anything you want to do differently?" Sunny rested her head on his chest, looking up at him.

"I enjoyed it a lot. More than I thought I would." He kissed her forehead, hesitating before he reminded himself that she wanted to hear his opinion. "But, can we come up with nicknames that don't remind me of my parents?" With a nod, Sunny laughed, cringing along with him. "And, no more drinking. I kept losing focus because you were so fucking cute and distracting."

She grinned. "Oh, was I? Tell me more."

"I kept thinking about how I wanted to kiss you. It was so hard to be bossy when I couldn't stop thinking about how cute you are, and how much I love you." Richard smiled, capturing her lips with his. Their tongues tangled as he kissed her. "I'm a lightweight."

She broke away with a grin, crawling over him to straddle him. "Wow, all I had to do to get you to talk like that is to liquor you up a bit? Dicky, have I told you what a fucking simp you are?"

Richard smiled as she kissed his neck, dreamy with bliss that erupted so easily around her. Maybe Sunny had been right; maybe this roleplay would be good for them. He'd already recovered from such a shit day in a matter of hours. "Only every day."

Tuesday, May Eleventh

Chapter Twenty-Eight

Meeting at Confession, without Chas and Freddie, to determine the fate of their own nightclub without their knowledge felt wrong.

But it had to be done. As the dinner rush started, Blanche ascended the stairs to the third floor, slipping in through the back without stopping to greet anyone along the way. Without Lee, Antonio, or any of the other lives caught in Confession's balance, aware that anyone was pulling the strings Blanche had gotten them all tangled up in. Confession had started as a pipe dream, but it'd become an institution, a legacy of Bellamy that Blanche refused to let Covey destroy.

It was Blanche's fault, this mess, this sword swinging over their necks. The devil in the shadows who asked threatening questions about payroll expenses and building code, under the guise of "learning the ropes." So Blanche would have to clean it up. Covey seemed as determined to keep his claws in Blanche as he had months ago, unapologetic for his role in the vigil, and unashamed of the disgust and resentment festering in Blanche every time his key turned the lock.

Unbeknownst to Covey, Blanche was desperately planning their move. Proposals had been written. Contracts had been drafted. Arrangements had been made. Unfortunately, the signs that had made Blanche confident that the risk was worth taking—the blossoming romance between Tara and Gabe—had fizzled out. Perhaps they'd made the wrong call, erred in their judgment.

But here they were anyway, about to propose a deal to their patron's wife to get them both out of this forced metamourship. Because Blanche wasn't sure how much more of Covey they could take, before they made a misstep and took themself down right along with him.

Opening the door to the third floor conference room they'd booked, Blanche paused, surprised to see someone already there. "Uh, hello."

"Oh!" A tall Black man with long locs and a devastating crooked smile rose, hand outstretched. "You must be Chad—or Blanche? What do you prefer I call you? You've been Chad in all of our emails, but Gabe said you go by Blanche, and I want to respect—"

Blanche raised a hand to stop his rambling. "Blanche is fine, thank you." His rings clicked together as they shook hands. "You must be Phineas. I have to say, you're not what I was expecting. I figured a Phineas would be older, and well, white."

"Likewise!" Phineas beamed. His roguish smile was so infectious that Blanche couldn't help but smile back. "You don't exactly look like a Chad Hermanson."

Blanche laughed. "That's a relief."

"Come, sit down!" He gestured to the conference table. "Can I get you anything? Water, coffee?"

"No, thank you." Blanche sat, feeling odd that he was offering them a drink, in a room where they'd framed the walls and hung the door a decade ago. Confession was Blanche's home, not Phineas's. They should be hosting him. "And thank you, Phin—if I can call you Phin—for doing all of this. I was expecting you to review the contract for loopholes, not draft ownership agreements and creep on someone else's prenup."

"It's no problem! A friend of Gabe's—and Richard's, and Tonio's, and Lee's—is a friend of mine!" he laughed. "This is more interesting than my usual estate planning work."

"Why do it, if you don't find it interesting?" Blanche asked, keeping an eye on the door for their guest.

"Between you and I, my Dad basically forced me to study law," Phineas shrugged. "And I don't mind. Being a lawyer is interesting, I'm good at it, and it pays well. But his plan for me was to be a prosecutor in Chicago, like he was before he was elected to the city council. And well, practicing estate law in Bellamy is my own way to rebel." He smiled, more halfhearted than roguish this time. "I set myself up so I can't practice in Illinois, so he can't push me to move back home. Going there for the holidays is exhausting enough, you know?"

Blanche nodded, more in sympathy than understanding. They'd rarely left Bellamy since they'd arrived, never contacted anyone in the Family again. But from what Lee had shared, reconnecting with his parents had been more draining than rewarding so far.

The arrival of Mrs. Covey to the communal work area brought Phineas to his feet again. His smile was less charming for her than it had been for Blanche, as he went through the show of offering her a beverage and inviting her to sit down.

Blanche nodded in greeting as Mrs. Covey sat across the table from them. Their relationship wasn't warm, by any means; Blanche was still technically the "other woman," so to speak. But they'd come to an understanding as Blanche was training her, sharing all of the tricks they'd acquired to manage Covey's emotional crises. They'd become business partners more than friends. Mrs. Covey had been open to hearing Blanche's idea over coffee, and later emailed over a copy of her prenup for Phineas to review for any loopholes.

"So, to get down to brass tacks," Phineas pulled a stack of papers out of a folder. "I've reviewed your prenup agreement, Mrs. Covey, and traced the ownership documents to prove your husband is the sole proprietor of the holding company he used to buy Confession. The good news is, because Confession was acquired by an LLC that your husband formed *after* your marriage, you legally co-own it. And therefore, you have the same authority over the purchase and sales agreements as your husband. So, you could sell his share of Confession out from under him. My client," he gestured to Blanche, "would like to propose that they purchase half of his share, and the other half be purchased by yourself directly, outside of the holding company. This would get it out from under your husband's jurisdiction—"

"Let me stop you there," Mrs. Covey cut in, her smile patient but firm. "I don't want it. I want nothing to do with Confession or your client," she glanced at Blanche, "No offense."

"None taken. The feeling's mutual," Blanche muttered. Disappointment leaked into their hope, turning their stomach like poison. Why had Mrs. Covey bothered to show up if she wouldn't even listen to the whole proposal? Their jaw clenched.

"I am willing to sell this impulse purchase of my husbands, but I will not be the buyer," she finished. "Why not just buy the whole thing?"

"Jesus, lady, I'm not exactly a bank!" Blanche scoffed, skin burning hot with anger and embarrassment; her classist dismissal wasn't just rude, it felt cruel. "Are you willing to sell for under market value? I'm putting all of my savings into this, except the half mil I need to break the contract. If I don't have that, we end up right back at square one, where he owns part of Confession, specifically, *my* stake in Confession." Their nails dug into their palms. "I'd be living out of this conference room and *still* have him breathing down my neck!"

"So, what I'm hearing is that you're willing to sell, but we need to find another buyer," Phineas smoothly redirected, his easy smile silently asking Blanche to calm down.

Arms crossed and toe tapping the floor, Blanche sat back in their chair, as Mrs. Covey confirmed that he'd understood correctly. She turned to Blanche, "Don't you have any other rich clients who could step in?"

Blanche's eyebrows raised, burning at the implication. "Are you fucking kidding me? Other than your husband, my clients are normal people. Professors, artists, surgeons, car salesmen! You think I just keep billionaires in my pocket?" They ignored Phineas's pleading look, burning with too much irritation to keep quiet. The problem with finally learning to talk and express their feelings from all the therapy bullshit was that now Blanche sometimes struggled to shut up. "Your answer to our mutual problem is that I tie myself to another rich man and hope this one is nicer? How'd that work out for you? You chose to marry the piece of shit who happened to be the only unmarried billionaire in Bellamy! We wouldn't be here if you hadn't confronted him earlier than we'd planned!"

"We're done here." Mrs. Covey rose. "Reach out again when you're ready to make a serious offer, instead of insulting me or questioning my judgment."

Phineas sighed as she swept from the room, slamming the door behind her. "Well, that could have gone better."

Blanche huffed, resignation sinking in that without Mrs. Covey's cooperation, they were no closer to a solution than they'd been before this disastrous meeting. "I was sure she would want to keep a stake in Confession to use as leverage against her husband."

"Then why not say that, instead of insulting her?" Phineas asked gently.

"Because her attitude pissed me off," Blanche muttered. They sighed, trying to rein in their anger. Phineas wasn't at fault, he was trying to help.

"I thought you were a dominatrix?" Phineas tucked the papers back into his folder. "Isn't self-control part of the job description?"

"Sure, but she's not a client." Blanche shook their head with a huff. "Domming didn't come naturally to me like it does for some people. I was trained for this, just like how you went to law school."

"Then why still do it?" Phineas asked.

"It's interesting, I'm good at it, and it pays well." They smiled as Phineas snorted. "I still do it because it's what I know, and some clients, some relationships, are more enjoyable than others. I like helping people, not being exploited by people."

"Well," Phineas nodded, his brown eyes soft and crooked grin earnest. "Let's fix that then."

"What, are you gonna pull a fortune out of thin air?" Blanche asked skeptically.

With a laugh, Phineas shook his head. "No, but I know people who can."

He must practice that smile in the mirror. Despite the bitter aftertaste of frustration left by Mrs. Covey, Phin's earnest grin left Blanche feeling hopeful. As Gabe had said last year—if anyone could get Blanche out of this mess, it was Phineas Watkins. With a nod, they smiled back, left with no choice but to trust him. Trust that somehow these unnamed benefactors, willing to cross one of the most powerful men in Bellamy, wouldn't be worse than Bryce Covey.

Sunday, May Sixteenth

Chapter Twenty-Nine

GABE

I'M FINE. FORCING HIS lungs to steadily inhale and exhale, like a normal person who didn't have to remind themselves how to breathe, Gabe ascended the concrete steps to Confession's third floor. *I'm fine.* His back burned from the imagined eyes watching him climb the staircase, but he ignored it. No one in the crowded dining room of brunch-goers—all laughing and tipsy and...happy—were actually watching him. *I'm fine.*

Gabe had never been up to the third floor before, but Tara had told him to meet in a conference room up there, so that was where he would go. Because he was a mature adult in full control of his emotions. Who could plan a bachelor party for his best friend, with the best friend of his best friend's fiancée. Even if, mere weeks ago, the best friend of his best friend's fiancée had torn out his heart and stomped it into the ground.

Stop—she did not stomp on your heart. Gabe caught himself before he started fucking up his hair again, gripping the strap of his messenger bag instead. *She simply does not want a relationship with you. She did you a kindness by ending it once she made up her mind. That's her choice. You can choose to handle it.*

Handling it sucked.

But he would be fine. He'd been through worse.

Meeting at Confession was better than being alone with Tara in his home again. Already he was reminded of her everywhere in his too-big house—the way she curled up on his couch with Hippo; her happy hums as she ate the food he made at his dining table; her moans when she came in his bed; the sobs that'd wracked through her in the kitchen, because he hadn't been there when she'd asked for the bare minimum.

Stomach curdling with regret and resentment, Gabe forced himself up the final flight, the concrete stairwell echoing his dread. Cheers from the drag show were silenced behind the door, directing him to the coworking space. He only wished Tara had done him the courtesy of admitting why she'd ended things, even though it was obvious why. He wouldn't want to be with him either after—

Stop—you are worthy of being loved. She said it wasn't about you. Don't go there again.

He found himself in a mostly empty office space, similarly decorated to Confession's lower levels—plants draped over the expansive windows, and suggestive art hung on the brick walls. But instead of stainless steel tables, small workspaces sat behind short cubicles. Leather chairs sat clustered together for conversation around coffee tables, and a long wooden conference table made for a homey office space. But there was no sign of—

"In here."

Gabe started as Tara's voice sounded to his right.

Looking as haggard as he felt in her stained hoodie and wrinkled sweatpants, Tara stood at the door of a small conference room. Eyes on the floor, she waited for him to follow her.

Back to being ignored. Great. His jaw clenched as he followed her in, leaving a chair between them. "How are you?" Gabe asked politely, keeping his face neutral as he waited for her to just *look* at him, while he opened his laptop.

Tara kept her eyes on her own computer. "I was thinking we should create an itinerary."

"Oh, okay." He huffed, tapping his fingers across the wood table.

"What?" Tara's defensive tone grated.

"Nothing. We can skip the pleasantries. Get right to it," he said with a shrug. It was easier that way. He wouldn't have to admit he was a fucking wreck. Or that he hadn't gotten a full night of sleep in three weeks, not since that restful night curled around her. Or that Tara had been co-starring in his already-constant nightmares, her sobs of terror mingling with his own voice as they begged for help.

"I just thought—" Tara shook her head, staring at her laptop harder than necessary. "It'll be easier if we stick to business."

"Right." Gabe forced his hand away from the ends of his hair and opened a new document. "This itinerary. How detailed were you thinking?"

"Nothing crazy like scheduling wake-up times, just when to order dinner and leave for the show on Saturday. Start making breakfast with enough time to check out by eleven on Monday. Just so we don't miss anything that we have planned."

Gabe nodded. "Makes sense."

"And..." Tara fidgeted as she picked a hangnail. "If it's easier, Blanche and I can ride with Richard and Sunny and get there early, if you want to drive Tonio and Lee."

"Why would we do that?" His voice was sharper than he'd intended, but how could he take that any way but personally? Add insult to rejection, now she didn't even feel comfortable riding in his car?

"Because—" Her green eyes finally flicked up at him. They both tensed. "Because."

Heart pounding, Gabe set his jaw, refusing to break away from her gaze. "Tara, I'll drive you and Blanche as planned. The cabin is in my name, so you won't get access to it without me, and I don't want Tonio and Lee to have to lift a finger the whole weekend."

"And *I* do?" Tara snapped, but she stopped herself, shrinking back. "Fine. If you're sure."

"I'm sure."

Drowning in awkward tension, Gabe was relieved they were in public. He couldn't help himself from staring, mentally daring her to look at him. As much as it hurt, it helped that she was pretending he was a disembodied voice. For her to see him—to acknowledge his existence in her physical space, to see what she'd done to his heart, and still not care—would be so much worse.

Tara's shoulders were stiff as her breaths became slow and deep. She sipped from a travel mug—*his* mug, the one he'd brought her coffee in, the day of the flower class.

Fuck, he should have brought something for her to eat. The sparkle in her green eyes, the vibrant energy that had drawn him in from the first moment she'd acknowledged his presence beside her at Confession two years ago, was dull. Normally, that was a sign for Lee to offer her his hand to hold, and Gabe would push some food in front of her to help stave off her dissociation. But that was before...

Before Tara had decided she would rather be friends. And as her friend, Gabe couldn't bear to see her so distant.

He put his hand, palm up, on the table.

Tara's mouth twisted, looking at his hand like it would bite her. "What are you doing?"

"If you need it."

"I don't—" Tara scoffed. "Why would I *need* it?"

"If you want it then!" Gabe snapped, keeping his hand still. "You were starting to dissociate, weren't you? And this helps?"

Tara stood up. "I can handle myself!"

"I didn't say you couldn't!" Gabe took a breath. "I'm saying that as your friend, if you need or want my support, you have it."

Tara's laugh could have been easily mistaken for a sob. "*Friend.*"

Gabe's jaw hurt from the pressure, but he sat silently. Calling the person he loved *friend* sat ill in his heart, but that was what she wanted. She didn't want his love. She wanted his friendship. That's what he would give her. He'd handle it.

"We can finish this through email." Tara closed her laptop and turned to go.

"Don't." Gabe rose, stopping her with a hand on her hip as she passed. "Let's pause and cool off. We can figure this out."

"We pause, and then what?" Tara looked up at him, green eyes swimming with unshed tears. Her lips were pressed thin in a stubborn twist. "I don't want to pause, Gabe. I have to go."

Gabe swallowed. His hand slid around her waist to her lower back, pulling her closer. "Please, Kitten, let's talk about this."

Neither of them was talking about the bachelor party any more.

"We will." Tara put her hand on his chest to keep from getting too close. "But not today. We'll figure out how to get through the fucking bachelor weekend, and the wedding, and then we'll figure out how to be friends. But I can't—not yet, Gabe."

"Okay." Fighting every instinct to hold her close, Gabe stepped back. His hand fell back to his side. She wanted time? Space, so that they could put their friends first? He could give her that. He would give her anything she wanted. "I'll drive you home."

Tara's laugh was bitter. "I don't need you to drive me home! I'm perfectly capable of walking a fucking mile!"

"I didn't say you weren't. Friends can do things like drive each other home, and I want to. Please let me—" Gabe huffed as he caught himself, hating how he was begging for her attention and affection. He had promised himself he'd protect the scraps of self-dignity he'd recovered since moving home. "You know what? Fuck it! I shouldn't have to convince you. You want to walk home? Walk, then!"

Blinking back angry tears, Gabe sat back down as Tara slammed the door behind her.

He didn't know how long he sat alone in the conference room, but eventually the blurry glow from his laptop went dark. No matter how much he reassured himself that this was for the best, that Tara was being kind, that he would be okay, it didn't make the ache in his chest any less profound.

He'd let Tara see his heart—an act of courage he hadn't known he'd possessed. And she'd said she understood. She'd accepted him, perhaps not wholeheartedly, but she had stayed through his moment of weakness. She'd said she wanted to hear his story, that her reluctance wasn't about him.

Only for her to turn around and erase him from her life the next morning. Yes, he'd screwed up, and he hated himself for it. But to be so wholly rejected after baring his soul, without even an explanation or conversation—without a chance to redeem himself, or truly apologize for his mistake...

A hand on his shoulder made him jump. "Gabey, you good? Tara told me you'd—Oh, shit. What's wrong? Are you okay?"

Gabe didn't respond, but Lee's arms opened and pulled him into his chest, holding him as he silently cried.

TARA

"Babes, you would not believe this new client I have! She is so sweet!" Blanche dropped their purse in the entry with a clatter. "I never thought I'd like being a soft domme, but she doesn't even want to have sex, just have me walk her through pleasuring herself. I couldn't have dreamed up a better client for me."

Tara grunted in reply, focusing on slicing the cherry tomato in front of her without squishing it. If *Gabe* were here, he'd probably show her how to do this faster. But he wasn't here, and he would never be here, so she sliced each one methodically in half. Assembling her lunch was painfully slow.

The back of Blanche's hand pressed to her forehead. Tara jumped, jolting the cutting board. Three cherry tomatoes scattered onto the floor. "Doesn't feel like you're running a fever."

"I'm not sick, Blanche!" Tara picked the tomatoes off the floor and rinsed them off in the sink. Again. Maybe she was supposed to keep them in a bowl? What had he done to steady the cutting board—put a towel under it or something?

"Your face is a little pink. I thought you might be running a fever."

"I got sunburned on the walk home from Confession."

"You got sunburned in a mile?" Blanche crossed their arms as they leaned on the counter. "And you're cutting tomatoes for what appears to be a salad. Now I know something's wrong."

"Nothing's wrong—I just want a damn salad!"

"Okay! You want a salad. Greater miracles have happened." Blanche looked around the apartment. "Is Lee here?"

"No. Why?"

Blanche gestured to the coffee table, where Tara's clean clothes were not-so-neatly folded in haphazard stacks. "Because apparently it's laundry day, so I figured he would be here, considering I didn't think you knew how the washing machine works."

Tara chucked the cherry tomato halves on top of the onion and kale layered in the mixing bowl—the only dish they had big enough to hold the springy kale. "I don't *need* Lee to do my laundry. I *let* him do it because he likes to fuss over me."

Blanche raised their hands defensively. "Sorry, I'll stop teasing. Nothing is wrong, and making a salad and folding your own laundry is perfectly normal behavior for you."

"I can do nice things for myself!" She grabbed another cherry tomato and carefully curled her fingertips around it. The same way Gabe had shown her, when he'd surrounded her in his arms and kissed her behind her ear. "I don't want anyone's condescending-ass favors!"

The knife pushed through the red skin of the tomato, oozing seeds onto the cutting board.

"I don't need anyone's support!"

One tomato half bounced off the kale when Tara threw it into the bowl, falling to the floor with a splat. Tara left it where it fell and grabbed the last tomato.

"I am fine on my own." The knife rattled the plastic of the cutting board as Tara cut the tomato with more vigor than necessary. She tossed the unevenly cut halves into the bowl anyway. "I can't rely on anyone but myself!"

Stabbing the salad with her fork, Tara stuffed the oversized bite into her mouth. The sharp burn of the onion and the bitterness of the kale made her gag. She spat it back into the bowl. "This is so gross! Why does he eat this shit?"

Blanche rubbed her back. "I think you're supposed to put dressing on it?"

Tara tossed the bowl back onto the counter and fell into Blanche's waiting arms. "I don't know how to make dressing!"

"We can buy some, Babes. You don't have to make it from scratch." Blanche held her as sobs wracked her body. "You want some tea?"

Tara nodded into their shoulder. "Yes, please. I hate feeling like this."

"Feeling like what, Babes?"

Like she hated herself for causing Gabe pain. Resentful, because she'd never asked him to do nice things for her, and conflicted because she was touched that he wanted to. Confused, because even when she'd made herself run, every fiber of her being had told her to stay. To pause like he'd said. To talk it out and let him bend her over the conference table to lavish her with kisses and praise, the way he always did.

For his sake—and her own—determination had won out. The mask she'd worn for nine months no longer fit. Being his friend was too uncomfortable, so she'd left, despite the hurt in his eyes and the pain in his voice. She had ended things because she didn't want to hurt him. Yet here he was, weeks later, with dark circles under his eyes, suffering in her mere presence, and still asking for more than she could give. She'd drink however many gallons of the nasty tea it took to soothe her conscience.

"Guilty."

Wednesday, May Nineteenth

Chapter Thirty

LIKE EVERY OTHER WEDNESDAY afternoon, Richard was early for his therapy appointment. And because he was usually Everett's last appointment of the day, Everett was always late. Richard tapped his foot on the sun-streaked carpet. The leather couch in the lobby creaked as he shifted impatiently.

He could do what the others were doing while waiting for their appointments: scrolling through social media (more specifically, watching videos without headphones in, which was rude and annoying). Instead, he was rehearsing how to tell Everett that he and Sunny had essentially started LARPing heteronormativity, and that he strangely liked it. Because while he felt spectacularly useless these days—Gabe was pretending he was fine, even though he clearly wasn't, and Antonio said that wedding planning was pretty much done, so there was nothing he could help with—Sunny wanted *this* from him.

The oddest part was that it was working. Setting aside time to plan and discuss their desires every week meant they were talking about stuff that they probably should have talked about months ago. She still got to annoy him to their hearts' content, and he got to make her come undone on new levels they'd never achieved before.

If only he could get Gabe to roleplay a friendship where they talked about their feelings—

"Hello stranger," said a cool voice.

Richard started at Blanche standing next to him; he hadn't seen them come in. "Please don't tell me you just left Everett's office."

Wrapping their knee-length cardigan around themself, Blanche laughed as they sprawled on the couch next to him. "Calm down, Dicky. I'm not poaching your therapist. No, I'm here to see someone named Shayla. She comes highly recommended with a six-month waitlist, so your therapist is safe from me."

"Another new therapist?" Richard asked, eyeing the other people waiting to make sure they were still absorbed in their phones. "How many is that?"

"Seven," Blanche scoffed. "In less than a year. I'm starting to wonder if I'm the problem, and I'm self-sabotaging my attempts at therapy, so I don't have to do the work to heal."

"Sounds like you've been in therapy," Richard muttered with a grin.

"Right?" Blanche snorted. "It's been hard finding someone nonjudgmental. Bellamy has a serious shortage of sex worker and kink-positive therapists. Or trans-friendly therapists. Or maybe just me-friendly therapists."

Richard nodded. "It took me a while to find Everett."

"So far, I've made three of them cry during the first session, and two referred me to someone else because I had too much going on." Blanche leaned back; their proud smile was undercut by a bitter look in their eye. "The rest have either been really judgmental about my life choices or my career, or they've been transphobic, or they said I won't heal until I end my contract with my patron. Which, yeah, obviously, but that's not really an option." They snorted. "So I think I'm beating therapy."

Richard snickered.

"But maybe it's working because I feel shit all the time now. And I can talk about hard shit when I'm sober, which is new. Getting me to *stop* talking is the problem now." Blanche pulled their hair over their shoulder, smoothing it out with their fingers. "Anyway, how is Gabe?"

Richard huffed. "Shitty. How's Tara?"

Blanche groaned. "She's a fucking wreck. As am I, because I haven't seen Hippo in weeks. Gabe used to let me dog-sit while he and Tara did their little driving lessons, and I miss my best friend."

Richard paused, tucking one leg under to face them. "Do you know what happened?"

"Not the details, but more than anyone else." Blanche leaned in with a conspiratorial smirk. "And I'm not telling you!"

"Come on!" Richard groaned. "Gabe won't open up about it, and I feel so...useless."

"Me too!" Blanche nodded in sympathy. "My shoulder has been cried on a lot, but I can't do much other than that. I hate feeling guilty."

"Why do you feel guilty?" Richard narrowed his eyes. "What did you have to do with it?"

"Nothing with their relationship," Blanche waved him off. "But I've been taking steps to extricate myself from my arrangement with my patron, and I figured when we got evicted, we could stay with Gabe. But now?" They winced. "Whatever happened has got Tara on an independent streak. She won't even let Lee do her laundry."

"Why would Lee do her laundry?" Richard asked skeptically.

"They have a weird friendship! Don't worry about it." Blanche shrugged. "The point is, her wounded pride will keep her from accepting his help, and the whole point of this arrangement is so Tara and Lee would have a roof over their head, and here I am, putting her at risk of homelessness again. I can only hope that whatever investors your friend Phineas can drum up leaves me enough to still rent us an apartment."

Richard frowned. "Investors for—"

"Blanche?"

Richard's question was interrupted by a woman, calling out Blanche's name from the hallway that led to the office.

"Ah, showtime," Blanche teased as they rose from the couch. "Let's see if I make this one cry."

"So LET ME GET this straight," Richard steepled his fingers from his seat in front of Phineas's desk. The sun had set, making the overhead lights obnoxiously bright. But the law office where Phineas worked was still bustling. "You need someone to invest in a gay bar to help a trans sex worker—and *friend* of mine—get out of an exploitative situation, and you didn't come to me? You know I love using my dad's money for shit like that!"

"Look, Dicky," Phineas sat back, blazer draped over the back of his chair. The top three buttons were undone, exposing the half-dozen chains under his shirt. He rubbed his eyes with a sigh. "You typically don't keep this much liquid, and your trust fund is basically dry after you bailed half of Bellamy out of jail. And besides, Miriam already agreed to it."

"How much?" Richard asked.

Phineas leveled a look at him. "Don't call him! You hate him!"

"Phin," Richard warned. He'd come here straight from therapy to get to the bottom of this; it had left him even more on edge than he'd been before his session with Everett. Who had suggested Richard find other ways to make himself useful, instead of waiting around for Gabe to be ready to confide in him. Unbeknownst to Everett, it gave Richard the excuse to show up unannounced to Phineas's office. "How much."

Phineas sighed. "Total? Just over a mil. Miriam is putting in five hundred, and Blanche says they can scrape together the rest."

"I'll get it," Richard blurted out. "The other five. Or however much Blanche wants."

"With what money?" Phineas asked. "Your investments are tied up, and your dad hasn't transferred you anything in two years. Because, might I remind you, you went no contact. And for good reason!"

"Phin, literally the only reason I haven't gotten more is because I haven't asked for it." Richard crossed his arms. If Gabe wouldn't let him help him directly, here was something he could do for Blanche. Helping Confession would indirectly help Tara, which would indirectly help Gabe. Kind of. "He probably doesn't care that I haven't reached out to him."

Phineas raised his eyebrows. "So you're just gonna call up your dad, who you haven't voluntarily spoken to since you stole his—"

"I didn't *steal* anything. He signed the papers. He just didn't read what he was signing," Richard clarified archly. "And yeah, I guarantee he hasn't noticed that I haven't been around. Watch." He pulled out his phone, took a deep breath, and hit the call button on his least favorite contact.

"What."

Delightful as ever, his father. Richard cleared his throat, forcing his pitch up. "Hey Dad!"

"Oh. Elizabeth. What's wrong?"

"Nothing's wrong! Just calling to say hi!" Richard had trained the upspeak out of his voice a decade ago; using it now felt like a cruel caricature of femininity.

Phineas cringed.

Richard shook his head at him, silently warning him to keep his face quiet.

"You know better than that. I'm a busy man. Get to the point."

"Well, you see... There's an investment opportunity Miriam suggested we go in on together." His dad's obsession with Gabe's mom was embarrassing on a good day, but Richard was never above exploiting it.

"Miriam, huh?" His dad's voice softened. "How much?"

Richard silently died inside as he chirped, "Just a million!"

Phineas's eyes bulged behind his glasses. Richard looked away to keep his composure within his most hated headspace.

"A million!" His dad coughed. "Jesus, Lizzie! What are the numbers looking like?"

Richard swallowed all of his pride and responded, "I can't remember off the top of my head, but Gabe told me they looked good when I asked his opinion."

"Ah, well. I suppose if Miriam is involved, and her son thinks it'd be good..." Dick sighed. "Where am I sending it?"

Richard gave Phineas a thumbs-up, who threw up his hands in annoyance. "My trust, please. Miriam is sending me the wiring instructions tomorrow, so it won't sit there long."

"I'll have my accountant send that over in the morning."

"Thank you, Dad!" Richard dragged out the singsong tone, as Phineas gagged.

"Oh, and Elizabeth?"

"Yeah, Dad?"

"Call your mom. She's been crying a lot."

"What's wrong with her?" Richard asked, his pitch slipping as concern flared through him. There was no love lost between him and his mom. But even after thirty years in Bellamy, Barbie didn't have many friends. Mostly due to her husband's personality, but also her own. Richard had always been her emotional support child; everyone in their social circle was aware that Barbie had never been Dick's first choice.

"Not sure. I figured you'd be better at all that than I would," his dad said dismissively.

So he hadn't asked. Typical. Richard wouldn't wish Barbie's life on anyone, not even his bitchy, transphobic mother. He sighed, "Yeah, I'll call her."

Phineas shook his head as Richard hung up. "You are the scariest dude I know, Dicky. Seriously. Watching that is uncanny as hell, every time." Opening his desk drawer, he retrieved a crystal glass and a bottle. "Here." He poured a finger of scotch, setting the bottle down next to it with a *thunk*. "Take the bottle with you. I'm taking a break from alcohol."

"Good for you." Richard threw back the scotch with a wince. He coughed, yawning a couple times to make sure his voice would come out at the register he wanted. "I hate doing that."

"That's why I didn't ask you, bro!" Phineas held up his hands. "Then again, you just got a million dollars for making a phone call, so what do I know? I'll iron out the details with Miriam and Blanche, but congrats. You'll soon own approximately one-fifth of a bar."

Saturday, May Twenty-Ninth

CHAPTER THIRTY-ONE

BLANCHE

In the middle of nowhere Wisconsin, Gabe stopped to fill the gas tank. Blanche eyed the dingy gas station with skepticism, an intuitive prickle of danger running down their spine. His Outback was dwarfed by the nearby pickups, parked on the gravel surrounding the log building. They sank back into the passenger seat, avoiding the gaze of three burly white men in overalls who reminded them too much of their Papa.

Just as Gabe climbed into the driver's seat next to Blanche, Tara got out, muttering something about the bathroom under her breath. Gabe huffed, waiting for the car door to slam behind her, before he asked, "Don't have to go?"

Their bladder was uncomfortably full, but Blanche was reluctant to leave the safety of the car. "I can hold it. You?"

Gabe raised an eyebrow at the yellow Gadsden flag, hanging below the American flag in front of the building. "Same. I'll let Richard know to get gas close to the freeway."

"You and Tara still not talking, I take it?" they tentatively asked, breaking the silence as they waited for Tara to come back out. Three hours into the four-hour drive, and already, Blanche had never had a more awkward car ride in their life. And they'd once hitchhiked from Marshall—the closest city to their small town in Minnesota—to Bellamy with a couple who had screamed at each other the whole way.

"Nope." Gabe's thumbs drummed on the steering wheel.

The only time Tara had spoken so far was to ask if she could change the music to something that didn't make her want to kill herself. Blanche—in the passenger seat, and therefore in charge of the stereo—had personally been enjoying the Alice in Chains album they'd picked. But they let Tara switch it to the R&B she preferred. Gabe apparently appreciated the change, humming under his breath, but otherwise he ignored both of them.

The GPS had been more talkative than anyone else.

"You doing okay?" Blanche asked.

"Fine," came Gabe's terse response.

Blanche glanced at him from the corner of their eye. "Can you fix it? Please?"

Gabe's jaw twitched. "Not sure what you want me to do."

"Whatever you need to! I can't take it anymore!" Blanche pleaded. "She's doing laundry every day! She already killed two of my succulents because she started watering the plants. I can't even finish my tea before she's washing the cup. She's eating salad, Gabe! Tara! Salad!"

His lips twitched, but he shook his head. "She asked for space, Blanche. I'm giving her space. Maybe after the wedding—"

"*After* the wedding? That's another month away!" Blanche groaned. "You guys would be so good together—she knows that! She's just stubborn and won't admit it to herself."

"So what, I should push her into something she doesn't want? Beg and grovel, until she gives in? How long would it last before she changed her mind again? A relationship like *that* would not be good for *me*." Gabe shook his head with a bitter laugh. "I would love to prove you right, but it's not my call. She said she wants to be friends again after the wedding, but until then, she wants space. And I will take her at her word. I refuse to be in another relationship—hell, even a friendship—where I feel like I'm not good enough."

Blanche touched his arm. "Tara would never make you—"

"Wouldn't she? Funny, I feel like shit now," Gabe's voice broke. He cleared his throat.

"Well, once she gets her head out of her ass, she won't." Blanche's heart went out to him. Lee had said that Gabe had been just as eaten up about their falling out as Tara, but it was different to witness themself. "Tara is so kind and loving and supportive once she lets you in."

"Then she can pull her own head out of her ass if she wants." Gabe turned the car on as Tara exited the gas station. "I can't—I *won't* make her do anything she doesn't want to do."

Blanche wanted to respond, but Tara opened the back door and climbed in wordlessly.

"Ready?" Gabe asked, his face solidifying back into a cold mask.

The click of her seat belt and a grunt from the backseat was Tara's only reply.

ANTONIO

"I WISH YOU'D LET us hire strippers for tonight," Tara pouted, adjusting her lounge chair to sit up. She sat near the sunbathing Antonio under a forest green beach umbrella, in running shorts and a tank top and slathered in sunscreen. Streaks of white stained the fabric of her clothes and clumped in her hair. More freckles seemed to erupt on her body every minute, despite her spot in the shade.

The small swimming beach in front of the cabin was exactly what Antonio had envisioned: gentle breeze, hot sun, and the peaceful lapping of tiny waves against the dock—interrupted by the occasional splash from a fish jumping. He'd wanted a retreat to nostalgia, to the long weekends when he and Gabe had gone up to the Cooper cabin, before they'd sold it to build the wedding venue at the vineyard. Board games, skinny dipping, and a sliver of peace. Tara and Gabe had done well with finding this place.

Contentment hummed in his chest as he stretched facedown in his lounge chair. The hot sun warmed his ass cheeks, peeking out of his barely-there speedo. He grinned up at her. "I know it's a bachelor party, Tara-Bear, but this is a small town. How many male strippers do you think live here? Lee will get plenty of lap dances from me this weekend."

Tara scoffed. "Who said anything about *male* strippers? They're for me, not you."

Antonio laughed, "Sorry, not happening. This weekend is for Lee and I. Your job is to be the supportive best man, who bends over backward for us."

"Yes, sir." Tara grinned as she smacked his ass. With how much she'd been complaining of sunburn lately, Antonio half expected her pasty arm to fall into dust like a vampire the moment she left the shade. "Whatever you ask, I'll deliver."

"Excuse me, please don't get sunscreen on the one part of my body that I'm trying to tan," Antonio teased. "I don't want a random handpri—" He paused. "Actually, *can* you give me a sunscreen handprint?"

Tara laughed and complied, rubbing fresh sunscreen on her hands and pressing a handprint into each ass cheek. "You really should be wearing sunscreen anyway. You don't want to get sunburned on your ass of all places."

"I'll take the risk. If it looks like I can't walk tomorrow, pretend it's sunburn."

Tara laughed again. She had been in surprisingly good spirits since they'd arrived, especially compared to what a mess Gabe had been the past month. And still was; Gabe had given the grumpiest tour Antonio had ever experienced. From what Lee and Blanche had said, Tara was just as emotionally fragile, but she seemed fine to Antonio.

Blanche pulled another lounge under the shade beside Tara. "Babes, can I have some sunscreen? Somehow my thighs burned through the sunroof on the drive here."

"You too?" Tara handed them the bottle. "My arm burned through the window."

"You don't have a weird contagious skin thing, do you?" Antonio asked, only half-joking. "If my ass falls off because you put sunscreen on it, I'm suing you for malpractice."

Tara laughed. "I don't think that's how it works. I'm a redhead. We burn easily. I don't know what Blanche's deal is."

"Maybe I am Swedish after all," Blanche deadpanned, tentatively pressing the bronze skin of their thighs with a wince. "They catch anything yet?"

Antonio twisted his neck around to where Lee and Gabe sat on the end of the dock. He had volunteered Gabe's expertise when Lee had mentioned he'd always wanted to learn how to fish (on the cabin tour, Gabe had pointed to the rods hanging on the walls with a grunted

"There's shit if you wanna fish"). They'd been sitting silently for an hour, drinking beers and watching their bobbers float in the water.

God, fishing was boring. "No. I don't think they even have bait."

"Where are the other two?" Blanche wiped their sunscreen-slick hands down their long legs, then covered them with their kaftan.

"Touching grass!" Antonio quipped.

Tara snorted. "On a walk. Apparently, the drive up here was enough to put Richard over the edge. Sunny mentioned something about too much car karaoke as she followed him."

"He has no appreciation for my talents." Antonio sighed.

"This is way nicer weather than your pool party last Memorial Day." Blanche slid oversized sunglasses under the large sun hat flopping over their face. "This is actually warm."

"I'm glad the weather cooperated. We had to drive hours to get here—it'd suck to sit inside all weekend," Tara said. "Finding a lake cabin close to a gay bar was a tall order, Tonio."

"But you and Gabe delivered perfectly, Tara-Bear." Antonio grinned as he rolled over, sitting up to take a sip of his sparkling water.

For an A-frame cabin, it was surprisingly spacious, with an addition that gave it three bedrooms and a loft. He and Lee had claimed the loft right away, ignoring Gabe muttering that he should have added earplugs to the packing list. The bed was clean and smelled like fresh linen and pine. Much nicer than the Cooper's old cabin, with the dusty bunk beds and spiders. But Antonio wouldn't trade those memories for anything.

"Babes, can you be a dear and take some photos of me for my socials?" Blanche crossed their legs on the lounge. "Let my subscribers know I won't be able to reply to their messages right away."

"Never stop grinding, huh, Blanche?" Antonio teased them. "I thought with Richard and Miriam buying Covey out, you could relax a bit."

"The papers haven't been signed yet," Blanche said with a shrug. "And assuming it all goes well, I might be able to afford a house, so I can't afford to slow down yet. The housing market is a bitch, even as a cash buyer. But I'll find a place for us, Tara, don't worry. Chas sent me the number of a realtor he knows."

"I'm not worried. We'll figure it out," Tara said cheerfully, pulling out her phone. "You look like someone's gold-digging stepmother in that getup."

Blanche laughed, winking over their cat-eye sunglasses. "I've been called worse."

"You know you're always welcome to stay with us," Antonio offered. If nothing else, he'd find a way to fix whatever had gotten between Gabe and Tara, and make him offer them a place to stay. *He has a big ass house just for him.*

"Please, you two are about to be married. We can't impose on that." Tara sat back, editing the photo on her phone.

Antonio shivered as the shade from the trees crept over his sun-warmed skin. The blue sky was hinting at the first streaks of orange when his stomach growled. "Gabey Baby! I'm hungry!"

Gabe scowled over his shoulder. "Yes, dear."

Lee and Gabe packed up their fishing equipment—pulling seaweed from empty hooks—just as Richard and Sunny strolled back, hand in hand.

"Let's pregame!" Antonio announced, throwing open the sliding patio door as he led the way inside. "Oh! We should play a drinking game!"

"I'm taking another walk." Richard turned around, but Sunny caught his arm with a laugh.

Lee followed Antonio up to their loft bedroom, teasing, "You know for someone who doesn't drink anymore, you certainly love to get everyone else drunk."

Antonio kissed him at the top of the stairs. "It's the only way I can get you all to my level."

Changed into a revealing white romper, Antonio slid down the railing as they made their way back downstairs. Lee had reluctantly agreed to wear a coordinating romper in black. Slightly more modest than Antonio's, yet Lee still left the top unbuttoned to show off his built chest. Despite his insistence that he didn't like to wear shorts in public, Lee hadn't protested when Antonio rolled up the sleeves and hems to flatter his muscular arms and thighs.

Still in their floral kaftan, Blanche had swapped the sunhat for a high ponytail, their silky bleach-blond hair flowing from the crown of their head. Their "Officiant" sash was draped over a shoulder as they lounged in a chair, a glass of whiskey in hand. "Don't you two look charming!" they exclaimed with a smile. "You're hoping for free drinks, aren't you?"

Antonio laughed. "I just want the glory of being a bachelorette. Any brown liquor I get is coming your way."

Wearing a tight black t-shirt and even tighter jeans that made Antonio drool a little, Gabe entered the house with a stack of pizza boxes, just as Tara walked past the front door with an ice bucket full of beer, sparkling water, and hard seltzer. They avoided eye contact, awkwardly dancing around each other so they didn't have to talk.

Oh, that must have been an awkward car ride. He glanced over at Blanche to catch their eye. They stared back with a deadpan expression and a heavy sigh in response. *Hopefully, drinks will help. Social lubricant and all that.* Antonio rarely missed alcohol, but it sure was useful for other people in dire need of loosening their inhibitions.

Richard and Sunny joined them shortly after, dressed sharply as always with Sunny in a cute red dress and her "Groomsmaid" sash. Richard was, once again, in his standard boring button-down and slacks under his "Groomsman" sash.

Antonio shuddered at the thought of wearing navy or black every day. *I want to put him in jeans. No, shorts!* He would find a way to make Richard dress down this weekend. Antonio gasped. *Jorts!*

As if sensing his thoughts, Richard narrowed his eyes. "Whatever you're thinking, stop it."

Antonio merely winked. "Food's here, drinks are here, we're here. Let's play Never Have I Ever!" He sat down on the love seat, pulling Lee next to him. "Take a drink with each one that applies to you, and then the losers—better known as the cool kids—have to finish their drinks."

"Eating in peace sounds fine to me," Richard muttered, but cracked open a seltzer anyway.

"At least it's not Truth or Dare again." Tara set her sash down next to her. "Never playing that with *you* again, Dicky."

Tara's chambray tank was unbuttoned daringly low, teasing a peek at her small chest and a generous view of her sternum. Her long legs were on display in khaki shorts that were tiny enough to pass as a belt. Freckles and damp leg hair decorated her pale skin. She must have rinsed the sunscreen off; her left arm was distinctly pink.

"I'll go first." Lee offered, elbowing him. Antonio blinked, grinning with a shrug when he realized Lee had caught him ogling Tara. "Never have I ever had PIV sex."

"That's a cheap shot," Antonio muttered, taking a sip of his water as everyone drank.

Lee grinned. "Gotta play my Gold Star card when I can."

Antonio went next. "Never have I ever... Damn." He'd done everything he could think of. "Oh, I know! Never have I ever been on a sports team."

Everyone but Tara and Blanche drank, including Antonio when Gabe reminded him that he'd played tee-ball when he was little.

Tara got everyone but Lee, when she said she'd never had a pet, and Blanche got everyone because they'd never gotten a degree.

Richard went next. "Never have I ever gotten a tattoo."

Everyone but Sunny, Richard, and Gabe drank. Sunny shot him an unreadable look.

"Hold on, let's show them off." Antonio held up his wrists, showing off the words "Not today" on one and "Not tomorrow" on the other. "Honestly, I don't know how it took me this long to get a tattoo, but Freddy did these for me when I hit two years sober."

"Freddy did mine, too." Blanche pulled back their kaftan, revealing a daisy along their collarbone.

"I can't show you my tramp stamp in this outfit, but I also got it from Freddy," Lee laughed, covering Antonio's mouth as he opened it to howl. "It's a paw print. I got it when I was nineteen. Not my finest moment."

"So *all* of us got tattoos from Freddy?" Tara asked. "Why does that not surprise me?"

"Wait, *Freddy* tattooed you?" Gabe asked, incredulous. "I can't say a word to him without Chas accusing me of flirting with her husband, but she let *that* slide?"

Antonio didn't know what Tara's first tattoo was, just that it was covered by her teeny tiny shorts. And the one she'd gotten with him was dangerously close to her titty. He cocked his head, curious how Gabe knew where Tara's sexy tattoos were.

"Chas supervised." Tara shrugged, not meeting his eyes.

Sunny cleared her throat. "Never have I ever had a threesome!"

Everyone but Lee drank.

Sunny gasped. "Dicky! When did you have a threesome?"

Antonio cackled. His suspicions about the tattoos could wait. "You never told her?"

Richard blushed. "I didn't think it was important."

Antonio tsked, offended. "Dicky, we spent a magical night together teaching Gabe how to eat vag properly, and you didn't think it was *important*?!"

Tara choked, coughing on her drink. "Wait, *you* taught *him*?"

Antonio waved her off. "I know, I come across as super flamboyant, but I'm honestly pretty equal opportunity. I was in my ho era back then, and Gabe... Well, no offense Gabey, but you weren't exactly a confident lover. Like, you could suck a dick like no other, but with pussy?"

"That's fair." Gabe shrugged. "I had no idea what I was doing."

"And I had no idea how to teach you." Richard nodded. "I was very sheltered."

Tara shook her head, staring stunned at the ceiling.

"Wait, I'm sorry." Sunny pointed at Tara accusingly. "Since when did *you* have a threesome? That's new, isn't it?"

"No. I told you about it. You just don't listen." Tara blushed so hard that the pale skin of her neck turned splotchy. "Pride weekend a couple years ago, this older lesbian couple invited me back to meet their dog. And you know I love dogs. So one thing led to another, and I met their—y'know... cats."

"Bitch, that is so corny," Antonio laughed along with everyone else.

Tara shrugged. "Whatever, second-best head I've ever gotten. They worked together, and it was sublime."

Curious as he was, Antonio didn't bother to ask who came first. Gabe's smirk told him plenty. *Oh, Gabey, what have you been hiding from me?*

"I feel like I'm missing out, but I don't want to share Dicky with anyone," Sunny sighed. "Gabe, this is your chance. Antonio and Blanche are the only ones who've done everything."

Gabe gave him a shit-eating grin. *Fuck.* Gabe knew all of his secrets. *Is it going to the BB gun? Or the time I pierced my own nipple? Or—*

"Never have I ever been engaged to someone I love as much as you two love each other," Gabe said, his smile softening.

Everyone aww'ed, no one louder than Antonio, whose heart melted. Sentiment washed away the manic excitement that had been fueling him. With everything so fraught between wedding planning, the anxiety about Confession, and Gabe and Tara still not talking, Antonio had been so focused on making sure everyone—especially Lee—could loosen up and unwind. But he'd forgotten that this weekend was for him and Lee, too.

"Oh Gabey, that's disgustingly sweet." He smiled at Lee, who drank with him before they shared a too-brief kiss. His future husband was always going to be weird about swapping spit in company. Antonio instead rubbed his back, a private display of the love fluttering in his chest, while he said to Gabe, "I thought for sure you were going to call me out for something embarrassing, like that time you had to drive me to the hospital because I got a bottle stuck in my ass."

"Thought about it, but it's your weekend, Tonio." Gabe smiled up at him.

Antonio was so caught up in his moment with Lee that he barely noticed Blanche downing their drink, too.

ON THE WALK TO the bar, Antonio pretended his shoes hurt as an excuse to meddle—not *too* much, just enough to ease the tension. "Gabey, can you give me a piggyback ride?"

"Isn't that what your fiancée is for?" Gabe bent down anyway.

Antonio climbed on his back, adjusting the "Best Man" sash around Gabe's shoulder so it wouldn't wrinkle. "Yeah, but I need to ride him tonight. I can't tire him out beforehand."

"Tonio, I swear if you talk about fucking your fiancée when your dick is pressed against my back, I'm going to drop you," Gabe laughed, despite his grumpy tone.

Once they were far away from the group enough to not be over-heard, Antonio asked quietly, "So, what do Tara's tattoos look like?"

"Oh, she's got like these abstract lines on her hips—" Gabe cut off when he realized exactly what he was explaining.

"Oh, Gabey. You walked right into that." Antonio kissed his cheek. "I fucking knew it! Did you see those abstract lines in my bathroom by any chance?"

Gabe didn't reply. That was all the answer Antonio needed.

"And you said you never had sex in my bathroom." Antonio shook his head. "You lied to me, Gabe? Me?!"

Gabe huffed. "I didn't lie. I specifically said I never *came* in your bathroom."

As happy as he was to finally have his suspicions confirmed, the pang of inadequacy that Gabe and Tara had kept their...whatever they were a secret from their best friends was bitter. Why were his friends so secretive about their relationships? First Dicky, now Gabey. When Antonio had first met Lee, he couldn't shut up about him.

"So if you've been boning Tara this whole time, why are you so upset right now?"

Gabe huffed. "We haven't been *boning* this whole time. More off and on. Mostly off. And it's off now, and it's probably going to stay off. So there's really no point in talking about it."

"Did you try telling her you love her?" Antonio gently teased. Gabe didn't have an Off mode once feelings were involved. He was an all-in, love-at-first-sight, heart-on-his-sleeve kind of lover.

As expected, Gabe didn't answer. He kept walking, hanging further back from the group.

While everyone knew Gabe and Tara had been carrying a torch for each other for at least a year, Antonio couldn't believe they'd been *fucking*. He and Lee had thought their argument was about the feelings they wouldn't admit for each other, not a full-on secret situationship and breakup. Sure, Gabe had those love bites. But before that, the only sign had been their longing stares and overly considerate attention.

That Gabe hadn't been worse over the past month surprised him, given how despondent he'd been after his breakups in the past; Antonio had moved to New York right after Justin had left, and had ended up staying with Gabe longer than planned because Gabe had been an utter wreck. Antonio had done his best to give him a reason to get up in the mornings—go to work, eat regular meals, *live*—but he'd been a mess himself. And Gabe's depression then had been the worst Antonio had ever seen, though Richard had said it'd been worse during his relationship with Emily.

"I wouldn't be too certain that it's off forever, Gabey." Antonio nuzzled his friend's neck, amazed by his resilience in what had been a worse time than Gabe had let on. "Lee thinks Tara caught feelings and got scared. She's been drinking this god-awful tea to help her mood, and working constantly and doing her own laundry and shit. Which is basically a cry for help when it comes to Tara."

Gabe's huff sounded more like a laugh this time. "She's been eating salad, apparently."

"Exactly," Antonio sighed, resisting the urge to meddle more. He couldn't bear to see his friends fight, especially when their feelings were requited. "Look, I know you don't like me in your business, but you've been moping and quiet for... Well, your whole life, but it's been *bad* the past month. I need you to get it together, for my sake." Antonio teased, hoping his go-to method for cheering up Gabe was more effective now than it used to be. "I can't have a sad best man in the wedding photos, after all."

Gabe grumbled, but when he spoke, his voice was husky. "Thanks, Tonio. Seriously, I love and appreciate you. Don't worry about me. This is your weekend, okay? Enjoy it."

Antonio kissed his cheek. "I *am* enjoying it. I hope you will too."

Gabe merely grunted in response.

CHAPTER THIRTY-TWO

TARA

TARA SCANNED THE CROWD as her family filed into the bar, searching for signs of danger in the dated wood-paneled venue, decorated with campy movie posters and rainbow beer ads. Two emergency exit signs were illuminated across the room, and the bar had good sightlines around the whole place. While small and badly lit, the space was acceptable enough to comply with Rule Eight (always have an escape route). Compared to Confession, the clientele was a little heteronormative and very white, but that was to be expected in a small town gay bar. *Seems safe enough for now, though. I'll stay alert.*

Their group would stick out like a sore thumb regardless. Thankfully, no one looked at their party with anything but curiosity and interest. As Tara lingered by the entrance, Antonio claimed a table near the stage. Before he could sit down, he was called up by the emcee, who recognized him from Confession; she'd apparently been a fan of Carlita Asada for years.

Tara settled onto a barstool instead of joining the table, desperately needing a moment alone before forcing herself to have fun. After spending all afternoon with a fake smile plastered to her face and a too-chipper attitude, her emotional reserves were depleted. This was going to be a long weekend.

The emcee ordered up shots for Antonio and Lee, who took both of them on Antonio's behalf. At the impromptu lap dance Antonio gave to Lee, the audience cheered for them enough that the knot in Tara's stomach began to loosen, ever so slightly. *Better than the bar we went to for Jazz's birthday. Hopefully Sunny won't start any fights today.*

Even though it was Saturday, Tara was determined to keep her wits about her tonight. Tempting as it was to drown her heart in whiskey, she needed to keep watch for trouble and creeps. She was the one who had brought her friends here; she had to make sure they were safe.

At least, that was the lie she told herself.

Mostly, she needed something to do. To focus on. Anything to take her mind off Gabe, because she couldn't exactly escape the bachelor party.

He'd barely looked at her since she'd gotten in his car this morning, but when he did, his brown eyes were mournful. Peak Puppy Dog Eyes, every glance was heart-wrenching. The hours-long car ride had been excruciating. She longed to see his dimples again, directed at her— *No, he needs to move on. Can't he at least pretend?* If Tara could suck it up and fake nice for everyone this weekend, why couldn't Gabe? For their friends sake, if not for hers. While she was determined to get through this the usual way, pretending she was fine had never ached so much before.

She swallowed a frustrated sigh when she looked behind her. Gabe must have had a similar idea: staying out of the way so as not to ruin the fun. He'd set himself up on a barstool a few feet away, giving her space, but his presence was undeniable. Despite her best efforts, her gaze kept pulling back to him.

Like her, Gabe seemed to be on guard duty. He craned his neck to watch Richard and Sunny dancing, and Blanche engaged in conversation. A group of short femmes at the next table were cooing over their kaftan. Blanche fawned over them in return, the bronze of their cheeks reddening. An affectionate chuckle escaped Tara. Blanche always acted so tough and untouchable, but a pretty femme giving them an ounce of attention turned them into a puddle every time.

"Can I buy you a drink?" Leaning on the bar between her and Gabe, some man smirked at her, wearing a dirty baseball hat and an unbuttoned flannel over a ratty gray t-shirt.

Tara blinked. "Oh, are you talking to me?" The guy must have thought she'd been staring at *him,* when she was sneaking glances at the sad brown eyes looking around the room.

"Yeah, who else would I be talking to?" The man snorted.

Behind him, Gabe glared into the middle distance, jaw working back and forth. Tara's chest tightened at the emotions clouding his face. Stomach twisting, Tara knew that she was about to make a bad decision. *This might be what helps him move on.* She forced herself to smile brightly, barely looking at the guy beyond his plaid shirt and grimy baseball cap. "Sure."

"So what's your name?" He handed her a beer.

Tara was over this already. Baseball Hat hadn't even asked what she wanted, just handed her an already poured beer. It was probably roofied. She frowned, dread and annoyance tightening her stomach. "Honestly, do you care what my name is?"

She was executing her impulsive, impromptu plan very poorly. If she was trying to piss Gabe off so he could stop moping after her, she had to at least pretend to like this creep.

Tara pretended to sip the beer with her lips tightly sealed. The bitter hoppy smell turned her stomach. He'd already been a walking red flag before he gave her a fucking IPA, objectively the worst beer. His cologne was another red flag, overwhelming and cheap. And the dirt under his nails? Tara set the drink down. Maybe she'd get to blow off some steam by beating the shit out of him after this. She only had to act interested long enough for Gabe to get turned off by what a disaster she was.

Baseball Hat laughed as if she'd said the funniest thing. "I guess I don't need to know your name. I already know everything I need to know about you."

Fucking kill me. "Oh? And what's that?" she asked, not caring.

"I came here looking for a good woman, but it looks like I found the best man instead," he cackled. "You might be the first man I take home with me."

She cringed as he traced a finger down the vee of her shirt, fiddling with the "Best Man" sash that hid her cleavage. She'd left her shirt mostly open, trusting the sash would cover the important bits, but that wasn't an invitation. His dirty nail scraped the skin of her sternum.

Her temper flared, *fight fight fight* coursing under her skin. After a month of being angry at herself, a punching bag would be a much needed relief. "Don't fucking touch me," she snapped, slapping his hand away.

With a scowl, he grabbed her wrist, and the adrenaline turned cold, dangerous.

"What the fuck did I just say, asshole?" Tara freed herself easily from his amateur grip, drawing back her fist. She fucking hated entitled-ass men grabbing her.

But before she could land the punch to his gut, he was gone.

Gabe grabbed him by the neck, swinging Baseball Hat around to his other side. Without leaving his barstool, Gabe pinned him against the bar, one arm pressed across his chest. The ratty gray t-shirt was balled in his fist.

Tara protested with a disappointed groan. "Dude, I had him!"

"She said don't touch her." Gabe ignored her, his deep voice going dark as he glared at the man, who scrambled for release from the arm pinning him to the bar. After a long moment, Gabe let him up.

"Jesus, dude, chill out! What are you, her boyfriend or something? We were just talking." The guy rubbed his neck where Gabe had grabbed him.

"Doesn't matter. She said don't touch her, and you did it again."

"Gabe, stop. Don't cause a scene." Tara placed a hand on his arm. Already, eyes from those nearby were turning in their direction. Fear and shame boiled in her chest at the attention of so many strangers spotlighted them. Thankfully the crowd around the stage where their friends were hadn't noticed. Any whisper of that cold anger, that drive to *fight fight fight*, was drowned out by the alarm to *run run run*.

"We don't tolerate fighting here, chief," the bartender said, his hands planted on the bar. "You've both been looking for trouble since you walked in. You gotta go."

"Seriously?" Gabe bristled. "That was hardly a fight. And he start—"

"Gabe! Let's just go. I'll text the others." Tara tugged on his arm. She had to get him out, before Tara got him in trouble too. The others would be fine. They weren't causing problems. Tara was. And now Gabe was at risk because of her shitty impulse control. *Not one lick of sense.* "Please."

A vein in his temple twitched, jaw still clenched, but he nodded.

Baseball Hat looked smug as Gabe followed her out. Tara held her head as high as she could as they walked past all of the eyes staring at them. The bouncer made a show of watching them leave, crossing her arms and glaring until they were back on the sidewalk.

As soon as they were out of earshot of the main street, past the last streetlight and back on the gravel road to the cabin, Tara whirled around. "What the fuck is your problem?"

"What's *my* problem? What the fuck is *your* problem?" Gabe retorted.

"What, I can't let someone buy me a drink?" Tara crossed and uncrossed her arms quickly, jamming her fingers into her pockets; they were too small for more than her fingertips. She tightened her hands into fists instead. Adrenaline coursed hot now that the danger had passed.

Gabe ran his hands through his hair. "Tara, you can do whatever the fuck you want, but really? Him? That *cologne*," he sneered.

"So I need your *approval* on who can buy me a drink?" Tara snapped. Gabe was right; she hadn't even scanned the guy first. But Tara didn't want to admit her lapse in judgment. Especially not to him. She was angry enough that he'd stepped in at all. Angry at herself for getting him into trouble. She was trying to keep him safe from her, and she'd fucking ruined it. Ruined everything. Like she always did.

After a month of suppressing it, all of her anger and hurt and heartache was on the verge of exploding, eager for release after the fight she'd been denied. Lifting her jaw to glare at Gabe, Tara took a step closer.

Gabe stepped back. Away from her. "It's not the drink, Tara. You can do what you want."

"So then, what was it, Gabe?" Her voice was low, steadier than she felt. "Why'd you go off on him like that?"

"Because he grabbed you—your *wrist* of all places—after you told him not to touch you!" Frustration leaked into Gabe's voice. "What was I supposed to do, let him?"

Tara crossed her arms again. "I can handle myself."

Gabe's laugh was sharp. "Oh, I know! Probably saved that dude from a fucking hospital bill. Instead, I get kicked out for fighting. *Chief.*" He spat on the ground and ran his hand through his hair again as he turned away. "Fuck this place!"

"Why'd you lose your cool, Gabe?" It wasn't fair to push him like this; Tara had no right. But she couldn't stop herself. Her pent-up frustration had broken free, making her even more impulsive and shortsighted than she already was. *Probably how I ended up taking a drink from that creep in the first place.* "The last time, you pulled me off the guy. This time, you threw him around by the neck! So what's your problem? Let's talk it out."

Gabe let out another cruel laugh as he whirled to face her. "Oh! You finally want to talk to me? Let's fucking talk!" He gesticulated between them, eyes full of hurt and anger. The moonlight made his tears shine silver. "Why'd you end things with me?"

Tara opened her mouth, but nothing came out. A month of telling herself she was right to push him away, and here Gabe was, making her fragile reasoning even shakier. He'd see right through her.

She looked down to the ground to avoid those damn pleading eyes.

"That's what I thought." He shook his head. "But whatever. *I'll* talk, even if *you* fucking won't. Yeah, I took it a little personally that you would reject me, and then entertain a creep like that!" He pointed to the bar, then jammed his finger against his chest. "And you kept fucking *looking* at me the whole time you were smiling at him! Like I meant nothing to you, like what we had together—what we *could* have had together—meant nothing."

Tara's heart ached at the hurt in his voice, wishing she had any defense, any excuse for the tremble of his lip.

"You can do whatever you want with whoever you want. I can figure out how to deal with my own fucking reactions and my own damn feelings." Gabe ran a hand through his hair again. "But I will not let some creep grab you like that. I would do the same for any friend. Maybe not quite with so much enthusiasm, but you *know* I would!"

A pang of hurt stabbed her right in the chest. "*Friend*, huh?"

"Yes, Tara. Friend!" He whirled back at her. She flinched, but stood her ground. He sighed, lowering his volume. Frustration was still audible in the cracks in his voice. "Because that's what *you* said you fucking wanted. So don't take that pissy tone about it now, not when I'm trying to respect what *you* fucking asked for!"

Turning away, Gabe stalked toward the cabin in the dark.

Blinking back tears, Tara swallowed the knot in her throat. Emotions flooded her chest as Gabe left her behind, coursing through her too fast to process. Shame. Anger. Hurt. Guilt. Longing. Fear. Above all else, regret. A deluge of grief she'd been holding back for decades.

In the heart of the whirlwind, in the quiet, determined calm, where the walls that had protected and caged her heart had stood firm her whole life, a crack formed. Tara trembled in the night air.

Chapter Thirty-Three

GABE

Despite his head roaring with anger, and his heart pounding with adrenaline, Gabe felt utterly ridiculous storming off in a huff. Not even his mom was this dramatic when his parents argued. What was he trying to prove?

That Tara had got under his skin? That much was obvious. She was embedded in his heart, and they both knew it.

That he couldn't stand to be around her? That wasn't true at all. Even now, it took everything not to go back. To sink to his knees in the sharp gravel and beg for her to give him a chance.

That when he got upset, he would leave?

Gabe stopped short with a frustrated groan, as shame forced him to look back. Silhouetted by the flickering streetlight yards behind her, Tara stood alone in the middle of the gravel road. Her face was masked by darkness, but the way her shoulders curled into herself made his heart ache. "Are you fucking coming or what? I'm not leaving you alone at night in this tiny ass town."

Tara jumped, hugging herself tighter.

For an excruciating second, Gabe thought she might turn and walk the other way, just to prove a point. But Tara gave a slight nod and hurried to catch up. He slowed his pace so she wouldn't have to rush in the dark. Eyes trained on the gravel in the dim light, he walked and kept his thoughts to himself.

A haunting cry called from the lake, splitting the silence with a sorrowful echo.

Tara gasped as she fell into step beside him.

"It's a loon," Gabe said softly.

"Oh."

The sound always brought him right back to one of many conferences his dad had dragged him to when he was still an angry teenager. Struggling to answer when everyone there asked him who he belonged to, or where he came from, he had to admit he didn't know. Everyone would put on a polite half smile and nod, but in a way that conveyed pity, doubt, and otherness—the way the other Jewish kids at school exchanged awkward half smiles, when he didn't get their shared slang or inside jokes.

As an adult, Gabe had found his footing. He'd learned to joke about being second generation Chilocco, that his mom had been raised Italian instead of secular. He followed his dad's approach of listening and observing to absorb everything like a sponge, and modeled his mom's incessant networking to find other people like him, who never quite belonged anywhere. But when he was a teenager, in that first year of being dragged to countless conferences and powwows, he had no answers. The constant feeling of being cast adrift, the disconnection from anything that might anchor him, had left him bitter.

The loon called again, piercing and sharp through the quiet night. Tara jumped beside him.

"Same loon, different call," Gabe murmured, his anger softening. "Announcing their territory. The first one was calling for their mate."

"It sounds so sad."

Gabe didn't respond.

In Vancouver, at what felt like the millionth conference in a year, Gabe had gotten bored listening to his dad and his friends tell the same stories about what they used to do, and complain about what was wrong with the world. He'd wandered out of his dad's shadow and into a small room, drawn by the voice of a Tsimshian elder, telling stories to a group of younger kids. Gabe had stuck out like a sore thumb like always—too big, too tall, too old, too young, too white, too brown—but he'd lurked in the back of the room to listen anyway. The elder had silently welcomed him with a smile.

Incorporating its calls with an uncanny accuracy, the elder shared how the loon was a granter of wishes and dreams. How a blind man had wished for his sight and, in gratitude to the loon for granting him this gift, had bestowed a precious shell necklace that scattered loose shells across the loon's back—

Tara slid her hand into Gabe's.

Gabe shook his head, choking out a wet scoff. "Tara—"

With a cold finger to his nose, Tara cut him off. "Pause. Please? I have things I want to say. Things I need you to understand about me. I owe you a dozen explanations." Her eyes fell to her feet. "And it's hard as shit to even think about it, let alone say it out loud, so I just need to get it out. Okay?"

With a nod, he turned back toward the cabin, slowly tracing her fingers with his thumb to warm them as they walked together.

"I'm sorry. For pushing you away. For hurting you. I know it was awful of me. It's just..." Tara hesitated, looking for the right words. "It wasn't nothing. *You* aren't nothing to me. And that terrifies me." Tara kicked a dandelion growing in the gravel. In the moonlight, the seeds exploded into a cloud of stars. "Lee returned some pictures of mine his mom kept after Auntie Alitrice died, when his dad kicked us out of her place. It was the first time I'd seen my parents' faces in years." Her laugh was bitter. "Can you believe that I forgot what my own fucking parents even looked like?"

This wasn't the explanation Gabe had expected. But the words were pouring out of her, and he clung to every one like the precious gift they were.

"I never even looked at them when I was younger. Even before my mom took off. I was too angry to want to. I kept lugging these damn photos around everywhere we went, because someone had to care about our family, even if my parents didn't. And then when I had to leave everything behind, I'd already forgotten their faces." Tara's voice lowered to a whisper, and Gabe held his breath to hear her better. "I didn't remember my dad at all. All of my memories of my mom are her dopesick and begging me for help. Or her sucking off the landlord so we could get another week to come up with rent. But she'd always spend it on fucking heroin, and we'd end up nowhere again. The clearest memory I have is her yelling at me to get lost, and I can only remember her voice."

Gabe squeezed her fingers as she trembled, though the night air was warm.

"Parents are supposed to take care of their kids. Mine left me to fend for myself. I'd go weeks without seeing my mom—and I was so hungry all of the time. But I still begged strangers to buy our food stamps to buy that shit for her. She needed heroin, and I could eat at school." Tara huffed, muttering quietly, "She's probably dead for all I know. My dad too. I search their names sometimes, hoping for a mug shot or police report so I'd know if they're still alive, but nothing ever comes up. I have no idea where they are or what they're doing. Or if they'd even want anything to do with me if I could find them."

Gabe's throat tightened when Tara blinked back the tears that threatened to fall. "But somehow, I was safer with her. After she left for good—I was almost fifteen and I'd already dropped out of school—I went to Saint Mary's because I didn't know where else to go. She'd gotten us kicked out of everywhere else, including Walter's camp. The deacon running intake asked me why my mom ran me off, but I didn't know. She never said. The only thing I could think of was that she caught me kissing a girl—someone I'd known from school. It's not like my mom ever gave a shit about anything I did, but I was a goddamn fool and just told him that."

Gabe could feel Tara's hurt in the way she clutched his hand. Hear her shame and anger in her voice. She exhaled as if trying to laugh, but her breath was shaky. "The deacon decided I needed to be saved from my queerness. He tried to get me to pray with him. I avoided him, tried to lay low so he'd leave me alone. Lee had been there about a week after his dad kicked him out, so the deacon sent him to convince me to attend the conversion therapy prayer group. Instead, I convinced him to stop going. By the end of the week, the deacon seemed convinced the only way to save me was to fix me himself."

Gabe froze as dread pooled in his stomach. "Tara, you don't have to—"

Tara glared up at him. Tugging on his hand, she walked determinedly on. "Don't you dare. You're paused. You told me your shit. I need to tell you my shit. I want you to understand this about me, so I never have to talk about it again. Okay?"

Gabe nodded, falling back into step. A splash broke the calm surface of the lake. A loon tremoloed their arrival.

"He came into my room on a night when I didn't have a roommate." Tara shook her head with a scoff. "I thought it was weird that any homeless shelter would have an empty bed, but he must have done it on purpose. I woke up when he pinned me down and kissed me, forcing his tongue in my mouth. He must have been drunk, because all I could taste was vodka." Tara looked up at him, a proud smile on her face. "So I bit off his tongue and screamed as loud as I could."

Gabe's stomach—already queasy from the memories of Derek doing something similar to him in the middle of the night—turned. His toe caught on the gravel, and he tripped over his feet. "O-off?"

"Just the tip, but it was bloody." Tara made a retching sound. "Then Lee came to my rescue. He heard me scream and hit the guy with my duffel bag, bashing his head into the wall. Knocked him out cold with one hit. Then Lee's weak ass stomach saw the blood and puked on the fucker." She snorted, a quick skip in her step. "It was the one and only time Lee's been useful in a fight, but it was a damn good one. So that's how we ended up kicked out of Saint Mary's, even though their employee sexually assaulted a teenager."

She laughed dryly. "The police wouldn't get involved, saying it was a church matter. Typical Eastside. It's a fucking joke. So we stayed with Walter and Wanda, until Auntie Alitrice tracked Lee down. Lee didn't even ask—he just told her that I was coming too." Her hand tightened around his again. "I never expected him to do that for me, you know? He was the first person who ever stuck around."

Her voice cracked, and Tara cleared her throat. "After she died, it was back to Walter's camp for a few months until the riots. We met Blanche that night, and within a couple weeks, they got an apartment for all of us. Blanche's is the first place I've stayed where I felt some stability. I never had a home before this one. I never had a family until Lee and Blanche." She leaned against his arm as a draft of cool air blew in from the lake, and Gabe fought the urge to wrap himself around her. "That's why I have my rules. I know I'm like my mom. I love the rush that comes with doing risky shit. I totally get how she got addicted, so I've built my life so I don't do the same shit and end up like her."

Gabe's heart broke for her; he forgot he was supposed to stay quiet. "You're nothing like—"

"I am, and you're paused," Tara insisted with a firm shake of her head. "That's what the rules are for, to keep me safe from my shitty impulse control. Only drink on Saturdays and never get drunk in public. Don't give people any information to use against me. Keep my duffel bag packed with anything I can't afford to lose. Don't use drugs—other than weed with Blanche." Tara snorted. "Don't waste food. Have sex when I need to feel a rush—no kissing, though, 'cause of the flashbacks. Don't get attached to hookups, so no repeats, no one from real life, and stay in public. Always have an escape route. Keep the circle small. Take pictures so I don't forget my happy memories."

Tara fell silent for a while as they approached the cabin, but she was still gripping his hand. Gabe wanted to pull her into his arms, hold her. Do everything in his power to reassure her that she'd never have to worry about any of that again. But her hand in his didn't mean anything had changed. Her trust in him didn't mean she wanted his love. She still had him paused.

Another loon wail echoed across the lake.

The two of them hesitated on the edge of the patio. Going through that sliding glass door meant returning to their new normal, the uncomfortable distance and painful silence. Gabe wanted more time with this open Tara, who trusted him with her past and wanted to hold his hand. He gave her a questioning nod toward the lake. Tara nodded back, and together they walked to the dock. Still hand in hand, they sat on the bench facing the water. Tara curled against him, her head on his shoulder.

The first loon wailed back to the second.

"Telling you all of that feels really shitty, but cathartic." Tara looked up at the stars. The moonlight washed out her freckles and the copper of her hair. "Only Lee knows some of this, but we never talk about it. I never even told Blanche most of it. Just enough to help me with the panic attacks." Her gaze rolled over to him, the curve of her cheekbone pale against the night sky. "And I'm not asking for help. I just want you to understand why I'm like this. Why I'm such a mess. Why it's so terrifying that I want you as much as I do. Because I've already broken all of my rules for you, and I still want more." She swallowed, her eyes flitting down to his lips as her own parted.

Gabe swallowed hard, fighting the urge to lean down those few short inches. He might have, if Tara hadn't just shared how much she didn't want any kiss, including his.

Tara looked away first. "But I have no idea how relationships are supposed to work. I don't know how to be there for you, when I don't even know how to be there for me." She blinked, her eyes bright with starlight. "I fucked up. I'm sorry for ending things and not telling you why. You didn't do anything wrong. I was scared, so I pushed you away because you're better off without me. And it sucks ass, because I want you more than anything I've ever wanted!" Tara sniffled. Gabe's heart wrenched at the sight of her beautiful eyes looking so desolate. Those thin, chapped lips he adored were downturned and quivering. "Because I love you. I'm in love with you, but you deserve someone good for you, and that's not me. I've hurt you, and I'll keep hurting you because I'm a fucking mess."

Gabe's heart pounded. Every thought rushing through his head burned on his tongue, desperate to escape. After a single, excruciating heartbeat, where the silence hung thick in the cool night air, Tara let go of his hand and made to stand. "Sorry, I'm gonna go cry by myself in bed. I'm sure none of that is what you wanted to hear, but thank you for listening."

No. Gabe's pulse roared in his ears. She couldn't just *leave* after that. Not without giving him a chance to think of how to begin to respond. With a hand wrapped around her neck, Gabe pulled her back down next to him. "Unpause me." His voice caught around the lump in his throat.

Smiling weakly through her tears, Tara poked his nose.

He wasn't sure which thought to say, what Tara needed to hear. So Gabe pulled her to his chest and held her. She cried quietly, fists bunching up the shirt at his waist as his hand ran across her back. "Thank you for trusting me. I'm here for you, and I'll always be here for you."

"As a friend?" she asked, with that same resentful tone that echoed in his heart every time she said it.

That hope—that irrepressible longing—was back, but he refused to nurture it. She'd said everything he wanted to hear and more. She loved him. He'd never believed anyone when they'd said those words as much as he believed Tara.

But that wasn't enough. Love wasn't enough.

He exhaled slowly. "As a friend, if that's what you want."

"And..." Tara hesitated. "If I don't want us to be friends?"

"You were right. You did hurt me." Gabe held her tight as she tried to squirm out of his arms with a broken sob. "Tara, you hurt me when you *left*, when you pushed me away. It's not about if I *need* you, Tara, or *deserve* you. I *want* you. Mess and all. I'm a fucking mess too, but I am *not* better off without you." He swallowed, murmuring, "Let me support you through a panic attack, let me be impulsive with you when we can, and trust me to keep us grounded when we can't. We can lean on each other." He drew her face to look up at him. Hand cradling her jaw, he struggled to resist the desperate look in her eyes. "But what I can't do is the hot and cold shit. I want us to happen, more than anything, but I need you to choose us even when shit gets hard. To stay with me, instead of running. To let me in like this. I can't do this if today you tell me you want to be with me, but then tomorrow you tell me you didn't mean it. My heart couldn't handle that.

"I meant what I said, I'm not going anywhere. I'm going to be here for you—as a *friend,*" they both scoffed, "or otherwise. Because I love you, and I've loved you from day one. However you want to interpret that, it's still true. I'm not asking for lifelong commitment, but I can't do casual, none of this off-and-on bullshit, not with you. If you aren't willing to be there for me or let me be there for you, then I deserve to know that now, and we will figure out how to be friends."

Joy would be so proud of Gabe. Hell, he was proud of himself. All the conflicting thoughts and suffocating emotions he'd been grappling with over the past month had come out far more coherently than they felt.

Tara's wide eyes blinked up at him, overwhelming him. Everything about her overwhelmed him. But he was tired of chasing and begging, of constantly giving her his heart, only for her to carelessly leave it behind like litter. She had to want him too.

She took a deep breath, lips parting. "Fuck being friends." Her throat bobbed as she swallowed heavily. "We're never going to be just friends. I've been miserable without you. I've made us both miserable. I want you. I want us. Together. Whatever it takes."

Relief crashed over him as he leaned in, pressing trembling lips to her cheek. "Tara, you've had me since the day we met. Even when I wasn't ready for us, I've always been yours."

Her long fingers traced his jawline, his ear, his throat. "You better be fucking patient with me while I figure out this whole relationship shit. I'm going to fucking suck at this."

"We'll figure it out together, Kitten." He laughed in relief, resting his forehead against hers. Their shared breath prickled his skin in the cool evening air.

The loons across the lake hooted softly.

"Fuck it," Tara breathed. "Don't use tongue." With the slightest tilt of her head, Tara brushed her lips against his.

CHAPTER THIRTY-FOUR

TARA

GABE'S LIPS WERE AS pillowy the night she'd stolen a kiss while he'd slept long ago. Tara sighed contentedly, eyes half closed as she let herself experience those fucking beautiful lips that had tempted her for months, years. Except... Gabe wasn't kissing her back.

Tara pulled away sooner than she'd wanted, looking up at him. Dread sank in her stomach as Gabe stared back, slack-jawed and frozen.

"Was that all right?" she asked, her throat dry. "Gabe?"

Gabe blinked rapidly, mouth working open and closed in silence, before he finally found his voice. "Uh... Yes. Very, very. More than all right, I mean. Um... I wasn't expecting— Does this mean I can kiss you now? Without tongue, obviously. I can do that of course, but I—"

With a laugh of relief, Tara cut him off. "Gabe. Just kiss me."

"Thank fuck!" He pressed his lips against hers firmly, the soft pressure perfectly slotting their mouths together.

Tara melted into a boneless puddle in his arms. This was more heavenly than she'd dreamed. Her chest grew so tight, her heart might explode. His hands weaved through her hair and around her back as Gabe kissed her over and over and over again, finding a rhythm between their contented sighs and quick gasps.

Smiling into his kiss, Tara climbed into his lap, desperate to get closer. His shoulders were firm and familiar under her arms, thighs comforting between her legs, curly hair soft between her fingers as they devoured each other. Tara couldn't believe that she'd held herself back from this bliss for so long.

Her phone buzzed in her back pocket.

"You need to get that?" Gabe asked against her mouth.

"Fuck no."

The buzzing continued as whoever it was called again.

"Shit, I forgot to text them!" As she retrieved her phone, Gabe's arms wrapped around her to hold her tight against him, as if she might try to escape. She glanced at the screen before answering it. "What the fuck do you want, Sunny?"

"Wow, bitch, I'm literally just making sure you're alive," Sunny's voice echoed. Music thumped in the background.

"I'm fine. Thanks for caring." Tara was unable to keep the sarcasm from her tone.

"Is Gabe with you? You both disappeared."

"Yeah, we got kicked out. We're back at the cabin." Gabe nuzzled her neck as she spoke, kissing her throat gently. Tara traced the shell of his ear with a smile.

Sunny laughed. "You got kicked out? What did you do this time?"

Tara grimaced as someone—Richard from the sound of it—vomited in the background. "We barely touched the guy. He deserved worse."

Gabe huffed a quiet laugh against her neck.

"Do you want us to come back? Antonio and Lee are having fun, but I bet I could drag them back to the cabin if you want company."

Gabe pulled away and shook his head emphatically, those brown eyes pleading.

Tara smiled, stroking his cheek with her thumb. Closing his eyes, he leaned into it. "No, don't come back on our account. We're just hanging out. About to play a board game."

"Okay, if you're sure."

"Yes, Sunny. I'm sure. Stay 'til close. Be safe. Have fun. Take lots of pictures." Tara hung up before Sunny could respond, tucking her phone back in her pocket. "I should be nicer to her. As bad as her timing is, she's a good friend."

Tara glanced back at Gabe, who looked back at her with soft eyes. Her heart melted, affection bubbling up. "So we probably have a few hours before they come back. What do you want to do?"

"I thought we were hanging out. About to play a board game," Gabe teased, leaning in to kiss her neck again. Tara rolled her head back, giving him more access as she tangled her fingers in his long hair. She yelped out a laugh as Gabe stood up. Gripping her ass, he carried her up the dock with heavy footsteps that echoed in the still night.

"I mean, we could. If you want. Chess? Cribbage? I saw an N64 lying around." Tara was half-worried he'd fall walking up to the cabin in the dark, but her back was soon pressed to the patio door. "I remember some rules for Strip Mario Party if you're into that."

He kissed her once more, sliding open the door with his elbow. "Oh, Kitten. I love it when you talk dirty." Tara laughed, clinging to him as he made a steady beeline for his room. "But right now, I want to kiss you." He pushed her against the bedroom door the second it closed behind them, kissing her hungrily and rutting his erection against her. "Preferably while we're naked and fucking."

She moaned into his kiss and pulled his hair, needing him closer. Gabe sucked her lower lip into his mouth and bit it gently, licking away the sting. Melting in his arms with a moan, Tara wondered if she could come from kissing him alone. She'd been depriving herself of heaven.

"Oh shit, Sorry." With a gasp, Gabe jerked his head back. "That was tongue."

Tara shook her head, chasing his lips. *Just when I thought I couldn't like him more than I already did.* In between kisses, she managed to reassure him. "That was good tongue. I liked that. Maybe we can work up to more tongue. In the future."

With a smile, he carried her to the bed. Pulling both of their stupid sashes off, Gabe lay her down gently, crawling over her. Unbuttoning the rest of her shirt with a hungry look that Tara would never get enough of, Gabe caressed her tits, kissing and licking until her nipples ached from desire.

Tara arched into his touch with a needy gasp. "Gabe, as much as I love what you're doing to me right now, I need you." Tara yanked his shirt off him to touch his skin. She dragged her nails through the coarse hair coating his chest, down his torso to undo his belt and zipper. With a grunt from Gabe, she pulled out his erection. Running her thumb over the rosy head, Tara stroked him gently, spreading the bead of precum that leaked from the tip.

"Tara, fuck." Gabe breathed her name into another kiss as he thrust into her hand. "Oh no, fuck!" His voice darkened in frustration. "I didn't bring condoms."

Tara laughed. "You didn't bring condoms to a bachelor party?"

"It's not like I was looking to get laid." He made a face at her. "I didn't think you wanted—I can't imagine wanting anyone but you."

Heart pounding, Tara smirked. "Blanche has some, but our room is awfully far away, isn't it? Do we need one?"

A hesitant smile spread across his face. "Do we?"

"You already came inside me once, and I'm still on birth control." She ran her thumb across his swollen lips, slowly stroking his cock with the other. "Can you stay with me without one?"

Gabe nodded, kissing her palm. "I'll try not to lose my head this time."

"I'll be here if you do."

His dimples deepened. "So, no condom. Color?"

"Green." The word had barely left Tara's mouth when he fell over her, planting too-quick kisses at every opportunity as he pulled her clothes off. She helped him kick the shorts off of her legs before he tore off the rest of his own clothes, carelessly throwing them across the room.

Mouth firmly on hers, Gabe plunged two fingers into her cunt. His touch was still the perfect stretch after a month of forcing herself not to think about him, not using any of the toys that had been his substitute. She moaned into his mouth as she bucked her hips against his hand, wrapping her legs around his waist. "Gabe, please. Just fuck me."

Gabe's groan was pained as he reached between them to line himself up. "I don't know how long I'm going to last. I've wanted to do this for so long."

"You literally fucked me raw twice already," Tara teased.

"Not while I could do this." With a biting kiss, he pressed into her slowly.

Holy fuck. Tara might explode merely from his lips devouring hers, while his cock stretched her, filling her inch by inch. "Gabe, you feel amazing." Tara panted against his mouth. He pulled out only to slam his hips into her, sending shock waves up her spine and down to her toes. "Fuck, I don't know how long I'm going to last either."

"Don't last. If you want to come, come," Gabe teased as he found a fast but steady rhythm, working a hand in between them to press on her clit. She loved how he always matched her neediness, as desperate for her as she was him. He moaned as he thrust into her over and over, gasping out her name into her ear. His voice was whiskey in her brain, intoxicating and burning and rough.

All of her pent-up energy, all of the emotions she'd been bottling up, had at last found their outlet, gushing out between her thighs as she came. Tara cried out his name as she writhed, spasming around him.

"Fuck, Kitten, you feel amazing." Gabe groaned in her ear, refusing to let up. Each press of his fingers and thrust of his cock sent wave after wave of pleasure through her. "Where do you want me to come? I'm so close."

"Inside. Come inside me." Tara barely managed to find her voice as she finally came down. This was the reckless behavior she'd held herself back from, the soft feelings and impulses that her fear had never allowed her to have. Now, she didn't care. She wanted all of him.

Gabe kissed her again as his hips stuttered against her. She swallowed his cries and moans as he came, painting her cunt with his cum. Like last time, Tara shuddered from the sensation, from his desperate whimper, from the weight of his body pressing against her, from the feeling of his mouth finally finally *finally* kissing hers. She wanted to keep all of it inside her, carry him with her always.

Neither of them spoke as they came down from their highs. They simply looked at each other, panting with equally dazed smiles. Tara stared into his coffee-brown eyes as long as she could stand, before surging up to kiss him again. Gabe kissed her back gently, still buried inside her, with her legs wrapped around his thighs.

Tara clung to him as he fell onto her chest, burying his nose into her neck.

"I'm pausing myself," he whispered. "I have too many things that want to come out of my mouth, and they're all going to ruin the moment. So I'm not going to say anything for a while."

Tara smiled, whispering back, "Okay. We can stay like this."

Tangled together and holding each other close, they kissed softly. Tara's body was screaming at her. Her hips ached and her bladder was full, but she couldn't find it in herself to ask him to move, to pull out, to end the afterglow.

Eventually, a buzz from somewhere in the room ended it for them. His phone chimed from somewhere else.

"We should check that. They might be coming back," Tara said, resigned.

"I don't care," Gabe said, but he slipped out of her. The trail of wetness that seeped from her sparked a glow of satisfaction. Giddy at the feeling of his cum oozing out of her, she found his shirt and threw it over her head, heading to the bathroom. Having him come inside her had been strangely thrilling the first time; without Gabe's unexpected flashback, she could enjoy the feeling fully.

Gabe stood by the dresser when she came back from the bathroom, a pair of boxers slung low on his hips. Her fingers itched to touch him there. "Tonio sent a picture. No actual messages yet."

As Tara passed behind him into the room, she looked at the screen. Richard was wearing Antonio's romper, one leg up on the bathroom sink in an outrageous pose. Tonio sent a caption of "Ducky in Shorts!" Richard was obviously drunk, his face bright red against the white romper, buttoned around his neck.

"Guess we have more time," Tara laughed, dropping the duffel bag that she'd grabbed from Blanche's room on the chair in the corner. She turned to face Gabe, suddenly anxious that she'd overstepped, that maybe he hadn't expected her to stay with him tonight. He'd insisted on taking the smallest bedroom, even though his feet would be hanging off the end of the full-size mattress. Tara's breath tightened in her chest; she fussed with the leather strap for reassurance.

"Moving in?" With a giddy smile that made her question why she'd ever doubted, Gabe nodded at the bag. He tugged her closer to gather her in his arms; the leather slipped from her hand.

"Pretty much." Breathing him in, Tara gave in to her urges and ran her fingertips along the soft skin of his hips as he held her. She could touch him whenever, wherever she wanted. Happiness glowed inside her at the thought. "Having my bag in here will help prevent a repeat of last time. I don't think I could find my way back to Blanche's apartment from here, so I'm not taking any chances."

Gabe smiled softly. "What do you want to tell them, Kitten? About us, I mean."

She sighed. "I don't want us to be a secret. But I also didn't want to detract attention from Lee and Antonio." She rested her chin on his chest. "Can we keep it low-key around all of them? Until after the wedding? Like, I don't want to cause drama because the best men hooked up at the bachelor party, but I also don't want to lie and pretend we're just friends."

Gabe nodded. "If that's what you want, Kitten. I'll keep my hands to myself for a while. At least around other people."

She grumbled. "That's a terrible idea when you put it that way."

Gabe laughed. "And what do we tell them if and when they ask questions? Are we partners?" His smile tightened into a wince. "Boyfriend and girlfriend?"

She snorted. "I'm sensing you don't really like the idea of being my boyfriend."

"I like the idea of being *yours*." Gabe kissed her forehead. "I don't really like gendered labels like boyfriend. Doesn't fit me."

"So still not Daddy?" Tara teased.

He groaned. "God, never! That's so much worse."

"Whatever you want is fine with me. The idea of being a girlfriend kind of makes me want to gag." Tara smiled at the relief on his face. "How about this—if they ask, we're together. But we don't intentionally draw attention from them until after the wedding. We already caused enough drama by getting kicked out tonight."

"Tonio might figure it out. He already called me out for knowing what your tattoos look like." He traced the lines on her thighs and hips, under the shirt that barely covered them. Tara shivered as his warm fingertips grazed the numb skin of her scars.

She smiled into his chest. "Blanche knows, of course. And Lee knows what a fucking wreck I've been the past month," Tara admitted, laughing. "I'm sorry I pushed you away. I didn't think I deserved you. I still don't."

"That's not how this works," Gabe replied. "You don't need to deserve me. Because I don't deserve you, either." He kissed her forehead. "I love you. That's one of the things I wanted to say earlier. I didn't trust myself to say it right after I came, because I probably would have kept saying other things we might not be ready for."

"I love you, too." The words were so unfamiliar, yet so effortless. Chest blooming with warmth, Tara smiled up at him. "So what now?"

He gave her a blank look. "What now, what?"

Tara shrugged. "Like, should we play a board game? Drink a little? Make it look like we actually hung out when they get back?"

Gabe smirked. "I was gonna suggest round two, but why not both?"

"So I *shouldn't* put shorts on before I sit on the couch?" Tara grinned, giddy from the hunger in his eyes, thrilled that they were each other's without reservation. Her head spun, light and carefree, because her heart was finally unrestrained.

"No, because you're not going to sit on the couch. You're going to sit on my thigh, and my cock, and my face." Gabe's hand swept down to her ass to squeeze her closer. "In that order."

Sunday, May Thirtieth

Chapter Thirty-Five

TARA

Tara stiffened as a large, warm hand, gently shaking her hip, roused her from her slumber. "Good morning, Kitten," a familiar deep voice rumbled, thick with sleep. *Gabe.*

Inhale, 2, 3, 4, 5. Plush lips sucked on her neck, melting her back into the sheets.

Too warm and sleepy to open her eyes, Tara burrowed deeper into the thick blanket and Gabe's chest behind her. She released her exhale as she spoke. "Where are we?" *2, 1.*

Gabe's hand slipped around her waist, pulling her closer. "We are at the lake cabin for the bachelor party. Your bag is safe on the chair where you left it. I'm about to start breakfast for everyone, but I didn't want you to wake up alone again."

With a smile, Tara inhaled. *1, 2, 3, 4, 5,* taking in whiskey and sweat, vanilla and oak, sex and Gabe. His heartbeat pounded against her shoulders, and his dick rested heavy and erect against her thigh.

She pressed back against it with a soft *Exhale, 4, 3, 2, 1.*

"Something makes me think you're not having a panic attack this morning," Gabe teased.

"Shut up. Just breathe with me," Tara said sleepily, rolling her hips against him. He matched her breaths as she reacquainted herself with her body the way she did every morning. Any remaining vestiges of fear melted under his hands roaming her stomach and hips. Her longing turned desperate when he cupped her tits. Heat bloomed between her thighs, the ache from the night before not enough to dampen her hunger for more.

Inhale, 2, 3, 4, 5. Gabe breathed with her, inhaling sharply into her ear as his erection slid between her legs. The head nudged her clit, and they groaned quietly together.

Exhale, 4, 3, 2, 1. Tara's eyes stayed shut, not willing to fully wake up yet, longing to stay present with Gabe in this bliss. She ran her fingers along his forearms and fingers, and down his side to his thick thighs, his firm ass.

Inhale, 2, 3, 4, 5. Arching her back, Tara nudged his cock into place to take him again. She shuddered at the sharp burn and pinch as he sank slowly into her without preparation, breathing through the pain and pleasure. His breath was ragged in her ear.

Exhale, 4, 3, 2, 1. His fingers found her clit with practiced ease, the familiarity making her melt even more. Tension climbed up her spine, vertebrae by vertebrae. Her skin burned as if doused in afternoon sunshine.

Inhale, 2, 3, 4, 5. Tara heard him curse under his breath, heard herself voice a soft cry of his name as a small orgasm shook through her.

Gabe nipped her ear. "We have to be quiet, Kitten," he murmured. Tara kept breathing, pretending not to hear. She didn't want Gabe to be quiet, didn't want to hold herself back.

Exhale, 4, 3, 2, 1. Her back arched to take him deeper. He gripped her hip, nails digging into her skin, his mouth on her neck, his cock dragging slowly inside her.

Inhale, 2, 3, 4, 5. His moan poured into her ear, her name from his lips.

"We have to be quiet, Coop." *Exhale, 4, 3, 2, 1.* With a quiet chuckle, Gabe slapped her ass in retort, muffled by the blanket. The promise of a powerful orgasm crept up her spine. Unwilling to force it, she kept breathing. Slow and steady, taking in everything happening in and around her, all of the thrilling sensations and loving affection Gabe brought her.

Inhale, 2, 3, 4, 5. Tension built in Tara's legs, her back, coiling like a spring in her belly, lust searing under her skin. The pressure on her clit, and Gabe's beautiful cock dragging in and out of her, hit every wonderful part of her perfectly. His deep timbre murmured wordless praise in her ear.

Exhale, 4, 3, 2, 1. Tara bit her hand to muffle her cry, shuddering as the orgasm overtook her. Wetness coursed out of her as she bore down around Gabe's cock. Her muscles convulsed uncontrollably. He choked on her name, his teeth sharp on the shell of her ear. They moaned together as he came, his cock flexing inside her.

Finally Tara opened her eyes, taking in the early morning light shining across the bed and wood-paneled walls. A glance over her shoulder revealed Gabe, delightfully wrecked behind her. Nostrils flaring, he caught his breath, brown eyes wide, his pupils blown out.

"Good morning," she murmured.

"No fucking kidding, Kitten." His head fell heavy into her neck. "I look forward to waking you up every morning."

"Blanche usually just gives me tea."

He laughed quietly, his exhale tickling her skin.

"What time is it?"

"Early, I don't think anyone else is up yet. They're probably all hungover, except Tonio."

As if called into existence, they heard Lee groan Antonio's name. Gabe pulled out of her, making a face. "And Lee apparently. Maybe I'll give them a few minutes before I start breakfast."

"I hope we weren't *that* loud," Tara laughed quietly, still in awe at the sensation of his cum leaking from her.

"We barely made a peep." Gabe kissed her shoulder.

She rolled over to kiss his lips instead, hoping her morning breath and the stale aftertaste of whiskey weren't as bad as they seemed. "I love you."

His dimples deepened as Gabe smiled softly. "And I love you madly." He didn't seem to mind her morning breath, because he kissed her again. She luxuriated in the softness of his lips against hers, until a rhythmic pounding from the loft shook the windows.

"I can't do this while they're doing that." Tara pulled away, cringing. Lee had never brought anyone back to Blanche's place. Before now, they'd lived in blissful ignorance of each other's sex lives. Lee would probably die from embarrassment if he knew Tara was awake and hearing this.

Undeterred, Gabe pulled her hands to his mouth. He kissed her fingertips and palms, pressing her hands over her ears to muffle the sound. "Here. Cover your ears."

"You're not going to block them out, too?" Tara raised an eyebrow, delighted by the adoration and hunger in his coffee-brown eyes. Her thoughts of Lee were replaced by daydreams of how wonderful waking up might be if they were at home in his bed. Instead of a cabin, with only thin walls separating them from the friends they needed to be low-key around. Less than a month, and they'd be free to be as openly affectionate and light and happy as Lee and Antonio upstairs.

She giggled as Gabe rolled her onto her back. Attacking her neck with his lips, he pushed her thighs apart so he could climb between them. He smirked, kissing down her body. "Keep your thighs closed tight enough, and I won't hear a thing."

Chapter Thirty-Six

TURNING DOWN THE FRUIT salad, veggie scramble, hash browns, and turkey bacon Gabe had offered for breakfast, Sunny nibbled a single piece of dry toast. No matter how good everything might have been, Sunny was suffering from the worst hangover of her life. Her stomach turned at the thought of eggs. She sipped her water to wash down the toast that stuck to her throat, unable to produce enough saliva to swallow. Her whole spine ached. "I'm too old to drink."

"Babygirl, you are twenty-six. It gets worse." Sprawled across the couch, Blanche pulled their sunhat low over their eyes. They even wore sunglasses, despite being indoors with the shades drawn. The whole cabin was quiet and still and dark, minus the faint music in the kitchen, and Gabe humming along off-key.

"Please stop talking," Richard whispered. Feet flat on the floor and hands pressing down on his knees, he took deep breaths at the table beside her. Sunny's stomach churned in sympathy at the green tinge to his fair complexion.

Poor Richard had gotten drunker than ever last night. Perhaps because he wasn't driving for once. Or, more likely, because between Sunny and Antonio handing him drinks, he'd had more than he'd planned. Maybe he hadn't been exaggerating about being a lightweight.

Though last night, Richard had been delightful, giggling with her while they'd made out in the bathroom—before he'd thrown up, anyway. *After* he'd thrown up, he'd been miserable for all of five minutes, before Antonio had egged him into a second wind. Sunny had blinked, and suddenly Richard was wearing Antonio's romper and busting the dorkiest dance moves. On a table.

Laughing softly, Tara dosed out pain relievers and antacids. "Gotta be honest, looking at you all right now makes me glad we got kicked out right away. I didn't even have time to get a drink."

Gabe followed her, refilling cups of coffee and water. "You kinda had a beer."

"Yeah, but I didn't actually drink any of it. It was probably roofied." Tara made a face. "And he had crusty ass nails."

"And terrible cologne."

"Again, this is a lot of talking." Richard sniffed his water, putting it down with a grimace. He looked at the antacids Tara had handed him as if they'd bite him. "Especially about smells and beer."

"Good morning everyone!" Antonio sang as he slid down the railing. Lee trotted down the stairs happily behind him, looking significantly more awake than everyone else.

Sunny wondered how he did it. Lee drank more than any of them last night, but managed to give Antonio a piggyback ride home, then still had energy to loudly fool around with his fiancée while everyone else tried to sleep. And from the sounds that Sunny had woken up to this morning, Antonio had not only woken Lee with morning head at the ass crack of dawn, but then fucked him hard enough to shake the whole cabin for fifteen minutes straight. *They're meant to be.*

Gabe handed them each a plate of food and steaming mugs. Sunny only half-listened as Antonio and Lee filled Gabe and Tara in about their night. She tuned out completely when Tara explained why they got kicked out, more concerned about Richard, looking paler by the minute. His nostrils were flaring as he tried to breathe. She winced. *No wonder he doesn't drink much.* "Richard, bathroom."

He nodded and left the room in a hurry. Wifey Material Sunny would probably go with to take care of him, but she'd also drank a lot last night, and her stomach was queasy enough. Sunny could be considerate and doting *after* he was done puking his guts out.

By the time Richard returned, refreshed and able to drink his coffee, Sunny felt human again. The medicine, toast, coffee, and the sound of Antonio chatting away had brought some normalcy back to her body.

Even Blanche had taken their sunglasses off, their green eyes less blood-shot than earlier.

Antonio forced them all outside on the porch, claiming the room smelled like sex and whiskey. Which—considering he and Lee had been the ones going at it in the loft—was a little oblivious of him, even by Sunny's standards.

Sitting around the table on the deck, they played board games as boats passed by on the lake. Sunny hoped that their hangovers hadn't ruined any plans for their bachelor weekend, but Antonio seemed content to sit in Lee's lap, as Gabe and Tara bickered over the rules. Their adventure with the creep yesterday seemed to have brought them closer again.

"Gabey Baby, I'm hungry!" Antonio sent Gabe a pleading look.

"We just ate," Gabe said. Antonio pouted until Gabe sighed. "I'll get lunch together."

"I can help!" Tara stood up as well.

Everyone groaned and laughed.

"Tara, we just started feeling better from our hangovers; we don't need food poisoning too!" Blanche teased.

"Or trips to the ER!" Lee added with a grin. "Remember that time you almost lost a toe?"

Tara took the shit-talking in stride with an eye roll. "Whatever, you survived the eggs I cracked for breakfast!"

"Don't worry. I'll keep everyone safe from food poisoning." Gabe steered her into the house with a hand to the small of her back. "Maybe we keep you away from the knives, though."

"I'm much better with a knife these days." Tara winked over her shoulder, where no one but Gabe might have seen it. And Sunny, whose curiosity was piqued.

Trying to catch Richard's eye, because he always saw everything and filled her in on what he'd noticed later, Sunny stretched casually, the picture of nonchalant. But Richard sat, manspreading on the porch swing, his head tipped back against the cushions. The slow rise and fall of his chest told Sunny he was asleep.

Sunny brightened. She might not have been the most responsible version of herself when he was puking this morning, but here was a chance to show that she could be just as observant and gossipy as he was. And Richard would have a lot of thoughts about that wink.

The banter was one thing, but a wink? A wink was *flirting*. Tara didn't flirt. Unless she was ready to drag someone to the bathroom for a good time, anyway. Burning with questions and more than a little bored with the movie trivia game Antonio had picked, Sunny sat quietly, waiting for an excuse.

Finally, Blanche emptied a water pitcher into their glass.

"I can take that in!" Sunny said, cheerily. Being considerate was much more fun with ulterior motives. "Anyone else want anything?" Not waiting for a response, Sunny raced into the house with the empty pitcher, sliding the patio door shut quietly behind her. She tiptoed through the cabin as laughter rang from the kitchen.

Poking her head around the corner, she saw Gabe and Tara dancing to the music. *Ugh, she's a terrible dancer.* They were cute though; Tara laughed when Gabe picked her up to pull her around the room. Tara smiling so freely was a rare sight.

"Well, don't you two look like you're having fun?" Sunny stepped around the corner, a grin on her face. Sunny half expected they'd jump apart. But Gabe spun Tara once more, before he resumed slathering mayo and mustard on the toast leftover from breakfast.

Tara picked up the knife to carefully slice tomatoes. "We *were* having fun until you showed up. What do you want?"

"Just here for some water, Tara-Bear," Sunny said innocently, holding up the pitcher. "What crawled up your ass and died? Am I not allowed in the kitchen?"

Tara opened her mouth to retort, but Gabe touched her nose. "Pause."

Tara shut her mouth, and turned toward him, waiting with a small smile.

Sunny blinked. Something about this felt familiar, but she couldn't place the déjà vu.

"Obviously, I would never dream of telling you what to do, but I distinctly remember you saying last night that you wanted to be nicer to Sunny. That's it. Play." Gabe tapped her nose again, leaving a smear of mustard behind.

"Did you just get mustard on my nose?" Tara elbowed him with a grin.

"Sorry, sorry." Gabe wiped it off with his thumb affectionately.

The correct tab in Sunny's brain finally popped open. She had jokingly told someone to pause a conversation like that before. But that wasn't anyone in person...

Sunny set the pitcher down on the counter with a *thunk*, jaw dropping.

"Sunny, you good?" Tara asked warily. "Want some ice?"

Sunny stared at Gabe. "*You're* Black Hawk?!"

Gabe looked up with a shrug. "Yeah, that was my screen name in high school, but I still use it sometimes. Why? Did Richard mention it or something?"

"Richard *knew*? This whole time?! I'm going to—" Sunny froze, realization after realization hitting her like a truck, tabs popping open like malware. She pointed at Tara. "Mind-blowing, life-changing sex. But that was before we met him!"

Tara looked at Gabe, confused. "Do you know what she's talking about?"

"Wha— I... You—" Gabe stared at Sunny, frozen in disbelief. His jaw opened and closed as he tried to force out words. "You seriously use your real name as your fucking screen name? You know, the hair in the drain thing right before you had a video with Blanche was a weird coincidence, but I told myself there's no way my Sunny could be Lee's Sunny. Because neither Sunny would use their real name on the internet!"

"*Your* Sunny?" Tara crossed her arms, narrowing her eyes at Gabe.

"Okay, but Sunny's not, like, my *real* name—Oh my god! You're real!" Sunny ran over to Gabe with a squeal, throwing her arms around him. "This is wild! You really aren't an incel neckbeard!"

Gabe hugged her back. But within seconds, panic struck his face. He took Sunny by the shoulders. "Fuck! Can you forget everything I've ever told you, ever?"

"Nope!" Sunny turned to Tara. "You two have seriously been together for two years, and you never told me?!"

"'Together' is a strong word. I told you that it wasn't anything official." Gabe ran both of his hands through his hair and started pacing. "Please, forget literally all of that. Everything I ever said. All of it. No one in real life was supposed to hear these things."

Sunny waved him off. "Whatever, you've had a *situationship* for two years then? Tara-Bear, why would you keep this to yourself? Does everyone else know, and I'm the last to find out?"

"I'm still stuck on the 'my Sunny' comment," Tara shot back, her green eyes flashing.

"He's Black Hawk! I talk about him all the time! He's, like, my online best friend, but I had no idea he was Gabe!" Sunny grinned, linking her arm through Gabe's as he let out a heavy, resigned sigh. "I didn't put it together until he did the pause thing I told him to do forever ago. My advice is amazing!"

Tara didn't look as thrilled. "Our pause thing is from Sunny?"

"'Our pause thing?' Stop! That's so cute, Tara-Bear!" Dots connected, adding links between the tabs. Richard's air quotes when he talked about Black Hawk, the mood swings that always lined up with Gabe's. Tara's evasive questions about getting over friends. Unrelated information fused as facts lined up that never had before. "Everything is making so much sense right now!"

Gabe looked embarrassed again. "I guess when you put it that way, yes, the pause thing was from Sunny? But I didn't know it was Sunny at the time. Is that going to be an issue?"

Tara pursed her lips. "No. It's useful. I suppose." She turned to Sunny. "Are you gonna be able to keep a lid on this? We were going to wait until after the wedding to say anything."

"Honestly, I'm about to cuss Richard out for not telling me that Black Hawk was Gabe, so no." She shook her head. "Anyway, you probably don't want Lee to be the last to know. Everyone's been encouraging this," Sunny waved her hand between them, "since we *thought* you met at the housewarming party."

"Maybe she's right," Gabe said to Tara quietly. "Still your call, of course. But I told you Antonio pretty much figured it out, and even though he *said* he'd give me space, that'll probably last about three more hours. Lee should hear this from you."

Tara nodded. "Blanche will probably be relieved. I felt so bad for them on the car ride here."

"Together? Like together together?" Sunny clapped. "I told you you'd work it out! Dicky's been shipping you. His nosiness makes so much more sense now!"

"I hate it when Sunny's right." Tara frowned. "But yeah, apparently everyone already knows anyway."

"Maybe after lunch, when we take the pontoon out?" Gabe suggested, wiping his hands on a towel before hugging her from behind. He even planted a kiss on top of her head.

"Where I can't run away? I see your plan, Coop." Tara smiled up at him. "We managed to keep this a secret for all of twelve hours."

"Honestly, it was longer than I expected. We weren't actually *that* quiet this morning," he teased. "And here, you thought we could go for a month."

SUNNY SPUN IN THE boat seat, enjoying the sunshine and fresh air as she waited impatiently for Gabe or Tara to start talking. He and Lee were fishing from the end of the pontoon in silence, while Antonio chattered about nothing in particular, spinning around in the seat next to her. Tara and Blanche huddled under the shade, commiserating about their sunburns. Richard sat apart from them, looking rosier than he had all day.

Still wrapping her mind around it, Sunny connected the dots to what little she knew about Gabe. And what that meant for their friendship. She had told Black_Hawk everything she couldn't tell people in real life. He'd done the same. They knew a lot of secrets about each other.

Before this, she and Gabe had been friendly, but not super close. He was Richard's friend, or Tara's secret crush. In the time it took to make lunch, Gabe had become one of Sunny's best friends.

Everything she had learned about his past relationships, his family, his mental health—it all made sense. That they both knew the same nerdy jokes *really* should have been a hint. But it was hard to wrap her head around. His sweet himbo personality in real life didn't mesh with the depressed, sarcastic neckbeard she knew online.

She couldn't believe she'd never made the connections before. Even the gender-affirming body sculpting link he'd sent her years ago was probably because he was training with Richard. And what Richard had shared about Gabe's experiences with kink was practically identical to what Black_Hawk had told her. She would have put it together sooner, if Tara had ever told her she was fucking him.

Oh god, what did I tell him? Sunny could be impulsive, especially where she was anonymous. *Ugh, I told him about our scenes. He even referred me to Blanche!* Realization struck her like an icicle in the gut. *Shit. We have a video on Blanche's channel! Did Gabe watch it? Does he know it's us?*

Desperate to find a way out of her train of thought, Sunny racked her brain to think of something she couldn't put together about Gabe and Black_Hawk. Something to distract her from just how much she'd revealed to him about her and Richard's sex life. "So Gabe, if you're not white, what are you?"

Richard choked. "Sunny, what the fuck?"

"What?" She shrugged. "It's the only thing I can't reconcile. I figured he was Greek or something. I don't exactly go around asking people where they're '*really* from' like your mom."

"I'm Native and Jewish. That's not a secret, and I talk about it pretty often." Gabe snorted, visibly confused. "But also, when did I tell you that?"

"You mentioned you could pass as white, then said how passing was stupid—which I completely agree with by the way, but I couldn't really say that at the time so you wouldn't figure out I'm trans," Sunny said, sorting through her brain for the exact conversation. "Back before I met Dicky's parents."

"Oh, yeah." Gabe barked out a laugh. "Wow, you really undersold it. If I had known you were talking about Dick and Barbie, I would have told you to run for the fucking hills."

Richard narrowed his eyes at Sunny. "You finally figured it out, I take it?"

Sunny tossed her hair over her shoulder. "Yes, no thanks to you. Why didn't you tell me?"

Richard narrowed his eyes at her hair toss; the hint of warning in his eyes sent a thrill through her. "You both appreciated the anonymity. I wasn't about to reveal all of your secrets to each other. Especially since you were telling Gabe more about our sex life than I wanted you to. And he was sharing more about *his* than he seemed ready to tell me yet."

Antonio stopped spinning his chair. "Oh? What did Gabe share about his sex life?"

Sunny pouted, ignoring Antonio. "You kept a secret from me. We don't keep secrets from each other. We keep secrets from *them*."

"And what secrets do you keep from us?" Antonio asked.

Richard's mouth twitched as he fought a smile. "I'm not going to apologize for keeping both of your secrets for you. Let's discuss it at home."

Sunny shook her head with a pout, playing up her obstinance. "On one condition—I want to tell one of your secrets."

Richard gave her a *look* that made her heart pound as he considered it. "Choose wisely, Doll."

"Yes, sir!" She beamed, giddy about the nickname he'd picked out for her, and the implied permission to be as bratty as she wanted. The promise in his voice gave her something to look forward to when they got home.

"Ugh, can you not do that around me?" Gabe shuddered, covering his ears. "Not kink shaming. It's just weird for me to know as much as I do about your sex life. Like, good for you, happy it's working. Do not want to hear about it again."

Sunny shot him a glare, about to retort that *he'd* been the one to recommend Blanche. But Antonio interrupted first, "Okay, someone fill me in."

"Gabe and Sunny have been friends online for years," Richard explained, his cheeks tinged pink from Gabe's callout. "They shared too much about themselves without knowing they knew each other."

"So does she know about you and Tara then?" Antonio asked Gabe.

"Whoa, way to put it out there, dude!" Tara huffed.

"You haven't exactly been subtle," Richard said.

Blanche added, "I can't be the only one who woke up this morning to you two going at it."

Sunny frowned, confused; she hadn't heard anything from the room next to them. But Tara shrugged unapologetically, and Gabe's face flashed with a mess of emotions as his jaw worked back and forth. Annoyance, embarrassment, joy, and pride took turns behind his eyes. He fiddled with his fishing rod, reeling it in a little. Sunny pouted; she'd missed the chance to hear Tara in her element.

"Is that what woke me up this morning?" Antonio beamed. "Thanks for the sexy wake-up call! Let me get up early enough to deepthroat—"

"Yeah, we *all* heard that, Tonio," Gabe replied. "So all of you know already. Great."

"That's one conversation over!" Tara nodded. "What's the secret about Richard?"

"Uh, no!" Sunny held up her hand, eager to play the only card up her sleeve. "Does everyone know the *whole* story?"

"For all I know, they might. I never told anyone except you anything, but everyone somehow figured it out," Gabe bit out sarcastically.

"I don't know the whole story!" Lee raised his hand.

"I do, but I still want to hear it." Blanche lowered their sunglasses.

Gabe exchanged a pleading look with Tara. "Do we have to?"

Antonio pouted. "Oh, come on, Gabey, I want details! I still don't understand how you and Tara had sex in our bathroom, but you didn't come."

"It *was* with you?" Lee smacked Gabe's arm.

"He just ate me out at your housewarming party. What's confusing?" Tara shrugged.

Lee cringed. "Maybe I don't want to know this story."

"What's confusing is that you two had met like, once, and for all of ten seconds," Antonio said. "Like, I'd expect that from you, not Gabe."

"They'd met *twice*," Blanche chimed in. "On her birthday that past April."

Tara whirled to face them. "How did you know that?"

"I distinctly remember a Mr. Tall, Dark, and Handsome who 'ate pussy so good it gave you a panic attack,' I believe was how you phrased it." Blanche shrugged. "I recognized him the second he walked into the housewarming party."

"*That's* where the two years come into the timeline." Richard tapped his chin. "Where was this, and why didn't I know about it?"

"Because I was impulsive and decided to go out in public by myself," Gabe sighed, turning away from his fishing pole with a resigned sigh. "Thought it'd be nice to surprise Tonio for his first performance."

"You said you didn't go!" Antonio exclaimed. "I gave you so much shit! Why didn't you say you'd come to see me?"

"Because I didn't see you," Gabe turned red. "Well, I caught the first ten seconds, but then... Figured you'd understand."

"And he caught feelings mid-nut," Sunny added. That phrasing had stuck with her.

Gabe shot her a glare, before turning back to look out at the water. "My first time going out since moving back home, and I fell hard for the first stranger with a nice ass. But she just wanted a onetime thing. And I took it personally."

Tara got up and sat in his lap.

Kissing her shoulder, Gabe chuckled dryly. "Basically, it made me realize I was still too fucked up to be putting myself out there yet. That sparked the CBT treatment with Joy that year." Gabe grinned at Antonio now. "And at your housewarming party, I couldn't help myself. So yeah, *she* came that night. I didn't. Might have had time for more, but we were interrupted." Gabe glared at Sunny again.

Sunny thought back to the party, when Tara had disappeared around midnight and hid in the bathroom, telling Sunny repeatedly to go the fuck away. "Is that why you sounded so sick?"

Tara's glare was replaced with a proud smile. "Yeah. You knocked while his tongue—"

"Ahhh!" Lee interrupted. "Please, no details!"

Gabe rested his chin on Tara's shoulder, fiddling with the fishing rod. "Anyway, we both agreed it'd be dumb to keep messing around."

Tara bumped his head with hers. "Didn't really stop us, though."

"True, but I wasn't in a great place, and you were a good motivation for me to get to a better one." He looked up at her with a soft smile. "You're just so fucking irresistible."

Fighting her own, Tara kissed him.

"Whoa!" Lee exclaimed as Sunny and Blanche gasped. "Buttercup, you don't kiss!"

Tara rolled her eyes. "I don't fall in love either, but here we are."

With a boom of laughter that echoed across the lake, Lee fell off this chair. "In love! And kissing! Oh my god!" Fighting a smile, Tara leaned forward to smack him on the arm.

"Anyway, that brings us to what we should probably tell you..." Gabe pressed a hand to Tara's waist to pull her back into his lap.

Antonio gasped. "You're pregnant!"

"No! Jesus Christ, dude!" Tara laughed, leaning into Gabe. "We talked last night and decided to be together. Like for real together, not just secretly hooking up."

"We were gonna wait until after your wedding, but then *Sunny* found out, and that plan went to shit." Gabe shot Sunny yet another look, and for a second, she recognized the sarcastic Black_Hawk in his surly expression. Unrepentant, Sunny smiled innocently. "So we also apologize for being the worst best men for getting kicked out of the bar and hooking up at your bachelor party." Gabe looked at Tara in adoration, shifting back to Antonio's best friend, night and day from her mysterious online confidant. "She feels so inevitable, you know? I'm tired of pretending I'm not crazy about her."

Tara blushed pink and kissed him again.

Richard sniffled, his eyes hidden behind sunglasses that he'd pulled out of nowhere. Voice strained, he muttered, "About time."

"Gabey, Tara-Bear, I'm happy for you. And this weekend is for all of us, not just Lee and I." Antonio stood up to wrap his arms around them both. "But if either of you hurt each other, I'm going to seriously injure whoever deserves it. You know I'm very protective."

"If I hurt him, I will gladly accept any punishment you dole out." Tara patted Antonio's shoulder.

"Me too," Gabe said softly. "But I doubt that will happen. I've never had to argue with someone so much to just let me do something nice for them."

"So, anything else, or can Sunny spill Richard's tea?" Antonio whirled around with a grin.

"I was hoping you'd forget," Richard groaned. "You're gonna tell them what I think you're about to tell them, aren't you?"

"You know it!" Sunny laughed and cleared her throat to announce, "Richard has nipple tattoos..."

Gabe gasped. "You got the zombie nips covered up!"

"...in the shape of roses," Sunny finished with a flourish of her hands, delighted to be the one to spill Richard's longest-kept secret. Especially after he'd kept not only Gabe's secret identity from her, *and* he'd had a threesome and never told her? Unacceptable. His nosy ass knew everything about everyone; it was high tide everyone else got to know him, too.

"No!" Richard groaned. "Now they'll want to see them!"

"Roses?" Blanche clapped in glee. "Show us your nips!"

Lee and Antonio joined in. "Show us your nips! Show us your nips!"

Richard glared at Sunny. "Almost ten years, I've kept that a secret! I had a big reveal planned and everything!"

"You called me Doll, I'm dolling. If you wanted control over the secret, *you* could have picked it! Or just said no!" With a sassy grin, Sunny brought her hair around to the front, just to flip it back over her shoulder. "Let this be a lesson in keeping secrets from me."

"You will pay for this later," Richard warned, his shoulders back with the easy swagger of his dominant side as he leaned forward.

"Looking forward to it." Sunny smirked, eager at the promise of the funishment in his tone.

"Show us your nips!" echoed across the lake. Folks aboard other boats turned toward them to see the commotion. "Show us your nips!"

"It's more than the nips." With a resigned groan, Richard pulled off his shirt with one hand, holding up the other in warning as their friends all rose to examine him. "Only look. Do *not* touch."

Everyone crowded around, oohing and awing at his heavily tattooed torso.

Except Antonio, who sighed and sat back down next to Sunny. "Boring. I saw all that last night when we traded clothes."

"You did?" Sunny asked. "Why didn't you say anything?"

Antonio threw up his hands. "I figured everyone already knew, and that I must have forgotten!"

Saturday, June Sixth

CHAPTER THIRTY-SEVEN

BLANCHE

NERVES HUMMING UNDER THEIR skin, Blanche buttoned the wide-leg slacks that completed their outfit, adjusting the pussybow collar of their blouse. They fussed with the stack of papers, neatly clipped on the coffee table. Tara was at Gabe's for the weekend, their sewing kit was packed away, and all the contracts were signed, but for one signature. As ready as they could be, given the circumstances, but Blanche felt as if they were on the precipice of a cliff. Sitting in their chair with both feet on the floor, they blew on their steaming mug and waited.

Only halfway through their honey-rich tea, the lock on the door clicked open.

Covey snapped, "Why aren't you dressed? I texted you I was coming two hours ago."

"I am dressed," Blanche said, the easy steadiness of their voice belying the bouncing of their feet. They forced their heels on the floor again. "Come and sit down. We're overdue for a talk about our arrangement."

"Don't start this again," Covey sighed. "Not after the day I've had. Please, Goddess—"

"Yeah, yeah, Goddess Divine, you need me, only I can forgive you, blah blah," Blanche interrupted, waving an irritated hand. Any sympathy they'd carried for his self-inflicted guilt had vanished when he'd tried to have their family arrested. The twisted love in their heart had calcified.

"I've heard all of your manipulation tactics dozens of times before. Sit down Bryce, we're talking."

He stood next to their chair, glowering down at them. "I can sue for breach of—"

"Go ahead." Setting their jaw, Blanche sat back in their chair, looking up at him. "Sue away. What's the fee, half a mill? I'll wire it to your joint account right now. Or maybe we can take it to court, so I can destroy your pathetic life on the stand, like you've so casually threatened mine." Blanche scoffed. "Luckily for you, I only want you to leave me alone." They pointed at the couch. "Sit down, stop pouting, and let's discuss this like grown-ups."

He sneered. "You're forgetting about your precious Confession."

"What does Confession have to do with this?" Blanche raised an eyebrow.

"I own it, and therefore I own you." Bryce leaned on the arm of their chair, his blue eyes digging into Blanche. They swallowed, stiffening their spine. "I will run it out of business—"

"And how will you do that, exactly?" Blanche asked, disdain dripping from their lips. "Even when you *were* invested, you didn't have majority control. Your only hope of doing anything was when Chas would be in labor."

His brow furrowed. "What do you mean, 'were'?"

"Oh, you mean your wife didn't tell you? How awkward." Blanche smirked as Covey's eyes narrowed. "She cleaned up your portfolio a bit, as is her right per your prenuptial agreement. Found new investors that fit better with Confession's mission and values." With a cold smile at the flare of his nostrils and the clench of his jaw, Blanche held out a stack of paper, relishing in his fury as he snatched it. "If you won't sit, you can stand and read then. This is your updated sub contract, a little less legally binding than the last one, other than the clause that releases me from our existing contract. I took the liberty of filling in your needs, limits, and preferences. Feel free to suggest any changes that you see fit."

"Why is my wife's name here?" Covey asked, tossing it on the coffee table. "I've told you both over and over that *you're* my domme, not her."

"No, she tried to communicate with you like any wife would, in a normal healthy relationship. You told her to mind her own business and then bought Confession," Blanche drawled. "I'd suggest couple's therapy next time."

"There is no 'next time'," Covey snapped. "I'm not signing this."

"Oh?" Blanche handed him another set of papers. "In that case, you can sign these."

"Divorce papers?" Covey laughed, derision scraping low and cold as a cinder block. "You really think I'm going to fall for any of this? She wouldn't fuck with my investments, and she sure as hell wouldn't divorce me."

"Wouldn't I?" His wife leaned against the doorframe to the playroom, wearing the scarlet robes Blanche had donned to hear this man's sins hundreds of times. Perhaps overconfident, Blanche had hemmed them to fit her smaller stature. It was a relief to see those velvet chains wrapped around someone who wore them with pride and dignity, who *wanted* the mantle Blanche had grown weary of.

Mrs. Covey's voice was patient but firm, the way Blanche had trained her. "Before we got married, you told me you needed one year to get your shit together. What's your plan when our anniversary comes around next month? Blackmail Blanche again? Lie to me some more? Hope I'll fold when you cry this time?" With a serene smile, she stepped slowly toward her husband, each click of her heel dragging against the wood floors. Covey's nostrils flared as his jaw ticked. "I let you walk all over me for the last year, but that ends now. You're going to sign one of these forms today, Bryce. Either let Blanche go, or let me go. Your choice."

"Don't do this, sweetheart," Bryce pleaded to his wife. "Our love—"

His wife scoffed. "Our love? It's as pathetic as you are, if it means so little to you."

With an approving nod that his wife had managed to make her degradation sound like true scorn, instead of the act it was, Blanche handed him the contract again. "You'll find the only difference between this and our existing agreement is the name of the dominant. The lease remains in your name, of course, and the apartment would provide a sense of separation between your marriage and your arrangement, if you choose to keep it separate. I've trained her thoroughly on your needs, and I can stay on as an advisor through the end of this month."

Covey scanned the contract, the vein in his temple twitching. "And after?"

"None of your concern," his wife answered sharply. "You'll have no reason to bother them again. And if you do, you can go through me."

"I will block you on everything," Blanche sighed dreamily, thrilled at his snarl. "You will be banned from Confession. If I hear so much as a whisper that you've contacted anyone I love, my lawyer has a restraining order at the ready. And I have so much dirt on you, you'll want to stay out of court."

"If nothing else, I already have these drafted." His wife tapped the divorce papers. "So what will it be, Bryce?"

Covey stared between his wife and Blanche for a long moment. They both waited, neither one backing down as the silence dragged on.

Blanche didn't dare breathe; this had to work. His wife had underestimated Covey the first time; *Blanche* had even underestimated how desperate he could get. But with the two of them united, with the schemes they'd pulled off and the leverage they'd built together, with Phineas and Richard and Gabe and his mother, this was their best shot. Blanche needed this to work, for the sake of everyone they loved, and themself.

"Fucking backed me into a corner." Covey shook his head as he pulled out a pen, pulling the cap off with his teeth. "Don't let me down, sweetheart." He signed the contract and pushed it at Blanche. They tucked it in a manila envelope and sealed it before he could change his mind.

"I won't if you won't." His wife smiled, caressing his cheek. "Now kneel, you pathetic piece of shit."

With one last glance at Blanche, who smiled innocently up at him as they leaned back to cross their legs over the arm of their favorite chair, Covey knelt and crawled after his wife to the playroom.

Bursting with relief that didn't feel real, Blanche sipped their cooling tea, unsure of what to do with themself. With Richard and Miriam buying Covey out of Confession, and Covey releasing them from their contract so they didn't have to pay the fine, Blanche was sitting on quite the nest egg. They'd been saving, and saving, and saving, and working their fucking ass off to get here.

Giddiness coursed through them, leaving Blanche floating in their chair, high on disbelief. They were finally free. Free from the anger and grief that had been dragging them down for decades. Free of the remnant links of the chains Daisy had kept them in. Free to heal and honor her with love instead of hate. Free to move on and work with clients who brought them joy instead of anger.

Free to live.

With Covey's cries of pain and the smack of the flogger as background music, Blanche smiled and opened their laptop to browse the listings from their new real estate agent. An old Victorian, baby pink with magenta trim, caught their eye. A fixer-upper that looked a little worn, perhaps even a little haunted; but that described Blanche too. A house like that may be exactly what they needed.

Thursday, June Seventeenth

Chapter Thirty-Eight

GABE

GABE HAD ANTICIPATED HIS best friend's wedding would be stressful. Between reining in Antonio's more whimsical ideas, and planning a huge celebration on a tiny budget (and it *was* tiny for a wedding this size, despite what Tara thought), Gabe had anticipated there'd be hard days.

Days like this one.

After a long, miserable day at work, he'd skipped the gym for one of the dozen scheduled practice sessions in Confession's empty venue. Because they couldn't simply walk up and down the aisle at Antonio Flores's wedding. No, they needed to do a choreographed dance.

What Gabe had *not* anticipated was how irritating Lee would be. Normally, Lee was cool. Gabe loved Lee. Respected Lee. Appreciated him and supported his relationship with Antonio completely and without reservation.

Then the countdown to the wedding shifted from months to weeks to days. With each passing day, Lee's temper grew shorter and shorter. Tara excused it as Lee finding solace in something he could control, and Gabe did his best to be as understanding as Tara. But the early warning signs had become red flags as the months passed: the overabundance of ideas that Lee wouldn't say no to, the meticulous attention to detail of each and every aspect of the wedding, the obsession with having the "perfect" day. There was no other way to slice it.

Lee was a Groomzilla.

And now, Lee was tearing Gabe's...*partner?* a new one, because Tara couldn't dance on beat to save her life—a quirk of Tara's that Gabe found extremely endearing. Lee, apparently, did not feel the same, at least right now. Which made Gabe not particularly fond of Lee at the moment either.

"I don't understand what the deal is. This is the simplest choreography!" Lee gestured to Daniel and Gracie—Antonio's youngest brother and his niece. "Literally children can get this!"

Sputtering, Tara threw her hands up. "Shocker! I still can't do it!"

Lee crossed his arms. "You could do it if you *tried*!"

"Bitch, you think I'm not *trying*?!" Tara lunged, but Gabe tightened his arm around her waist to hold her back for the third time this rehearsal. Thrilled as he was for the excuse to hold his partner close without their friends teasing them for how affectionate they were, Lee was really getting on his nerves.

"If you were, you would learn it!" Lee replied testily. "Gabe, you can dance! Can't you make her—"

"*Make* me do what, motherfucker?!"

"Okay, I'm done. I'm not getting in the middle of this." Gabe dropped his arm as Tara dove for Lee again. "Good luck, man."

Shouting obscenities, Tara took off after Lee, chasing him around Confession's second floor. Cassie, Antonio's older sister, covered her daughter's ears. Daniel glared up at the rest of the wedding party, daring them to do the same. Gabe and Richard looked at each other and shrugged; in the Flores family, the eight-year-old had heard worse.

"Should we do something?" Jazz asked.

"Nah." Sunny shrugged. "She won't actually hurt him."

On stage, Blanche examined their fingernails as Antonio fidgeted, watching them tear around the venue.

Cornering Lee against the stage, Tara leapt as Lee backed up the stairs to escape her. Slowly, Lee fell to the floor under her weight as Tara climbed up his shoulders. Pinning his arms to the floor with her knees, she straddled his chest.

"Damn, that's hot."

Richard elbowed him. "Keep it together, Cooper. You're in public."

Gabe elbowed him back. "*Jazz* said it, not me."

"You were thinking it, though."

Gabe shrugged. Tara climbing him like that, albeit preferably not in anger, was not the worst idea.

"Leland Aloysius Jones!" Tara yanked Lee's glasses off. "I am not a fucking robot! Get your fucking head out of your fucking ass, and stop being a catty bitch to your friends! We are here to support you because we love you, not because we want you nitpicking us to death!"

"But I want the wedding to be per—"

"Do you want your *wedding* to be perfect, or do *you* want to be perfect? Either way, nothing is ever perfect! Neither you nor your wedding has to be fucking perfect!" Tara pointed at Antonio, who shifted his weight anxiously. "Tonio, imagine it's your wedding night. You're in the hotel suite with Lee, and everyone else went home—what will you care about most?"

"That we're...married?" Antonio glanced around at everyone else, as if seeking validation that he'd gotten the answer right.

"Hear that, Lee?" Tara cupped Lee's cheek, forcing him to look at her. "He isn't going to care if I fuck up your corny-ass processional dance! He isn't going to care if my speech at the reception is awkward because I'm going to fucking cry the whole time! He isn't going to care if I beat the shit out of your dad—"

"Oh, I kind of care about that one!" Antonio piped up.

"Okay, but if I beat the shit out of him *after* the wedding, is it the end of the world?" Tara asked. Antonio shrugged. "No! Because Antonio isn't marrying you to be fucking perfect, Lee. He's marrying you because he loves you, and if your friends can't dance on beat, or give a speech without crying, or if they commit assault after the reception, he understands and accepts that, because we're part of your life! You don't need a perfect family or a perfect life or be the perfect husband to deserve him!"

Lee lay on the floor silently.

Tara put his glasses back on. "Get it together, Lee. Stop taking your shit out on us."

"Sorry, Buttercup."

"I know." Tara kissed his forehead and marched back to Gabe, putting her hand on the small of his back. Gabe draped his arm around her shoulders, chest glowing with warmth from her open affection in front of everyone, and pride that she'd managed to get through to their tightly wound friend. Together, they led the group back to lineup, taking it from the top as the music started again.

"You want to talk about anything from earlier?" Gabe asked as they washed dishes together, wearing a dazed smile he couldn't be bothered to hide. Even if this was their nineteenth dinner since their relationship had started less than a month ago. Tara in his home, sharing a meal they'd cooked together, staying the night with him more often than not—he hoped the joy of their new routine never wore off. But Tara had been quiet since the rehearsal, and he could see her frustration.

Tara shook her head. "Can we practice the damn dance?"

Gabe raised an eyebrow. "What happened to 'nothing is ever perfect'?"

Tara scoffed. "I can still try harder."

"Too bad dancing is free," Gabe teased, pulling up the wedding playlist. Tara didn't really need to practice—no one would truly care if she messed up—but he wouldn't pass up the opportunity to dance with her in private. "Otherwise, we could have talked them out of this. I don't think anyone has choreographed a processional dance since Obama was in office."

"Be hard on me, please?" Tara asked. They waited for their cue at the end of the hall that flowed through the main level of the floor, leading from Gabe's bedroom. It continued on past the stairs and the basement door, through the living room, and out of the kitchen into the mudroom. Not as long as the central aisle of Confession would be, but they could double back and still come out to the right timing.

"Permission to smack your ass every time you get it wrong?" Gabe winked.

"That'd just encourage me to fuck up," Tara laughed. "How about if I get this perfect within five tries, I win. If it takes more, you win."

"Name your stakes, Kitten."

She grinned. "Anal, of course."

Gabe laughed as he led her in a simple line dance down the hall on their cue. "Deal. But if I win, we have to wait until next week to claim my prize."

"Why?" Stepping a little too wide, Tara winced as she smacked a picture on the wall. The framed photo of Hippo wavered on its nail.

"I have an appointment with my wax lady on Sunday," Gabe admitted, steadying it smoothly as he guided her back to center. "I'm sure you wouldn't judge, but I can't in good conscience have my ass that hairy the first time you fuck me."

"Yeah, I really don't care— Wait, I thought if *I* win, I get to fuck you?" Tara laughed.

"Sounds like either way, I'm winning." Gabe's cheeks heated as he smirked. "But you just forgot your shoulder lean before the step touch, so I'm pretty sure you're losing the bet."

"Fuck!" Tara froze.

"Just keep dancing." Gabe spun her under his arm. "You freeze when you mess up, but you have to keep going. Any missed steps are less noticeable if you don't react."

Tara grumbled, then asked, "Where did you learn to dance?"

"My parents like to dance together. And Antonio's whole family is big on dancing. Picture Angie at fifteen teaching a thirteen-year-old me how to bachata."

Tara shook her head. "I don't even know what a bachata is."

Gabe tsked and pulled her closer, weaving their thighs together. His lips teased her ear as his hands directed her hips to follow his. "This."

"Oh." Tara coughed, a flush creeping up her neck. "That's um...close."

Lips trailing down her neck, Gabe hummed in agreement.

"Did you do that with Angie, too?" Tara teased. "Kiss her neck?"

"No, I was terrified of her."

Tara laughed, tightening her grip around his shoulders. "I think I'm better at this than the stupid processional dance."

"I'm doing all the work, Kitten," Gabe teased, picking her up off the ground to emphasize his point. Tara responded by wrapping her legs around his waist and kissing him. "I thought you wanted to practice," he whispered against her lips, cupping her ass to carry her to the kitchen island.

"We can practice kissing," Tara replied, tracing his lips with her tongue.

Groaning in a heady rush, Gabe parted them, letting her explore without pushing his tongue back. His hand roamed up her torso to pinch her nipple.

"Ow!" Tara smacked his hand.

"Sorry, too rough?" Gabe bent to kiss it through her shirt.

With a hiss, Tara pushed his head away. "Even *that* was too much. They're not used to getting this much action."

Gabe pouted, kissing her lips instead. "Sorry."

"Don't be. I enjoyed every minute." Tara smiled against his lips. "But my tits need a few days off."

BLANCHE

I can't believe I'm thinking about moving out of Eastside. Blanche lit a joint as they looked at photos of the pink Victorian again, still in disbelief that this fantasy could be their home, but not daring to hope too soon. After seeing the old, glorious house in-person, Blanche had made an offer above asking price, despite all of the house's "cons" their realtor had pointed out. And now, they waited. It'd only been a day, but every hour felt like an eternity.

Near the U, up in the hills north of downtown, the house was located on a busy street with a bus stop in front of it. With five bedrooms, it was way too big for them. The porch was half rotten, and the glass atrium off the kitchen was long destroyed in a hailstorm. The floors were scratched to hell, and the pink paint peeled from the wood siding. Obviously rented to college students for decades, based on the sheer amount of stains and holes in the walls, the last owner had tried to renovate it, but only got as far as the attic.

A sane person wouldn't even consider such a money pit.

But it was under budget, with good bones and character. The wood siding under the paint was solid. The floors were mostly level, and the space had a nice flow. A list of kids' heights marked the door frame. Later tenants (presumably college students) had added to it, leaving a big jumble of heights clustered between five and six feet. The corner lot's white picket fence and arbor bordered the property, with old hedges that created privacy.

If they managed to fix it up, Blanche could imagine themself living there forever. Growing roots and growing old in the charming pink house. Adding their own height to the door frame. Maybe getting a dog. Or a whole pack of dogs.

Ugh. I never thought I'd live this long, let alone grow old in fucking Iowa. Blanche wasn't sure entirely why they were so opposed to leaving Eastside. They'd ended up here by sheer accident twenty years ago. As they'd told therapist after therapist until the long-repressed memories became rote, thirteen-year-old Chad—on the run from his cult back in Minnesota—had figured he'd be harder to find in New York.

He'd ended up hitchhiking only as far as Illinois. The couple who'd picked him up had broken up and parted ways in Bellamy, leaving Chad stranded in a park in Eastside. There he'd met Daisy, who'd said that kids could slip through the cracks there, and Chad decided then and there that's where he wanted to be. With Daisy.

In the cracks, Chad wouldn't be forced to go back to the parents who made him sleep in the barn, because he wasn't the white son they'd thought they'd adopted. Or to the cult that wanted to mutilate his changing body. In the cracks, Chad could be free and whole. And Daisy had been the first person to tell Chad that he—no, *they* were perfect—that their body was perfect, just the way they were.

East Bellamy (and Illinois in general) was never where Blanche had intended to spend the rest of their life; they wanted to be wherever Daisy was. The local government was corrupt, out of touch, and had made misstep after misstep for longer than East Bellamy had been incorporated. It was the armpit of Illinois, where the undesirable and invisible had lived for over a century.

But Eastside was close to everything and everyone they cared about: Chas and Freddy's house, the feral cat colony in the alley, Lee and Antonio, the island where Daisy's ashes had been scattered into the river, the weed guy at Kum & Go, and Confession, just across the river. Eastside had character.

Or it used to. The graffiti on the boarded-up warehouses had more color and life than the sterile luxury condos they were being replaced with. The barber shops, panaderias, and nail salons were being replaced with art galleries, craft breweries, and GMO weed shops where the indica didn't have seeds.

Eastside had changed from when Daisy and Blanche had spent their days on park benches by the mounds. They would hang out, waiting for a john to ask if they wanted to go for a walk in the woods along the bluff, out of sight from the road, or go for a ride with them in their car somewhere. Or when they were older, Daisy would find Blanche a roster of assholes who got off being humiliated and beaten by a "chick with a dick."

Blanche supposed they had changed too. Instead of sucking dick amidst an ancient graveyard so they'd have something to eat, Blanche now made videos where they dominated halfway decent people and streamed it to thousands of paying fans across the globe. Blanche was buying a house in fucking Iowa. In cash!

I wasn't supposed to make it this long.

Taking a deep pull on their joint, Blanche wondered what Daisy would say if she could see them now. *She'd think it was the funniest shit she'd ever seen.* Daisy would call Blanche a revolutionary. She'd say they were fucking capitalism and patriarchy, all while making money from it. She'd say Blanche had truly found their calling.

And Blanche would have smiled and accepted her praise, even if they'd only did all of this because Daisy wanted them to. Blanche never had a calling—just Daisy. As much as they resented her, hated her sometimes, she was still the love of their life.

She would have loved to live in this old pink house with me. Pink was her favorite color, even though Daisy always pretended she liked red better, because pink was "too girly."

Daisy had adored the old fourplex they used to live in, even if their tiny studio was awful. Three hundred square feet of mystery stains and roaches. Daisy had been so excited, so proud, of a place that was their own—no stepdad, no pullout couch in Freddy's apartment, no sleeping in a tent next to Walter and Wanda's bus. Blanche hadn't appreciated it at the time. Now, a place of their own was all Blanche could dream about. Even if it meant they'd have to take the bus to Confession.

I should write Covey's wife a thank you card. Blanche hit send, asking their realtor to waive the inspection if needed. This pink house—this pipe dream of growing old—was only possible because of her. But Mrs. Covey probably wouldn't appreciate a reminder of Blanche's existence past the end of the month when Blanche moved out; they'd been a shadow over her life for long enough.

Instead, Blanche took another hit and opened their script for the wedding. They'd rehearsed it dozens of times, but they wanted to do at least a dozen more run-throughs over the next week. Poor Lee was already a wreck, the peace from the bachelor party long forgotten. The least Blanche could do was make the ceremony perfect for him. So they cleared their throat and recited the sweet words about Lee and Antonio's whirl-wind romance. How, in standing up for Antonio and their relationship, Lee had learned to stand up for himself. How Antonio's persistence, devotion, and patience had finally convinced Lee that Antonio meant it when he said he loved him, and how Lee had shown Antonio he was capable of shedding his old ways for good.

It was cute and romantic, but tame. Lee and Antonio had vetoed most of Blanche's snarky comments, or any one-liners about their sex life. Lee had also made Blanche remove all shit-talking about his parents, since they'd be at the wedding. Leland Sr. still sounded like a piece of shit, but he was trying, so Blanche would give him some grace, for Lee's sake. Tempting as it was to add in a few subtle reads.

They managed one more run-through before they glanced at the clock, wondering if Tara would be home tonight and knowing she wouldn't be. Lately, she was spending most nights at Gabe's. Blanche missed her. The apartment was too empty without anyone else. Too quiet.

God, and here I am trying to buy a bigger place. It was for the best though—both the fresh environment and Tara presumably shacking up with Gabe. Tara deserved to be treated sweetly, like Gabe treated her. And based on how loud they'd both been the one time Gabe stayed overnight in her tiny ass bedroom, the sex was phenomenal. And fun. There'd been a lot of laughing.

Blanche sighed. They missed fun sex. Other than their brief fling with Sunny, Blanche had been painfully single since Daisy had died—clients intentionally excluded. And with Sunny, any intimacy had been mostly for Sunny's sake; Blanche hadn't paid attention to their own wants. They hadn't really been present. They hadn't let themself enjoy it.

They let their loneliness float away with another hit of the joint.

I need more love to fill my pink house. Even if she moved in with them, Blanche was sure Tara would eventually move out. They'd both be moving in with Gabe after the wedding weekend—temporarily, until Blanche closed on whatever house they found. Though their relation-ship was only a few weeks in, Blanche wouldn't be surprised if Gabe asked Tara to stay once Blanche found a place. Tara had already prac-tically moved in, leaving behind only a couple storage bins of clothing whenever she dragged her duffel bag back and forth. She had never truly moved into their apartment, never quite settled in the way Lee and Blanche had. Tara lived out of her duffel bag and storage bins, instead of hanging her clothes or decorating her space.

Blanche, on the other hand, had no idea what was theirs, and what technically belonged to Covey. They didn't want to give him any reason to get in contact, so they'd probably have to start from scratch aside from their clothes, plants, and instruments from their set. Even the video games that had provided so much entertainment would stay behind.

Without Tara, Lee, or Sunny to fuss over, Blanche would have to find new ducklings to adopt. Maybe cats or dogs or plants, or college students, or more street kids who needed a place to live and wouldn't judge Blanche for their occupation. There was always more love to find, even if Blanche knew they'd never have another Daisy to grow old with.

Blanche stamped out the end of the joint into the ashtray. No, it was for the best that they couldn't. They had loved her, but that hadn't been a healthy love. Reciting their history over and over and over again to every therapist, including the new, promising one (who had not cried, but instead sworn under her breath and made Blanche laugh), had made Blanche's growing awareness of their toxicity inescapable. Maybe now that they were free of Covey, they could find a better way to love. But they would need to start with themself, before anyone else.

Thursday, June Twenty-Fourth

CHAPTER THIRTY-NINE

TARA

BLANCHE HANDED TARA HER morning tea, as had become their ritual over the past months. At first, Tara had been more energized from drinking it—or perhaps that was just from the bitter flavor and her stubborn delusion. Now, the effect seemed to have plateaued; she'd been exhausted for weeks. Maybe because she'd been staying at Gabe's so much, skipping her morning tea more often than not (and expending significantly more energy when she stayed the night).

Despite her exhaustion, Tara found herself smiling into the steam rising from her mug. A dam had broken in her after she'd finally voiced everything that had been building for months—years, really. All of the urges and desires she'd been holding back were still flooding out. She couldn't stop smiling, constantly horny and floating on air. Luckily, Gabe seemed to have just as many feelings and urges and desires as she did. They couldn't keep their hands, or mouths, off of each other. *Somehow, I still always have energy for him.*

He'd looked glorious the night before last: hair spread across the bed, shouting her name into the pillow as she fucked him with their new strap-on. She'd left the dildo in his ass when she'd turned him over to ride him, relishing in the dazed and wrecked expression on his face when he came.

It was more than the sex, though that was thrilling. They were so comfortable with each other. Somehow, Gabe had a sense for when she was overthinking something, and Tara could get him to open up about the private heartaches he nursed. Even the hard conversations, and her occasional morning panic attack, were manageable once she finally let herself enjoy him—enjoy the lightness she'd envied in Lee since meeting Antonio.

"You're thinking about him again, aren't you?" Blanche teased.

Tara nodded, smiling as she brought the tea to her lips. "You caught me." She took a sniff and wrinkled her nose; it smelled worse than usual. "Is there no honey in this?"

Blanche nodded, sipping their own. "There is. I even added a second teaspoon for you. I noticed you didn't like the taste yesterday. I left the milk out. It's expired, but it passed the sniff test if you want to risk it."

"No!" Tara took a hesitant sip. Her stomach turned. "There's something wrong with it."

"It tastes fine to me—well, no worse than usual." They chuckled. "Are you coming down with something?"

Tara tried again, taking another sip in hopes that it was merely the smell. *Nope.* Her mouth watered in warning that her stomach was threatening to revolt. She put the tea down with a hard swallow.

Blanche pursed their lips. "You feeling okay there, babes?"

Tara nodded. "Yeah, I'm fine. I'm just not feeling it this morning. Weird."

The suspicious expression remained on Blanche's face. "Any other symptoms, or only a random bout of nausea?"

"I'm a little tired, I guess," Tara conceded. "I'll probably take it easy today, in case I'm coming down with something."

"And how are your tits feeling?"

"Excuse you?" Tara covered them protectively.

"Are they still sore?" Blanche asked, calmly ignoring her offended look. "You were complaining about it last week."

Tara squeezed them gently, hiding her wince. "They've been getting more attention lately."

Blanche raised an eyebrow, their voice steady. "And what is the date of your last period?"

"Why the interrogation—" Tara's heart leapt to her throat. Her period had come early, starting a few days before the placebo pills. It had been light too, just some spotting for a couple days. *But that's not unusual.* She often went several months without a true period. Or she *had*, when she was younger. But the last few years, it had been more consistent;

especially since she'd been eating regularly over last year. She groaned. "But I take birth control!"

"And is that your only form of protection these days?" Blanche's half smile stayed firmly on, stoic as always.

Tara nodded.

Blanche grimaced. "Not judging, but is he pulling out?"

Her cheeks heated, thinking of all the times she'd begged him to come inside her.

"I'll take silence as a no." With a sigh, Blanche stood up, ruffling her hair as they passed. "Wait here. I'll go buy a test."

"Thank you," Tara whispered.

Motionless on the couch, she waited for Blanche to return. But her thoughts and feelings were racing, clambering for space in her head. Tara focused on her breathing, training her concentration on her senses, but her head kept spinning.

Stop it. There's no point in stressing until I take the test.

She wrapped her hands around the horrible-smelling mug. The heat seeped into her palms. *What would I do if I was?* The stench of dirt and rotten mulch threatened her stomach again. Tara put the mug back down. *There's no point in worrying yet.*

The plants filtered the morning sunlight through the bright windows, splitting around the sharp points of an aloe and encircling the spider plant. *Would Gabe want to stay with us?* The sound of traffic drifted in from the street below, as someone wailed on their horn at the busy intersection. *Shit—us? No, there's no point in getting my hopes up yet.*

Wait. Get my hopes up? Tara was startled to realize she *was* hoping. She was... *Y'know.* She couldn't even think it out loud yet. The prospect was terrifying enough without hoping for it. *If I am...y'know, I'm glad it's with Gabe.* Hopefully, he felt the same. Hopefully, he'd want to...*y'know* with her. The idea that he might not...

"Fuck!" They hadn't even talked about any of this yet. Gabe hadn't mentioned any future life plans he might have. Tara had never even considered her own future, let alone theirs. If they even had a future after...*y'know.*

She shook her head to clear the negative train of thought. She could overthink after Blanche came back.

The acidic flavor festering in her throat grew worse. Still unable to bring herself to drink her tea, she got up to find something to eat. Maybe one of the muffins Gabe had made would sit better. *Could I support us if I am…y'know? If he doesn't want to…y'know?*

During her month of moping and pining, she'd begrudgingly followed Gabe's advice to raise her fees. Annoyingly, he'd been right. Fewer clients with higher fees was a change she hadn't dared try, but it was paying off. She was making better money, while doing less work. *I could do this. If I am…y'know, anyway.*

Blanche came back as she was nibbling on the muffin, which didn't smell great, but it wasn't as revolting as the tea. They handed her a bag from the drugstore down the street. Inside were mint chip ice cream, ginger candies, Tums, condoms, and a pregnancy test.

"Oh, sorry. Those are mine." Blanche took the condoms out of the bag. "I'm not trying to be shady. Your pussy, your choice. The cashier was hilarious though. She told me it's a little late for these, if I'm buying the rest of this."

Tara managed a laugh and thanked them with a hug, before taking the test to the bathroom. A familiar fog steadied her as she followed the instructions in the box—like she was watching herself in a movie, and this wasn't really happening to her. Normally, her dissociation spiked her fear to awful heights. But right now, it was the only thing allowing her to keep going.

Fuck, I never thought I'd have to deal with this shit. She set the test down on the counter without looking at it, and sat back down next to Blanche.

"What did it say?" Blanche asked, handing her a spoon and the ice cream.

"I don't know. I couldn't look." Tara scooped out a large bite. The artificial mint flavor was comforting—sharp enough to bring her back to her body, and sweet enough to keep her there. It didn't turn her stomach like the tea had.

"What do you want it to say?"

"I'm too scared to think about it," Tara admitted. "I don't know how to be a parent. I'm still figuring out how to be *with* someone. I never learned all of the shit that everyone with normal lives learned when they were young." All of the social norms and expectations. All of the life skills, like driving or cooking. How relationships work or how to love people. "I shouldn't want this."

But faced with the possibility, "no" would inexplicably be more disappointing than "yes."

Tara wanted a family—people to belong to—and she'd always liked kids. Unexpected as this was, this might be her chance to have a family of her own. And maybe Gabe *would* want to...*y'know.*

Her eyes filled with tears.

"Shit. Why do I always fucking cry?" Tara couldn't bear to lose Gabe now that she'd finally let herself have him. They'd only just begun, and it might be over already, all because she told him to leave it in all of the fucking time!

"Maybe I don't have to tell him. Maybe I just won't tell him and..." Tara floundered for the words. And what? Secretly terminate it, and pretend she wasn't upset, when Gabe would see right through her? Somehow keep it a secret for nine months, and hope he'd forgive her for lying? Leave him to do this on her own?

Blanche waited patiently, rubbing her back slowly.

"Fuck, what if he hates me for this?" Tara swallowed, fighting to still the tremble in her voice. She'd let herself trust too much, let herself get too reckless now that she'd finally let herself have something she wanted. But she'd still fucked it up, and he'd resent her for forcing this decision on him, when they weren't ready. They had never even talked about their future yet.

Tears streamed hot down her cheeks. Gabe would want her to be honest with him about it. He'd be more hurt by her not trusting them. Even if it was negative, he'd want her to lean on him to process her feelings. Tara owed him that. She'd promised him that they'd work shit out together, instead of running. Curling around herself, Tara shook her head. "How am I supposed to tell him?"

"Well, let's start by looking at the test, so we don't get ahead of ourselves." Blanche's hand kept a steady pace, running up and down Tara's back. "But no matter what it says—no matter what you do—you have me. And Gabe. And all of us. We're here for you. And you might have hit the baby daddy jackpot by getting knocked up by an investment banker with a trust fund, but if something doesn't work out, you'll always have a home with me, okay, Babes? Not that I think Gabe would ever—"

"Oh god, what if he thinks I did this on purpose?" Tara whirled to look at Blanche, chest aching harder than ever. The thought hadn't even occurred to her. "I told him I'm on birth control. I mean, I *am* on birth control! But what if he thinks I lied?"

Shushing her gently, Blanche wiped her tears away and cupped her face. Their green eyes were serious. "Tara, remember to breathe. That joke was in poor taste. Forget I said it. Gabe knows you wouldn't lie about that. If you are pregnant, I don't know why your birth control failed, but Gabe is over the moon about you. He'll understand and be supportive of whatever happens. And if not," Blanche poked her nose with a wink, "I will destroy him and wipe every trace of his existence from the earth!"

Tara laughed through her tears, putting her hands over Blanche's. "Thank you for being here for me, always. It's nice to know I have you ready to kick ass for me."

"Do you want me to go get the test?" Blanche offered.

Tara nodded. "I'm scared to look on my own."

Blanche rose and headed to the bathroom.

Tara stared at the ice cream melting slowly, refusing to look up when Blanche came back in, until they set the test on the coffee table in front of her.

Chapter Forty

Gabe

GABE ANSWERED HIS PHONE, not bothering to look at the screen, with a cool and terse, "Gabe Cooper."

If Leigh Anne would stop calling me every five fucking minutes, I might get some fucking work done. His boss had been breathing down his neck all morning. He'd never imagined his mortal enemy would be a forty-something white woman from North Carolina with an obsession with chinchillas, but this was where life had brought him. He'd been in worse places; he could handle Leigh Anne.

"Blanche Van Horne. Do you always answer your phone with your name? Not even a hello or anything?"

Gabe looked at his phone in confusion. "Oh shit. Sorry, Blanche. I thought it was my work cell. What's up?"

"Listen, darling, any chance you can swing by sometime today? On your lunch or after work or something? Tara needs to talk to you. It's kind of an emergency."

In the background, Tara retorted that it wasn't an emergency. He smiled at her argumentative tone, before dread took over. "What's wrong? Is she hurt?"

"Everything is fine. No one is hurt. But come over when you have a minute, so Tara can fill you in." Blanche's voice was calm and soothing. "No rush though—just at some point today."

Gabe didn't feel reassured. As Blanche hung up, he set an Out of Office and sent Leigh-fucking-Anne an email that he had a family emergency, and that he may be unavailable the rest of the day. She would be pissed that he didn't call her to inform her, but Leigh Anne could go fuck herself. If she ever *read* her email, she might not need to call him so damn much.

Increasingly dark possibilities ran through his head as he packed up his belongings, each more nonsensical than the last. *What if she's hurt? Or what if I did something to piss her off? Or maybe they're getting kicked out early.* As they'd been gradually moving Blanche's belongings out of their apartment (Blanche had already claimed two guest rooms: one to sleep in and one to stream solo stuff until they moved out), Gabe had been fantasizing about what it'd be like when Tara came to live with him. How she might stay in his room, instead of a guest room. How she might settle in in the weeks to come. How she might decide to stay. But he wanted them to make that decision together, not out of necessity on some whim of Blanche's sugar daddy.

Gabe made it to Blanche's building in record time, taking the steps two at once to their third-floor apartment.

At his knock, Blanche opened the door. "Wow, that was quick. I meant this afternoon or something." They beckoned him inside. "I'll be in my room if you need me."

Gabe followed them in, stopping short at the sight of Tara, wrapped in the weighted blanket on the couch. Eyes red and puffy, she was eating ice cream out of the container.

He rushed over to take her in his arms as Tara broke into fresh sobs. "What happened?"

"Can you take this off?" She clutched at his blazer, shaking. "Don't wanna cry on your nice clothes."

"It's just clothes." Gabe shrugged the stiff jacket off anyway, tossing it on the arm of the couch. Pulling her into his lap, he rubbed her back as Tara wrapped him into the blanket with her. Worry quietly curdled as he waited for her to speak.

"I'm sorry," Tara eventually said. "I'm trying to get myself under control, but I can't get the words out. I haven't been able to say it out loud yet."

She grabbed something off the table and handed it to him.

It was a pregnancy test.

A *positive* pregnancy test.

Gabe stopped breathing as every nerve in his body lit up. "Kitten, are you? Are we?" He shook the test to finish his question. "Shit, I can't say it out loud either."

Tara nodded, lips pressed together tightly. "Seems so."

The possibility of him and Tara having kids hadn't even crossed his mind. He'd been too caught up in the newness of their love, so focused on their Now that he never looked into their Future, beyond knowing he wanted to be in hers.

But now that a family with her was possible, Gabe couldn't consider anything other option. Images of ultrasounds, Tara with a round belly, him holding a tiny baby flashed in his eyes. Of a cute kid with freckles and curly dark hair, learning to walk and crawling over Hippo. Gabe let out a shaky exhale.

Tara eyed him anxiously with tears in her eyes. Gabe blinked, realizing he was still staring blankly at her. Lost in the swirling thoughts in his head, he searched for the right words to say—running through the story his parents had told him of their own unwanted pregnancy with him. How Gabe had been an unexpected surprise, and even though they'd decided not to have kids, they supported each other's decision to be the best parents they could. Even though they didn't know how.

If his parents had figured out how to be supportive, loving parents all on their own, then maybe he and Tara could too.

Gabe swallowed, praying to whatever Creator or higher power might exist, that whatever he was about to say came out right. "I support you and love you, no matter what you choose to do. I will always want to be part of your life. Their life too, if that is what you want. If that's what you decide." A smile spread across his face as he spoke. "And if you want...this, I'd be so fucking happy, Kitten. And if you don't, my love for you will be unchanged."

Tara smiled through her tears. "We're getting better at this shit. You didn't even need to pause." Her laugh was cut short as she whispered, "I don't know how to be a...mom."

"I don't know how to be a...dad." He choked out a laugh. Tearing up, he pulled her close to rock her gently. Kissing her neck and shoulder, he breathed her in as they clung to one another. It was a strange feeling, trying that label on for himself. "Dad" felt uncomfortable.

"Do you want to be a dad?" Tara asked.

"Whatever you decide. You have my full support and whatever level of involvement you want."

"No, I mean—the word. You don't like the boyfriend label and gendered shit." Tara snorted. "Or have we found the one circumstance where I could call you Daddy?"

Gabe laughed into her neck. "How could you tell I hated it?"

"There was a hint of disgust in your voice," Tara teased. "Probably the same queasiness I got when I said 'Mom.' Maybe we can just be parents for a while?"

"'Parents' does feel better." Gabe pulled away just enough to smile at her. "Does that mean you...want to?"

"I think I do want...this?" Tara whispered, gesturing to her stomach. "And I definitely need you to be involved, but I don't really know what that means. For me or for us. Or for," she paused, panic crossing her face, "the baby. Oh god, we're having a fucking baby!"

Gabe nodded, laughing in relief. He hadn't lied; he would've supported her no matter what. But he'd just been slapped in the face with a glimpse of their future, and Gabe wanted it more than he could have imagined. "What'd you bet that their first word will be 'fuck'?"

Tara laughed. "I am not taking that. I'd lose."

Gabe smiled against her neck. "I meant it, I want to be involved as much as you'll let me. I want to come to all of the doctors' appointments. I want to be there when they're born. I want to rub your back when you're throwing up in the mornings, cook all of your meals for you, and make them a bottle in the middle of the night. I want to take care of you, of the baby." He looked up at her, hoping he wasn't overstepping before Tara was ready. "You can move in with me if you want. I mean, you're moving in already, but I'd love it if you stayed. Baby or no, I want you around all the time. I've been wondering if I should ask you anyway, and now this... Well, it seems right."

"Gabe..." Tara nuzzled her head against his.

"I know it might be too much to take in or decide right now. We have time. Take whatever time and space you need. Move out, move back in, stay with Blanche. Hell, I'll move in with Blanche, too. Whatever you choose, I'll be here." He considered a second, before adding, "Although having tried to sleep here before, maybe ask if Blanche's new place has a bedroom bigger than that closet you have now."

"I love my closet, but you barely fit," Tara chuckled. "Can I think about moving in with you? But yes to everything else you said, because I don't know how to make a doctor's appointment—Oh god, I have to get health insurance!" She buried her face in his shoulder.

Gabe shook his head in adoring exasperation, because of course she didn't have health insurance. "I'll add you to mine. Anything you want or need, consider it done, Kitten. And don't do that thing where you overthink it and say no, because you're too fucking proud to let me do nice things."

"You're too nice, but it's not just about me anymore, is it?" Tara grumbled. "Fine—you can spoil our kid, but not me."

"Give me time, Kitten. I'm going to make your life *so* comfortable." The glow of happiness in his chest extended far beyond comfort, but no words he could find would do it justice.

Tara settled against him, wiggling in his lap. "Fuck, how am I going to get away without drinking at the wedding this weekend? Sunny will say something if she notices."

"There will be mocktails and sparkling grape juice for the toasts. We can pass it off as alcohol unless someone looks too hard—a benefit of having one of the grooms in recovery. We don't have to tell them until you're ready."

Tara shook her head. "We should tell Lee and Antonio in case it comes out. I don't want them to think we're making their wedding about us. Especially after we caused all the drama at the bachelor party."

"Fuck." Gabe froze, guilt and dread tightening his chest.

"What?"

"My parents." He had been planning to introduce Tara as his...*partner?* But now? "You'll need to avoid them, too."

"You don't want me to meet your parents?" The timidness in Tara's voice hurt his soul.

Gabe winced, hating himself for even suggesting it. "Please don't take this the wrong way, Kitten, because I absolutely want you to meet them. But my mom is very encouraging of me dating anyone, so you'll get interrogated. She'll notice within seconds that you're not drinking and jump to conclusions, and everyone at the wedding will know within minutes, because she'll make it a big fucking deal."

To his relief, Tara laughed. "Your mom announcing our pregnancy at Lee's wedding is not best men behavior. I'll do my best to stay away from you during the reception."

Gabe groaned. "That sounds horrible."

Tara kissed his cheek. "Besides, I want to ask the doctor if they have any idea how my birth control failed before we tell anyone, especially your parents. I don't want them to think I lied or trapped you somehow.

Because I take it at the same fucking time every morning, with the tea Jazz made for Blanche. I haven't skipped my pill in years."

An eerie sense of déjà vu crept up Gabe's spine. "Is there St. John's wort in this tea?"

Tara nodded. "I think so? Jazz would know for sure. Why?"

Gabe laughed. The universe could be frustratingly opaque sometimes, but this message was loud and clear. "St. John's wort can interact with birth control, which is exactly how I happened. My dad found this emotional stability tea to help my mom after her mother died. And nine months later, they had a moody-ass baby to figure out how to parent."

Tara patted her stomach. "They're already taking after you."

Gabe smiled, putting his hand over hers. "The poor kid."

"Hey now, I happen to like you quite a bit. They'll be lucky to take after you." Tara looked at him with adoration swimming in her lovely green eyes.

Gabe's heart lurched. "Hopefully, they take the best parts of both of us. Mostly you," he added before he kissed her, pressing his heart into her lips. "I love you."

"Love you, too." Her tongue tentatively sweeping over his, Tara kissed him back.

A buzz from his jacket pocket split harshly through the quiet room.

"Do you need to get that?" Tara asked between kisses. "Or go back? I didn't mean to drag you away from work."

"Fucking Leigh Anne can sit on a damn cactus," he growled against her lips. "I told her I had a family emergency." He kissed her again before adding, "You're more important than that fucking job."

"I like that. Us being a family. Not the emergency." Tara smiled, getting a mischievous look in her eye. "How long do family emergencies usually take?"

Gabe grinned. "However long it takes to figure out a way to fuck you in your tiny ass bed." Standing up, he carried Tara to her bedroom, leaving the phone buzzing angrily on the couch.

***

"So, let me get this straight." Jaida, his friend in HR, folded her hands on her desk and took a deep breath. "You need to add your domestic partner to your health insurance."

Adjusting his shirt collar to cover the hickey Tara had left a mere hour ago, Gabe nodded, wondering why Jaida was looking at him like he'd grown a second head. Maybe he had. So many thoughts were flying around his brain, it felt like he had two of them. "Right. How do I do that? What information do I need?"

Jada frowned. "Gabe, Richard can't have insurance through the same provider twice. Is there a reason he doesn't have enough coverage? Maybe there's some other resource we can look into."

Gabe blinked, confused. "What does Richard have to do with this?"

Blinking rapidly, Jaida asked slowly, "Is your partner not Richard?"

"No? Her name is Tara." Gabe's mouth hung open. Did Jaida actually believe he and Richard were together? Richard had made it very clear to everyone at work—especially their lunch friends—that they were not.

"*Her*?" Jaida threw her pen down. "Aren't you gay?"

Gabe shrugged, masking his annoyance behind feigned confusion. If Jaida was going to be *that* obtuse, he'd make it uncomfortable for her. "Yeah. What does that have to do with anything? I didn't think that'd matter, seeing as Tara and I aren't the same sex, but she's queer, too, so—"

Jaida held up a finger. "Sorry, are you sure you want to add this new person to your health insurance? I heard Richard was dating someone new, but you two broke up so recently. Is there a reason you're rushing into this?"

"What? Richard and I broke up fifteen years ago. Not that we ever really dated." Gabe scratched his head, wishing he had taken the time to detangle the snarls Tara had left before coming back to the office. "What does any of this have to do with Richard? Sunny has her own health insurance through work." It was still weird that he knew things like that about Sunny. His Sunny had complained a lot about her health insurance. Lee's Sunny had never brought it up once.

"Wait—who is Sunny?" Jaida groaned. "I thought you said her name was Tara? Why do you need to add her to your health insurance, if she gets it through work?"

"I need to add *Tara* to mine. *Sunny* is Richard's girlfriend." Gabe stared blankly at her, searching for some spark of recognition. "They've been together for like a year and a half?"

Jaida picked up her pen just to throw it down again. "Am I being punked?"

"No. What is happening right now?" Gabe ran his hands through his hair. This was why he never talked about his private life at work. Like everyone else had his whole life, his coworkers would see what they wanted to see, hear what they wanted to hear, and assume what they wanted to assume. Sure, they were nice, but they didn't care to know the real him. "I just want to add my partner to my health insurance as soon as possible!"

Jaida looked at the ceiling, as if the explanation might be written there. "Everyone here, myself included, is under the impression that you and Richard have been in a serious committed relationship since you transferred here *together* from New York."

"Who thinks that? Why?" Gabe had never taken Richard seriously when he'd said that people thought they were dating, but this conversation was going nowhere because of it.

"Literally everyone, Gabe!" Jaida smacked her desk. "Everyone thinks you're gay. Everyone assumed you and Richard were together, until he was caught texting other girls last month. And since then, everyone has been trying to find you a new man who will treat you better than Richard!"

Gabe buried his face in his hands; he should have stayed in Tara's cramped bedroom, where he was happy and understood. "All of that is wrong! Richard is a very close friend. He was texting his girlfriend—Sunny—who is also a close friend." He shook his head with a derisive laugh. "Just because we're both queer men doesn't mean we're dating!"

"If you're," Jaida paused meaningfully, "*gay*, then why are you adding a *woman* to your health insurance?"

"Because we're in a relationship?" He knew he had a reputation for being a little slow; sometimes playing it up came in handy in making awkward situations awkward for everyone else, too. But he was running out of patience waiting for Jaida to remember bisexual people existed. "I'm not gay as in homosexual. I'm queer. I guess you could call me bi or pan or omni, but I prefer queer." He leaned forward, making sure Jaida was actively listening, because he'd apparently overestimated her comprehension skills in the years they'd been work friends. "You can say that word, you know. Some people might feel it's a slur, but I'm literally telling you my label."

Jaida sighed and rested her head in her hands. "Okay. Sorry for making assumptions. I'll do my best to shut down the Richard rumors, since you're in a new relationship."

"Oh, no need to go that far!" Gabe held up a hand. "I don't want Richard knowing I'm adding Tara to my health insurance yet."

"I wouldn't tell him anyway, but, out of curiosity, why not?" Jaida pulled out a vape pen. "Don't tell anyone I smoke in my office. I just can't deal right now. It's like I don't even know you! I was going to set you up with my spin instructor!"

Normally in their workplace friendship, Gabe would listen and validate her feelings. But as much as he enjoyed the office gossip with his lunch friends, Jaida was still his HR rep, and that's who he needed her to be right now. "Richard will jump to conclusions, and I don't want him to find out Tara's pregnant yet. Speaking of, what kind of parental leave do I get? How does all that work?"

"She's *pregnant*?!"

"Yup! Kinda why I'm adding her to my insurance outside of the enrollment period." Gabe leaned back in his chair, as Jaida dramatically sucked on the vape. "I think most people would say congratulations at this point."

"Gabe, you are killing me today." Jaida let out another long-suffering sigh as she exhaled, sickly sweet vapor wisping from her nose. "God, I wish I was allowed in the betting pool, but allegedly, I have an insider advantage working in HR."

"There's a betting pool? About *me*?" Gabe gasped, his sarcasm probably going over Jaida's head. Of course there was a betting pool—that explained why Bella had been extra nosy whenever the others weren't around lately. He leaned forward conspiratorially; maybe he could have some fun with this. "Can I get in on it?"

Friday, June Twenty-Fifth

Chapter Forty-One

Lee

WITH THEIR FINAL DRESS rehearsal finished, Lee and Antonio hurried to hide away their décor, before the venue opened for the night's show (so the burlesque dancers wouldn't be tempted to use it), carefully stacking box after box in Confession's storage room. If any of the inventory he'd been carefully managing for months went missing before their wedding tomorrow, Lee might throw up. Chas and Jackie had reassured him the storage room would be locked until after the brunch show tomorrow, when they could set up the venue for the ceremony.

That was where Tara and Gabe cornered them, blocking their exit with too-bright smiles.

"Hey, how about we drive you two to your mom's house for the rehearsal dinner?" Gabe offered, his hand falling heavily around the back of Antonio's neck.

"Great idea!" Tara looped her arm through Lee's as he locked the storage room door. "Let the best men chauffeur you around all night!"

Antonio and Lee exchanged a suspicious glance. Jazz had already headed home to ride to the rehearsal dinner with their parents. Antonio's sister Cassie had left to run some last-minute errands for their mom, taking her daughter Gracie and their youngest brother Daniel with her. And Blanche had ridden with Sunny and Richard, rushing them out strangely quickly.

Lee narrowed his eyes at Tara's passive smile. "Is *Gabe* chauffeuring us, or are we about to die tragically in a car accident the night before we're married?"

Tara smacked him. "Fuck off. I can drive. Kind of."

"I will be driving," Gabe said, guiding Antonio down the stairs. "Tara doesn't know how to follow the speed limit on the freeway yet."

Tara scoffed, pulling Lee after her. "Isn't the point to go fast?"

"Not *that* fast."

"What about our car?" Antonio asked, breaking free from Gabe's grip on his neck once they were outside. Instead of where Gabe's car would be parked in the ramp, he headed toward the employee parking lot. Tara tightened her hold on Lee's arm before he could think to do the same, dragging him toward the ramp.

Gabe grabbed Antonio's shoulders to steer him after Tara. "We'll make sure it gets safely to your hotel, so you can drive home on Sunday. Your nerves are probably going crazy, so don't worry about how you'll get anywhere for the next forty-eight hours. *I* will drive you wherever you want."

"My nerves were fine until you said something." Antonio held up a trembling hand. "Is this what being gaslit feels like?"

"No, this is us being your best men," Tara said cheerily.

Lee's skin prickled with anxiety sweat. "Buttercup," he hissed. "What's going on?"

"Nothing!" Tara hissed back.

This was too forced. Something had to be wrong. He'd been trying to remind himself that it was okay if things went wrong, if things weren't perfect. Antonio would still love him, still marry him. His future in-laws probably wouldn't think much of it. His parents would not withdraw their reluctant acceptance of him. Probably.

And yet, their best men were acting like they were in denial that the venue was burning down, while they were still in it. *Oh God, what if Confession burns down?* "Did we check if the candles lining the aisle are up to code? What if someone knocks one over?"

"They're LEDs," Tara smiled through gritted teeth, opening the car door for him. "Everything is fine. We just need to talk, and I'll explain in the car."

"You can't say 'everything is fine' in the same sentence as 'we need to talk'," Lee grumbled. "Nothing is ever fine when someone says 'we need to talk'."

"Lee, I love you, but shut the fuck up and get in the damn car!" Tara pinched his elbow, pushing him into the backseat. "Everything. Is. Fine."

Lee tried to keep the panicked intrusive thoughts at bay, until he was buckled into Gabe's Outback with Antonio. "Okay, spill. What the fuck is going on?"

"Everything with the wedding is totally fine," Tara said, exchanging a look with Gabe.

Gabe turned back to face them. "Right. We have something to tell you—"

Antonio gasped. "Oh my god, you're pregnant!"

"Babe, you always think Tara's pregnant," Lee snorted, but Tara and Gabe's forced smiles made him freeze. He left them an opening to deny it, but their smiles only widened. "Oh, damn—you are pregnant!"

"Probably, yeah." Tara's joy turned manic as her eyes widened. "Took a test yesterday."

"We obviously didn't plan this." Gabe rubbed Tara's arm. "And we promise to do everything in our power to keep it under wraps so the focus stays on you and your wedding."

"Gabey, that is the least of my concerns!" Antonio squealed, before he stopped short. "Wait, just to make sure—we're congratulating, right? Not commiserating?"

Tara and Gabe exchanged nervous smiles. "Yes. This is good news."

"Terrifying, but good."

Jaw still hanging open, Lee stared at his platonic soulmate, his twin flame, who swallowed nervously. Tara's smile seemed genuine, but he'd never been great at reading her good moods.

"Dude, your mom is going to figure it out in two-point-five seconds," Antonio said. "No one can keep secrets from her."

Gabe sighed. "I know. Which is why we're telling you now, in case she figures it out and makes it into a thing. We don't want you to think we're making your wedding about us."

"Especially after we made your bachelor party about us." Tara chewed her lip, her green eyes still trained on Lee; his mind was racing too fast to do anything but stare. "I don't want to steal any attention from your day, okay?"

"Our bachelor weekend was perfect, and our wedding will be, too." Antonio waved it off. "But your parents aren't going to let Tara escape the night without an interrogation."

"Which is why as far as my parents are concerned, I'm still single," Gabe sighed. "Hopefully, if Mom senses there's a secret, she doesn't dig farther than finding out Tara and I are together."

"Ooh." Antonio pursed his lips. "And how do we feel about that, Tara-Bear?"

She made a face. "Not great, but I get it. It was a mutual decision."

"I hate it," Gabe muttered, taking Tara's hand. "But only our close friends know we're together, and Richard and Sunny agreed to keep our relationship to themselves for a night. They don't know why, because we aren't telling anyone else until after the first doctor's appointment. We just wanted to give you the heads-up before everyone else in case it came out, so you know we tried and don't hate us."

"Gabey Baby, I could never hate you. Especially for such good news!" Antonio leaned forward, hugging Tara and Gabe as much as he could through the gap between the seats. "I can't believe you're going to be a daddy!"

"Oh, no. Let's not do that," Gabe groaned. "Can we try to keep the mom and dad shit to a minimum? We're going to be *parents*. We're already going to have to deal with everyone else thinking we're a straight couple with a kid."

"What is your kid going to call you, then?"

"Tonio, we have a very long time to think about that," Tara said. "What we're worrying about now is keeping this secret until the doctor's appointment. Can you keep this quiet for a few weeks while we wrap our heads around this?"

"A few *weeks*?" Antonio gasped, hand pressed to his chest. "I'll do my best!"

"Lee?" Tara asked softly. "You've been quiet. Are you—are we okay?"

Lee's mouth twitched. "You're going to be a mom."

"Parent," Gabe and Tara corrected together.

With the pressure building in his chest and behind his eyes, Lee half expected himself to cry from the mess of feelings he wouldn't have space to process until after the wedding. Instead, a loud laugh burst out of him. "Buttercup! We're going to have a kid!"

Tara smiled, her eyes shiny. "You're going to be an uncle!"

"If only Auntie Alitrice could see us now. She must be rolling in her grave laughing." Reaching for her hand, Lee laughed harder, tears springing to the corners of his eyes. "Imagine us—having a baby!"

"This is my kid, too, right?" Gabe snorted.

"It better be," Antonio teased.

Lee ignored them. "I'm gonna be the best damn uncle this kid could ever want! Not that I know shit about babies!"

Tears spilling from her eyes, Tara laughed with him. "We'll learn together. Along with Gabe."

"Oh good, I'm still involved," Gabe chuckled.

Lee smiled through the laughter choking him. "I'm not changing shitty diapers."

Tara snorted. "Yeah, no. Not with your weak ass stomach."

AN HOUR LATER, LEE stood in the whirlwind of laughter, dancing, and music of Antonio's mom's backyard, rubbing his palms on his thighs. There were more people here than he'd expected, considering the rehearsal dinner was limited to "family, out of town guests, and wedding party."

Antonio's extended family was already deep into the fun by the time the wedding party arrived from Confession, turning their rehearsal dinner into one of their many "Any Excuse for a Party" parties. While Lee normally loved the Flores family gatherings, today his stomach was in knots just imagining how his parents would handle meeting strangers in such a chaotic environment.

Well, strangers and Sunny, technically. Although the last time his parents had seen Sunny was the day he'd gotten kicked out, and she'd since transitioned. Lee winced, pushing his glasses up his face. He really needed everyone to get along. At least until after the wedding was over. Then the arguments could come out.

Lee turned to Tara, Sunny, and Blanche, who had congregated around a table in a quieter corner of the backyard. They were practically tucked under the deck to avoid the kids running around underfoot. "You guys are going to be nice, right?"

"I'm always nice. However, I make no promises about *staying* nice if they start talking shit." Sunny tapped her peach acrylics along her beer bottle. Most of the wedding party had gone with Antonio to get matching nails for the wedding earlier that week. They looked cute, but Lee couldn't bring himself to do it. Richard had opted out, too.

"Agreed. I won't start anything, but I sure as hell will finish it if they do." Tara tried to look tough, but her soft smile called her bluff. Lee fought a dopey grin. His Buttercup deserved these satisfied smiles for once in her life. He forced himself to look away, not trusting himself to control his laughter or his tears.

"I'll try to keep them in line," Blanche promised. "As much as I can, anyway."

"Thanks for the half-assed promises, guys," Lee laughed. "I feel loved knowing you won't commit felony assault unless I ask."

"For you, Lee?" Sunny squeezed him tight. "I'd kick his ass a hundred times."

He hugged her back. "But it won't come to that, right?"

Sunny merely smiled and pointed with her chin; Jazz was entering the backyard, Althea and Leland in tow.

The Joneses were dressed appropriately for a rehearsal dinner in their Sunday best. Which meant they were overdressed for a back-yard cookout. The rest of the wedding party were in the same boat, but Lee and Antonio had changed into their rompers again. Until now, it had seemed like a cute idea. Antonio's skintight ensemble teased Lee with too much thigh and good memories. But now Lee felt exposed, his bare legs, arms, and chest crawling. Around the Floreses, this was nothing. But the Joneses? It was too late now; his parents would have to deal.

Antonio and his mom met Lee halfway across the yard. Lee squeezed his fiancée's hand as they approached.

"Welcome!" Paula greeted enthusiastically. "You must be Lee's parents! It's so lovely to finally meet you. And you must be Jazz!" Paula beamed, revealing no hint that she'd ever met Jazz before (even though Jazz had been to a few cookouts already).

Lee would never stop appreciating Antonio's mom, or his whole family, for protecting his sister. For understanding how nervous Lee was about this. It was one thing to have lunch with his parents in public; introducing them to the rest of the people in his life (who he loved significantly more than the parents who raised him) was going to give him an ulcer.

Althea and Leland smiled tightly and said nothing. Jazz rolled her eyes behind their back.

Paula gushed as if they'd been just as enthusiastic as her. "We absolute-ly adore Lee—he's been such a wonderful addition to the family!"

Lee's cheeks heated at the undeserved praise.

"It's so nice to meet you," Althea said finally. His parents were obvi-ously out of their element. The chaos of the backyard was exciting for him, but his parents had always preferred structure and quiet. "Thank you for welcoming us to your home. You have such a big family!"

Lee tried not to be resentful, but part of him had hoped that seeing Lee with Antonio's family made them feel a *little* guilty for not inviting him and Antonio to his mom's family reunion. Not that he'd *wanted* to go to the reunion. Or *could* go, because it had been the same weekend as the bachelor party. But still, it would have been a nice gesture for the estranged son they claimed they wanted to reconnect with.

Jazz had been reluctant to talk about the reunion after, so Lee assumed that his parents hadn't told anyone that they were back in contact. His mom's extended family had never bothered to reach out in all these years, either. Proving once again that his friends and Antonio's family were the ones who really mattered.

Still, Lee would keep trying. And maybe his parents would try harder one day, too.

"Mom, did you want to meet Tara?" Jazz asked, as Paula waved them into the backyard.

Before Lee could panic, Antonio's hand squeezed his in reassurance. Hazel eyes smiling up at him, Antonio turned to Althea and Leland. "Yeah, let's introduce you to everyone."

Antonio led them to the corner of the yard where his friends stood. Gabe and Richard had joined them, bringing food and beverages for everyone around their little table. Lee loved his wallflower friends, but they were probably overwhelmed too; Richard and Gabe were used to the cacophonic chaos.

Antonio introduced everyone, while Althea and Leland nodded po-litely. Until Antonio got to Tara.

"Oh! I recognize you from the pictures," Althea said excitedly.

With a confused smile, Tara nodded. "Thank you for keeping them safe. It meant a lot to see them again."

"I'm sorry that I ever put you in a position to leave them behind," Leland said suddenly, interjecting as if he'd rehearsed it. "I made many mistakes, and kicking you out of Ali's home like that was cruel of me. Thank you for taking care of my sister in her last days."

Maybe Lee was too cynical about his dad, because Tara's eyes went misty. "I mean, getting evicted wasn't exactly fun, but it worked out for the best. We never would have met Blanche here otherwise." She linked arms with Blanche. "They took us in after Auntie Alitrice passed."

Althea smiled hesitantly at Blanche. "Thank you for taking care of our son."

Blanche's polite smile softened. "Lee and Tara have helped me far more than I've ever helped them. And I'm glad at least one of us is back in touch with their family. Maybe there's hope for Tara and I, too."

This is going way smoother than I expected. Lee smiled in relief that everyone was getting along, albeit awkwardly. When he was a kid, his parents had seemed strict and threatening. But now, he saw them for who they truly were: socially awkward rule followers. How Jazz had turned out so curious, impulsive, and slightly manipulative, he'd never understand.

"Dad, you remember Sunny, don't you?" Jazz put her arm around Sunny's waist.

Speaking of! Lee shot her a look. His sister smiled innocently, as if she wasn't casually dragging up memories of Leland physically dragging Sunny out of the house.

Leland froze as his shoulders tightened. "Sunny. Looks like you're doing well. You've certainly...grown since the last time I saw you."

Sunny covered her laugh with one hand. "That's one way to put it."

Lee met Antonio's hazel eyes with a smile. They just had to get through tomorrow—however imperfectly it might go.

Then they could start the rest of their imperfect life.

Together.

ONCE THEY WERE BACK home from the rehearsal dinner, Tara made herself a blanket cocoon on the couch. They'd all had a long day, but the weariness in Tara's eyes was a cause for worry. Weddings and secrets were exhausting, even without growing a human.

"Too tired to go to Gabe's tonight?" they asked. They half expected Gabe to stay the night, after the sloppy kiss Tara had given him before she'd climbed out of the car. "Did you actually find someone with a higher sex drive than you?"

"Honestly, I'm exhausted, but no. We're pretty well matched," Tara laughed. "We have to be up early, and I want some alone time to think about stuff. There'd be no sleep or alone time if I went to his place tonight."

When Tara made no effort to go to bed, Blanche sat on the couch beside her. Normally, this was when they'd pull out the weed and whiskey to fuel a heart-to-heart. *I suppose those days are over. At least for now.* "Do you want to talk about it?"

Tara shrugged. "I'm feeling sorry for myself, I guess. Meeting Lee's parents reminded me that my own parents won't even know they're going to be grandparents, you know? I don't even know if they'd care that I made it this long."

"You're going to give this baby so much love, Tara," Blanche said softly. "I know you didn't have anyone looking out for you, but this baby is going to have all of the aunts and uncles they could want. We're all going to look out for them. And you."

Tara nodded. "I know. I'm— *We're* so lucky."

"Besides, from what I've heard about Gabe's parents, they're going to have the most enthusiastic involved grandparents a kid could hope for," Blanche teased as they pulled up their laptop to check their email, so Tara could have the illusion of alone time. Maybe their realtor would finally have an update.

Tara sighed heavily. "I hope they like me after Gabe and I spend the whole wedding lying to them. I'm not good at being low-key."

Blanche doubted if Tara and Gabe *could* be low-key, but it was cute that they thought they could try. "I'm sure they'll love you, babes." The subject line on the latest email from their realtor made them squeal with joy. "My closing date is set for the end of July!"

Tara brightened. "Is this the pink house you were talking about?"

With a rush of giddy relief that made their head spin, Blanche opened a tab with the listing of the house. Their home, where they could choose who had access to them. First freeing themself of Covey, and now this? Happiness was so...uncomfortable. "Yes! See? It has five bedrooms and three bathrooms, including a monster primary suite that someone added in the attic. I'm going to make that my filming area. It's got a giant walk-in shower and a tub big enough for three people. And look, it's got a porch swing and a garden and a cute wooden fence. It needs some TLC of course, but it's mine! And you have your pick of the bedrooms for you and the baby."

Tara hesitated. "I might not be coming with you. Gabe asked if I wanted to stay. Like permanently move in, I guess?"

"I expected nothing less from him!" Blanche was thrilled for her sake, even as they swallowed a preemptive pang of loneliness. They hadn't lived alone since their loft bedroom in the barn as a kid— They shook their thoughts clear. *Not the time to think of that. I can always get more roommates for company.* "Do you think you will?"

Tara shrugged. "That's what I'm thinking about tonight. Deciding what I want to do. It's scary. And I don't want to leave you alone."

With a wink, Blanche waved a hand. "Don't worry about me. Besides, I still need your help with editing my content. You're not allowed to leave me completely." They set their laptop down to face her. "I'm proud of you—I know it's scary. Remember, you don't have to decide tonight, and you can always change your mind later. You *and* your whole family will always have a home with me."

Tara smiled. "Thanks, Blanche. I am scared, but this will be good for me. For us. And you will always have a home with me, too."

Blanche laughed. "Tara, I love you. I love Gabe. But I'd rather stay with Lee and Antonio on their wedding night than live with you two for longer than I have to."

"Come on, we're not that bad." Tara laughed. "Are we?"

Blanche snorted, searching "how to repair a porch" on their laptop, as they raised an eyebrow at their most hedonistic duckling. They were going to miss Tara very much in their new, old home that was far too big for just one person. Even if it was a relief that she wouldn't be around to "help" fix up their pink house without supervision. "I had my music up full blast on my noise-canceling headphones yesterday, and I still considered filing a noise complaint against my own apartment."

"Poor Hippo." Tara laughed. "That was us trying to be quiet."

Saturday, June Twenty-Sixth

Chapter Forty-Two

ANTONIO ADJUSTED THE WHITE leather harness around Lee's chest, fiddling with the buckle. Lined up in Confession's stairwell, the wedding party waited impatiently for Chas's cue to get the show on the road. But no one was more jittery than Antonio. Standing still in the quiet, dark stairwell was impossible. Lights, flowers, music, and their loved ones waited for them around the corner. Even the murmur of their guests was dulled by the door separating them, leaving the wedding party in another world.

"Babe, that is the eighth time in five minutes you've adjusted that strap." Lee stilled Antonio's fidgeting by lacing their fingers together. "If there's something wrong with it, it's too late now."

"I just need something to do with my hands," Antonio admitted. The anticipation was killing him. Anxiety gnawed at his gut, panic threatened to rise up his throat, and tension coursed through his limbs. Even his toes were wiggling. But despite his nerves, irrepressible joy was making his head float. He wanted to get this over with and be fucking married already.

"I'm nervous too, but fussing with my outfit over and over is not helping. Can you do something else with your hands instead?" Lee teased. Smirking down like that, with his hair in fresh twists and that *beard,* Lee looked positively scrumptious. Dressed in an all-white tuxedo with a peach flower decorating his lapel, the white leather harness underneath the jacket gave his sweetness an edge.

With a bite of his lip, Antonio ran his hands up Lee's chest and tugged him closer by the harness. "Something else, huh?"

"Boys," Blanche warned. The entire wedding party watched in their coordinating navy ensembles with varying degrees of amusement. Blanche's jumpsuit—low-cut with floor-length cape sleeves—was stunning. Their updo was adorned with blue rosebuds. "Hands to yourself until after the ceremony."

With a pout, Antonio smoothed the sash of his ensemble. Menswear was too boring, and he didn't want to get married as Carlita. So, like Blanche, he'd designed his own. A peach boat-neck blouse matched the stripe down the side of his white cigarette pants and patent leather platforms. An elaborate boutonniere was pinned to the white and gold jacquard sash draped over one shoulder. Around his waist, it fanned out to create an asymmetrical half-skirt.

In the other room, the music began to swell. Everything quieted as the chatter faded away, leaving only Antonio humming to himself.

"Ready, everyone?" Blanche asked, looking at Lee and Antonio for approval. "Chas says it's showtime."

At their nod, Blanche led the procession down the stairs to an instrumental of "Bittersweet Symphony". Antonio's niece followed arm in arm with his youngest brother, in matching navy suits (because Gracie refused to wear a dress if Daniel didn't have to). The very tall Jazz and the very short Cassie went next. Looking like muses in infinity dresses with orange bouquets, they disappeared around the corner.

Antonio patted Gabe's shoulder and loudly whispered, "You and Tara really outdid yourselves with the flowers."

Gabe exchanged an amused look with her. "You're welcome."

Sunny and Richard followed, looking adorable together. Richard wore the most boring suit imaginable, but Sunny looked gorgeous in a satin cocktail dress. Gabe wore the same suit as Richard, but at least he knew how to accessorize without looking like an old man.

Lee leaned in. "I was a little worried that telling people to wear 'navy' would leave everyone uncoordinated, but they all look stunning together."

"Yeah, we knew you were a *lot* worried. That's why we went shopping together." Tara snorted, looking unusually curvy in a corseted jumpsuit. Her cleavage was positively voluptuous for once. "You cannot comprehend how many thrift stores we went to."

"Kitten, this is our cue."

"Ah, shit!" Tara scrambled into place, exchanging a grin with Gabe. Antonio and Lee peeked around the door as Tara and Gabe nailed every spin and slide. Tara missed only a few steps, but Antonio could barely tell on account of how hard she and Gabe beamed at each other the whole way up the aisle.

"They really should stop eye-fucking each other if they're trying to stay low-key," Lee snorted as the music smoothly shifted into Frank Ocean's cover of "Moon River," cueing them to stand in the doorway as everyone stood and turned toward them.

"Honestly, they're so obvious." Antonio slid into Lee's arms for their slow dance up the aisle. "Tara nailed the dance, though. They must have practiced."

"Freddy is really nailing these transitions today too," Lee murmured as they stepped into the spotlight. "He got it at the right timestamp and everything."

"Chas must be doing sound right now," Antonio whispered back as they boleroed up the aisle. Of course, Lee could tell he needed a distraction. "This lighting is all Freddy."

"That makes a lot more sense." Lee smiled at him, ignoring the photographer clicking away as he dipped Antonio. "I didn't think Freddy had it in him."

As they reached the stage, Lee—ever the gentleman—held out his hand to help Antonio up the steps. Instead, Antonio rolled into an effortless flip onto the stage, to the delight of their guests. "Angel, you know I can do that in my sleep. With or without heels."

"Such a show-off," Lee muttered playfully as he hurried after him.

From the moment he stood on his mark in front of Blanche, Antonio's mind was lost. The exact details in the ceremony escaped him as they flew by. But he remembered the feelings—the love and devotion, the commitment and joy—they shared with their loved ones.

He tried to pay attention to Blanche, but for the life of him, he couldn't retain a word they said, even as tears sprang to his eyes whenever Blanche said something particularly poignant or tender. Joyful excitement erupted over his body, leaving no room for anything but the thrumming of his heart. He listened intently to Lee's vows and recited his own flawlessly.

Everyone in their world—their family, friends, coworkers, and community—witnessed the most deliriously happy moment when Antonio was suddenly kissing his husband. It was real. He was married. To wonderful, patient, devoted Lee. Joy bubbled up in his chest as Antonio kissed him with everything he had. He'd been waiting for this moment—waiting for Lee—his whole life. Now the life they'd built together would go on, the same as it had since they'd met. And that was exactly the way Antonio wanted it.

The opening bars of "Crazy in Love" reminded them to stop making out in front of everyone and lead the recessional. Lee descended the stairs first, holding out his arms for Antonio to jump into. Antonio clung to his husband's neck as Lee spun him around. They kissed again, before Lee carried him down the aisle as everyone cheered and clapped. The others in the wedding party presumably danced back up the aisle with them as they'd practiced, but neither he nor Lee bothered to check; they only had eyes for each other.

The rest of the evening passed in a whirlwind, greeting guests Antonio hadn't seen in years and posing for photos. During dinner (which he barely got a chance to eat, but the three bites he'd had tasted amazing), the endless stream of happy moments flew by without any lasting impression, beyond the ache of his cheeks from smiling so much.

Gabe did his toast first, making the guests laugh with his funny and sarcastic speech. Only to be outdone by Tara, who choked up immediately as she shared how much Lee and later Antonio meant to her. There'd barely been a dry eye in the room.

Chas made jokes about them as he emceed the evening. Later, Antonio's dad and stepdad gave an unprompted, rambling, and tequila-inspired joint speech, full of stories that were probably supposed to be embarrassing. But Antonio and Lee simply laughed with them.

All was forgotten as it passed, leaving love in the wake of Antonio's memories. Their first dance ("Can't Take My Eyes Off of You" by Lauryn Hill) was a moment of stillness in the blur of the evening, and even that he barely remembered—other than the feeling of being exactly where he was meant to be.

Normally times like this frustrated Antonio, who fought so hard to retain his happiest moments. He'd cling to them, squish them into silly little song lyrics, forcing his brain to memorize everything it could, so he wouldn't forget something important. But today was too joyful for him to worry. That was what the photos were for; Lee would remind him of everything important later. Instead, Antonio welcomed each brief and blissful moment after another, until they disappeared. Floating in his joy, his heart soared with love for Lee.

My husband.

Chapter Forty-Three

Richard

"Dicky, that woman is trying to get your attention," Sunny muttered as they stood off to the side, far from the dance floor, to eat their cake. "Older lady, brown hair, pearl necklace. Very tall man next to her."

Richard didn't need to look. He hadn't even needed the description.

Miriam Cooper had been trying to corner him all night.

But Gabe had asked him to keep his relationship with Tara a secret. And if Richard spent any time with Miriam or John, they would get it out of him. He couldn't trust himself to hide anything from them.

Pretending to fuss with the last crumbs of his cake, Richard shifted over a couple of inches. Perhaps the flower arrangements on the tables would protect him from the burning between his shoulder blades, where Miriam's eyes were laser-focused. "I'm avoiding her."

Avoiding Gabe's parents was worse than ignoring Dumpster when she wanted attention. Both were heart-wrenching feats of pure will. He loved the Coopers. They'd become his second family since Gabe had taken pity on the awkward weirdo trying to flirt with him freshman year. Instead of being creeped out that Richard's dad had basically sent him to Yale for the sole purpose of coercing Gabe into marriage, the Coopers had adopted him as a member of the family.

In fact, he had been looking forward to introducing them to Sunny, but another opportunity (after the last attempt had ended in disaster) hadn't come up. It'd been too long since Richard had seen them, and

Antonio's wedding was a great opportunity to catch up. To find out if Sunny and Miriam would get along as swimmingly as he'd imagined.

Except *Gabe* had asked him to keep a secret from his parents. As if *anyone* could keep a secret from Miriam and John. Avoiding them would be stupid and fruitless, but it was all Richard could come up with.

"Who is she?" Sunny licked the frosting off her fork.

"Gabe's mom."

"Why are we avoiding her?"

Richard huffed. "He doesn't want his parents to know about Tara yet, for some reason. Literally, we had this conversation yesterday."

"I remember *that*, Dickhead." Sunny snorted. "So instead of lying, we're just gonna avoid them all night?"

"I cannot think of a single other way to not tell them," Richard huffed. "I don't trust myself to keep a secret from them."

"Oh, Dicky." Sunny tsked with a toss of her hair, a silent invitation to be more dominant with her. "And deprive me, Tara's best friend, of the chance to talk her up to her future in-laws? Come on, introduce me!" She grabbed his plate and left it on the table, dragging him behind her by the elbow. "I can keep a secret."

Dread sank in his stomach. Sunny was an adequate secret keeper, but Miriam was scarily good at uncovering them. Especially out of Richard. Squaring his shoulders, he pulled her back by the elbow before they got too close. "Doll."

Smirking, Sunny raised an eyebrow. "Yes sir?"

"Be good, and you'll get a reward when we get home," he murmured quietly in her ear, using that raspiness that fit better than the sharp edge Blanche had shown him. Maybe he could roleplay someone capable of keeping a secret from the Coopers. "Spill the secret, and it's edging."

With a grin, Sunny flipped her hair over her shoulder again. "Lucky for Tara, I hate being edged."

"That's why I picked it," Richard snorted, his dread growing as Sunny dragged him closer. Sunny didn't know Miriam; she would probably underestimate her. Hopefully, Richard could change the subject quickly if he needed to. Or get them talking about some mutual interest that he hadn't come up with yet. Why wouldn't Gabe tell his parents about his new partner? *Miriam would be over the fucking moon—* No, he had to be in better control of himself if they were going to pull this off. How could he dom Sunny while panicking? Richard cleared his throat, trying to collect the confidence needed to keep Sunny (and himself) in line.

"You've been avoiding me, Richard." Miriam greeted him with a warm hug, as did John. For them, Richard didn't mind the affection. Hugging Gabe's parents felt so natural, compared to his own family. "Is that any way to treat your newest business partner?"

Richard didn't bother to pretend. "I was giving you a chance to catch up with Antonio's parents before hogging your time."

"Bullshit. You were trying to keep this lovely young lady away from me, so I wouldn't scare her off," Miriam teased, turning to Sunny.

"You caught me." Richard politely introduced everyone. *That would have been a better excuse. I should have thought of that.*

"Don't worry. I don't scare easy." Sunny smiled.

Miriam laughed. "You must not have met his parents yet then."

Richard let out a sardonic laugh. "She has, actually. They beat you to the MAI fundraiser last year. It went about as well as you'd expect."

"Is that why security was escorting them out?" Miriam's mouth dropped open in shock and delight. "And you stuck around? I'm impressed. Don't tell me Dick actually turned a new leaf and finally gave up on his weird obsession with you and Gabe?"

Sunny laughed as Richard shook his head. "No, as if that would ever happen. But I've barely had contact with them since. It's been quite nice."

John eyed him thoughtfully. "That's a big step for you. You should be proud."

Richard's cheeks burned. He pulled his shoulders back a little more.

"So, Sunny!" Miriam turned her attention to his girlfriend. "I can't believe you've been dating Richard for over a year, and this is the first time we're meeting. Tell me all about you!"

Sunny grinned. "Let's see, I'm a software engineer. I like gaming—I actually play with Gabe all the time—and I make apps for fun. Our cat's name is Dumpster. She's orange."

Richard perked up. That was the subject change Gabe and Tara needed. If anyone could help connect Sunny to a good cause to sell her next app, it was Miriam. Even if Sunny wouldn't let Richard pay for anything, he could at least help her earn money indirectly. He interrupted as politely as he could. "Her apps are more than a mere hobby. She recently sold a supply chain transparency app to an international human rights NGO to track human rights violations in the fashion industry."

"Is that so?" The light in Miriam's brown eyes said she was hooked, just as Richard had hoped. She loved a good cause and a new protégée. "That sounds impactful. What are you working on now?"

Sunny beamed, visibly excited to have a new audience. "A self-improvement app that modifies the kanban model, so people can use the methodology on their personal goals. But I'm stuck on how to keep people's personal information from being data mined."

Richard glanced at John, who gave him a barely visible nod as Miriam and Sunny exchanged ideas rapid-fire. They stood silently by while the two chatted, like John and Richard both preferred.

Eventually, Gabe joined them. "You got Mom on a roll, huh?" he muttered in Richard's ear, silently handing his mother a glass of wine. Miriam took it without looking, engrossed by Sunny's ideas. "I came over to run interference, just in case."

Richard snorted. "Sunny did that all on her own. She's doing better than I thought at avoiding *certain* topics."

"Gabey Baby, I'm surprised you're not dancing." Miriam turned to her son. "What happened to that lovely woman—Tara, was it?—the one you were paired with during the ceremony! You looked like you enjoyed dancing with her."

"You know, Ma, when you're right, you're right!" With a laugh, Gabe grabbed Sunny's hand. "Sunny, want to dance?"

Richard huffed in annoyance as Gabe pulled *his* girlfriend to the dance floor. But Gabe couldn't ask Tara to dance. They couldn't keep their hands to themselves for two seconds; it'd blow their whole cover. Richard could take one for the team, while Gabe made his escape.

"Give her my number, Richard," Miriam said. "I have some projects she might be interested in."

Richard nodded, pleased Sunny had earned her approval, even if he felt off-balance without Sunny to keep an eye on. He knew Miriam would approve, but it was nice to have confirmation. Unlike his own parents, he actually cared what the Coopers thought.

"So, how has Gabe been?" John asked. "We've been so busy with wedding season at the vineyard, this is the first time we've spent much time with him in weeks."

"He's good. Genuinely." Richard was glad he could reassure them of that at least. He'd been the sole line of communication between Gabe and his parents in New York, after Emily had made Gabe cut off contact with them. He'd never undersold Gabe's misery in those years, but he still felt guilty that he'd failed to protect their son. Not that the Coopers would ever blame him, but Richard wished he could take away the burden of their anger and guilt.

"And would *you* tell me if something was going on between Gabe and the pretty redhead?" Miriam asked, eyeing Tara, who was devouring cake next to Blanche across the room. "Or at least if there's a chance his feelings are reciprocated? It's strange, Gabe has never mentioned her, but he seems taken with her. I'm worried, given how blind to flaws he can get when he's infatuated," Miriam narrowed her eyes as she swirled her wine. "Tonio ran away like a fucking coward when I asked him."

"I wouldn't worry." Richard shrugged, trying to stay nonchalant, but his shoulders curled in with the movement. He trusted himself to keep Sunny on topic. But himself? "Her background check was...understandable." *Fuck.*

John hummed. "Background check? It's serious, then?"

"Fuck," Richard muttered, sweat prickling his back as he tried to think of any response that wouldn't completely backfire. Desperate for an escape, he glanced over his shoulder; Phineas and Antonio were talking a safe distance away. "Uh...Tonio is calling me. God fucking dammit."

"Richard—"

"I'm sorry." Holding up his hands in surrender, Richard squeezed his eyes shut. Miriam Cooper was so hard to lie to; he always felt compelled to tell her everything. And lying to John was impossible; one look and he could see into Richard's soul. Even leaving would give them too much information. But it was the best he could do. This was Gabe's fault for taking Sunny away; Richard needed her presence to keep himself focused. "Just...talk to Gabe after the wedding. I've already said too much."

Avoiding their eyes, Richard backed away a few feet before practically running to Antonio, weaving through the crowd in hopes that they wouldn't follow him.

"If Miriam asks, you needed me for something, and I wasn't avoiding her questions about Tara," Richard muttered to Antonio. "And if Gabe asks, his parents didn't hear anything from me."

Antonio laughed. "I barely got away."

"So the redhead is off-limits, I take it?" Phineas asked with a waggle of his eyebrows.

Antonio rolled his eyes. "Can you *try* to not be a horny creep for once? Especially at my wedding? Especially not about someone who is basically Lee's sister?"

Phineas shook his head. "No. Can't turn it off. Although I'm trying to mostly date other queer people these days. Apparently, it makes the sexuality issue easier."

"Did your therapist tell you that?" Antonio teased.

"I didn't know you were in therapy." Richard narrowed his eyes at Phineas. He'd stopped drinking, *and* he was going to therapy? Maybe he'd been neglecting Phineas too much. He really should invite him to dinner with Sunny one of these days. "About fucking time."

Phineas adjusted his glasses. "I've only had one session so far, so no—that advice came from Gabe. Seems to be working out for him. I should probably give it a try."

Richard snorted. "It certainly is, but if his parents ask, he's single. And no, I don't understand why he's not telling them." Richard looked out at the dance floor, where Gabe danced with Sunny. He tamped down his jealousy when they both burst into laughter. Gabe and Sunny's suddenly close friendship was strange, but they'd been friends for longer than Richard had known her. It'd be unrealistic to expect them to not be closer, after figuring out who they were in real life to each other.

But Richard wanted to dance with his girlfriend.

"On second thought, maybe it's good that the redhead is off-limits." Phineas nodded across the room.

Tara, unapologetically enthusiastic as always, danced terribly as Lee laughed with her. *Gabe must have practiced with her for hours. She actually looked like she could dance for all of two minutes.* "At least she's dancing," Richard said dryly. "I haven't seen you take a turn yet, Phin."

"Oh, and have *you* danced yet, Richard?" Phineas shot back.

"No, Gabe stole his dance partner." Antonio teased. "Do you miss your girlfriend, Dicky?"

"*Girlfriend?* Since when?" Phineas asked. "Damn, am I the only single one left?"

"I told you about Sunny!" Richard scoffed; Phineas was just as bad as Sunny. Did he need to make a damn slide deck about his life for everyone? "She's the one who didn't start that bar fight."

Phineas smacked his arm. "You didn't say she was your girlfriend, asshole!"

"Why else would I call in a favor?" Richard returned, but doubt sank in. He was sure he'd said Sunny was his girlfriend. Hadn't he? Maybe he *should* make a slide deck. They were working pretty well for scene planning with Sunny. He'd been printing off the agenda they'd discussed and sticking it to the fridge on Friday mornings. Sunny read them before he came home.

"They've been together for over a year," Antonio said. "Sunny even met his parents."

"What?" Phineas smacked Richard again. "Why didn't you tell me?"

"I basically did," Richard muttered. "Maybe you need to work less and spend more time with your friends."

"Yeah, well..." Phineas shrugged. "How'd your parents take the news?"

"Other than that one conversation with my dad, I haven't spoken with them since."

Richard had reached out to his mom to make sure she was okay, but they hadn't been able to get more than a few minutes into a conversation, before she'd crossed one of the many boundaries he was finally enforcing. They'd barely made it past hellos because she'd insisted on using his deadname, even after he'd corrected her twice. He'd given up on his father and brother, but his mom... Richard worried about her enough to give her a chance. And Barbie had let him down, just like she always had. He'd called from Everett's office, though, so at least he'd had the reassurance that he'd communicated his boundary appropriately.

"That bad, huh?" Phineas teased. "Well, Sunny sounds like she's exactly what you need."

"As if I didn't know that already." First the Coopers and now Phin; it was nice to hear the people Richard cared about supported him. Even if his parents didn't.

"Is Blanche off-limits, too?" Phineas asked, nodding to where Blanche sat at the bar next to Chas and Freddy. "Since I'm technically not their lawyer anymore?"

Antonio laughed. "Yes, but more for your sake than theirs. Blanche would destroy you. Mentally. Emotionally. Physically."

"Don't forget financially," Richard added.

"Sounds hot, but message received." Phineas pouted. "Who *can* I dance with?"

"Phin, there are literally two hundred people here," Antonio said with a tight smile. Richard could tell his patience was wearing thin. Gabe was usually the one who validated Phineas's insecurities, not either of them. "Just ask anyone not related to me if you're going to be a creep."

"Tonio! There you are!" Jazz appeared with her parents in tow. "We wanted to let you know we're heading home soon. Once we can get Lee off the dance floor to say goodbye, of course."

"So soon?" Antonio didn't look that upset that his new in-laws were leaving so early.

"We have to get up early for church." Althea smiled politely.

"Are you going to introduce us, Antonio?" Phineas smiled at Jazz.

Jazz shot him a skeptical look back.

Richard rolled his eyes. For someone so well-trained in social norms, Phineas did not know how to read the room. Jazz was obviously a lesbian. Even if her septum ring was hidden, the obvious difference in length of the acrylics on her middle fingers was a neon sign that screamed sapphic. *I just wish Sunny had done the same.*

"Oh, this is Phineas, and you met Richard yesterday." Richard nodded politely as Antonio reintroduced him. "These are Lee's parents, Leland and Althea, and his *little sister*, Jazz."

Richard snorted; as if that would stop Phineas from hitting on her.

"Pleasure to meet you, sir." Phineas turned on his charming fake smile as he shook Leland's hand. Richard thought *he'd* been well-trained as a kid, but Phineas's politically ambitious father had ingrained manners in Phineas that couldn't be turned off. He was just as charming with Althea, complimenting her as he greeted her. Phineas nodded politely at Jazz. "I don't suppose you'd care to dance."

Jazz's nose wrinkled like she'd rather clean a toilet. "I'm good, thanks. Like I literally just said, we're about to leave."

"Phineas Watkins!" Antonio flicked water at him, speckling his glasses with droplets. "You know very well when I said find someone to dance with, that didn't mean to ask my new sister-in-law! If Tara and Blanche are off-limits, why would Lee's sister be an option?! There are *So. Many. Reasons* that would be disturbing!"

Leland and Althea's smiles were still forced on, though they exchanged a confused look.

Phineas grinned, taking off his glasses to wipe them on his shirt. "What, who else can I ask? You said no one you're related to, but that's everyone here!"

"Watkins?" Leland asked. "I don't suppose you're a relation of Phineas Watkins, the city council member in Chicago?"

Phineas nodded, his Politician Son's mask sliding back over his face.

Richard sighed. *Poor Phin. There's no escape for him even in Bellamy.* Watching the anxious, chatterbox he knew morph into a charming, confident stranger was always unnerving.

Speaking in his slow, resonant lawyer voice, Phineas said, "Yes, he's my father. I take it you've met him?"

Althea nodded. "He was at our family reunion last month."

The mask slipped briefly. A flash of panic crossed Phineas's face. "Wh—What?"

"I am about to scream!" Antonio announced before bursting into laughter. "Family reunion?! Phin!" Antonio doubled over, cackling loudly, stomping his feet in his heels.

Jazz, Althea, and Leland looked as confused as Richard.

Sweat beaded on Phin's forehead and his eyes widened, despite the polite smile on his face. His anxiety leaked through his lawyer voice in a barely-there tremble, "I wasn't aware I had a family reunion to attend last month."

"Oh no, he was campaigning at *our* family reunion. He's no relation!" Althea explained with a polite laugh. "Most of my family lives in his ward. They're all going to vote for him, don't worry. He's such a great man. A real leader."

"Oh! Right, that's good." Relief flashed over Phineas's face, before the mask went back up. "My family appreciates the support. I have to ask, Lee didn't…meet my father by any chance, did he?"

Leland and Althea exchanged uncomfortable glances.

"Lee wasn't invited," Jazz explained, her voice and expression neutral, other than a barely-there roll of her eyes. Richard's jaw tightened, angry on Lee's behalf; Lee must be as appreciative as Richard was of the Flores family. No one was left uninvited from their home.

"Ah." Phineas nodded politely. Turning to Antonio, he hissed in his real voice, "Stop laughing, you know how my anxiety gets! There's no relation!"

Antonio dabbed his eyes. "The look on your face was the best wedding present! Oh, my side hurts!"

Richard wondered what he'd missed as Antonio said his goodbyes to the Joneses, and Phineas excused himself to get some air. Whatever it was, it was probably not his business.

Out the corner of his eye, his gaze was drawn by Sunny's smile. She was apparently enjoying dancing with Gabe, but Richard wanted her to enjoy dancing with *him*. Miriam had already seen how Gabe looked at Tara anyway. The cat was basically out of the bag. And really, he should probably confess that *he* deserved to be edged when they got home. Sunny was really taking to this roleplaying much faster than he was, but he'd be damned if he wouldn't hold himself accountable, too.

"Tonio." Richard held out his hand. Cutting in without leaving a partner for Gabe would be rude.

Antonio grinned and took his hand eagerly. "I thought you'd never ask, Dicky."

BLANCHE

"I NEVER THOUGHT I'D see my baby this pretty," Chas said, his voice husky with emotion as he looked out on the dance floor from his perch on Freddy's knee at the bar. Freddy wore the same suede suit he'd worn to his and Chas's wedding, and Chas wore a matching blazer over a drag getup that accommodated his bump. Candles flickered in hurricane glasses, and a riot of flowers in varying shades of pink and orange decorated every surface. "Through the ministry of love, we are granted a glimpse of the divine. Let us rejoice and bear witness to her beauty!"

Freddy and Blanche exchanged an amused look. If Chas hadn't been six months pregnant, Blanche might have thought he was drunk. But between the festive atmosphere and the relief of freedom from Covey's manipulation, Blanche could understand his sentimental mood.

Besides, Chas's emceeing duties for the reception were over, as were Blanche's officiating duties; they could finally both relax. While officiating Lee and Antonio's wedding was an honor, a weight had lifted the second Blanche had pronounced them married. Their responsibility for the night was done, their advisory with the Coveys would last a mere five more days (not that Mrs. Covey had needed Blanche's guidance), and in a month, they'd have a home of their own. Nothing paired so well with jubilance as fifteen-year-old single malt scotch and shooting the shit with their oldest friends.

"Will you actually let me take care of Confession while you're on leave this time?" Blanche teased between sips. "Between Miriam, Richard, and I, you two don't actually have to micromanage anything."

Chas guffawed. "You know, this is my last pregnancy, so maybe I'll actually relax this time and enjoy it."

"What, five kids is enough?"

"We will take all the blessings the Lord gives us," Chas said, his eyes drifting upward. "But five blessings in seven years is a lot—" His eyes widened as the song changed to something Blanche didn't recognize. "Freddy, it's our song!"

Freddy and Blanche exchanged another amused look. Clearly, he'd never heard this song either, but he politely followed his spouse to the dance floor.

With a sigh, Blanche sat alone at the bar. Moments like this—everyone celebrating love through dancing and laughter, through clinking glasses and kisses—often reminded them just how alone they were. They sipped their scotch, trying to focus on their good mood, instead of extrapolating their wallflower tendencies into what their life would feel like in a big, empty house alone.

"Good evening, Blanche," Phineas approached them, pulling his waist-length locs over his shoulder with that devastating smile. "That was a lovely ceremony—"

"Nope." Lee materialized out of the crowd and steered him away with a hand on his chest.

"Bro, come on!"

Blanche laughed as Lee guided him back across the room. Charming or not, Phineas never stood a chance. After pushing themself past their limits for so long to save up for a house, Blanche was really looking forward to only having a few select clients, including any recorded sessions. The ones they liked, the ones who were useful, the ones who deserved their time and energy. They planned to focus on themself—

"You have a beautiful laugh," A familiar-looking woman, with a torrent of loose brown curls cascading around her elegant neck, looked over from a couple barstools away. "And he's right. That was a lovely ceremony." Her full red lips parted as she smiled.

Blanche's heart pounded. "Th—thanks. Have we met?"

"I'm Angie." She held out her hand. "If I recall correctly, we had a brief conversation at Stormé's last year."

"Ah, I remember. Blanche." Blanche shook it.

"Yeah, I gathered that from the program." Her fingers were more calloused than Blanche expected; they lingered when Blanche let go. Her hazel eyes were teasing. Hazel eyes resembling Antonio's...

"You're the florist cousin." Blanche should have guessed anyone here would be related to him somehow. Antonio would likely not be thrilled if Blanche indulged in Angie's flirting.

Angie laughed. "I am. You've heard of me?"

"Tara and Gabe mentioned you."

"Ah, yes." Angie's eyebrows rose, and she took a sip of her wine. "*Those* two."

Blanche might be more than a little drunk, but Angie's bitter tone wasn't subtle. "Oh?"

Angie shrugged. "Don't get me wrong, I bear no grudges—they're both sweethearts. They're both really attractive, and neither of them was into me. I got rejected back to back. It was a rough night for my ego." She waved a hand. "They're cute, though. Glad they finally got together."

"Did *they* tell you they're together?" Blanche tried to sound more curious than suspicious.

"They didn't have to." Angie smirked. "How far along is she?"

Hackles up, Blanche set their scotch down and raised an eyebrow. They'd forgotten how damn direct this woman was.

"Oh, don't be like that!" Angie laughed. "Gabe can't keep his eyes off her, and Tara keeps touching her stomach and smiling."

Anxiety in their chest unwinding, Blanche laughed with her. "They are hopeless. But they're also not far enough along to tell anyone yet."

"Don't tell anyone what?" Jazz popped out of nowhere, taking the barstool between them. She patted Blanche's arm. "Sorry I've been avoiding you all night—I ran back to 'look for my phone' while my parents are fighting in the car." She pulled her phone out of her bra. "I figured this buys me at least ten minutes where I can enjoy myself."

Angie raked her eyes over Jazz, landing on the shortened pink nails that the Joneses would never notice.

Some of Lee's protectiveness must have rubbed off on Blanche, because they shot Angie a warning glare as they greeted Jazz with a hug. With a smirk, Angie turned to sip her wine.

"I'm glad you could get away, Beautiful! I hate that you have to act like you barely know us around your parents." Blanche took Jazz's hand. "Just curious—are there any side effects I should be worried about with that tea you made for me?"

Jazz pondered as she mindlessly tapped on Blanche's palm in a quick triad. "Let's see. Perhaps some nausea if you drink too much, from the ashwagandha. The Saint John's wort can interact with some medications and cause sun sensitivity."

"Is *that* why I've been burning?" Blanche tsked. "So, let's say, hypothetically, if Tara was drinking it regularly and getting rawdogged every other day, her birth control might fail?"

Jazz shrugged. "Sure, I suppose that could—" Her fingers curled around Blanche's forearm as her jaw dropped. "Oh my God, are you saying what I think you're saying?"

Blanche put a finger to their lips. "I'm not saying anything. But let's say in a month or two, perhaps we might expect an announcement."

"Oh no!" Jazz's mouth fell open. "I feel horrible! I had no idea—"

"Nope." Blanche shut Jazz's jaw with one finger, giving her a stern look to quell Jazz's panic before it started; her anxiety could get worse than Lee's. "Tara and Gabe are in a very different place in their lives than you. Trust me, they're both over the moon about it. But only your brother, Antonio—and Angie here, apparently—know about it. I wanted to let you know, in case any other customers of yours find themselves in the same boat."

Brown eyes swimming with anxiety, Jazz groaned out a, "Thanks."

"No, thank *you*. The tea has done wonders, I promise. We'll just keep it away from Tara from now on." Blanche took Jazz's hand. Maybe something to look forward to would distract her; Blanche's hand shook from how hard hers were trembling. "And subsequently, since my current roommate is presumably moving in with her baby daddy, and I'm about to move into a big, empty house by the U—"

"Yes!" Jazz tightened her grip.

"You don't even know what I'm going to say," Blanche laughed, relieved at Jazz's eagerness. They'd felt a twinge of shame for needing companionship so desperately, but Jazz was a rare friend. Someone Blanche had never felt a need to take care of like Lee and Tara, with no debt of loyalty like Freddy and Chas. Jazz needed nothing from Blanche but space to be herself. And Blanche now had three extra bedrooms in a big, old house, where Jazz could do just that.

"You're about to ask if I'll move in with you, right?" Jazz nodded with them. "The answer is yes. I don't care how much the rent is. I don't care what crazy chores you have for me. Get me out of my parents' house, please!"

Blanche tsked. "I'm not going to charge you rent. I just hate living alone."

"Seriously?" Jazz asked. The tremor in her hands stilled. "For *free*?"

With a nod, Blanche waved her off. "I never charged Lee or Tara rent, but they insisted on paying for utilities and food. Don't worry about that, though. Just don't judge how much weed I smoke, or any screams coming from the attic."

Jazz laughed. "I won't say a word. Can I have...friends stay over?"

"Of course!" Blanche raised an eyebrow at her emphasis on friends—as far as they knew, Jazz was single. But Jazz was twenty-one; she *should* be dating. With how strict her parents were, Jazz had probably never been able to bring anyone home before.

The phone in Jazz's lap buzzed. She rolled her eyes. "That's my cue. Blanche, seriously, thank you! Let's talk more about this living situation, okay?" She kissed Blanche's cheek before she answered the call. "Hi Mom! Yeah, just found it in the bathroom. I'm on my way back to the car now."

Angie smirked into her wineglass as Jazz walked away. "You offering everyone a place to live, or just her?"

Blanche shrugged. "I don't know anyone else who might want one."

Angie's smirk twitched. "Sure."

Her tone struck a nerve. "She's Lee's little sister."

"I didn't say anything." With a wink, Angie set down her empty glass. "Excuse me. Lee looks like he needs a dancing partner. Pleasure to meet you formally this time, *Beautiful*."

Any attraction Blanche might have felt for Angie was replaced with irritation. Blanche huffed and ordered another scotch. Angie's presumptuous tone dug under their skin. They weren't inviting Jazz to live with them under any nefarious intentions; Jazz needed freedom, and Blanche needed company. They were friends. That was it.

CHAPTER FORTY-FOUR

TARA

"THAT'S A LOVELY OUTFIT you're wearing."

Tara tore her eyes away from the dance floor, where Gabe and Antonio were floating effortlessly together. Next to her stood a stout middle-aged woman, a bit shorter than herself, looking expectantly at her. Her curly brown hair, streaked with gray, was coiffed neatly beneath pearl pins that matched her earrings and rope necklace.

Tara had seen her talking with Sunny earlier, but wasn't sure who she was. Richard had hugged her though, which was frankly unusual for him.

"Thank you." Tara smoothed the satin jumpsuit over her hips, trying not to let her hands linger over her belly. Blanche had already called her out on doing that enough. "It has pockets. Lucky find at the thrift store."

"Very sensible. Weddings cost so much money these days. We spent about a grand on our wedding back in the eighties, and that seemed like a fortune then." The woman laughed, still inspecting Tara with a curious but friendly look, beaming as if she'd found something to get excited about.

Tara couldn't imagine this woman had ever considered a thousand dollars to be a fortune, even that long ago. Her floaty lilac gown was tailored to fit like a glove. Those pearls looked real. "Weddings are way more expensive than I expected. Luckily, Lee and Tonio had a lot of generous people help them out." Could she ask who this woman was?

She didn't remember seeing her at the rehearsal dinner yesterday, so she probably wasn't a Flores. But Richard had *hugged* her, so she must be closely connected to Antonio somehow. She certainly wasn't there as a guest of Lee's; she'd finally met Hot Barber and Mo earlier—the only people in Lee's life she'd had yet to meet.

"They do indeed." The woman sipped her glass of wine.

Tara looked at it wistfully. Her Saturday indulgence was on hold indefinitely. Tara never imagined she'd be a wine drinker, but Gabe had been splitting a bottle with her every weekend; this was her first Saturday of indefinite dry Saturdays. The Cooper house red the woman was drinking was her favorite, but she wasn't going to risk even a sip. *I won't do to my kid what my mom did to me.* Tara fought the urge to touch her belly, shoving her hands in the pockets instead.

"So, how do you know Lee?" the woman asked.

"We've been best friends since we were teenagers." Tara didn't want to give more detail than that to a stranger, even one who seemed nice. She set her empty mocktail glass down, scanning the room to catch Gabe's eye. They exchanged a smile; he and Antonio had stopped dancing to talk to someone else she hadn't met yet. He glanced at the woman next to her, quickly turning back to the tall, handsome man with locs.

Tara turned back to the woman to find her beaming at her, dimples deep in her cheeks. Something about her was familiar, but she couldn't place it. Tara belatedly realized she was probably expecting the same question herself. "And how do you know Antonio?"

"Our families have been good friends since he was in middle school. Can I get you a glass of wine?" The woman offered.

"Oh no, thank you. I'm staying sober to drive the grooms back to the hotel." It was the best excuse she and Gabe could come up with. "Luckily, there's a great mocktail selection."

"Yes, indeed. And anyone else who might not be drinking...for whatever reason." The woman's warm brown eyes dug into her with a knowing smile.

Tara forced her hands to stay in her pockets and away from her stomach. She didn't think any of the signs were obvious yet. Mostly her tits ached, especially in this corset top (which she had never gotten around to taking in, though she didn't need to anymore), but this woman wouldn't know they were bigger than normal.

"That's quite enough, dearest." A tall man that Tara hadn't noticed spoke up on the woman's other side. How he could have escaped her notice was beyond her. Almost as tall as Gabe, he had a lanky build, with straight black hair cut short and styled the same way Richard wore his. He had nice eyes, too—a dark, smoky brown.

The resemblance with Gabe was uncanny.

Oh, shit. Tara froze, her heart thumping.

"Let's take a turn on the dance floor, shall we? A much safer activity than jumping to conclusions. Excuse us." The man gave Tara a nod and a smile, before he led the woman away, who was already whispering to him excitedly.

Panic and dread flooded through her. *Did I just meet Gabe's parents? Did she figure out I'm pregnant? Oh no, I probably made a horrible first impression!* Her breath shallow, Tara hurried away to find someone who could take her mind off of it. Maybe it would get less embarrassing if she replayed it in her head. But Tara struggled to find anyone she knew but Gabe—as wonderful as it'd be to bury herself in his chest, that would be very counterproductive. Her eyes kept going back to him as her mind kept replaying the interaction, getting worse every time.

With a rush of relief, she found Lee talking to a familiar face by the head table. "Angie!" Tara cried enthusiastically. "So good to see you!"

Angie, looking radiant in a green wrap dress, hugged her. "You're looking good, Tara! I love that outfit on you." She winked.

With a laugh, Tara shook her head. *She really does act just like Tonio.*

"I was just telling Angie what a great job you and Gabe did on decorations. I can't believe how you pulled it all together like this on the budget we gave you." Lee waved his hand toward the centerpieces and fabric, draped over the tables and walls of Confession.

Angie grinned wryly at her. "Yeah, how on earth *did* you and Gabe pull this off?"

Tara winced apologetically. She figured Gabe would tell Lee and Antonio; she'd only told them not to worry about it. "So, Gabe might have convinced me to splurge a little. His money, of course, not yours. And we decided to splurge on Angie. And as you can see, she did a truly amazing job."

"At cost, of course. Can't go overcharging family." Angie affectionately put her arm around Tara's waist, her hand drifting around to her belly. Tara's cheeks burned. She'd forgotten how flirtatious Angie was.

Lee grinned. "Buttercup, did Gabe seriously convince you to voluntarily spend money on something without an argument?"

"Please, if he wants to spend money on *you*, I'd never stop him." Tara shrugged. "Though, there was an argument about it. Several, in fact. I'm not that easy."

Angie squeezed her closer. "I dunno, you seemed pretty easy to me. All I did was show you a brochure and some cleavage."

Tara laughed. "True. The cleavage is what sold it." She put her own arm around Angie. Angie knew she and Gabe were a thing; flirting was harmless fun.

Lee shot her a questioning look. "Well, however it happened, it looks beautiful!"

"Beautiful? I'm right here!" Antonio dramatically spun in front of Lee, who caught him around the waist as Gabe joined them. Tara was envious of how smoothly they danced together. Even after all of her practice, she still had two left feet.

"Come dance with me, Angel!" Antonio grabbed Lee's hand. Unabashedly eager, Lee followed, leaving Gabe standing in front of Tara and Angie, still with their arms around each other.

"Am I interrupting, or can I cut in?" Gabe smiled at them, holding out a hand to Tara. With a questioning look, she took it, giddy to have his hand in hers again after hours of keeping her distance.

"You are interrupting, but I know where I stand. She was already *glowing*, but she damn near lit up when you came over." Angie sighed dramatically. "I'll go find someone else to flirt with tonight. There's gotta be someone here I'm not related to." She kissed Tara's cheek, then walked past Gabe, who jumped as she passed.

"She just pinched my ass," he muttered as he drew Tara to the dance floor.

"Can't blame her," Tara laughed as he pulled her close into a slow bachata. A satisfied glow erupted in her chest from having him so close, though an unsatisfied heat bloomed between her thighs. She grinned. "It's been hard to keep my hands off you all night."

With a lazy smile, Gabe murmured, "Trust me, Kitten, you have no idea."

"What, all it took to break you was me flirting with Angie?" Tara teased. She counted steps as best she could, trying not to care that she was making a fool of herself.

"Out of pure curiosity—if we weren't a thing—Angie, smash or pass?" Gabe asked quietly, his voice pouring down her neck. Fighting a laugh, Tara listened for anything akin to jealousy in his tone, but his tone was light and teasing.

"Honestly? She's my type." Tara shrugged as she tried to keep up with his steps. Talking and counting at the same time was hard. "But when the chance came up, I couldn't stop thinking of you. So, hypothetical smash. In reality, pass. Why, would you?"

"If I didn't know you? I don't think it'd go anywhere serious, but probably. So same, hypothetically smash. She's hot, very forward, and I definitely had a crush on her before Antonio and I got together." Gabe grinned, then teased, "Tell me more about this type of yours."

"Long hair, pretty eyes, thick thighs. You have nothing to worry about." She tugged affectionately on the braid over his shoulder.

"Trust me, Kitten. I'm not worried. Just curious is all." He smiled softly at her. "For how long we've known each other, I feel like I'm still getting to know you."

"True. We haven't talked about a lot of things. Like having kids." She smiled back before adding, "Or life goals. Or religion."

Gabe cocked his head. "Are you religious?"

Tara winked. "I used to get on my knees in the Confessionals a lot. Does that count?"

"You might make a convert of me," Gabe laughed, then quieted. "In a significantly less-hot change of subject, how was your conversation with my mom?" He searched her face cautiously.

"Fuck, I thought that might be her. God, I hope I didn't make a fool of myself," Tara groaned. "She was really nice, but she seemed very suspicious of why I wasn't drinking."

Gabe shook his head. "Of course. And that's exactly why I'm not introducing you to them tonight. She tried to corner me at the bar, but I made her promise to stop harassing people for information on you, and I'd answer all of her questions soon. Dad decided they should probably go home to be on the safe side."

"Is *that* why we're dancing?" Tara raised an eyebrow. "Because they left?"

"Well, and because there's half an hour left of this wedding. I want to spend it with you." Gabe grinned sheepishly. "It's a relief though. Because you think I'm a lot? Just wait until Mom finds out—she will smother you."

"You're not a lot. You're perfect," Tara smiled. "And I want our kid to get all of the love they can get. She can smother away."

She wondered if she could kiss him now that his parents had left, but they'd agreed to keep any affection to a minimum during the wedding. *Not that that's keeping his hand from my ass.* His fingers were drifting progressively lower. Maybe they could pay a quick visit to the Confessionals before the end of the night.

"I'm so happy we're doing this, Kitten." Gabe drew her closer as a slow song came on. He rested his cheek against her hair. "You have no idea how excited I am."

Tara melted against his chest, breathing in the comforting musk of his body, the vanilla of his lotion, and the wine on his breath. "I have some idea. I'm happy too. Even if you still haven't told me the secret ingredient in the family cheesecake recipe."

Gabe snorted. "I see what this is. An elaborate plot for cheesecake."

"You caught me. Catching feelings and getting knocked up were all part of my master plan. I'm not after your money—just the cheesecake."

He whispered in her ear, "Add a teaspoon each of almond extract and cardamom to the sour cream, and whip it before you add it to the filling. There. Now you can leave me if you want."

Tara looked up at him with a grin. "I don't even remember the sour cream. I guess I still need you to make it."

Gabe's brown eyes smiled down at her. "Oh, lucky me."

Tara rested her head back on his chest to keep herself from kissing him, relishing in the peace and softness. "Is that offer to stay permanently still on the table?"

Gabe stepped back with an earnest smile, leaving his dimples on full display. "Of course! Does that mean you're considering it?"

Any doubt that he wanted this as much as she did was swept away in Gabe's eagerness. Tara nodded. "I'm willing to give it a try. Like I said, I want our kid to have all the love they can get, and living apart would make that harder. Plus you're a way better cook than Blanche or I. This baby shouldn't eat ramen every meal."

Gabe beamed, his dimples deeper than ever. "Whatever you want, I'll make it happen. We can set up a nursery and put a playground in the backyard, anything you want."

Tara shook her head with a laugh. "I just want you to be there. You don't need to buy stuff. You're always throwing money at everything," she teased.

"I like to do nice things for the people I love," Gabe whispered in her ear as he drew her close again. She shivered. That voice, those words, made her soft feelings sing. Fear and Hurt and Loneliness had been quiet lately. Never gone, but quieter. The lightness she felt with him was a soothing balm she hadn't realized she needed.

"I love you," she murmured into his neck. All of the confusing soft feelings she felt for him, they all made him feel like home. Safety. Family. He felt inevitable, undeniable, irresistible.

She only realized he'd stopped dancing when his hand grazed her jaw. Tilting her head back, Gabe looked earnestly into her eyes. "I will never get tired of hearing you say that." His coffee-brown eyes shined with a deeper hunger and reverence than that first time they'd locked eyes in the mirror, two years ago. "I love you too, Kitten." Gabe captured her mouth in a kiss. All of their worries about making a scene vanished amidst the crowded dance floor, his lips on hers promising that the love in his eyes would never fade.

Sunday, June Twenty-Seventh

Epilogue

Gabe

Gabe had checked all the usual spots for his wallet—the dining table, the entry hall, his jacket pocket—but to no avail. He was running out of time. He ran back to the stove and flipped the turkey bacon and hash browns before they burned. The cinnamon rolls were already on the tray with the coffee, veggie scramble, and fresh fruit.

He'd timed everything to return to the bedroom before Tara woke up, but his missing wallet was threatening that plan. He hadn't woken her up to tell her where he was going; she'd looked too peaceful sleeping, and she'd been so tired the past few weeks. He'd let her sleep all day, as long as he could be there when she woke up.

Plating everything carefully, he loaded the food onto the tray, adjusting everything to perfection. A vacuum for anything edible, Tara wouldn't care how it looked, but Gabe had standards. Carefully, he carried the tray to the bedroom as quietly as he could.

Tara sat cross-legged on the bed, stark naked and eyes closed.

"You're up!" Gabe winced. "Sorry, I didn't wake you. I went to make breakfast."

She nodded without opening her eyes, breathing deeply. "I figured. I could smell the coffee and potatoes."

"No panic attack this morning?" Gabe asked. He'd been so careful to be with her every time she stayed over, waking her up before he left for work to let her know where she was, that she was safe. He'd grown fond of the morning ritual, holding her as she slowly came back to the world with him. Way better than his usual insomniac routine of lying awake half the night, alone with his thoughts. Plus, she usually woke up just as horny as he did. He'd been late to work several times.

Tara shook her head. "I managed. Gonna have to learn to do it on my own eventually."

"I'll still wake you up in the mornings until you tell me to stop, Kitten," Gabe smiled, setting the tray on the bed before climbing in carefully next to her.

"Considering you wake me up with an orgasm or two every morning, don't hold your breath." She grabbed a cinnamon roll, moaning as she shoved it in her mouth.

Gabe speared a pineapple on his fork. He always ate his fruit first, then the veggies, and lastly, protein. Emily had insisted it was better for his digestion. The science behind it was questionable, but it was a familiar ritual by this point. Then again, Emily also never let him eat carbs at all, so that bitch could go fuck herself. He stabbed a bite of hash browns to reclaim a bit of agency over what he put in his own damn mouth. Tara'd been right; he still followed so many of Emily's rules without realizing it.

Hesitantly, Tara sipped her coffee, practically water compared to his. She'd been queasy off-and-on; the usual thick sludge he made hadn't been sitting well with her. She nodded approvingly, sitting back with the mug under her nose.

"By the way, any idea what happened to my wallet?" Gabe asked. "I'm trying to order room service for Tonio and Lee, but I can't find my credit card."

Tara nodded to her duffel bag on the chair in the corner. "I put it in the bag. Everything important goes in there, just in case."

Gabe's heart twinged at the thought of her leaving in the middle of the night without a goodbye. He forced himself to keep his tone light. "Planning on stealing my wallet, Kitten?"

She smacked his arm. "What if we have to leave in the middle of the night? Searching for your wallet and shit in the dark would slow us down."

His chest warming, Gabe got up and found his wallet on top of her laptop in her duffel bag. "Oh, I'm invited in this hypothetical evacuation?"

Tara shot him a confused look. "Well, yeah! I have Hippo's spare leash and a baggy of food in there, too. Although..." She paused. "You'd probably want a change of clothes, too. And shit, we'll need stuff for the kid eventually. I might need a second bag!"

Fighting a laugh—because how could he doubt that he'd ever be left behind by Tara, now that she was determined to keep him—Gabe pressed kisses up her neck as he climbed back into bed. "Kitten, that is the sweetest, most fucked up gesture I think anyone has ever done for me."

"What, hiding your shit in my getaway bag?" Tara teased.

"Exactly." He took out his phone to finish the room service order.

"I'm glad you think it's sweet." Tara leaned on his shoulder. "Because that bag will be staying here from now on, so other than my clothes, I'm basically all moved in."

"Good." He set his phone and wallet on the bedside table and speared another bite of pineapple. "I cleared a few drawers for you and moved some stuff around in the closet."

"Already?" Tara asked.

"Maybe a few weeks ago," Gabe admitted.

Tara grinned. "We just found out I was pregnant like three days ago."

Gabe shrugged. "I was optimistic. For once."

His phone buzzed, a confirmation that the room service order had been accepted.

"Any messages from your parents?" Tara asked, glancing at his phone with no small amount of trepidation.

Gabe scoffed. His mom had sent more than a dozen texts by the time he'd woken up. "Mom sent a few. Her first was a screenshot of a picture that Antonio's mom took of us kissing on the dance floor. Then she said 'mazel tov,' but in the 'about fucking time' way, not the 'congratulations' way. Then she told me I need to bring you to the next family dinner we have, whenever it is. It's the busy season at the vineyard. She kept suggesting dates and then remembering she had plans." Gabe grinned. "Eventually my dad chimed in and said they'd let me know, just that I need to bring you. Which I was already going to do. Welcome to the shitshow. At this rate, it'll be autumn by the time you meet them. Maybe we should have made a scene yesterday."

"Too late now." Tara snorted. "Believe me—the Cooper shitshow is a welcome change compared to the Sanderson shitshow. I have no idea how to be a part of a normal family, so I'm relying on you to help me with this shit."

Gabe looked at her skeptically as she finished her cinnamon roll, because Tara had the most loyal family he'd ever known, even if they weren't blood-related. If anything, she'd be teaching him. "That's not how this works. We'll figure it out together."

Tara smiled sadly, nibbling a piece of turkey bacon. "I kinda wish I could tell my parents. At least my mom. I don't know if she'd care, but the rare times when she was trying to get sober, she'd ask about my future dreams. What I wanted to be when I grew up, where I wanted to live—that kind of thing. Neither of us expected a baby and a dog and a house though. That shit's too American dream." She reached for the second cinnamon roll.

Gabe gently smacked her hand. "Excuse me, that is mine."

Tara looked at him with mock horror. "Are you seriously depriving me of a cinnamon roll? I'm eating for two, Coop!"

"There are more in the kitchen. This one's mine!" He picked up the cinnamon roll and took a bite to claim it. Not that it would stop her. He ignored the turkey bacon he was *supposed* to eat next, instead stuffing half the cinnamon roll in his mouth. *Damn. Tara was right. This is really good.* He couldn't hold back a moan either.

"You really need to eat your own baking more often." Tara eyed him like she was ready to eat him, instead of the cinnamon roll. She bit her lip as her eyes flicked to his mouth.

Gabe took another bite to tease her. As insecure as he was, she made him feel wanted in a way that no one else ever had. She just wanted him as he was—nothing in particular from him, no service demanded or judgment made—as if his mere presence was enough. It was the easiest thing to give. With Tara, Gabe could simply be himself.

Putting the pastry down, Gabe playfully sucked the cinnamon and sugar off his fingers. Tara stole his hand away before he could finish. Sucking his thumb in her mouth, she licked the sweetness away, green eyes bright with mischief. Finally, the universe had brought him to a place filled with hope and love. With Tara as part of his life, his family, his home. Just like he would be hers. Together, they'd figure out how to provide all the stability, affection, and love they'd craved when they were young, for the family they were building together.

With an irrepressible grin, Gabe drew Tara into a sticky, sweet kiss.

Also by Cozy

If you enjoyed this book (or if you didn't!), please kindly show your support by leaving a review and telling your friends about it. Honest reviews and word-of-mouth recommendations make it possible for indie authors to keep writing. Thank you!

Want to read more by Cozy? Check out their books at cozydubois.com

Confession Series
Book 1: *Loving Lee*
Book 2: *Love on the Sunny Side*
Book 3: *Tempting Tara*
Book 4: *Carte Blanche*
Epilogue: *Finally Phineas* coming soon!

Standalone Novels
Earthly Ties

Summer Weddings in Solberg
Petty Roots
Familiar Faces

Long Nights and Bright Futures
Glimmer in the Dark
Dancing in the Snow coming November 2026

Sleighbell Springs
For Luck's Sake
Happy (Endings) for the Holidays coming December 2026
Searching for Starlight coming November 2027
More Happy (Endings) for the Holidays coming December 2027

Short Stories
"Dad, Are You..." — part of *Bi All Accounts: Volume 1.*

About the Author

Cozy DuBois (they/them) thought writing fiction was a long-lost hobby. A longtime lover of romance novels, Cozy has renewed their love for writing by telling stories for and about LGBTQ+ people. They hope to bring more books into the world that represent the complex and entangled relationships between friends, lovers, and chosen family found in the queer community they love.

Based in Minneapolis, they enjoy life with their partner, two hound dogs, a regal queen of a cat, dozens of houseplants, and a garden that has seen better days. Find them with a beverage in hand on a patio anytime the temp is above freezing or planning their next vacation when it's not.

Connect with Cozy on social media or via email updates at cozydubois.com for announcements about upcoming releases.

Acknowledgements

First of all, a huge shout out to my editor, Mikko Lahna. Without their support, encouragement (and ability to reconcile the English language with my own dyslexic brain who literally cannot figure out where those damn commas go), I would never have gotten the Tara's book into the shape it is now. I feel like With every book, my standards for myself get higher, and I fully attribute that to Mikko's feedback!

I also want to give kudos to Marta Susic, for creating such beautiful and striking covers for this series. I often just sit and look at them when I'm supposed to be working, because I love them so dearly.

A huge thanks goes out to my beta and sensitivity readers. It goes without saying that these books would be a complete, cringey mess without the feedback everyone provides along the way. I deeply appreciate every early reader who helps shape the series, especially those who reassured me that accidental pregnancy tropes are not inherently bad. Because queer people get knocked up on accident in real life too!

I also want to thank the readers of Loving Lee and Love on the Sunny Side who reach out to me and tell me what the books mean to them. It's so wonderful (and slightly surreal) that the figments of my imagination resonate with so many people, because that is why I wanted to publish these books, to connect with people. So thank you for loving these books, because without the external validation, I'd cry. (Kidding. Kind of)

My partner also gets their usual shout out, even though they still haven't read anything I've written. From the random questions of "how would you phrase this?" to the many many massages after I've been sitting in shrimp mode for hours, I deeply appreciate their support.

www.ingramcontent.com/pod-product-compliance
Lightning Source LLC
Chambersburg PA
CBHW061104310726
48974CB00002B/387